POLLY OF PENRYN

POLLY
of
PENRYN
Dor Stacey

UNITED WRITERS
Cornwall

UNITED WRITERS PUBLICATIONS LTD
Ailsa, Castle Gate, Penzance, Cornwall.

British Library Cataloguing in Publication Data:
A catalogue record for this book is
available from the British Library.

ISBN 1 85200 091 0

Printed in Great Britain by
United Writers Publications Ltd
Cornwall.

To my daughters Linda and Rosemary
and my old friend Pauline.

Chapter One

'Tea in bed! It's a good thing I don't have a wedding anniversary every day . . . I'd be thoroughly spoiled, Mary.' Polly Pendleton pushed tumbling dark tresses from her face as she sat up.

'Mr Pendleton has left for the granite quarries,' the maid said. 'And there are letters on the tray for you.'

'Thanks, Mary.'

The maid left and Polly poured tea, then scanned the writing on the envelopes. One from Jessie, one from Great Aunt Elizabeth and . . . Oh! . . . Her trembling hand spilled tea into the saucer and her heart somersaulted as she recognised the writing on the third envelope. It was from Joss!

Hastily Polly gulped from the tea remaining in the rose-patterned china cup, willing it to steady her trembling. She had not felt the least bit trembly on her wedding day, yet the sight of Joss's writing had such a disturbing effect.

Unsteadily she replaced the cup and saucer on the tray and lay back against the frill-edged pillows. Memories raced through her head and pictures of herself as a child came unbidden to her mind's eye . . . The encompassing white smock protecting her dress and the straw hat mother made her wear in summer she made her way up the winding lane. The high granite hedges were covered with all manner of wild plants, making the air heady with scents of flowers and blossoms, all protectively overshadowed by Oak, Hawthorn and Ash trees. Everywhere was the soft soporific drone of bees.

To Polly, Joss had been one of the family and in her mind she retraced the walk up Tiggy Lane to where she waited for him to return from school, when he would swoop her up into his arms and sit her on his shoulder, calling her his 'little friend'. She would laugh and playfully pull his thick black hair.

Joss was always around to amuse her, to tease, comfort, and take her for walks. Jack would come too, and sometimes Joss's older sister, Lottie. But Lottie was too old to spend much time with children. She was an apprentice in the dressmaking department of Corfield's Draper's Shop in Penryn, and was paid nine pence a week!

Joss and Lottie lived with their parents in the cottage adjoining the one where Polly lived with her parents and younger brother Jack, some two and a half miles from Penryn. The two families shared a well which was the water supply. There were no other dwellings nearby, and the Renfrees and the Pascoes became very close.

Later, when Joss reached the age, his Uncle Ben, a miner who became wealthy after emigrating to Australia, sent money to enable Joss to attend Camborne School of Mines. This meant that he had to stay in Camborne, returning after school on Fridays for the weekend. To Polly, Friday was the highlight of every week.

When Joss's schooling ended there was a party when his studies and those of a number of other students were finally over. A room was booked at a hotel on the fringe of Camborne and apparently several young ladies were present. It was at the party that Joss met Miss Clementine Du Cane. She was pretty and high-spirited and all the young males vied for her attention. But it was the good-looking boy from the rough lower classes who intrigued Miss Du Cane. Her family were reputed to be well-off and she lived in a manor. Her parents were condescending where young Joss, the poor student from the humble background was concerned. After all, he was presentable and quite handsome, the worst of the rough edges had been smoothed off by the years of mixing with rather better class young men at the mining school. Now, as a qualified mining expert, he could make big money especially in the colonies as well as the United States of America.

Right from the start Polly resented the haughty Miss Du Cane and sensed the danger that she might entice her hero away, though she would never have allowed Joss to know she thought of him as her hero. She wasn't sure she knew why Joss might prefer the disdainful young lady to herself. She had a feeling it was the feathered hats and voluminous shiny gowns which so held his attention, for he too was now smartening himself up with a new

8

suit of the latest style. Didn't Clementine du Cane know that Joss belonged to *her* family and was *her* best friend, and nice people didn't take away other people's best friends. But she had to face the fact that Joss still went off with Clementine, who wore Sunday clothes every day of the week, and when Polly protested and sulked, Joss only laughed and patted her head, acting all grown-up like father when she wanted to be allowed to stay up late.

It was on the day Joss and Clementine became engaged that Polly felt the first stirrings of love and the heartbreak of knowing Joss belonged to someone else. Love, heartbreak, hatred and jealousy were all mixed up together and Polly did not know how to handle the despair, the sadness, and the bitterness. Joss was amused then perplexed at her moods. She was small for her age but nevertheless, she was now twelve. Mother told him she was reaching a funny age and this Joss seemed to accept as one of the mysterious and secret differences between male and female.

Joss and Clementine Du Cane married and subsequently emigrated to the United States where his Uncle Ben had connections with a large mining company. Meantime, Polly grew up. The puppy-love died and the broken heart mended. She was courted by and married Edwin Pendleton who worked with his now elderly father as partner in the granite quarries old Mr Pendleton owned . . .

With a start Polly realised she had not opened the letter. Gracious! She must have been reminiscing there for at least half an hour. Her dark brown eyes glanced at the clock on the bedside locker. No; less than five minutes had elapsed since she replaced the teacup on the tray. How time played tricks! The letter was still in her hand. She again read the envelope. Heavens! Joss was already in this country . . . the postmark was London! Polly tore it open and took out a single sheet:

Dear Polly and Edwin,

You will be surprised to learn Clementine and I have decided to return home, bringing our son, Theodore, with us.

We sailed on the S.S. *Castleton* and disembarked at Southampton a couple of days ago. Clementine wants to stay a while in London with friends and I have business here, so I don't know when we shall be returning to Penryn.

We are looking forward to seeing you again in the not too distant future.

With warm good wishes from us both.

Joss.

When Polly went downstairs she found a huge bunch of red roses from Edwin awaiting her on the breakfast table. Also there was a dainty white, fine Lawn blouse wrapped in tissue paper.

'This must have been made by Lizzie Tripp,' Polly said to Mary. Only Lizzie could do pin-tucks quite like that!

Sometimes Edwin returned from the quarries at Gwarda to share a mid-day meal with Polly, and today was a must. He greeted her with a hug and a kiss and Polly gave him a box of cotton handkerchiefs with his initials embroidered in blue in a corner of each. After eating, when they were enjoying their tea Polly produced the letter from Joss.

Edwin was delighted and said, 'We must invite them here, though I expect it would take several visits to cover all the lost ground.'

Polly's thoughts turned to Clementine Du Cane, forgetting the lady was now Clementine Renfree. Would the imperious Clementine of Manor Withiel look down her nose at their home? She looked at Edwin, studying his gentle expression, the long, strong nose, hazel eyes, brown hair greying at the high temples and spare figure.

How could she think such thoughts. Edwin had provided her with a beautiful home. She was the envy of all her contemporaries. Had it not been for Edwin she might have married someone who could not do better than a tiny two up two down cottage with a solitary tap in the backyard. Here she was installed in a lovely home with four bedrooms, and a bathroom with a huge cast-iron bath, a sitting-room, dining-cum-living-room, kitchen and scullery. There was gas lighting throughout, though Polly kept a few oil lamps − just in case, a flush lavatory was incorporated in the building but entered by a door in the backyard a few feet from the kitchen door. There was a small granite-walled rose-garden to the front and a flower-bordered lawn at the rear, behind which was a herb and vegetable garden. To the rear and side was stabling for at least three ponies, though Edwin kept only one, a nut-brown

10

mare named Bessie. Behind the granite hedge at the bottom of the vegetable garden was their own field where Bessie grazed. To top it all she had a maid. How dare she, even for one instant, compare her home unfavourably with Clementine's. There wasn't a happier more blessed wife in the whole of Penryn.

'Penny for 'em,' Edwin said, passing a hand in front of her unseeing eyes.

'They were worth much more than that,' Polly said with a start. 'I was thinking what a lovely home you've given me.' She stood and looked into his face. 'Edwin, you've made me so happy.'

He beamed at her. 'You've made me very happy too, dear.'

After a brief pause and with his eyes still holding hers in his gaze, he added, 'My cup of happiness is filled. Just one more thing and it would be overflowing.'

Polly lowered her gaze. 'A baby,' she said, not looking up and her voice barely audible. Then her chin tilted as she looked back into his face and her dark brown eyes engaged his hazel ones. 'I want a baby too, you know, Edwin.'

'I know, my darling. There's plenty of time and you're young.'

'So are you young.'

'Not so young when you consider what a long-term project having a baby and bringing a child to manhood is.'

Manhood . . . Yes, he did so want a son. Polly felt a flush of guilt and again withdrew her gaze. 'Darling . . . I'm sorry.'

'What have you to be sorry for, my love? I shouldn't have said that . . . I didn't mean to. We've had a wonderful year and I should be thankful, which I am, that nothing has happened to interfere with our first year together.'

'It was a wonderful year, wasn't it?' Polly agreed.

'The best year of my life.' As Edwin spoke he pulled her to him, kissing her with fervent intensity; She experienced the return of the sense of being totally safe and secure which had momentarily deserted her; the good, happy, snug feeling which had been hers the whole of her year as Mrs Polly Pendleton.

The close members of the family were coming to have a little celebration evening with Polly and Edwin. Polly and Mary had prepared boiled ham and pork with pickles, an assortment of small savouries, saffron cake, sponge sandwiches and Cornish splits with blackberry jelly and clotted cream.

This was spread on the dining-table in advance and covered with a crisply starched white Damask tablecloth. There was a large moustache cup for Edwin's father but it was uncertain whether old Mr Pendleton would be well enough to come, and he had now handed over ownership and running of the quarries to Edwin. The lace curtains had been freshly laundered and crushed strawberry coloured velvet curtains hung on either side, topped with a deep scalloped pelmet. Against one wall was a large chiffonier topped with two port-wine-coloured lustres from the tops of which hung long rectangular crystals, pointed at the ends, and wedding and other photographs, all in silver frames.

Promptly at 7 p.m. the guests began to arrive. Edwin's dark-haired, matronly sister, Agnes, was first, with her husband, Caleb, a gingery-haired, pink-faced dumpling of a man with pale blue eyes, and Mary Jane, their nine-year-old daughter, also plump and pink with frizzy ginger hair . . . a replica of her father. Caleb was a teacher at the local Council School. They were accompanied by Edwin's mother, his father still being house-bound with a bad spell with his rheumatics. Cordelia Pendleton was tall and slim and looked elegant in a chic silver-grey dress which matched the colour of her immaculate wavy hair. Her distinguished appearance was not at all intimidating, for Cordelia had a gentle air and a smile which quickly dispelled any unease.

Next to arrive was Polly's mother, Nell Pascoe, grey-haired and petite, Polly's father having died almost three years before. She was accompanied by Joss's parents, Emily and John Renfree, the Renfree's always being regarded as 'family'. The two ladies were of similar build and could have been taken for sisters. John Renfree, whose once large frame was now bowed and somewhat shrunken, wore his navy-blue Sunday suit. His smiling dark eyes looked out from under bushy black brows streaked with silver.

After the customary greetings Emily apologised for her daughter, Lottie, who was unable to come as Nora, Emily's grand-daughter, was poorly with a tummy upset.

Agnes promptly expressed her disappointment. 'I'll never forget that gorgeous wedding-gown she made for you, Polly.'

Polly nodded agreement while Emily and John Renfree smiled with pride.

Whether Polly's brother, Jack, would put in an appearance was uncertain as his young lady, Milly Bartlett, who was one of nine children and whose father was a labourer, was both sickly and shy and Jack had confided to Polly that she was overawed by Polly with her middle-class husband, large house and maid, not to mention the presence of the parents of Joss Renfree, who was a rich and important man and married into gentry.

The ladies engaged in presenting Polly with small gifts of cotton such as handkerchiefs or muslin coverings beaded round the edges, for the tops of basins and jugs, etc. Most household items were made of superior linen. They also complimented Polly on her new coffee and cream coloured satin cloth dress trimmed with Russian braid which she had purchased for the occasion from N. Gill & Son at Truro. She was accompanied on this expedition by Edwin and he had wanted her to have a tussore silk dress she had admired, but this cost two and a half guineas and was an extravagance Polly could not allow.

Edwin, who looked impressive in well-tailored grey trousers and a wine-coloured velvet smoking jacket, poured port and lemon for the ladies and whiskies for the men. Before he had finished a knock on the front door signalled the arrival of Jack and Milly.

Polly hastened to welcome them, kissing both and hoping to reassure the pale, thin-faced girl she was indeed welcome in the Pendleton home. Edwin appeared in the hall and warmly grasped Milly's cold hand in his, saying how pleased he was to see her. A smile transformed Milly's face. She really was pretty. Polly took her coat and could not help noticing the rubbed cuffs and buttonholes. The garment had been well-worn before ever it got into Milly's possession. They joined the others in the sitting-room.

All eyes turned to greet the last arrivals. 'Hello everybody, this is Milly,' Jack announced unceremoniously and with one of his engaging smiles. 'I expect you all know her, but if you didn't . . . well, you do now.'

'Hello Milly,' they chorused.

'Hello.' Milly's reply was almost inaudible and she sat in a chair indicated by Polly.

'Milly's got something for you,' Jack said to his sister. Polly turned to Milly who handed her a small package. Eagerly Polly removed the wrapping to reveal a beautifully embroidered cotton traycloth.

'It's lovely,' Polly enthused. 'Who did this gorgeous embroidery?'

'Milly did,' Jack interjected.

'Did you?' Polly said.

Milly smiled and nodded, her cheeks now flushed bright pink.

The traycloth was passed around for all to admire and Milly was showered with compliments which both embarrassed and pleased her.

Following the traycloth the drinks were passed around and Jack quietly asked Edwin for Milly to just have lemon . . . the strength of the port might set off the cough which troubled her.

After ensuring everyone had a glass Edwin addressed Emily and John Renfree. 'We had a letter today, bringing us the good news.' Two pairs of eyes sparkled with pleasure.

'Yes, 'tis grand news. We heard today too,' John Renfree said.

'What news is this?' Agnes was agog.

'Joss and his wife and our grandson are coming home,' Emily Renfree beamed.

'Coming home . . . how exciting!'

Warmed now by the drink and excited by the bombshell of news, the conversation began to flow in an uninhibited manner. No one exactly said anything against Clementine, but no one said anything in her favour either. Everyone had reminiscences about the old days when Joss was a boy and when he was a student, and there was veiled speculation on how big was the fortune he had made in the United States. Someone had heard rumours that Clementine's parents were now in poorer circumstances. Emily and John Renfree had heard nothing of this, but showed neither surprise nor interest. They had not seen their son's parents-in-law in a very long time.

After much discussion of this and all other items of news of the townsfolk and neighbouring villagers, right down to the progress of Marcus Treloar's sick cow, they all admitted to being ready for refreshment. All trouped to the dining-room to discover young Mary Jane not only already there, but tucking into sweet things with cream, before even starting the savouries! Agnes, however, was too abstracted with all the latest news to remember to reprimand her daughter for this double misdemeanour.

Eating did little to reduce the pace of conversation, and talk of the suffering of Great Uncle Harry with his chronic indigestion did not impair hearty appetites. Milly's face betrayed astonishment at the sight of so much food. Plates of meat patties, sausage rolls and sandwiches disappeared in a twinkling and were replaced just as swiftly. But the girl herself ate little and took a long time over the little she had.

'Eat up, Milly,' Polly encouraged. 'We don't want all this left on our hands.'

She saw the tightened lips and swift small shake of Jack's head and knew she must not press her young guest.

'Milly can't take a lot of rich food,' Jack said.

'Oh well, you just have what suits you, Milly,' Polly replied and moved to talk to Edwin's mother and sister.

A few minutes later Milly began to cough, then rushed from the room into the hall, followed by Jack. Polly waited a few moments then followed them into the hall where Milly, with a large handkerchief pressed to her mouth, was racked by coughing. Jack had an arm about her, but could do nothing. The spasm passed and Milly pushed the handkerchief into her handbag. Her face was wet where watering eyes had overflowed onto her cheeks.

'I'll take her home,' Jack said to his sister.

'Edwin can take you in the wagonette,' Polly said.

'Thanks, Pol, but it isn't far to Shute Lane and the fresh air will be good for her,' Jack replied.

'Would you like to rest a little while?' Polly asked, turning to Milly.

'No. I'll be all right, thank you, Mrs Pendleton.'

'Polly,' Polly corrected.

'Polly. You've been so kind to me. It's been a wonderful evening.'

'Say cheerio for Milly,' Jack said.

'I will,' Polly replied. 'Be sure you both come and see us again.'

At this Milly smiled, and with good-byes over Polly returned to her guests.

'Jack's taking Milly home,' she announced when she entered the dining-room. 'He asked me to say good-bye for Milly.'

'What's wrong with her?' Agnes asked. 'Something go down the wrong way?'

'Something like that,' Polly said, but thought that poor girl is

15

far from well.

By now the biggest appetite was sated and the guests returned to the sitting-room while Polly made tea and coffee to complete the refreshments.

For a while tongues wagged, then returned to the topic uppermost in the thoughts of Emily and John Renfree . . . Joss's homecoming. Apart from wondering whether Milly was all right, it was uppermost in Polly's mind also.

'I expect you'll be pleased to see Joss again, Polly?'

Polly was too shaken by the question to know who had spoken. 'I . . . I . . . ' she stammered, searching for an appropriate reply. But the sudden return of Jack saved the situation.

Polly was curious to see Joss, to know how he looked, hear again the sound of his voice. But she didn't want old memories raked up and brought to the surface . . . or did she mean old loves? There was the nagging fear that Joss's arrival would herald change, and she was happy with her present life. She had a doting husband whom she loved . . . she *did* love Edwin; a beautiful home here in Penryn among friends and family. It was perfect. Perhaps Joss would have changed a lot and she wouldn't like him as much as she once did. That would be good . . . wouldn't it?

'How's the little maid?' Polly's mother asked Jack.

'She's tired,' Jack said. 'Milly was off work sick last week,' he explained. 'And she's still feeling the effects.'

Polly gazed at her tall, lean, fair-haired brother and felt a pang of sympathy. The girl he had fallen in love with was far from well. It looked like he could be taking a big burden onto his young shoulders.

'Glad you came back, Jack. Now we can "strike sound",' said John Renfree.

They sang a number of popular tunes and favourite hymns. Polly's voice was mezzo-soprano, Agnes contralto, John Renfree had a deep plumb bass voice, Edwin was a baritone, Caleb's voice was second tenor and Jack had a sweet tenor voice which, as his mother so often described, soared like a bird.

Cordelia, Emily Renfree and Nell Pascoe preferred to sit and listen, joining in now and then with a chorus. The final song was *Loves Old Sweet Song*, sung in honour of Polly and Edwin's anniversary, and causing both Cordelia and Nell to reach for their handkerchiefs.

*   *   *   *

The last guests now departed, Edwin shut the front door, his arms encircled his wife and he kissed her.

'Thanks again for a wonderful year, my love,' he whispered, when at last he withdrew his lips from hers.

Polly smiled up at him and nodded. 'Yes, it was wonderful,' she agreed.

'Let's get to bed,' Edwin said.

'There's the dishes.'

'Mary can do those in the morning.'

'I'll just stack them, ready for her,' Polly replied, and moved to go to the dining-room.

But Edwin caught her arm with a firm restraining hand. 'It's our wedding anniversary,' he said, looking down at her intently. 'We're not going to end the day bothering with dishes.'

Polly recognised the determination in his voice and manner. Edwin definitely had other ideas on how the evening would end.

Together they mounted the stairs, Edwin with a spring in his step, Polly slowly, suddenly tired. At the top of the stairs Edwin pulled Polly to him and kissed her again, hard and passionately. Then his lips released hers and he stood back a little, gazing down at her. She saw the light of desire in his hazel eyes, desire and something else . . .

Polly read his mind. The first year of married life was over. Tonight the real married life, *family* life, would begin. Tonight he was going to start a family. Tonight he was determined to make his wife pregnant!

Suddenly Polly felt slightly faint. She was tired and she didn't feel like love-making.

Edwin's jacket was already off. With a single swift tug his tie was removed and flung in the direction of the jacket. He turned to her and with fingers slightly trembling with urgency, helped undo the fastenings on her dress. Usually responsive, always compliant, for the first time Polly braced herself. Silently she issued a command . . . Polly, you mustn't fail him this time!

17

Chapter Two

The days which followed seemed flat, an anti-climax. Polly's main concern was to learn she was with child. This must have accounted for the hideous dream, from which she awoke with a despairing sob.

She had a baby, Edwin's baby, a boy, and she had lost it. She was frantically searching everywhere but the infant was nowhere to be found. Then, with a sickening jolt, she was suddenly awake to the realisation that the baby she and Edwin so fervently hoped for, especially so since the night of their wedding anniversary, was still only a dream. Familiar cramp-like pains low in her abdomen, and other signs, told her the longed for addition to the family, the natural result of the union of man and wife, was not taking place within her.

For a while she lay with her back to Edwin, so that even though he was asleep and it was dark, there would be no chance of him seeing the unstoppable tears which flowed from half-closed eyelids, wetting her cheeks and the pillow, and filling her with despair and grief for the loss of the baby that never was.

After what seemed a long time, Polly slid from the bed and silently removed a handful of handkerchiefs from the top drawer of the dressing-table, then left the bedroom.

Downstairs in the kitchen she made herself tea, tears still flowing as she went through the motions of filling the kettle, warming the brown teapot and putting milk into the blue and white cup. As she sat at the kitchen table, lost in her own misery, she did not hear Edwin enter. Swiftly he was at her side, a comforting arm about her shoulders.

'Darling, whatever is the matter?' Concern filled his hazel eyes as he gazed down at her face, her eyes red and swollen with weeping.

Polly, knowing the disappointment she was about to inflict on him, choked on a sob and was unable to speak. Edwin held her to him, her wet face buried against his chest and her tears saturating the front of his striped linen pyjama jacket.

Comfortingly he kissed her long, tousled black hair. 'Darling, what is it? Nothing can be this bad,' he soothed.

Oh but it can, Polly thought as she remembered the anniversary night, just three weeks ago, when Edwin's lovemaking reached a new pitch of double-desire to both enter and be one with her and to leave within her the beginnings of new life . . . the continuation of himself, of his own flesh and blood in a son, his son, his and Polly's. She swallowed noisily and tried to speak.

'Go on, sweetheart.' He held her slightly away from him where he could read what was written in her face.

'There isn't any baby!' Polly blurted the words and promptly again buried her head in his chest, unable to bear the sight of his disappointment.

They clung together for a couple of long seconds before Edwin spoke.

'Is that all, darling?' His voice was unnaturally flippant. 'I told you there was plenty of time. You're only twenty-two years old . . . and sweetheart, I intend to be making love to you for umpteen years to come . . .' He forced a laugh. 'For the rest of my life!'

'It's good of you to make light of it, Edwin,' Polly said, knowing that what he had just said was quite out of character. Edwin did not talk that way, nor did he make risqué jokes.

'Here, let me dry your eyes,' he said, producing a dry clean handkerchief. He dried her face and put the handkerchief to her nose. 'Blow,' he ordered as though she were a child. Dutifully Polly obeyed, and yielded up the sodden handkerchief she held in her hand.

'Now,' Edwin said, making his voice sound cheerful. 'You didn't drink your tea and it must be cold. I'm going to make us both a fresh cup and you must have some aspirin. You'll feel better in no time,' he went on talking as he moved about the kitchen. 'You really have got all this out of proportion and I know why,' he chatted on. 'I do know that ladies are not quite themselves at certain times,' Edwin enlarged as he put three spoonfuls of tea into the pot. This was not a subject normally spoken about by him. 'You are a very clear-headed lady, my darling Polly, and you will be right as rain.'

19

Dear Edwin, Polly thought. He is trying so hard, and hiding his own disappointment so well. But underneath I know it is there.

Edwin poured Polly's tea and passed it to her along with some aspirins he had taken from a bottle. He sat facing her.

'You are just like my mother,' he said.

'Oh, how?' Polly had at last stopped weeping and was more composed.

'She and my father were married more than two years before Agnes was on the way.'

'I didn't know that.' Polly at last was able to smile at Edwin. This bit of information really was cheering. Cordelia had borne four children; as well as Agnes and Edwin there was a brother who drowned in a shipwreck several years ago, and a sister who was married and settled in South Africa. And he was right. She really had got it all out of proportion. The dream had seemed so real. That was what made her so upset, that and disappointing Edwin. He had given her everything and a son was the one thing she could and should give to him, and that she desperately wanted to do.

She suddenly realised that since the letter and the news from Joss of his imminent return to Penryn, she had been continually reminding herself and going over in her mind how fortunate she was to be married to Edwin. She was just an ordinary girl who lived with her mother and brother in a small granite cottage with shared well-water at the rear of the house. Now she was mistress of Villa Gwidden – the White House – with a position in the community of Penryn. How on earth could a letter from Joss make her so suddenly aware of how blessed she was in having Edwin for her husband. No . . . no . . . it wasn't the letter from Joss. . . It must have been the effect of the wedding anniversary, reminding her of how different her life now was to what it was like when she worked in Councillor Corfield's Draper's shop.

She drained the remains of the tea, suddenly aware that Edwin had been waiting for her to finish.

'Come back to bed,' he said, and taking her hand they returned to the bedroom. Edwin put an extra pillow on Polly's side to raise her head to allow the congestion of accumulated tears to drain away. Wearied by emotion, they lay side by side, hand in hand, Polly now feeling more relaxed, more composed, more hopeful. She *could* bear a child, she just *knew* she could. One day she'd have a son . . . one day she'd give Edwin the son he'd set his heart on, one day . . .

Chapter Three

The two-carriage branch-line train rumbled as it slowed, then screeched to a halt at Penryn Station, which nestled on a flat wide ridge, half way up a high hill, aloft of the town. Doors opened and there was a minor flurry of activity as seven or eight passengers alighted.

Among them, carrying a small overnight case, was a tall, big-framed man who looked different from the others. It was his clothes, though his dark good looks and bearing would have ensured that he would never be overlooked. His dress did not have the slightly drab, dark sameness about it as the suits and working wear of the people about him. His suit was a fawn colour with a darker thread running through it both vertically and horizontally, forming little squares. His coat was not of heavy, dark, durable worsted material, which kept out the east wind, but was a fawn colour and of lightweight material, which was something of an extravagance, keeping out neither wet nor wind, and served only to add a modicum of protection and to look smart. But Penrynians were used to seeing emigrants returning from America to visit home and kith and kin. The only difference was, there was usually a crowd of relatives waiting to greet a returning son of Cornwall.

The man looked about him, drinking in the scene and filling his lungs deep with Cornish air, mingled with smoke from the engine. Then, close by, a voice addressed him.

'Why, bless my soul. 'Tis Joss Renfree or I'm much mistaken.'

The soft burr and sing-songy lilt of Cornish voices were music to his ears. Joss turned and saw a short, stocky young man with shiny round cheeks.

'It's never Jim Paull, Ron's young brother who used to plague me to sit on my shoulder to get a better view of Ron playing rugby?'

'The very same,' said the young man, his artless face beaming as he extended a hand to shake Joss's and with his other hand warmly grasped Joss's arm. Joss instantly reciprocated. By now two couples – George and Cissic Trembath and Ben and Olga Pellow – were standing, also waiting to welcome Joss, who was bombarded with questions on how he had fared on the other side of 'the pond', how Clementine had fared, and Theodore; had he seen Willy White, Skeet Harris, Jenny Mossop and a string of other emigrants, was he home to stay, etc?

The small gathering was growing into a big one and Jim Paull invited them to his mother's cottage, little more than a stone's throw away in Helston Road, for a cup of tea and a piece of his Ma's saffron cake.

Joss thanked him, but refused, pointing out the welcome he expected from his mother would turn into a hiding if he was much later. The mental picture of tiny, Mrs Renfree laying into her hefty six-foot son set them all laughing, and although Joss declined to stop at Mrs Paull's cottage, the others accepted the invitation to have tea and cake, and no doubt sit and talk over the latest and one of the most successful of the many Penryn boys, and some girls, who had crossed the great Atlantic to seek their fortunes in the new and exciting land of opportunity.

Greetings and farewells over, Joss went in one direction and the gathering moved in a body in another. Joss could have taken a cab, but had looked forward to walking the two and half miles. On the way he would pass within half a mile of Villa Gwidden where Polly his 'little friend' lived with her husband, Edwin Pendleton. Joss had been glad to learn the little girl he had always regarded with brotherly affection, had made such a good marriage. Edwin, he had always considered to be a really decent chap, a tiny bit stodgy, but nevertheless honest, upright and loyal. The respect in which Edwin and his parents were held in the community was richly deserved. He was a good employer too, Joss's own father had worked for old Mr Pendleton.

But Joss had seen to it that his parents were now independent with their own nest-egg, half in the bank, the rest invested in four cottages which brought in an income in rent. He would have liked to give them a nicer home, but they did not wish to leave the tiny house which held so many memories.

As he walked Joss paused now and then, not because the road was uphill most of the way, but to look about him, to drink in the views, to turn and look where Penryn was hidden under the steep hill but the more distant Penryn River shone pink and golden in the light of the setting sun. Further along the river curved, and on the right were the hills which led down into Falmouth, while opposite, nestling at the foot of the surrounding hills and protected from all but the soft wind from the south was the village of Flushing. Beyond the curve of Flushing the river widened into one of the best, one of the deepest, and most beautiful natural harbours in the world. Here was a miscellany of craft and vessels of every description, nationality and appearance from breathtakingly beautiful schooners, clippers, windjammers, cutters, yawls, sloops, packet ships and brigs to steamships, coasters, barges, dredgers, pleasure boats and ferries, fishing boats, etc. The harbour abounded with masts and small local boats weaving from one vessel to another, plying their wares and some exchanging English for foreign money.

The sheltered waters were known to seafaring men the world over for safe haven. How good it was to be back in Cornwall.

Joss had told his parents not to come to the station to meet him, saying he was unsure which train he would be travelling on and thoughts of them and 'home' made him turn his back on Penryn and the river, and hurry the last three-quarters of a mile, noting as he went the familiar fields, farmhouses and landscape scarred by granite quarries and quarry spoil.

Who was the figure coming towards him, a familiar form but bent and old-looking. The man waved.

'Father,' Joss shouted, and ran towards him, his father struggled to run too. The distance was rapidly covered by Joss and the two stood middle of the road, hugging each other and laughing, and when at last they managed to extricate themselves from each other's embrace, to look at last into the face of the other, Joss saw with a pang the craggy, lined face, beaming with joy and wet with tears of happiness. His father's stiff, gnarled fingers fumbled for his handkerchief to wipe away the tears, laughing as he did so and saying, ' 'Tis good to see you, Joss my boy, 'tis so good to see you.'

'Good to see you too, father,' Joss said, noting he was now

taller than his father's shrunken frame.

'Mother's home waiting, with Lottie and George and little Nora.'

'How is mother?'

'Looking forward to seeing you, my boy. How are Clementine and Theodore?'

'They're fine. They're staying a few weeks more in London, but they're anxious to see everyone at home.'

Joss's mind was working on two levels, carrying on a conversation and thinking how much he had to reduce his pace to suit his father's slow progress. This was not as he remembered. All his life father had seemed exactly the same unchanged by years or circumstances. Without giving it a thought, he had expected to find him unaltered. His pleasure at returning home took on a deeper significance. It was time he came back. Thank God he did before it was too late.

They walked along, talking and laughing. The countryside was unchanged. Here was Tiggy Lane and there was the spot where 'little friend' used to wait for him to come home from school and later, on Fridays, from Camborne School of Mines.

He took his father's arm as he stumbled slightly in a rut. Then, round a bend by the elder tree he could see the two cottages. There was mother. How tiny and frail she looked! She and Joss started to run toward each other and in seconds Joss had clasped her in his strong arms, sweeping her feet off the ground while she shrieked with joy as her arms encircled his neck. At such times minds seem to function with a speed exceeding that of lightning. In a split second, along with the joy of seeing his mother, Joss registered his sister Lottie and her husband, George, with a little girl who must be his niece, Nora; Mrs Pascoe and a tall, pleasant-looking young man who must be Polly's young brother, Jack Pascoe. How those absent years had flown! What changes! How feather-light his mother was! How much older she looked! Both he and his mother were now laughing as he whirled her round in a spin, before coming to a standstill, when the two released their hold on one another sufficiently to enable them to look each other directly in the face.

As with his father, his mother's face was wet with tears as she stared joyously at him; but he gazed into the same shining brown eyes which had last looked into his when he bade her good-bye around ten years ago.

'My Joss is a boy no longer,' Emily Renfree said in a soft voice. 'And I didn't even see the changes.'

'If I stayed at home, mother, you never would have noticed the changes,' Joss replied, his voice equally soft.

'Oh yes I would,' she answered. 'You've become your father all over again.'

Hugs and kisses were exchanged with the others and a special greeting for the little niece he had never seen before, as well as news for Lottie and George of their two sons, Eric and Oliver who lived and worked just outside the London area. Joss had already visited the two nephews he last saw as small boys, and who were now both 'learning their trade in the motor business'.

They moved into the cottage which was even smaller than Joss remembered, and Nell Pascoe poured tea, leaving Emily to feast her eyes on her son.

'Best cup of tea I've tasted in years,' Joss pronounced as he drank from the special occasion only, rosebud-covered bone china tea-set he remembered so well.

Joss apologised that his presents from the distant United States were in the trunks in transit, but he did have a present with him for little Nora, his niece. Nora jumped up and down with excitement as Joss took from his pocket a manilla envelope with a jeweller's name on it.

The eager child ripped it open and took out a small flat box. She lifted the lid and sitting inside, on a satin padded base, was a dainty gold bracelet with a chased pattern.

'It's too small!' she exclaimed, disappointed. 'I can't get it on!'

'Let me show you,' said Joss. 'See this?' He showed her a tiny gold protrusion which he pressed and, hey presto, the bracelet opened out and expanded to show an inner gold extension which allowed a hand to be inserted, and then clicked shut again, making a safe and perfect fit.

Nora was delighted. 'I'll only wear it on Sundays,' she promised, and promptly put it on again, holding out her chubby arm to admire the effect.

Joss's bedroom was the one at the rear of the cottage. With a sudden welcome feeling of peace and repose, he sank into the

b

soft, feather-stuffed mattress. He luxuriated in his boyhood surroundings. Humble though they were, they gave him a sense of security and well-being, of comfort, of safe haven, surrounded by people he could totally, utterly trust. In the recesses of his mind he drew a comparison . . . unlike Clementine, or her father, or her brother, or . . . The whispering of the west wind soughed around the eves close to his ear, lulling him to sleep.

'Morning Joss, my handsome. Did you sleep well?'

Joss crossed the living-room to where his mother stood by the Cornish range, and kissed her.

'Morning, mother. Best night I've had in years,' he replied, beaming.

Emily smiled. 'Sit down, dear,' she said. 'Would you like your breakfast now, or will you wait for father?'

'I'll wait for father,' Joss said, taking a seat at the large kitchen-style table which stood opposite the range and which was covered with a snow-white, starched tablecloth.

'He'll take a while,' Emily warned. 'He's always stiff in the mornings, but he'll loosen up as the day goes on. I'll pour us a cup of tea and while we're waiting you can tell me all about my grandson. There didn't seem to be much chance last evening with everybody talking.'

Over breakfast, when at last John Renfree joined them, he suggested they go for a stroll in the afternoon.

'Do you feel up to it?' Joss asked. He had been shocked to discover how long it took his father to get down the stairs for breakfast. Yet clearly breakfast in bed, as his parents had said, would only worsen the problem.

'I like to go for a walk every day,' his father replied. 'Don't want to rust.'

'Have you any idea where you intend to live, Joss?' Emily asked as they finished their eggs, bacon and sausages.

'Yes, mother, we are going to live in Clemmie's parents' home,' Joss replied.

The smile disappeared from Emily's face. 'Going to live with your in-laws!' Surprise, disapproval and concern all mingled in her voice.

'No, mother. Clemmie's father's textile business has suffered losses and they are going to sell their home to us and live in a smaller place. There will then be some money left over to see them through a difficult patch.'

'Buy Manor Withiel! What do you want with a barn of a place like that? All those big damp rooms, they'll cost a fortune to heat and keep aired. And one maid, like Polly Pendleton has won't be enough to look after it, even if Clementine helped with the housework every day of the week.'

Joss had never known Clementine to help at all with the housework, but did not say so. 'It's Clemmie's *home*, mother. She doesn't want to see it go out of the family, and we have to live somewhere. It seems the obvious thing to do.'

Neither of Joss's parents replied to this observation and Joss knew from their silence they did not think it a good move. He too, knew it was foolish and would prove expensive, but it was what Clemmie wanted, and they were trying to repair the rift in their marriage. To refuse her entreaties to buy the home which she desired so much, and at the same time, to help her family in a difficult financial situation . . . a crisis, apparently . . . was not something he could refuse, though his head told him he should.

Joss shot a glance at his mother. He could read her thoughts. It seemed odd to buy Clementine's parents' home when eventually half of it would become hers anyway. Or was the situation so bad her parents were in danger of losing Manor Withiel?

The brief silence was ended by the quiet, gentle voice of Joss's father.

'It's just the way it sounds to us, Joss, not knowing the full facts,' his father said. 'If you think it is the best thing to do, then you have your reasons, and you must do what you think is right.' He looked into Joss's face and smiled at him, confident his son knew what he was about.

His mother nodded agreement. 'That's true,' she said.

There was a knock on the back door. ' 'Tis only me,' said a voice.

'Come in, Nell,' Emily shouted, and Nell Pascoe entered from the door to the scullery.

'I just dropped in to say "good morning".' Her face beamed.

'Good morning, Nell,' the Renfree's chorused.

Emily had started to pour the last cup of tea for each and passed a cup to Nell.

'Come here and sit beside me, Nell,' John Renfree said, and Nell squeezed in at the table between Joss and his father.

'We've been having a leisurely breakfast,' Joss said to Nell.

'Don't blame you, my handsome,' she said. 'How does it feel to be home?'

'Wonderful,' Joss replied. 'Makes me wonder why I ever left.'

Inevitably they reminisced about old times. At last Emily looked up at the clock on the high mantelpiece. 'It can't be that time!' she said in disbelief.

'I'll wash the dishes for you,' Nell volunteered, and started clearing the table.

Emily Renfree had invited the Penhales and Sam and Ellen Thomas to spend the evening at the cottage as they were eager to see Joss. By the time John Renfree, now more mobile, was ready for the walk, Emily decided to stay at home.

'If I come with you I shall be all behind,' she said to John and Joss.

'Just like the cow's tail,' Nell laughed. 'Can I help you?'

'No, dear, you're going to the vicarage. The pastry is made for sausage rolls, and I've only got to do splits, saffron buns and make sandwiches. But you know what it's like cooking with yeast; you have to wait for it to rise, and it doesn't pay to rush it.'

'If you're sure,' Nell replied.

Joss and his father were late returning from their afternoon walk.

'I thought you'd forgotten the way home,' Emily said when at last they returned.

'We were passing Marcus Treloar's farm and he asked us in for a chat,' John explained.

'Here's a dozen eggs and a dish of clotted cream he insisted on giving us,' Joss said, as he looked about for a space on the table which was covered with baking for the evening's visitors.

'That was good of him,' Emily replied. 'Put them in the scullery where it's cool.'

Joss disappeared into the small back room and grabbed a Saffron bun as he returned. 'These buns smell gorgeous, do you mind if I help myself?' he said, having already taken a bite out of a large warm bun streaked red with strands of saffron.

'Will it make any difference if I do?' Emily laughed.

There was a knock on the cottage door.

'Come in,' Emily shouted, as Joss, swallowing the remains of the bun, went to greet the caller.

'Edwin!' he said, warmly clasping Edwin Pendleton's hand.

'Come in and have a hot saffron bun,' Emily said. 'Try and stop me,' Edwin replied. 'I could smell them halfway down the lane.'

'Didn't expect to see you at this time of day,' John Renfree said to Edwin.

'I would have called on the way home from work at the usual time, but I've left early to give a message to Polly's mother before she leaves to go to the Vicarage to cook for the vicar, only she's not there. Still, I expect you can pass it on for me, Mrs Renfree.'

'Yes, I'll do that,' Emily replied. 'She went early because the vicar has two guests tonight and she wanted to cook something special. What's the message?'

'Polly had a letter from Lerryn. Her Great Aunt Elizabeth is very poorly and a neighbour wrote to inform us. Polly feels she should go, otherwise her mother would have to, and she has her part-time cooking job to consider. It would be better for her if Polly went.'

'Nell didn't say anything,' Emily said.

'We only heard today,' Edwin explained, 'and Polly went out this morning to enquire about train times.'

'I'll tell Nell as soon as she gets home,' Emily assured.

Edwin turned his attention to Joss. 'Polly will be disappointed to miss you. Are you free to come and see us this evening?'

'We've got the Penhales and the Thomas's coming to see Joss this evening,' Emily interrupted.

'I'm sorry, Edwin, but mother has already invited them,' Joss said. 'I'm not going to be here long, just a week or two, then I shall return to London until Clementine has seen everything and everyone she wants. After that we shall be back for good and there will be all the time in the world.'

Edwin was interested in the things Joss had done in the United States, especially local people he met in America. Mining experts were in demand in many parts of the States and where there were mines there were Cornishmen. Joss met quite a few Penryn boys. Arthur May had married an American girl and had become integrated into her large family. There were the Datsons, along with two of the Francis family from Penryn, Absalom and

Jane — Elisha, Elijah and Harry having returned home with their mother who refused to stay — also Tom Andrew, who was doing well.

But Joss detected no desire on his part to strike out and try his luck in the 'land of opportunity', the 'great melting-pot', nor any regret that he had never given it a try. It wasn't that Edwin did not possess a venturesome streak; although a trifle stodgy he was game to try his luck, pit his wits. There could be only one reason for his seemingly complete satisfaction and contentment with life, Joss thought. Edwin was a happy man. He had not married young to the first girl who came along. Oh no. He waited for the one who was just right. And clearly he had found her in Polly. Good for Polly! For what else could make a red-blooded, if cautious, man in his mid-thirties that content. Only a very special woman. Lucky Edwin, Joss thought. Edwin sometimes appeared hesitant in latching on to new things and ideas, but in the long term he usually came out on top. He never did anything in hot blood. He was cool enough to distance himself, to consider all the pros and cons, before deciding which way to act. Edwin was not rich like Joss, but he had all the money he needed to make life good, and he had a good marriage with the woman he loved. What more could any man ask? Joss felt a tinge of wistfulness. He continued with his tale.

'There is one particular thing which might interest you.'

'What's that?'

'Do you remember Bill Boaden, his father had a small farm over Mawnan Smith way . . ?

Edwin paused to think. 'They used to sell lovely crusted clotted cream?'

'They're the ones. Bill had a restless streak and thought he'd do better mining in the U.S. than keeping cows in Mawnan. Well, he had to spend a fair time in California in The Great Kalmoosh Mine up to his waist in water and it affected his health. He was warned that in future he must work above ground. He knew of a ranch with good pasture in Michigan that he really wanted to work, only he had no capital. He told me all about it, talked so much I went with him to look, and it really was attractive . . . not like here, of course, the ranch-house was made of wood for a start, but I thought, "Well, it's a good investment, and it's good to diversify." I bought the ranch and . . . '

'But you know next to nothing about farming,' Edwin interjected.

'True, but *Bill* knows about it and I don't think he'll let me down. He's running it for me. He gets his pay for running the ranch, hiring and firing, buying and selling, and gets a good percentage of the profits. He'll make a good job of it. If I don't get a profit, he doesn't either. It's the next best thing to owning it himself. He could never have done that and he knows it. Bill might have had a wandering streak when he went to the U.S. but that illness changed him, that and the passing of the years. He has discovered a latent interest in farming, just like his father before him.'

'I seem to remember hearing he was a bit of a rip when he was young,' Edwin agreed.

'Yes, well Bill's also got a fancy for a widow he's met. She sounds just right for a farmer's wife. I'm sure he's really ready to settle down.'

'Well, Joss, it sounds like a good investment. A sort of background safe bet I'd say,' Edwin concluded.

Edwin looked at his watch. 'Must go or the meal will spoil and Polly won't like that.'

Joss laughed. 'It's not wise to upset the wife.'

All went to the door to bid Edwin good-bye and he departed. 'Be sure to visit soon,' Edwin shouted from the cottage gate.

'I will,' Joss replied.

'You're not eating your breakfast, Joss. Aren't you hungry?'

'Yes, mother, I'm hungry. It's just that I was miles away,' Joss replied.

'You were looking thoughtful last evening. Is everything all right at Manor Withiel? . . . I'll never get used to the idea of you living in a manor . . . doesn't seem fitty, somehow,' she remarked.

'That's true,' Joss said, and swallowed some tea.

'Ah yes, 'tis what Clementine wants,' she said, pointedly.

'Now mother,' Joss's father said, mild reproof in his tone.

'It's all right, father,' Joss said. 'Mother's right. But I've already explained, it's Clemmie's home. Only it's in more of a mess than I expected.'

'The Manor?' his father asked.

'The whole situation,' Joss replied.

Joss's mother hit the nub of the matter. 'It'll cost a lot to put right!'

'One way and another,' Joss confirmed. He had been at Manor Withiel several days. 'I've dealt with everything. Work has already started on roof repairs, there are fairly extensive general repairs, then there will be some decorating; some of it I can do myself. I've sorted out the finances with the solicitor and Clemmie's family, and they know where *they* stand,' he added, meaningfully. 'With a bit of luck everything should now be straight-forward.' His face broke into the familiar smile. 'Don't look so worried, mother. It's just that now and then I have to make Clemmie understand that where money is concerned, every pit has a bottom.'

Emily Renfree sniffed. As a wife, she did not hold a high opinion of her exalted daughter-in-law. When Joss became engaged to the high-flown young lady, she had viewed the prospect with a mixture of awe and 'Aw!'

'I'll spend a few more days here with you, and looking up old friends, mother,' Joss said. 'Then I'll go back to London and bring Clemmie and Theodore home . . . and that will be that,' he added with a tone of finality.

Chapter Four

Edwin, with Bessie and the small beautifully crafted wagonette, was at the station to meet Polly on her return from Lerryn.

'It's good to be home, Edwin,' she said with a grateful sigh as they entered Villa Gwidden.

Edwin, who had kissed her with restrained propriety when she alighted from the train at the station, threw with abandon his black bowler hat at the hat-stand in the entrance hall, and kissed his wife tenderly and long.

'I can't tell you how good it is to have *you* home,' he murmured. 'These last three and a half weeks seemed like eternity.'

'They were for me,' Polly admitted, reflecting that Great Aunt Elizabeth was not the easiest person to nurse and care for. I don't know how anyone can get so out-of-temper in such heavenly surroundings,' she added. 'And all the neighbours seem so pleasant.'

'Never mind.' Edwin kissed her cheek comfortingly. 'You're home now.'

Polly had already put thoughts of Joss's return behind her. The stay with Great Aunt Elizabeth which seemed interminable, made her long to be at home, enjoying her old lifestyle. It no longer seemed true that Joss and Clementine were returning. It was unreal and dreamlike. Edwin was her own dear husband. She was Mrs Pendleton, mistress of Villa Gwidden. She was going to bear Edwin's children, preferably two boys and two girls. And nothing was ever going to change.

She would love to see Joss once more. Just one look, when natural curiosity about how he really had fared and how he now looked, would be satisfied. The stay at Lerryn had made her even more aware how lucky she was to be married to Edwin. Thankfulness flooded her bosom. How happy she was to be home.

Mary had gone off duty, but left a prepared tea-tray on the kitchen table, awaiting her arrival. Polly had found it both strange and pleasant to get accustomed at Villa Gwidden to the simplicity of heating a kettle on the gas stove instead of on a Cornish range, which required regular black-leading as well as having the ornamental brass parts polished. Then there was the daily raking out of cinders, the removal of ashes, and relaying to kindle and to start the whole process over again.

With typical thoughtfulness, outright indulgence some thought, Edwin had seen to it that his bride had both.

With the tray of tea, and scones plastered with soft yellow butter from Marcus Treloar's farm, they settled side by side on the sofa in the sitting-room.

'And how was Lerryn?' Edwin enquired.

'Lerryn was idyllic, out of this world,' Polly said. 'You really must go there sometime, Edwin. It's so pretty, low down in the valley sheltered by the steep hills either side, it seems shut off and distant from the present-day world. A little hump-back bridge straddles the river, where there are unusual breeds of duck and they sit on the banks sunning themselves, with their ducklings all around them, quite unconcerned and unafraid of whatever else is going on about them. The small quaint cottages are intermixed with larger, more grand houses on the river banks, and all have the most colourful flower gardens, some flowers I've never even seen before. Even those with practically no garden seem to find patches of soil and containers to grow all kinds of blooms. The air is so balmy and everything blooms early. I don't think the weather can ever be unkind in Lerryn.'

'Well, there's an encomium, if ever I heard one! You paint such a pretty picture, darling, but I really meant "How is Great Aunt Elizabeth?" ' Edwin was smiling with amusement at what seemed to be a speech.

'Oh,' Polly paused, embarrassed, and tried to call to mind the right word to describe her Aunt. 'Crotchety,' she said. 'Otherwise much better and really able to manage very well now.'

'Her cough is better, then?'

'Almost gone.'

'Did you give her your favourite cough mixture, the one with wine and treacle?'

'It's more than wine and treacle, and it's not any old wine, either,' Polly said defensively.

'What is it then, darling?' Edwin grinned.

Polly feigned annoyance. 'You're not really interested, you're just trying to humour me.'

'No I'm not,' Edwin lied gallantly, 'I'm really interested!'

She gave him a playful slap. 'Shan't tell you.'

He laughed, loving it when his wife got rough with him. To think that when he was single he would have considered such goings on to be unseemly. How marriage changed a man! He never wanted to be single ever again.

'Go on, tell.'

Polly, whose lips were tightly pressed together trying to suppress a grin, folded her arms across her chest in a gesture of defiance. Edwin seized his opportunity and, placing his hand on her stomach, dug his forefinger into the soft curve of her belly. This was Polly's vulnerable spot, the one place where she was ticklish. With a yelp she collapsed, laughing, screaming, and trying with flailing arms and legs to fend Edwin off, until they both sank exhausted and convulsed into a heap on the sofa. Edwin, having the vantage position of being over Polly managed to get both her wrists clasped in his narrow strong hands. Rugby tackles were never this good!

He lowered his face close over hers. 'Tell,' he commanded, squeezing her wrists even tighter.

'Shan't,' came the plucky reply, along with a shower of spittle caused by trying to speak and suppress a laugh at the same time. Edwin received the droplets full in the face and, weakened with uncontrollable laughter, eased his grip to swiftly wipe a blinded eye. Polly, laughing, succeeded in raising herself a little. Edwin's arms promptly encircled her, and his mouth was over hers, pressing against her, his arms encasing her body which he crushed to his own, little ecstatic squeaks and moans now and then escaping his throat. At last his mouth released her lips sufficiently for him to speak.

'Come upstairs.' His voice was both coaxing and commanding. His mouth again clamped hers and Polly instantly computed her thoughts. Edwin's arousal, midway of tea and scones, was unplanned and overpowering, and caused his natural sense of the conventional – there was a proper time and place for everything, and late afternoon was not the time when married couples of rectitude and probity did that – to scatter to the four winds.

His hold slackened and he relinquished her lips, all laughter now replaced by the strength of a more urgent overwhelming need. He held out a hand and took hers, drawing her up from the sofa.

'Come on,' he said, and kissed her once again, then, with one arm encircling Polly's slim waist, guided her out of the sitting-room and towards the staircase.

On waking from a deliciously relaxed, hour long sleep which followed their impetuous love-making, it occurred to Polly that their union, prompted by nothing but the sheer joy of being together, was the best, the most ideal way for a start to be made in founding a family. She snuggled deep into the pillows, a feeling of delicious contentment pervading all her senses. She had not been the least bit anxious about it, neither had Edwin. She was relaxed, happy and unconcerned. All she and Edwin had thought of was their happiness in being together again, and the unique pleasure of their being one. The portents were good. Surely this time their union would be blessed.

She smiled to herself at the prospect, unaware that Edwin, who was lying beside her, was watching, propped on one elbow. Lazily she opened her eyes and he brushed her cheek with a kiss. Her eyes stared up into his. He too was smiling the same happy smile. Polly instinctively knew they had both been thinking the same thoughts. Unspoken hopes were high.

A fortnight after, Polly again made the discovery that she was not pregnant. She shed no tears; gave no outward sign that anything was amiss.

That evening, with less emotion than if telling him the mayoress's cat had toothache, she imparted the news to Edwin. As if tuned in to her mood, he said nothing, but just stared for a few long seconds into her face, reading the message in her deep brown eyes. Gently he kissed her, then grasped both her hands,

36

crushed them briefly in his and that was that.

Neither referred again to the subject of parenthood.

For a time Polly carried on as usual, doing the same things in the same way, but she felt she was in some kind of limbo, numb with the shock of bereavement, not for a baby that was, but for one that never would be.

At last she concluded she must not continue in this way. She had ceased to look forward to parenthood, but she did have a husband who was loving and generous in every way. He deserved something from her. She could not go on wallowing in self-pity. What then was she to do?

One thing was obvious. If she were not to occupy herself in parenthood she must do something else. She supposed the only alternative was to dismiss Mary and devote all her time to domesticity and being a housewife.

It was fortuitous that a few days later Mary succumbed to an attack of influenza and had to stay at home for over a week. Polly commenced with zeal to tackle all the housework, the black-leading, doorstep-scrubbing, the Monday wash, the polishing of brasswork and furniture, the cooking and the tedious washing-up. She would have done some gardening, but Jim Jenking, who was retired and spent one day a week working the garden, would have resented the intrusion.

Half-way through the week Edwin protested, but did not insist on getting temporary help. She guessed he realised her need to be more occupied.

By the time Mary had recovered and was able to return, Polly had concluded being the perfect housewife was not the answer. The housework, the laundry and cooking did not occupy her mind. That was still engrossed in thoughts of a baby, the son she could almost but not quite visualise.

Polly asked herself what other wives in her situation actually did do? Mrs Morcumb, who was herself the eldest child of a large family, counted herself fortunate that no children resulted from her marriage, and took pleasure in a life of comparative ease and doing fine embroidery. Mrs Spargo threw herself heart and soul into work for the church, including being a Sunday School teacher; Miss Agnew, a thin middle-aged spinster of small private means, was musical and played piano for the chapel whenever and wherever required. Two or three others enjoyed a life of ease and took interest, mostly unwelcome, in the business and goings on of all their neighbours and friends.

Polly thought about good works, feeling this was something she ought to do. But the thought did not spark any interest, much less enthusiasm. What she needed was a challenge. Was her only challenge to be to bear her disappointment stoically and to be a good wife? She was sure she could do those things better if there was something additional she could accomplish.

But what else was there? Married women were not expected to go out to work, except for the extremely poor who did washing or charring. Their ordination was clear and unmistakable – to care for husband, home and family. And who, apart from those needing help with charring and washing, would employ a married woman. It was widely accepted that any woman or girl who decided to wed would terminate her employment immediately upon marriage. If not, she could be sure of being dismissed.

Any woman who did not have to go out to work to keep body and soul together would *prefer* the luxury of being at home during the cold, wet, dark winters, likewise in summer, when they could take walks out in the fresh air and enjoy the sunshine instead of being enclosed in some shop or stuffy workroom. This, together with the near certainty that at any time a newly-married woman could become pregnant, made it obvious the woman was an unwise selection for any employer. Besides, it did not conform with convention. And how would all the poor spinsters fare if married women kept their jobs?

Polly pondered the situation. She had to think of something. But no solution came.

Adding to the gloom, one Friday shortly following this period, Jack called on Polly. Edwin was just returning to the quarries and only had time to exchange a few words.

'You look worried, Jack,' Polly said after Edwin's departure. The two sat together on the sofa.

'Milly's been off sick all week. She's been off work a lot lately.' Jack told her.

'Oh, I'm sorry,' Polly sympathised, looking into his anxious face, and privately thinking the poor girl's chance of recovery was slim.

'I didn't see her today, the doctor was there.'

With sinking heart Polly realised it must be extremely serious. People like the Bartlets didn't call in the doctor unless the situation was desperate . . . they couldn't afford to.

'Let's hope he can do something,' Polly said in an effort to be comforting.

'I've been calling in my dinner-break, just for a few minutes,' Jack said, as though to himself. 'A call seems to cheer her up . . . her face lights up when she sees me . . . she's got such a lovely smile . . .' His voice faltered and Polly put an arm around her brother and clasped his hand in hers, silently communicating her sympathy.

A week later Milly died of what the doctor called 'galloping consumption'.

Chapter Five

The sad death of Milly Bartlet seemed to have deepened Polly's gloom. She became aware that for Edwin's sake, she must jolt herself out of this almost melancholy state.

A few weeks later there was a day mid-week when Edwin was extra busy. He had to go to Redruth to see a builder with whom he had already had business dealings, and who had been selected by Redruth Town Council to erect a large public building. Edwin would not be coming home at mid-day. He was hoping to have a successful negotiation for the supply of the required granite building material.

Polly's mother was at the vicarage that morning. Mary was now quite fit. Polly had done her ironing and shone the brasses. She had the rest of the day to fill. She picked up the four short knitting needles on which she was knitting Edwin's socks. Drat! The stitches had fallen off the end of one of the needles! With clucks of annoyance she struggled to get the small loops of wool back onto the needle without letting the stitches 'run' and without allowing stitches to drop from the other needles. Mrs Morcumb could knit on four needles with her eyes shut! 'Why can't I do that,' Polly said aloud, irritated with herself and her awkwardness. But Polly knew the answer. It's because you're too impatient, and you don't like knitting anyway!

So saying to herself, Polly, having retrieved the endangered stitches and knitted another row all round to make the stitches feel right, flung the half knitted sock back into her knitting bag, thankful she had at least 'turned the heel'. She put on her hat and coat and went to the kitchen.

Mary looked up, surprised to see Polly standing in the doorway ready to go out.

'I'm going out Mary and I'm not sure what time I'll return.'

'Yes, Mrs Pendleton.'

Polly was about to shut the kitchen door when Mary spoke again.

'Mrs Pendleton.'

'Yes, Mary.'

'I like you in that hat and coat. It looks so smart and it's such a lovely colour.'

'Thanks, Mary.'

Polly smiled with pleasure. She also liked the plum coloured, well-cut coat with velvet collar and trimmings and a matching velvet hat. It was purchased on a day out in Truro with Edwin, when she saw it in the window of Roberts Draper's and fell in love with it. Edwin, against all her protestations that it was much too expensive, insisted on buying the two. He was so proud of her when he saw her wear it to church the next Sunday though he was not aware, but Polly was, that Howard Sinclair, one of the upper classes, kept casting appreciative glances in her direction. Polly always felt good when she wore the coat and hat. Perhaps it would work its magic for her today.

She walked down the road, deciding as she went that she would take a trip to Falmouth, some two miles away, by horse bus. The bus left at regular intervals from Market Street, just above the narrow, ancient Town Hall. This building stood alone in the middle of the wide street and divided it into two narrow ones, which linked up again at some point beyond the other end of the Town Hall, and narrowed to a bottleneck before widening into Broad Street.

Penryn was an old town, an ancient Borough no less, having been granted a Charter in 1236 which was confirmed in 1275. From where the swing bridge straddled the Penryn River, the main part of the town rose upwards on a ridge-like hill, roads and openings which accommodated a hotchpotch of tiny cottages huddled together as though for warmth. These roads and opes descended from either side of the main streets. The terrain in and around Penryn made life difficult for the work-horses which pulled all manner of carriages, carts, buses and Jersey cars.

When Polly arrived at the pick-up point in Lower Market Street, Charlie Polmeor and his horse-bus were already waiting at the side of the road, Charlie a mustachioed wiry man in his fifties

41

who wore breeches and leather leggings, was standing on the pavement near the entrance to the bus.

'Morning Polly, you're looking very smart,' he said cheerfully as he held out a hand to help her step up into the bus. 'Having a little outing this morning, then?'

Polly smiled. Even a man could see she was not dressed to go out to buy a bag of potatoes!

'Morning Charlie. Yes, I'm going to Falmouth to see if there are any bargains to be had.'

'Very nice too.'

By the looks of disapproval on the faces of two elderly matrons who sat inside, Polly concluded they did not approve of young wives having morning outings. Dutiful young wives were at home attending to the needs of husband, house and family at that time of day.

'Good morning, Mrs Bray, Mrs Mason.'

The po-faced two simultaneously nodded and bade her 'Good morning.'

'I haven't brought my umbrella, I hope it won't rain.'

'Be a shame to spoil your nice velvet hat,' Mrs Bray said, implying that this was the time of day for working wear, not dressy velvets.

A shrivelled-looking old man removed a smelly pipe from his mouth. ' 'Tisn't going to rain, so the hat will be safe.'

Mrs Bray turned and shot him a withering glance. 'How do you know? Been consulting your corns?'

The old man ignored this and silently replaced the pipe in his mouth. Penryn Town Clock, which rose from that end of the Town Hall, struck ten o'clock. Charlie Polmeor looked up and down the street to ensure that no further likely passengers were approaching, climbed up into his seat, picked up the reins and gave the instruction to move off, making a double clicking sound out of the side of his mouth which the horses understood, followed by an interpretation in English.

'Gee up.'

With a clatter of hooves and a rumble of wheels, the bus moved forward, proceeding slowly until they had passed the bottleneck beyond the other end of the narrow Town Hall building.

The horse, from habit, slowed at the bottle-neck, then, as no

42

one was outside the Kings Arms waiting to board the bus, trotted the length of Broad Street and the Square, passing as they went, the fire station, the Liberal Club Rooms, a bank, a few small shops and many rather splendid houses.

After the Square, Charlie Polmeor applied the long-handled hand-brake to assist the horses descend Quay Hill, at the foot of which the road merged with the end of Commercial Road immediately prior to crossing the swing bridge over the lower reaches of the Penryn River.

Polly's timing for the outing to Falmouth had been unwittingly good. With only a brief delay they were able to cross the bridge. A man at the back of the bus, whose resonant voice could be heard by all, told his companion that half an hour earlier there was a tedious delay as the bridge had opened to admit three craft. The wait caused some congestion among the assortment of horse-drawn vehicles, cyclists, a few people on foot and a newfangled motor car, the show-off driver of which honked his large horn to signal impatience and almost caused a nearby horse to bolt from fright.

The flat stretch of road beyond the bridge closely followed the river which gradually widened as they approached Falmouth. The first houses within the boundaries of Falmouth were Ponshardon Cottages and soon they reached Greenbank, where dignified houses on the landward side benefited from a magnificent view of the harbour, and the assorted craft, including a number of stately ships.

Polly always felt a little thrill of excitement when going on one of her occasional trips into Falmouth.

At Prince Street the view, except for occasional glimpses, was blotted out by buildings on the harbourside. They were on higher ground here and slowed to negotiate the descent at the High Street, a hotchpotch of buildings, huddled opes and mews, a Congregational Church and an Old Town Hall, now supplanted by a magnificent new Town Hall in a more central part of the town.

At Market Strand, in the open area which formed the entrance to the Prince of Wales Pier, most passengers, including Polly, alighted. She walked a few steps towards Market Street, then slowed by the portico of the Kings Hotel, remembering the scene at the Pier when the Prince and Princess of Wales came to lay the foundation stone of the extensions to Market Strand Pier, which was subsequently to be known as the Prince of Wales Pier. What a wonderful day that was! Neither Polly nor her mother had ever seen such crowds, nor so many elegant ladies, but Princess Mary outshone them all.

'Madam, you look a trifle lost. May I be of assistance?' Polly looked up, startled. Gazing down at her stood a tall, blue-eyed, fair-haired Customs Officer.

'Oh . . . I was just wondering where . . .' Her voice trailed as she searched in her mind for a suitable reply.

'Which way to go?' he asked, his penetrating gaze not leaving her face. Polly was not accustomed to this type of male. She must gather her wits.

'I know exactly where to go. I just can't think of the name of the shop.'

'Ah. What sort of shop was it? Would it be a dress shop?'

He evidently was familiar with the shops ladies preferred to visit.

'Yes, it is . . .' There wasn't any shop she really had to visit. It was just an outing.

'Was it . . .' The officer began to reel off a list of names of draper's shops. Polly promptly interrupted him.

'It was Gedney's. But I shall look at several before I finally decide,' she said, pretending she was considering making a purchase.

'Ah, yes, of course.' He turned slightly in the direction of Market Street, and Polly noticed the handsome lines of his profile, the high forehead, the fine straight nose and clean-shaven slightly jutting chin. He certainly was handsome, and she neither liked nor trusted him one little bit.

'I am going in that direction myself. May I walk along with you?'

'If you wish,' Polly said, concluding she had no grounds for refusing, except an instinctive distrust of the man and his intentions.

'In that case I'd better introduce myself. Charles Brendon Copeland at your service,' he said with an ingratiating smile and a slight click of his heels. Almost without realising, Polly found herself having her hand encased in the warm clasp of his large one. The handshake over, Polly tried to withdraw hers, but he held it entrapped.

'May I know *your* name?' he asked, still smiling.

'It's Polly Pendleton,' she said, and Customs Officer Copeland released her hand.

'Polly.' He seemed to caress her name with his voice. 'Polly Pendleton. It suits you,' he said and, as though on impulse, seized her left hand and raised it that he might inspect her fingers. 'I see you are married. How sad!'

Again Polly removed her hand from his. This time she was amused by his antics.

'It's not sad at all, I'm very happy to be married to Edwin.' She laughed.

'I meant sad for me, not your fortunate Edwin.'

Polly turned to move along Market Street, which was thronging with people. She couldn't help wondering whether this handsome officer, who obviously had an eye for the ladies, would have singled her out for attention if she had not been dressed in the smart clothes of the middle-classes, but had on the poorer well-worn outfits that had been hers before she became Mrs Pendleton.

Charles Copeland followed closely, his hand lightly holding her elbow, supposedly to guide her path through the thoroughfare which bustled with housewives, seafaring men, genteel and fashionably dressed ladies, businessmen, a sprinkling of foreigners speaking to one another in strange languages and men making deliveries to and from shops, as well as an assortment of horse-drawn vehicles and errand boys with bicycles equipped with large baskets for carrying customers' goods.

Across the street Polly saw Mrs Bray and Mrs Mason. This will set their tongues wagging, she thought and smiled in amusement, noticing out of the corner of her eye that as they passed by, the two heads turn to ensure they really could believe their eyes.

At the entrance to Gedney's Polly stopped and turned to bid the officer good-bye and to thank him. She was not sure for what, but it seemed the appropriate thing to do. But he was not to be so easily dismissed.

'Couldn't we cross over to the coffee shop opposite and fortify ourselves before we part company?' he pleaded.

'I'm sorry, but I really don't have the time to spare,' Polly protested.

'But you've come all the way to Falmouth, you must be in need of refreshment.'

'All the way!' Polly echoed. 'It's only two miles. I could have walked here *and* back to Penryn, and would have thought nothing of it.'

'Could you really, Polly.' He gazed deep into her eyes. 'Yes, I'm sure you could do anything if you wanted,' he breathed.

'Mr Copeland, I think you tease me,' Polly laughed. 'I must again say thank you and good-bye.'

'If you insist, dear lady,' he replied, exaggerated reluctance in his tone.

Polly laughed, finding his tomfoolery both irritating and, in turn, amusing.

'Good-bye then,' Polly said, laughing. He was about to again take her hand, when something on the other side of the narrow street distracted him.

'Dear lady, I think someone on the other side of the street is trying to gain your attention.'

At a glance Polly took in the mane of jet black hair streaked with silver, the wide grey eyes and slightly matronly but shapely figure of Joss's older sister.

'Why it's Lottie,' she said. 'I must go and speak to her.' Since her wedding Polly had scarcely seen Lottie.

'Allow me to escort you across this busy street,' Officer Copeland insisted.

Any excuse to hang about, Polly thought as he steered her across the narrow choked thoroughfare. Polly's smile was increased by the thought that perhaps Officer Copeland thought her elbow was a tiller.

'Thank you, Mr Copeland,' she said, dismissively.

Again Officer Copeland was not to be so easily dispensed with.

'May I be introduced to your charming friend,' he said, as they stood with Lottie outside the coffee shop.

Polly had no choice but to do as he asked.

'It's a rare morning indeed that I am fortunate enough to be introduced to two such lovely ladies, and all within the space of less than then minutes,' he said as he deliberately looked into Lottie's laughing eyes.

'I thought you two must be old friends,' Lottie said.

46

'Alas, no. But who knows, perhaps one day we shall be, all of us.'

'I'm afraid we really must part company,' Polly insisted.

'I'm afraid of that too, dear Polly.' Officer Copeland feigned a sad expression, and Polly and Lottie struggled unsuccessfully to suppress their giggles.

With an effort to regain control of herself, Polly looked at Lottie. 'Perhaps you could spare the time to come into Gedney's with me, Lottie,' she said. 'I'd be glad to benefit from your advice on a suitable dress.'

'I'd be happy to,' Lottie said.

'Then I suppose I must say good-bye to you both,' the officer said in a sad tone as he once more escorted the ladies across the road.

'Whoever was that?' Lottie said, as soon as he was out of earshot.

Polly explained.

'I can see you would have difficulty in shaking him off,' Lottie said. 'But I think he's harmless. He's too obvious to be anything else.'

'Yes,' Polly agreed. 'I think with him it's just a game.' They went up the thickly carpeted staircase and idly inspected Gedney's collection of dresses.

'Do you need any help, madam,' the sales assistant asked.

'We'll let you know if we do, thank you,' Polly replied.

'I could make them all for a fraction of the cost,' Lottie whispered.

'Let's go and have a coffee,' Polly said. 'I didn't really want a dress.'

'Yes, let's. I love your coat and hat, Polly.'

'Edwin likes me in it,' Polly said.

'It seems the Customs Officer did too,' Lottie laughed.

They retraced their steps, again crossed the street, and went into the coffee shop. Polly pushed open the coffee shop door which had a curved metal bracket attached to the inside near the top of the door. When opened a spring caused a bell to clang loudly.

Most tables were occupied, mostly by ladies taking coffee, with just a sprinkling of gentlemen, mostly elderly except for one naval officer and a lady who both rose to leave. Lottie and Polly took the small table and Polly ordered coffee and scones from the young waitress who was dressed in the customary black dress with white apron, cap and cuffs.

'Joss was sorry he didn't see you when he was home,' Lottie said.

'Yes, I was too,' Polly agreed. 'I had to go to Lerryn to look after Great Aunt Elizabeth.'

They chatted for a while about Joss and Clementine. Polly already knew George, Lottie's husband, and Clementine didn't get on well. Perhaps after so many years apart, the situation would now be improved. Polly learned that George, who worked in an office in Falmouth Ship Repair Yard, had not been well for some time, and was suffering of late with heart trouble.

'It runs in his family,' Lottie said resignedly. 'I sew for a few neighbours and friends, but I've really been doing it because with George like he is, well, I don't know what I might need. It's as well to be prepared.'

'What a good idea,' Polly enthused. 'You were apprenticed to dressmaking and it would be a shame to let it all go to waste. After all, you only have yourself, your mother and Nora to sew for.'

'Enough of me and my doings. What have you been doing with yourself?' Lottie said. 'Are you going to be a lady of leisure for much longer?'

This was her way of saying, any signs of a family yet?

Polly's gloom, temporarily banished, returned in full flood.

'I don't think I'm ever going to have a baby,' she blurted out.

'And you want babies?' Lottie said, studying Polly's tensed face. Momentarily unable to speak, Polly nodded her head.

'I haven't told Edwin. I haven't told anyone,' she said. 'But I just know it.'

'You're over-anxious,' Lottie soothed.

'But I haven't always been. Oh Lottie, I don't know what to do. I want a family and so does Edwin. He's given me so much. The least I can do is . . .' Her voice trailed.

Lottie stared at Polly, weighing up the situation.

'Polly,' she said. 'It would be better for you to put thoughts of a baby right out of your mind. Take up new interests and if, sooner or later, a baby does arrive that will be that. You can't will it to happen or not to happen. Try to let things take their natural course.'

'That is exactly what I have already decided,' Polly answered.
'Only I can't think what to do.'

'Did you have any special purpose in coming to Falmouth today?'

'No. No special purpose. I came on a sudden impulse.'

'Just for distraction,' Lottie said.

'Just for distraction, something to do,' Polly agreed. 'But talking to you, I'm beginning to wish I'd learned dressmaking in the workroom at Corfields instead of doing shop-work.'

'I've heard Mr Corfield thought you were excellent on the business side.'

'If he did it wasn't reflected in my pay,' Polly laughed, her equilibrium restored. 'Do you have many customers?'

'There's no shortage of those,' Lottie said. 'I could do a lot more work if I set my mind to it.'

'Did you make the dress you're wearing?' Polly had observed the smart navy and white garment visible where Lottie had unbuttoned her coat in the warmth of the café.

'Yes,' Lottie laughed. 'It cost me less than half a crown.'

'It's fine lawn material, too,' Polly said. 'It would sell for at least fifteen shillings.'

'In a shop, yes,' Lottie said, then suddenly realised Polly was not taking this interest out of idle curiosity. 'Polly, what are you saying?'

'And you've saved the money in case George's health gets worse?'

'Yes, I have,' Lottie confirmed. 'I know Joss would be only too glad to help if times got hard, but there's been an atmosphere between us all. It's such a pity and has nothing to do with Joss. The fault was Clementine's. It was all a long time ago, but George is very independent. He said he could keep his wife and family without their help. Although he's never had a cross word with Joss, he's quite unforgiving!' Then she added, 'But I can't say I blame him.'

Evidently Clementine had done or said something George found quite unpardonable.

'Edwin says anything I save out of the housekeeping money is mine,' Polly went on. 'But I've only been married a year, so it doesn't amount to a lot. Still, he might . . .' She stopped,

49

c

wondering whether Edwin and George, more particularly George, might be persuaded to agree.

'Just what are you saying, Polly?' Lottie demanded.

'The thought struck me, Lottie, with Eric and Oliver no longer living at home, George at work all day and Nora at school, you have the day to yourself.'

Lottie looked at her gold wrist watch, a present from Joss. 'Nora comes home from school at mid-day,' she said. 'Normally I would be at home now, preparing a meal for her, but she's arranged to go to George's sister's house today. They live close to us and their daughter, Madge and Nora are good friends as well as cousins.'

'That needn't make a difference,' Polly said, as though to herself.

'I don't know what you are talking about,' Lottie muttered.

Polly caught the attention of the waitress. 'Could we have two more coffees, please.'

'You did need reviving,' Lottie said.

'No. I've an idea.'

. The waitress returned with the coffee.

'I see there is a closing down sign in the sweet shop next door,' Polly said to her.

'Yes, madam. The old lady who ran it had a stroke and died a few days later. It's only going to stay open until the end of the week.'

'That's interesting. Thank you,' Polly said.

'Are you interested in selling sweets?' the waitress asked.

'No,' Polly answered with a slight shake of the head. Again, Lottie was staring questioningly at Polly. The waitress departed.

'Polly, what are you up to?' Lottie demanded.

50

Chapter Six

Polly leant over the small table in order to draw closer to Lottie. 'Lottie,' she said, looking into her companion's face. 'Between us we could run a dress shop! . . . High quality clothes!'

The volume of Lottie's reply rose. 'In that grubby old sweet shop! The inside can't have been painted since before you were born, nor dusted either I sometimes think.'

Polly's reply was low. 'It would look quite different decorated and without that large high counter taking up so much space right down the middle, and all those shelves with bottles and glass jars of sweets. It could look so different, Lottie!'

For long seconds Lottie stared at her without speaking, then: 'Edwin would never agree.'

'I think he would. He hasn't said anything, but I can tell he feels I must have something to occupy me. We've both realised we're likely to be . . .' Polly's voice became almost inaudible, 'childless . . . no baby . . . I must have something to do . . . and Lottie, you already do a lot of sewing and you're so good at it.'

Lottie's impatience melted. 'Of course you must, Polly. You're not the type to enjoy a life of idleness. But opening a dress shop, that takes a lot of thinking about and, more to the point, a lot of money.'

'It wouldn't cost anything to take a look at the shop, Lottie, and if it's not too expensive, to go into the pros and cons. After all, if George's health worsened . . . I don't want to look for trouble . . . but if it does it could be an alternative source of income.'

'It could be another millstone,' was the sharp reply.

'With your expertise, surely not. Remember my wedding dress? You told me to let you know exactly what I wanted, and

51

that was the first time I had a really serious try at designing anything. And you made it so beautifully, Lottie, it looked better than I ever envisaged.'

'Yes, everyone was talking about it, even the men,' Lottie admitted, smiling with satisfaction as she recalled that special day.

'Edwin was so impressed, "bowled over" he said.' They debated the idea.

'The coffee's cold,' Polly said, draining her cup.

'Who's fault is that?' Lottie came back with a wry grin, and Polly knew Lottie had not set her mind against the idea . . . she was open to persuasion. They got up to leave. 'I want to buy some sweets,' Polly said, as she closed the coffee shop door behind them.

'You don't think you'll get round Edwin by buying him a box of chocolates, do you?' Lottie came back, a mite impatiently.

'No, not that.'

Lottie saw the 'For Sale' sign and nodded knowingly, 'Oh, I see.'

The girl who was serving in the sweet shop looked no more than fourteen.

'I'd like half a pound of Clotted Cream Toffees,' Polly said. The girl took a scoop and started to weigh the toffees.

'I see the shop is for sale,' Polly remarked to the girl. 'Where is the Auctioneer's Office?'

'It's here in Market Street, opposite Downing and Son's Draper's shop,' the girl replied, obligingly.

'Have you had many people interested?' Polly asked.

'Two or three people have been shown around.'

'Did they seem seriously interested?'

'Don't know,' came the reply. 'Fourpence please,' the girl said as she handed over the bag of toffees.

'Have we time to go along to the estate agents?' Polly asked Lottie, when they were outside.

'I can see there's no holding you,' Lottie said. 'But don't go making any rash decisions. Don't commit yourself. Information only, remember?'

'I'll remember, I promise,' Polly said, and they walked the short distance to Rowe and Corlyon's Auctioneer's office.

Polly and Lottie were greeted by a Mr Evans who had a

welcoming smile despite the gloomy darkness of the interior of the office.

Mr Evans was fully acquainted with the situation, and knew all about the shop and its owner, Miss Hope Barnard. Polly remembered her well, she had always stood behind the counter, half hidden by large jars of humbugs, aniseed balls and an assortment of the more popular lines. 'Miss Barnard,' he said, 'was the youngest and last surviving sister of a family of four, three spinsters and one who had married leaving no issue. The solicitors dealing with her estate were anxious to wind up her affairs and the shop is to be sold by auction at the end of the month. The proceeds will go to charities, mainly the church.'

'The end of the month's in two and a half weeks,' Polly said.

'Quite so,' Mr Evans replied. 'Would you like me to show you around?'

Polly looked at Lottie questioningly.

'Go on,' Lottie said. 'You won't be satisfied until you have a look.'

Mr Evans selected a bunch of keys from a long row of hooks and they retraced their steps.

The shop had a large window with a display shelf, and would have let in quite a lot of light had it not been cluttered with so many bottles, jars and chocolate boxes, which rose up in tiers from the display shelf. The dingy interior looked small. A door led to an inner room with what was once, and still could be, a rather handsome staircase, and a window overlooking a small walled courtyard. It was a clutter of boxes, bottles and an old desk which Polly thought probably contained invoices, ledgers and old records. Part of the building extended beyond this room and was a good-size kitchen with a gas cooker, kitchen sink, rickety table and two chairs, a built-in floor to ceiling cupboard and a freestanding cupboard . . . all in grubby condition. Lottie's nose wrinkled in distaste. At the rear of the courtyard was a privy . . . surprisingly clean and light, despite having no window, it being whitewashed and the large gap at both top and bottom of the door let in sufficient light.

'Are you ready to go upstairs, ladies?' Mr Evans asked, when both Polly and Lottie had silently inspected everything. He led the way up the stairs. To the front was a large room which was evidently the late Miss Barnard's living-room. The large window overlooked the busy Market Street. It was filled with heavy Victorian furnishings, and a large table in the centre took up a lot of space, giving the room a cluttered look. Nevertheless, it was, or could be with a bit of dusting and cleaning, a pleasant room.

To the rear of the small top-of-stairs landing was a bedroom with a bed, a wardrobe, a bow-fronted chest-of-drawers and a high-back padded chair covered in faded green velvet. A window in the corner overlooked the courtyard and there was a door to another room which was over the kitchen. A door on the landing to what appeared to be a floor to ceiling cupboard revealed a surprise. It afforded access to a steep narrow staircase which led to the attic.

'Do you want to go up?' Mr Evans asked, dubiously.

'Yes, please,' Polly replied, and led by Mr Evans, up they both went, hoisting their skirts with one hand and holding onto the handrail with the other. The stairs led to one large, surprisingly light attic room with two dormer windows to the front and one to the back. The floor was bare of covering, but under the dust was stained polished wood. There were boxes and cobwebs, and to one end lay a roll of linoleum. Polly and Lottie gazed appreciatively about them.

'Quite a handy space, this,' Mr Evans said.

Polly gazed about her. 'It would make a wonderful workroom, wouldn't it, Lottie?'

'It would indeed,' Lottie agreed.

'What sort of price are you expecting?' Polly asked.

'As it's to be auctioned it's hard to say,' Mr Evans said.

'We can't afford a lot,' Polly said.

'Then you could be lucky,' said Mr Evans. 'As there is now no actual owner, and the money is to be shared among charities. The solicitors have set a ridiculously low reserve price to ensure a sale because they are anxious to get the business settled and wound up.'

'I see,' Polly said, then turned to Lottie. 'It's worth thinking about.'

Lottie nodded.

'You're welcome to come back for another look,' Mr Evans encouraged. 'As many times as you like.'

'What about all the furniture and boxes?' Polly said.

'The furniture will be sold off and I could get someone to

remove the boxes,' he assured.

Carefully Polly and Lottie made their way down the staircase, took a final glance around, then descended the wider curved staircase to the ground-floor.

Once outside the building Mr Evans shook hands with them, raised his hat and assured them he would be delighted to be of any further assistance.

'What do you think, Lottie?' Polly asked.

'I don't know what to think,' Lottie replied. 'The place is in an awful mess.'

'But you think it's got possibilities?'

'Well, I . . . I haven't had time to think,' Lottie spluttered.

'Can we talk about it?'

'Yes, we can talk about it,' Lottie said. 'But talking and doing are two different things.'

'When?'

'Er . . . er . . . Would you like to come back to my house now?'

'It's nearly time to eat,' Polly demurred.

'If you don't mind sandwiches you're welcome.' Lottie offered.

'Thanks, Lottie. Sandwiches will be fine.'

They walked from Market Street along Church Street and Lottie stopped at the butchers to buy ham and hogs pudding to make the sandwiches. Then they ascended the steps to the side of the Church of King Charles the Martyr and went up the path which led into New Street, then up a flight of steps into the parallel Gyllyng Street. 'Nearly there,' Lottie said as they climbed higher to Wodehouse Terrace.

Lottie's house was in a road leading off Wodehouse Terrace. The house, like all the others in the row, had a small neat garden with a low wall. Lottie took the front door key from her bag and they both entered, passing the sitting-room and through the small dining-room which Lottie always referred to as 'the middle-room', to the kitchen which, as in so many houses, projected from the rear of the house. Lottie poked the fire in the Cornish Range.

'The fire was getting low,' she said, adding a few lumps of coal.

'But it's nice and warm in here,' Polly remarked as she removed her hat and coat.

'That's what I like about a kitchen,' Lottie agreed. It's always warm. She went out to the scullery to wash her hands, then set about making the sandwiches. They began to eat in silence. After a few minutes Polly could contain herself no longer.

'What do you think, Lottie?'

'My head is swimming . . . I can't take it in,' Lottie said.

'Could we work out between us how much money we can offer.' Polly suggested.

'We can't offer all we've got . . . and that will be precious little,' Lottie said. 'We'd need to have someone to rip out shelves and things and redesign and redecorate the place.'

'I'm sure Jack and his friend, Vic Trewin, he's a mason, would do that very cheaply in their spare time,' Polly said.

'Your brother, Jack, is a carpenter,' Lottie said. 'How is he? It was so sad about his young lady.'

'He's sad, but he doesn't say much. I think for some time he was prepared for it,' Polly said, 'but Milly never suspected.'

'Just as well, poor little soul,' Lottie said, sympathetically.

'Yes, he's a very good carpenter. I'm sure they wouldn't mind if we couldn't pay them right away. And it would keep him occupied, which would be a good thing, stop him quietly brooding.'

'We'd have to buy paint and, I expect, a lot of wood, even if we don't pay them for their work immediately, and there are bound to be things we hadn't thought of.'

'If we're catering for the upper end of the market we've got to have the premises looking really good, otherwise I don't think it will work,' Polly said, thoughtfully.

'Yes,' Lottie agreed. 'The idea does appeal to me, but I just don't know what we'd be letting ourselves in for.'

'Do you think George will object?' Polly asked.

'If he thinks it's feasible I don't think he will. Like Jack, he doesn't say much but I think he's conscious that both his father and grandfather died fairly young and I might have to manage on my own if the same happened to him. But I'm far from convinced myself that we can manage it . . . I don't know what we would be letting ourselves in for.'

'I'm sure I haven't saved as much money as you, Lottie,' Polly said. 'But I think Edwin would be willing to at least make up the difference.'

'Let's work out what we've got,' Lottie said, as she fetched a sheet of paper from a drawer in the kitchen table, and the two set about doing calculations. 'We mustn't forget I would have to make a good stock of clothes for us to open. We shall need materials for that, and good materials.'

'I'll be able to get onto the wholesalers,' Polly said. 'And I'm sure I could help with simple straightforward stitching.'

'If Edwin makes up my £65 to match your £205 we shall have £410 between us,' Polly said gloomily. If we make an offer of £375 and that is low, it will leave us with £35 for everything.'

'Even with the barest essentials that's not enough,' Lottie said. 'And I doubt they'd consider an offer that low anyway.'

'You're right, Lottie,' Polly glumly agreed. 'It's no good.'

They sat in silence for a few minutes, then Polly looked up at Lottie.

'Why, Lottie . . . you're really disappointed too, I can see.'

'It's just thinking that with a bit more money *I* could have made a real success of the dress-making,' Lottie said. 'And you would have been so good with the business side, plus you're good at designing clothes.'

'We'd better put it out of our minds.' Polly said flatly.

Five days later Polly and her mother both received a letter informing them that Great Aunt Elizabeth had died suddenly of a stroke. They and Jack had to make hurried arrangements to be at Lerryn in time for the funeral, overnight accommodation being offered by the neighbour in the adjoining cottage.

A small group of relatives and friends gathered at the cottage for the customary post-funeral refreshments. Their late aunt's solicitor asked that Polly's mother, Jack, Polly and a niece who had come from Plymouth remain behind afterwards. it was then Polly learned that each had been left £165 by their Great Aunt Elizabeth and that the cottage was to be sold and the proceeds shared among the four of them!

She was amazed. She had no idea that Great Aunt Elizabeth would leave her more than a token bequest, nor that her Aunt was so well off.

With luck the shop might still be theirs!

Chapter Seven

After the excitement of Polly's unexpected windfall she and Lottie, each with trepidation, realised the time had come to reveal to their respective husbands what they were thinking of doing. Both felt that after a good evening meal had been consumed was the best time to broach such a delicate proposition. They met together in Falmouth next morning.

'I expected Edwin to be flabbergasted,' Polly told Lottie. 'But he didn't say a word or bat an eyelid!'

'Well George was flabbergasted,' Lottie expostulated. 'Flabbergasted and fair near dumbstruck! When he was able to say anything he said he thought we'd get above ourselves,' she went on. 'Then he concluded that Edwin, being a businessman, would weigh up the situation and persuade us that it couldn't be done . . . He's got a very high opinion of Edwin, and all the Pendletons for that matter.'

'I'm afraid Edwin didn't react as either I or George expected,' Polly giggled. 'He just said if anyone else had come up with such a suggestion he would have been surprised, but as it was me . . .'

'I know what he means,' Lottie interrupted, grinning.

'I think he spent the evening turning it over in his mind, then true to form, slept on it,' Polly went on. 'This morning he said he thought he and Jack should inspect the premises. Jack is very knowledgeable about the building trade. He thought it would be a good idea if George could be there too.'

'I think that's a wonderful suggestion,' Lottie replied. 'And I'm sure George will go along with that.'

'Good,' said Polly.

The three men inspected the property, Edwin and Jack pronouncing it to be 'sound'. Edwin thought it a little small, but his business head appreciated the advantage of the prime situation in the heart of town. He reasoned that after alterations and redecorating had been carried out, if the business of selling clothes should fail, and the worst happened the premises could be resold with more time spared to advertise and to attract bidders at no great loss, probably at a profit.

On this basis, but even more because he wanted to see Polly happy, he promised to make up Polly's saving of £65 to Lottie's £205, and to allow her to borrow from him a further £160 until such time as the money from Great Aunt Elizabeth's legacy was forthcoming. The legacy itself would be larger than £160 with a quarter share of the proceeds of the cottage.

Lottie's husband, George, seemed bemused by the whole thing. He did not express any firm opinion but listened to what Edwin had to say and the lines on which Edwin reasoned his view of the possibilities. He apparently assumed Edwin was right . . . Edwin knew what he was talking about. Polly privately hoped George wasn't the sort of person who was always wise, but only with hindsight.

Polly and Lottie were going together to the auction, which was to take place in a room in the Royal Hotel further along in Market Street. Edwin offered to go in their place, but Polly knew he was busy organising the loading of the traction engines and ensuring that tan was laid on a section of the road in Broad Street to lessen the sound of traction engines passing the home of old Mr Thomas who was seriously ill. She insisted that with Lottie to accompany her the two could cope very well.

On entering the hotel they were directed to the auction room, which was not much bigger than Polly's sitting-room. The sound of conversation within was instantly silenced, and they were aware of a number of men present and that all eyes turned to stare at them. The two made their way to the rows of chairs which were placed across the middle of the room, and sat in the row third from the back. The men's conversation resumed and the hostile eyes which had stared in disbelief, turned away. They were intruders! So what, Polly thought. Our money is as good as theirs.

'Not very friendly-looking, are they?' Lottie whispered.

'Seem to think an auction is a gentlemen's club,' Polly replied.

'We shan't stand a chance against all these,' Lottie said, apprehensively.

There were about a dozen men but in a room of this size, they seemed more. The ten minutes until 10 o'clock when the auction was due to start dragged. The two spoke in whispers, each having the feeling that for them to jabber and clack like the men would offend or break some unwritten rule.

At last the auctioneer took his position to the front, behind a narrow table where a clerk was sitting to one side. The auctioneer picked up his gavel, banged it on a block on the table, and there was silence.

'Would you take your seats please, gentlemen. I'd like to get on with the business now.'

There was a shuffling, and banging of chairs as the men took their seats, all carefully avoiding the row where Polly and Lottie sat. Polly was the one who was to bid and she and Lottie had been well and truly briefed not to move a muscle, except to either put a finger up or nod to make a bid. Lottie had a terrible sudden fear she would sneeze and that would be taken as bidding. Both Polly and Lottie had noticed there were quite a few businessmen present, mostly shop-keepers.

'Er . . . Ladies and Gentlemen . . .'

The auctioneer went over the details of the property . . . then:

'I would like to start the bidding at £300 please . . . Anyone bid me £300? . . . Any bids . . . Come on, gentlemen . . . er, sorry . . . ladies and gentlemen . . . Someone bid me £300.'

'Two hundred,' came a thick phlegmy voice, with the emphasis on *two*.

'It'll do for a start,' said the auctioneer. 'Any advance on £200?'

There was absolute silence. The auctioneer's eyeballs seemed out of control . . . 'Two hundred and twenty I'm bid . . .' Silence. 'Come on Gentlemen . . . and ladies . . . Two hundred and forty in the back row.' Silence.

Neither Polly nor Lottie had heard a sound . . .

'£240 I'm bid . . . £250 . . . £270 I'm bid. £270 . . . Any advance on two hundred and seventy pounds . . . Come on gentlemen, we can't give the premises away . . . two hundred and eighty . . . two hundred and eighty pounds . . . three hundred pounds . . .'

There was silence, the auctioneer's eyes combed the faces, whilst Polly's gaze was fixed on the auctioneer's face. She nodded.

'£300 I'm bid. I have £300 . . . come on gentlemen . . . you're making me work very hard . . . Anyone bid me £325? . . . £320? . . . Be reasonable my friends, you know it's worth much more than that . . . Three hundred I'm bid . . . any advance on £300 . . .'

Gradually the bidding rose. At £375 Polly nodded again. By this time she and Lottie had discerned there were two men bidding against her. The others had apparently come to watch the proceedings and to exchange gossip, presumably of a business nature.

The bids had been slow in coming, and were now rising by £5 and £10 at a time, as though with each bid the bidder was scraping the bottom of the proverbial barrel.

£380 someone bid at last.

Clearly and distinctly Polly promptly said, 'Four hundred pounds.'

There was the sound of several sharp intakes of breath, but quick as a flash the auctioneer seized on it.

'£400 I'm bid . . . the lady in the plum-coloured coat . . . Come on gentlemen, any advance on four hundred pounds? I now have a bid of £400 . . . any advance?'

Silence.

The auctioneer hustled for an increase, the auctioneer cajoled. Stony male faces stared back at him. He raised his gavel. 'Going,' bang . . . his eyes darted . . . 'Going,' bang . . . again his eyes darted . . . Four hundred and five pounds I'm bid . . . Any advance on £405? . . . Any . . . '

'Four hundred and twenty pounds I'm bid.'

A murmur went round the room.

'Any advance on £420?'

After more requests for an advance and more lengthy waits the auctioneer again raised his gavel, 'Going,' bang . . . 'Going,' bang . . . eyes darting, 'Gone!' bang . . . 'Sold to the lady in the plum-coloured coat!'

At the words 'Sold to the lady in the plum-coloured coat', both Polly and Lottie experienced a sudden shiver of excitement and trepidation, leaving them goose-pimply.

The men slowly dispersed, but Polly and Lottie scarcely noticed. They felt too stunned to move a muscle until the auctioneer smiled and signalled to them to come to him at the table in front. He confirmed there were only two other bidders. The others were mainly regular attenders, who just liked to 'be in the know'. One bidder was wanting to open a furniture shop and thought the premises too small but would have bought if very cheap. The other wanted to open a cycle shop but there were two already in the nearby High Street area and again, unless it was cheap he didn't want to risk it. There was no one totally set on buying the shop, and this had been to Polly's and Lottie's advantage.

The auctioneer congratulated them both on having made an excellent buy at £420 and said he admired Mrs Pendleton's strategy. If the bids continued to rise in dribs and drabs he thought at least one of the other bidders would have gone further.

Polly and Lottie came away from the auction bursting with excitement.

'Let's go and have a coffee in the shop next to ours,' Lottie said, staggering slightly, drunk with excitement. 'We need something to steady us.' They gazed at the grubby premises as they passed by, but in their eyes they saw it clean and freshly painted, with beautiful dresses displayed on models in the window. Today was an historic day . . . that's how it seemed to both Polly and Lottie . . . a turning point. They were now joint partners. A different life lay ahead, a challenge, an adventure.

You can do anything if you try, Polly thought as the waitress placed a cup of coffee in front of her, the auction episode vivid in her mind. Then, momentary sadness . . . anything except have a baby.

Chapter Eight

The morning after Clementine, Joss and Theodore arrived at Manor Withiel Joss was up at his usual early hour. He decided to have a look around before the workmen put in an appearance. The restoration and redecoration of the property were almost completed and he was anxious to inspect.

All the family were still abed. Joss strolled about, hands in trouser pockets, head tilted to survey the roof, etc., thankful to be able to inspect without distraction the work on what was now his house. He liked what he saw. Good progress had been made and gas lighting had been installed in all rooms. The roof repairs appeared to be finished. Work on window repairs, all of which were set in columns and lintels of granite, had been extensively carried out. Chimney stacks could be a problem, but he had confidence that the men he engaged knew the job. At least something seemed to be going well. With good and thorough repairs and replacements the manor would carry on without further major work for a good many decades.

The greyness of the granite building, along with its stables and coach-house seemed to merge with the sombre hills and trees. The manor stood on a small flat area and was encompassed around with gently sloping ground. There was a protective hill behind and a descent in front with a small lake at the bottom. Clumps of trees and assorted shrubs, including many tall rhodo-dendrons, magnolias and camellias gave an attractive aspect to and from the house, which was not ornate, but impressive never-theless. The house looked long and low, with a raised terrace along its front and sides. There was a large, heavy mahogany door at the front with three long windows on either side. Manor Withiel, Joss thought, was well-named, for although only a

63

quarter of a mile from the hidden narrow road, the grounds were completely encompassed by trees.

Except for the cook, now cook-cum-housekeeper, and one part-time cleaning woman now a general factotum, all indoor staff had been dismissed by Clementine's impecunious parents. One gardener had been retained. He was assisted by the stable-boy. With only two horses left to look after and the rarely used assorted carriages, he had time to spare.

The crisp, early-morning air whetted Joss's appetite and he strolled towards the kitchen. Evidently the household were late risers. The cook had not yet put in an appearance and Joss busied himself finding food and a few utensils to prepare his own breakfast on a much used gas cooker. There was also a large Cornish range, looking sad and unwelcoming with ashes and cold burnt out cinders waiting to be raked. Across a large open fire-place was a spit which had probably not been used for decades, if not generations.

Joss sat at the large deal table to eat his breakfast and, glancing about the grimy half brown half yellow-ochre walls, was glad the kitchen was next in line for redecoration. I might do some of it myself, he thought, for although he had not yet bothered to look closely, he suspected the two very large dressers which housed enough crockery and kitchen gadgets to stock a shop, had been painted around when last someone had the job of smartening up the kitchen. Joss was just finishing the toast he had made with the grill of the gas cooker when Miss Trembath, the elderly cook, put in an appearance. She looked as though she had overslept, Joss thought. Her grey hair was pinned haphazardly into a lopsided bun, and her encompassing long white cook's pinafore was inside out, the stitching where there was a pocket was clearly visible.

'Good morning, Miss Trembath,' Joss said.

The deep voice and the sight of the new master of Manor Withiel in the kitchen, seated at the bare kitchen table, eating a breakfast he had to cook himself, threw Miss Trembath into a state of complete fluster. Her tired face seemed to shake with agitation.

'Oh . . . sir . . . oh, my dearie me . . . If you'll go to the dining-room, sir, I'll bring the rest of your breakfast and a pot tea and coffee to you straight away. Yes, indeed I will.'

'My dear Miss Trembath . . . it's all right . . . calm yourself.'

Joss soothed. 'I've just about finished my breakfast, and I've already made a pot of tea . . . Here, let me pour you a cup.' Joss rose as he was speaking, and poured milk into a cup he took from the dresser.

The tip of Miss Trembath's pointed nose seemed to twitch.

'Sit down, Miss Trembath, and drink this.' He indicated a chair at the table, cornerwise to him.

'Mr Renfree, sir. I can't do that. It isn't fitty.'

'Fitty or no, I've poured the tea, so sit and drink it.'

'Yes, I suppose so.'

Joss resumed his seat when the cook sat down. 'Sugar?' he asked, pushing the sugar bowl towards her.

'No . . . yes . . . I think I'd better, thank you . . . I'm all of a doodah . . . and, oh dear, sir . . . you're using the servants' cheap crockery.' She looked towards an adjoining room. 'The special fine china for the household and guests is in there.'

Joss threw back his head and laughed. 'I don't think the cheap crockery affected the taste of the bacon very much,' he said. 'Anyway, these cups and saucers and plates are just like ones my mother uses.'

This remark had the effect of reassuring the bewildered cook, the trepidation disappeared from her brown eyes and she actually smiled.

'Tell me, Miss Trembath,' Joss said. 'How many staff have been dismissed? There doesn't seem to be enough here to cope.'

Miss Trembath's eyes lit up at the possibility of having help.

'I used to be a proper cook and do only cooking,' she said. 'I had a girl to help me in the kitchen and do the washing-up, and extra help when we had guests staying, or here for a meal. Then there was one looking after the house, a housekeeper the mistress called her . . . and Mrs Solomon, the gardener's wife, did rougher work. Again, there was extra help when we had guests. Mrs Du Cane had her own personal maid, but that was a long time ago when they had a lot more social life. There were two gardeners and a groom who looked after the horses and carriages, and a man who used to come in from Stithians for maintenance work.'

'And now there is only you, and part-time help with the house, a gardener and stable-boy.'

'Yes, that's right, sir. Tom Solomon the gardener – he and his wife live in the lodge.' Involuntarily, the cook gave a long,

65

weary sigh.

'And which is your day off, Miss Trembath?'

'It was Mondays, but I haven't . . .' her voice dwindled.

'You haven't had a day off lately?'

'Circumstances are different now, sir,' she replied with a resigned expression.

'How long is it since you had a day off.'

The cook's voice was hesitant. 'It was the day of my sister's funeral.'

Joss's light-heartedness had sobered. There was silence, and Joss sensed Miss Trembath's discomfort. He realised she had to put up with the situation or run the risk of being dismissed, as the others had been. And who then would engage an ageing cook who was a spinster with probably no close family she could turn to for help.

'Don't worry, Miss Trembath,' he smiled. 'We'll do something about it.'

'Thank you, sir. Thank you . . . Sir,'

'Yes, Miss Trembath.'

'Mr and Mrs Du Cane like their tea brought up, if you will excuse me. And I expect Mrs Renfree would like the same.'

'Yes, you carry on, cook,' Joss said.

The sound of male voices told him the workmen had arrived.

'Cook, would you tell Mrs Renfree I have already breakfasted?' he said.

She nodded. 'Yes, sir. Certainly.'

'And I or Mrs Renfree will speak to you later in the day about help.'

It was almost an hour later that Clementine and Theodore left the bedrooms to go downstairs to breakfast. Before they descended the stairs Clementine's parents appeared.

Clementine and her parents exchanged greetings. 'Good morning Theodore. Did you sleep well?' Margaret Du Cane cooed.

'Morning, Theodore,' his grandfather echoed.

'Good morning, Grandmother; good morning, Grandfather. I slept very well, thank you,' Theodore replied and was promptly smothered by a kiss from his grandmother.

'Did you like your nice big bed?' Margaret asked.

'It was fine, I guess . . . They have big beds in America too.'

'But do they have big houses like this?'

With childlike logic Theodore answered, 'I don't know. I haven't seen this one yet.'

He suddenly made sounds which were recognisably an imitation of a motor, circled around, then whizzed downstairs, jumping the bottom four or five.

'He's a real Du Cane,' Clementine's father remarked with a laugh.

'He's got my fair hair and blue eyes,' her mother said. 'Yes, he takes after our side,' her father affirmed.

Margaret Du Cane lowered her voice to almost a whisper. 'He's going to have style. Not much Renfree in him.'

Clementine laughed almost uncontrollably at the remark, and the inference that Joss did not have polish, class, breeding.

They had reached the bottom of the truly beautiful curved staircase and were about to cross the spacious panelled hall to the dining-room. Theodore, who was circling the hall, still pretending to be a motor, zoomed towards them.

'By the way, where is Joss?' Clementine's father asked.

'Daddy always has breakfast before us,' Theodore interjected, before Clementine had time to answer. He gazed about him as he spoke.

'This is a big house,' he conceded as they entered the dining-room. He had been asleep when they reached Redruth Station the previous evening and had little recollection of his arrival the previous night.

'Do you like it?' his grandfather asked.

The boy again surveyed his surroundings and pouted. 'It's gloomy . . . but I guess I'll get used to it,' he said, grudgingly.

'This is where I was born, and my father before me and his father before him.' Albert du Cane smiled with pride. 'So I hope you will grow to like it, because one day my home will come to you.'

Theodore stared at him unblinking. ' 'S'not your home . . . It's my daddy's,' he said with a directness only found in young children. Clementine's parents pursed their lips slightly but the arrival of breakfast broke the awkward silence.

But Theodore had not forgotten the conversation.

'Daddy said he's had a cottage built for you.' His grandparents remained silent. 'So why are you still living here?'

'Be quiet and eat your breakfast,' Clementine said.

'Don't like it,' he flashed back, jumping from his chair and running from the room as he spoke. Clementine ignored this.

'Oughten you to go after him?' her mother asked.

'He often won't eat his breakfast. I expect he just wants to look around. He won't sit still and wait for us to eat while there are so many things he hasn't seen.'

She glanced about the room at the panelled walls.

'Not much has altered, but it does seem kind of brighter,' she admitted.

'The ceiling has been replastered and redecorated,' her father said. 'The door and panelling stained and a new window has been put in.'

'Did any of the panelling need replacing?'

'No. The builder said it was good well-seasoned wood and would last many more years.'

When breakfast was over the grandparents showed young Theodore over his new home and the grounds. Joss had intended to do this, but when he found Albert and Margaret Du Cane thus engaged, merely gave an almost imperceptible shrug of his shoulders. It was of no consequence. Meantime, Clementine made a start on the unpacking.

The next day Joss took Theodore in a horse drawn break to see his other grandparents. He left the horse and break a quarter mile down the road in Ben Spargo's farm. Emily Renfree had made pasties so that the little grandson could be introduced to some Cornish fare.

The boy was intrigued and greatly amused by being able to eat a main dish without plate, knife, fork, or even a spoon. Joss's mother wrapped the bottom half of the pasty in a clean napkin, and Theodore learned he could hold the pasty and eat it from the top, working his way downwards. To Joss's delight, not to mention Joss's parents, he ate every bit, thoroughly enjoyed it, and announced he would like another tomorrow.

'And so you shall,' said his Grandma Renfree. I made two for you, just in case you liked it. You can eat them hot or cold, though most people prefer them hot, so you can have it warmed up, if you like.'

After the meal they talked for half an hour and Emily Renfree imparted to Joss the news that Lottie and Polly intended to go into business together. They had even bought a shop in Falmouth, though much work needed to be done. Joss was interested, pleased and amused.

'Good for them,' he said, then added, 'But have they the capital to set up in business?'

'Apparently the property went for a very reasonable price for a quick sale and was too good an opportunity to miss.' Emily Renfree said. 'She and Polly Pendleton intend to go into partnership. It was Polly's idea and it seems Edwin is prepared to put up the same sum as Lottie, plus Polly has been left a legacy by her great-aunt. Lottie has been taking in dressmaking and tailoring at home and she had saved the money for a rainy day, George not being in the best of health.'

'Lottie and Polly,' Joss said. 'They'll make a good pair . . . But will Polly have the time?'

'She hasn't said anything, but Nell Pascoe told me she hoped for children and none have come along.'

'She was around twelve or thirteen when I last saw her, so I only knew her as a child. I'm hoping to see her soon. She had to go away when I was home before.'

By now Theodore was becoming restless.

'Would you like to see the quarries where I used to work?' his grandfather said.

'Are they like Botallack?' Theodore asked.

'The tin mine? No. They're nothing like that, my boy; it's just a very big pit with men working in it and outside it.'

'There are really men working in a pit?' Theodore said incredulously.

'That's right.'

'Yeah, I'll see it.'

'I'll get the horse and break,' Joss said, a hint of anxiety in his voice.

'It'll do me good to walk,' his father replied, excited at the prospect of going out with the grandson he was seeing for the first time. Emily Renfree came too; she wasn't going to miss a minute of time spent in the company of her son and his son. John Renfree had to pause several times on the way, to what he called 'draw breath', but the afternoon passed pleasantly.

Theodore was intrigued by the depth and size of the quarries, also the size of the large cumbersome-looking machinery. It surprised him to discover there were tramways and a Blacksmith's shop. The men stopped work to chat and be introduced to their old workmate's new grandson, and were amused by his American accent and clothes which they thought made him look like a grown man in miniature instead of a small boy. Theodore in turn, pronounced he couldn't understand a word they said and turned to his father.

'Tell them to speak English, Daddy,' he demanded, at which some men went into paroxysms of laughter and a couple patted his head.

Jim Coad, speaking to Joss, said, 'He don't look like your side of the family . . . I suppose he takes after his mother?'

'Yes, he's got my wife's colouring and blue eyes,' Joss agreed, then added, 'Just as well, she's the good-looking one.'

'Aw, yes,' Jim Coad laughed revealing a shortage of teeth. 'The ladies are always better-looking . . . leastways, that's what I think.'

'I agree with you, Jim,' said a voice. It was Edwin, who had just returned after involvement with a shipment of granite to Cadiz.

'Mrs Renfree, John, Joss,' he said, warmly shaking hands with each. 'Good to see you.' The workmen returned to their work. Edwin bent and warmly shook the boy's hand. 'And this is Theodore, I take it?'

'Pleased to meet you, sir,' Theodore replied with easy composure.

'And what do you think of my quarries, Theodore?'

Unhesitatingly he replied, 'They sure are big.'

Edwin's smile broadened to a laugh and the faces of Joss's parents shone with pleasure and pride at their quick-thinking young grandson with the American accent.

'Is the granite really going on a ship?' Theodore, not sure whether he was having his 'leg pulled', looked up into Edwin's face.

'Yes, it's going all the way to Spain.'

'Will people build houses with it?'

'When it goes abroad it's usually for more important things than houses . . . big official buildings, but a lot is used to build

70

dockyards . . . and bridges.'

'Do the horses take it to the ship?'

'Yes,' Edwin said with a smile. 'They took this shipment but we also use traction engines.'

'Theodore, you mustn't take up so much of Mr Pendleton's time,' his grandmother remonstrated.

'Don't worry, Mrs Renfree. I enjoyed it,' Edwin said, and again directed his gaze at the boy.

'You must come and visit me and Mrs Pendleton, Theodore.'

'Mrs Pendleton . . . is that Polly?'

'You've heard of her?'

'Sure I have. She used to live with Mrs Pascoe in the cottage next door to Grandpa . . . When Daddy lived there.'

'You've learned a lot in the short time you've been here,' Edwin said.

'I knew that when I was in America. Daddy told me. Daddy told me a lot about the mines, and going to school at Camborne . . . Uncle Ben paid for that.'

'I think you'd better stop before you give away family secrets,' Edwin tried to conceal a smile as he spoke.

'What secrets? Have you any secrets, Daddy?' But he didn't wait for a reply. 'I think Mummy has, because she doesn't tell Daddy everything.'

Joss laughed loudest at this remark and said to Edwin, 'I think some of her dresses are a bit more expensive than she lets on.' The men smiled knowingly, as though they were all aware that that type of little deception was the kind of thing husbands had to expect from their wives, but Emily Renfree said nothing, and her smile was a mite tight-lipped.

Joss felt his father was tiring and said they should leave. He would look forward to a good chat next time they met. They exchanged a few pleasantries, during which Joss twice noticed Edwin's glance linger on Theodore, then left to make their way back to the cottage.

'Good timing,' Polly said as, with a kiss, she welcomed Edwin home from work. The chicken pie and accompanying vegetables were cooked to perfection.

'Guess who visited the quarries today?' Edwin said as they sat

71

at table. 'Joss and his parents and his little boy.'

'How were they?' Polly asked. 'And what was Theodore like?'

Edwin proceeded to relate, dwelling mostly on Theodore, his grandparents' pride in their grandson, and the boy's surprise to find there were tramways and a blacksmith's shop where tools were made as well as repaired, and how deep the quarries were.

'Joss must be proud of him,' Polly said, a note of wistfulness in her voice.

'He is,' Edwin replied. 'But it did not prevent him from giving the boy a slap before they left.'

'Joss slapped him!' Polly said, astonished.

'I watched them depart, Joss held on to him while they paused to again stare down into one of the quarries. But after they'd walked on a little distance the boy turned and ran back picking up stones as he went, then throwing them down into the quarry where men were working. I was about to run and stop him. As well as injuring someone, he could have fallen himself, but Joss forestalled me. I could hear Joss lecturing him on how dangerous it was, and apologising to the men down in the quarry. While he was speaking to the men, Theodore produced more stones from his pocket and was about to throw them, but Joss prevented him just in time and slapped his legs, which made him yell. It was a very dangerous thing to do.'

'It certainly was,' Polly agreed.

'The boy continued to bawl as they all continued on their way, but I saw Mrs Renfree surreptitiously give the child a sweet from her bag and the crying instantly stopped.'

That evening, when dinner was over and Theodore had gone to bed, Joss and Clementine had a number of matters to discuss.

'Clemmie, did you sort something out with cook about staff?'

'Yes. And I've written asking the scullery maid if she would like to return. The housekeeper already has a post, but Solomon, the gardener, is going to ask his wife if she would like to work in the house and Solomon also knows a good man who will help him with the grounds.'

'You haven't tried to re-engage the groom, have you?'

'No . . . you didn't ask me to, and anyway, it's your place to deal with that sort of staff.'

'It wasn't a matter of whose place it was,' Joss replied. 'I just don't know whether we shall require one.'

'Go on,' Clementine said, her mouth pursed.

'Before I say anything further, I think we should discuss Theodore's schooling.'

'You surely don't imagine he'd go to one of those awful local Council or Church Schools, like you did.'

'No, I didn't imagine that,' Joss replied.

'And I'm not having him sent away to some boarding-school. He's too young.' Clementine added.

'I agree.'

'Then what's there to discuss? You must engage a tutor to live in.'

'He's an only child, Clemmie. He needs the company of other children.'

Clementine remained silent.

'Nell Pascoe was telling me this afternoon that the vicar's brother-in-law sends his two children to a boarding-school at Cresby, that takes day boys. Cresby is a tiny place about two miles from here. Not far from Ponsanooth.'

'I know where it is,' Clementine interrupted, irritably. 'I'm not having him walk over two miles to school every day.'

'Plenty of children do,' Joss retorted. 'I walked further than that and before I was seven years old . . . it didn't do me any harm.'

At this last remark Clementine adopted a long-suffering expression.

'But I wasn't thinking of suggesting he should walk,' he went on. 'I'm thinking of buying a motor.'

Clementine's face and tone of voice were instantly transformed.

'Oh, Joss, dearest, are you? I think that's a marvellous idea. That'll teach them.'

'Teach who?'

'All those friends who sneer because father has had a temporary unfortunate patch with his finances.'

'Speaking of your parents, when do they intend to move into their new home?' Joss asked.

'Darling . . . they've been here looking after the place for us . . . keeping it going. They want to be with us and their grandson for

73

a little while.'

'Oh, yes.'

'Besides, I want them to stay here to help me.'

'Help you what?'

'Listen, Joss dear. To invite all our friends to visit here individually would take forever . . .'

Joss waited for her to continue.

'I want us to give one big party and get it all over with, and I want mother and father to stay here and help me with the arrangements . . . You know you would find that tedious.'

Joss was silent for a few seconds, quickly turning over the pros and cons. Perhaps it wasn't such a bad idea. It would get all the invitations Clementine would undoubtedly want to make, over in one event and keep her sweet.

'All right,' he said. 'How soon can you arrange it?'

Chapter Nine

Jack and his mason friend, Vic Trewin had spent their spare time making the necessary alterations to the old sweet shop premises. Vic Trewin was saving to get married and Jack needed to fill his time instead of brooding alone over Milly. So everyone was benefiting from refitting and redecorating every inch of the property.

The shop and the room behind it were to be made into one to form the ground floor showroom at the entrance to the premises, and the other showroom was to be upstairs where the late Miss Barnard's living-room was, but now incorporating the landing and the bedroom, which made a surprisingly spacious showroom. The room over the kitchen was to be the fitting room.

Lottie was working on the clothes stock at home and Polly helped with designing and plain straightforward stitching, as well as starting up business records. The room at Villa Gwidden which Polly had mentally reserved for a nursery was now a depository for the growing stock of dresses, skirts, blouses, etc. Excitement mingled with sadness as Polly's dream of having her own baby or better still babies sleep in this room was replaced with the sales stock for a dream which in that first honeymoon year she had never ever contemplated. She tried not to let herself dwell on the comparisons.

Polly and Lottie were going to do the painting and papering themselves, apart from ceilings. Jack considered his sister to be good with these skills and, as Lottie said, he should know. But now Polly was growing exceedingly anxious about how the carpets would look. She and Lottie had jointly decided on plain soft grey-blue walls and a deeper but still soft shade of plain blue-grey carpet. Polly was convinced it would show off to advantage the garments which would be displayed and she had been successful in persuading Lottie this was a good idea.

But at the carpet department of the high-class furnishing shop, the department manager looked askance when told what was required.

'*Plain* blue-grey carpet, madam?' He raised one eyebrow. 'We don't stock plain colours, there is no demand. Of course, it could be ordered if you are sure that is what you really want, but we have some very *popular* lines in carpeting here, if you care to have a look.' He indicated a display at the side of the wall. 'Very nice *patterns* with quite a *variety* of colours.'

Polly would have ignored his remarks but Lottie was weakening. 'It wouldn't hurt to have a look,' she muttered. Lottie never could quite envisage the effect as Polly saw it, and now Polly suspected she was having doubts.

So Polly and Lottie looked at the samples of carpet stocked.

'They're not right, Lottie,' she said, after complying with Lottie's suggestion.

'No . . . I suppose.'

Lottie was definitely unsure, but offered no resistance to standing firm on the plan already agreed, and the man took note of the special order which he said might take a little longer than normal to expedite, being a somewhat unusual request.

Although at the time Polly was glad she had not been thwarted by the man's attitude, afterwards she began to doubt her ideas. Carpets were expensive and these were to be fitted carpets, not ready-made carpet squares or rectangles, but purchased in long wide strips and subsequently joined together. How awful she would feel if her ideas for decoration were all a ghastly costly mistake. They were spending money as if there were no tomorrow. Had being Mrs Edwin Pendleton and having a legacy from Great Aunt Elizabeth gone to her head. Her mother would never dream of the extravagances in which she was indulging. And not only Polly herself, she had persuaded Lottie to join in her . . . her what? Folly? Oh, God, I hope not, she thought. So on the day the carpet was to be delivered she was, unbeknown to Lottie, a bundle of nerves.

Lottie was quite delighted with the effect of the pale grey-blue wall-paper and confessed surprise at how much bigger than she expected the showrooms now looked.

Lottie stayed at home and got on with her sewing on the day

appointed for delivery of the carpet. Two men arrived promptly with the carpets. Ernie, the senior of the two, said they would start with the lower showroom then work their way up the stairs, the opposite to the way in which painting and papering were tackled.

Once they started Polly spent an hour in the attic on straight forward machining work, then went out to buy groceries to both help with the shopping and make the time pass more quickly. On her return to make coffee for herself and the two men, Ernie opened the door at her approach. 'The downstairs is laid; what do you think of it, Missus?'

With heart thumping, Polly increased her pace, then gasped audibly as she stared about her.

'Oh . . . Oh . . . It's beautiful,' she said as though to herself. 'And so spacious looking.'

The elegant simplicity surpassed even her imagined vision of how the showroom would look.

'It do look nice, don't it?' the man agreed. 'I never thought 'twould make such a difference, or look so smart. And don't it light the place.'

'Yes, it does. It looks really fine,' Polly replied.

Ernie stood rocking backwards on his heels and surveying the effects of his work with obvious satisfaction.

'You like it, don't 'ee Horace?' The carpet-layer addressed his assistant, who stood in the staircase.

'Aw 'es, 'tis handsome,' Horace agreed. 'Proper job!'

Ernie and Horace tread with unaccustomed delicacy to the kitchen, awaiting their coffee and biscuits. They were unfamiliar with Polly's idea of 'plain and simple decoration', most people having dark patterned or embossed wallpaper, and patterned dark carpets, usually in assorted sizes of squares and rectangles, and in colours which did not show the dirt.

Polly explained she thought plain quiet colours a good idea for a dress shop to focus attention on the clothes displayed.

'I never thought of that,' said Ernie. 'Did you think of that Horace?'

'No, I can't say as I did,' Horace replied.

It was quite late by the time the two men finished and Polly rode home on the bus, now contemplating Lottie's reaction with a measure of hope.

She was at the shop early next morning, anxious to learn how

Lottie would react. The shop looked so different from anything she had seen before. Lottie would either love it or hate it; no one could be indifferent. Polly fervently hoped she would like it. Surely she would, wouldn't she?

Once inside the shop Polly removed her hat and coat and waited in the kitchen, from where she could clearly see Lottie's face as she let herself in through the door. Minutes ticked by, then she heard Lottie's key in the lock, and the door handle squeak very slightly as she was about to enter. Suddenly there was Lottie, her jaw dropped, her mouth opened. 'Oh . . . Oh, my goodness!'

Unnoticed, Polly emerged from the kitchen while Lottie's head rotated slowly, gazing about her, mouth still open.

'What do you think of it, Lottie?' Polly asked in a small voice.

'What do I think of it?' Lottie turned her face toward Polly, mouth still open. 'It's gorgeous!' she said, quietly. 'You could knock me down with a feather! I think it's fantastic!'

Relief flooded through Polly and she ran and flung her arms about Lottie's neck.

'I'm so glad you like it, I was afraid you might not,' she confessed at last.

'How could I help but like it . . . it's beautiful!' Lottie went on to extol the lightness, the airiness, the illusion of space, and repeatedly admitted she never thought it would look so good.

'I can't believe it's all happening,' Polly told Lottie. 'Every once in a while I need to pinch myself. It's not when I'm asleep that I think I'm in a dream, it's when I'm awake!'

'Well brace yourself for the latest news,' Lottie said.

'Good?' Polly asked, suddenly fearful that the dream would be shattered.

'Let's put the kettle on,' Lottie answered as she moved towards the kitchen, intent on not revealing the special news until there was a cup of coffee to accompany it.

'Are the dresses coming along all right?' Polly asked, as they waited for water to boil.

'Oh yes, no problem there. Gosh, your brother Jack and his friend did a good job with the set-in clothes rails and display areas. Those were your idea, Polly.'

'Jack's a good chap. He's good to mother too. He's been tremendously interested in our venture, and it's helped occupy his mind.'

'Yes, poor Jack,' Lottie said. 'We've both got good brothers.' She placed two large cups of coffee on the small table, and Polly drew up a chair. 'Out with it, Lottie. What's all the big news?'

'I had a visit from Joss yesterday.'

'Joss! How is he?' Polly's head took this news calmly, so why did her heartbeats suddenly flutter?

'Oh, he's well, but at the moment quite busy. He asked for you and has actually called but you were not at home, plus it is taking a while to get the domestic arrangements sorted. Then he has been busy seeing about Theodore's schooling . . . he's not allowed to go to a Council School like the rest of us, you know.'

'I didn't think he would be,' Polly said, the fluttering subsiding. She remembered only too well the arrogant Miss Clementine Du Cane. Each stared into the other's eyes, smiling and knowing exactly what the other was thinking regarding Joss's supercilious wife.

'Well . . . he seemed thrilled we are going into partnership together. Mother and father told him about it and he thinks it's a marvellous idea. He wanted to give me money towards the expenses; but George is so touchy and unforgiving.'

'It wouldn't do to upset him,' Polly observed. 'After all, he was agreeable to you risking all your money in the idea.'

'Yes. Come to that, Polly . . . I didn't think Edwin would consent so easily when you asked him. He let you have your half of the money needed without even bothering to check if the figures were right.'

'Yes,' Polly agreed, her eyes suddenly downcast. 'I think he understands the reason behind it.'

Lottie paused momentarily, her dark eyes reading Polly's sudden wistful expression.

'I don't want to get George's back up. But he is a *bit* unreasonable. None of it was Joss's fault, and he is my brother. I don't wish to throw his kind intentions back in his face.'

'Of course not,' Polly murmured, dipping a biscuit in her coffee.

'So he has decided to give me an advance Christmas present to use for the shop . . . not cash . . . but he is crediting us with some money in three firms which are top suppliers to businesses like ours, to cover the cost of more dress-maker's dummies, three display models and the latest sewing machines, chairs, etc.'

Polly's jaw dropped with astonishment. 'No!' she shouted in near disbelief, and flung her arms about Lottie in an impetuous hug. 'That's marvellous!' Polly enthused, when she released her hold on Lottie.

'The reps for this area will call on us with samples and all the information,' Lottie said, then added, 'I'm not going to tell George exactly. I'll just let him know my Christmas present from Joss is going to be a new piece of equipment for the shop or workroom. He won't be interested in precisely what it is. He's my husband, and I don't want to be deceitful. But as I said, Joss is my brother. He's never harmed anyone, certainly not George, and I'm not going to hurt him by refusing to let him help. Sometimes it pays a wife to know when to keep her own counsel!'

'It rather depends on the husband, but I think you're right there, Lottie,' Polly agreed. She did not include her Edwin in that category of husbands.

'I'm glad you know the situation,' Lottie said, then added, 'And why wouldn't he want to help his own flesh and blood . . . he's done enough for *her* parents . . . buying that great barn of a manor just to get her parents out of a mess!'

'Did he really?' Polly asked, incredulously.

'Didn't you know?'

'Mother said Mrs Renfree mentioned something, but I thought she must have got the story wrong.'

'It's true all right . . . Hey, what else do you think? . . . the whole road was agog . . .'

'What else?' Polly held her breath.

'He turned up in a horseless carriage. It was in the road outside the house.'

'A motor!'

'It's not so odd really. He had one in America . . . they do out there, you know. And then he's got to take Theodore to school every day and Joss will want to be able to get over to see my parents quite often. It's not to be a "show-off". '

'Of course not,' Polly agreed. 'Different from Jack and Vic Trewin though. Not only do they walk back to Penryn from Falmouth, when the horse-bus goes up the High Street and the horse finds it heavy going, they put their shoulders to the rear to help the horse!'

They giggled at the comparison.

'I think your news was worth a few minutes celebration,' Polly said.

'Yes, indeed. We should be able to make this a really smart establishment.'

'I think if we can make the fitting-room as smart and attractive as the "show" areas it gives a good impression . . . a feeling of quality.' Polly went on.

'That's good thinking, Polly,' Lottie agreed. 'Usually fitting rooms look about as attractive as a broom cupboard. No cutting corners, high standards in everything.'

'We shouldn't go over the top though, this is Falmouth, not Knightsbridge.'

'Agreed.' Lottie stood to emphasise chat over, work about to recommence.

Time sped. Polly was noticeably happier. She threw herself into the project. She now had thoughts for other things as well as the baby she so desired, and pored over catalogues, advertisements and pictures of society ladies, then started making a portfolio of designs from which customers could choose.

Chapter Ten

Neither Lottie nor Polly had illusions about leading fashion. They would *follow* fashion, only with a few distinctive touches.

'We'll try to go with the trend,' Lottie said. 'But leaving fashion aside, I know my present customers. A lot of them know exactly what they want and what suits them, irrespective of fashion trends. And I try to give them what pleases them.'

'I wouldn't think you could go wrong with that,' Polly approved.

'It occurred to me with the spacious showroom upstairs we could have a millinery section,' Lottie suggested.

Polly did not care for this suggestion. 'Millinery,' she said. 'That's a very individual thing. You need quite a lot of stock to attract customers, which would be unproductive capital being tied up. Besides, styles are changing. Hats are not as big as they were. We are to be an exclusive concern. Do you know of a milliner, Lottie?'

Lottie placed a hand to her chin to think. 'I believe you've hit the nail on the head, Polly . . . Madam Delia!'

'The name rings a bell.'

'She had a milliner's shop in Boscawen Street in Truro, but sold the business when she married. She's a widow now and lives somewhere in Falmouth.'

'Perhaps she would make the occasional hat to order for our customers.'

'*And* perhaps using or incorporating material I used to make the dresses,' Lottie said. 'That could be so smart. Madam Delia would have a supply of feathers and other embellishments.'

'That sounds wonderful, a customer for every hat sold and we take a percentage. No wasted space and no tied up money.'

'I'll find out where she is.' Lottie promised.

Both Polly and Lottie made a point of being at home well before their husbands at the end of the men's working day. This enabled them to get a meal under way. Lottie always cooked. Polly and Mary took it in turns to cook the meal. Polly did not wish Edwin to feel she had abandoned housewifely pursuits and duties.

She instinctively felt, and she knew Lottie did too, that it was prudent to keep the home routine running as smoothly as possible and not to let their husbands' home life be affected by their activities.

On this particular day Edwin arrived home around 5.45 as usual. He took off his bowler hat and dark overcoat, and went to the kitchen to deliver Polly a kiss. This was his daily order and ritual, and Polly knew that coming home each evening to her and a meal together was the highlight of her husband's day; the reason why despite all his deep interest in his granite business and all the attendant activities, he was always happy to leave it at the end of the working day, and hurry home.

After the main dish, Polly produced from the kitchen plum tart, made with plums she had bottled, and clotted cream. Edwin did not immediately 'tuck in'.

'I've had a gentleman visit me today, complaining you are elusive . . . although he tries hard to time his calls when he thinks you are sure to be at home, it is always to no avail.'

'A gentleman!' Polly sounded both surprised and intrigued, though her heart lurched. 'Who was he and what did he want?'

Edwin placed a hand inside his jacket and, with a flourish, produced an envelope from an inner pocket.

'He asked me to give you this.'

Polly took the envelope and hastily opened it.

'Oh! . . . It's from Joss . . . and Clementine,' she added. 'It's an invitation to a party at Manor Withiel to "meet old friends and renew old friendships". How lovely! We *can* go, can't we?' Her voice rose animatedly. Why did her cheeks feel suddenly warm?

'Of course, my love.'

Polly leant forward and kissed Edwin, glad to bury her face in his collar to hide the tell-tale flush of excitement, or was it

83

apprehension?

She was happy with Edwin. It didn't make sense that seeing Joss would change anything. But Joss was inadvertently right. She had been elusive, like the time Lottie dropped a hint that he might call next evening and she went to visit her mother. And she *had* been relieved to go away to Great Aunt Elizabeth, only at the time she would not admit it, not even to herself. Swifter than the speed of light the thoughts flashed through her mind.

She felt Edwin plant a kiss on her hair. She must conceal her illogical fears and not under nor overdo her pleasure at the prospect of this social event. She must also give thought to the opportunity to promote the shop, very discreetly of course, nothing obvious. Wasn't it odd . . . to think of the shop at such a time. But thinking of the shop was her mental 'port in a storm'. Every time she felt sad that there was no baby, she turned her mind to the shop.

Polly raised her head from Edwin's shoulder and smiled up at him. He comfortingly kissed her head.

'I think you're tired, my dear.'

'I am a little,' she admitted.

Polly, her arms still around Edwin's neck, snuggled closer. 'I'm keeping you from your pudding!' she murmured.

'The pudding can wait,' Edwin said.

Next day Polly arrived late at the shop, and as she unlocked the door to let herself in, her gaze fell upon Lottie.

'Morning Lottie. Have you heard the news?' she said, excitedly.

'I think I can guess . . . you've had an invitation.'

'Yes. Did you get one?'

'No. Joss came around to see us last evening. He had a long talk with George and asked if he might forget, or at least overlook his differences with Clementine, and come to the party.'

'Did George agree?'

'Eventually. Joss said it was putting a strain between him and me. He didn't think Clementine remembered the incident anyway. After all, they had both been abroad so many years. It would be so good for my family if we could show willingness to be friends.'

'So he's going to the party?'

'Yes, he said he'd go.'

'I'm so glad.'

'So am I. Joss and I have always been close.'

'Isn't it a good thing some of the material arrived last week?'

'Why?' Lottie said, slightly startled at what seemed a change of topic.

'You'll have to drop everything and make us both new dresses.'

'For the party?' Lottie looked perplexed. 'I don't think we've time to stop for that.'

'We've got to, Lottie. We need to be the two best dressed ladies there. Clementine and her family know a lot of County people. Think what a shop window it will be!'

'Why Polly! You're right. I was so pleased George and Joss parted company on such good terms, I haven't thought of much else. You'll have to help me, though.'

'I'll be glad to,' Polly said. Let's have a look at those materials. 'Oh, my goodness. There's another delivery of something, coming right now.'

'Good, because most of what came last week was the heavier materials for skirts and suits,' Lottie said.

Polly went to open the door wide enough to admit the two men who delivered display models, dressmaker's dummies, a long table, a box of assorted equipment and ten more bolts of dress material.

Being of superior quality, the bolts had special wrapping, and eagerly Polly and Lottie, with the party in mind, partially opened each one. Lottie, spotting a roll of flimsy material which took her fancy, wrested it from its protective wrapping. 'Ah . . . this pink is lovely, Polly.' She unrolled a length of the variegated wild silk and held it against her cheek. It was cool as balm and soft as a floating feather.

'I don't like pink for adult dresses,' Polly answered indifferently, without looking up.

'Oh, feel it, Polly. It's heavenly,' Lottie insisted, still holding the material, just enjoying its filmy softness.

Reluctantly Polly shifted her gaze to the material which Lottie still held. 'Why, Lottie, that's not pink, it's . . . it's . . . It doesn't look pink to me, it's almost mauve.'

'Yes, it does look sort of mauve,' Lottie agreed.

'I've seen a colour like that before, only I can't think where,' Polly said.

Lottie began to open another roll. 'Look, here's a roll of the same material, only it's plain.'

'It's gorgeous,' Polly murmured. 'Anyone would feel special wearing that.

'Go on . . . have it,' Lottie said. 'You could wear that colour.'

Polly's face lit up. 'Shall I?'

'You know you want it. You'll regret it if you don't.'

'Thanks, Lottie, I'd love a dress made with it. But whatever colour is it?'

'There's a hanging label,' Lottie said.

Polly detached it. 'It's "Sundown",' she read.

'*That's* where *I've* seen it before,' Lottie exclaimed. 'When George and I were married we stayed a long weekend with my Uncle Harry at the Lizard, after the wedding. He had a little shop which sold things he made from Serpentine. There were some beautiful sunsets and as the sun dipped down below the sea out at the horizon, the distant sky took on that lovely pinky-mauve colour.'

'Oh yes, I've seen it too at times,' Polly said pausing, a dreamy look in her eyes.

'There's a booklet here. It's got details on the latest dresses and outfits in the London and Paris Fashion Houses.'

'Let me see,' Polly said eagerly, the dreaminess banished.

Lottie held the booklet up. The cover read 'This Season's Styles'. She flipped through the pages. One in particular caught her eye. It was basically simple, yet a very smart evening dress.

'How about this style, Polly?' Lottie held up a picture of the dress.

'I love it!' Polly said.

'I'll make you one that's very similar . . . *This* is nice . . . ' Lottie had pulled off another layer of wrapping to reveal a roll of deep blue voile. 'What do you think of this one?'

'It's gorgeous, Lottie. And you could carry that colour off beautifully.'

'I think I'll have it.'

'Good.'

They both felt its softness and admired the way the opaque

quality of the indigo blue, streaked here and there with muted purple, caused the blue to seem both soft and vibrant at the same time.

'It's just . . . just beautiful,' Polly said, adding, 'And here's a dark blue lining material.'

'I'll need that,' Lottie grinned. 'George would throw a fit if I appeared dressed in a gown you could see through!'

'What's this, there's another little booklet enclosed,' Polly said.

'Have they put in two of those fashion booklets?' Lottie asked.

'No. This one says we can order shoes and evening bags in matching shades,' Polly said, excitedly.

'That's a nifty idea,' Lottie came close to inspect. The booklet showed designs to choose from in both footwear and the evening bags.

Polly read aloud: 'Dainty evening footwear, also evening bags could be supplied in bulk or individually to complete your smart ensemble . . . The essence of style . . . '

'It sounds marvellous,' said Lottie.

'We'd better make up our minds and place an order for the shoes and bags right away,' Polly observed. 'The party is in less than three weeks.'

'It's going to be a bit costly,' Lottie pointed out.

'That's the prudent housewife in you coming out, Lottie,' Polly said. 'It's just . . .' Staring heavenward, she searched in her mind for the appropriate expression.

'A sprat to catch a mackerel,' Lottie supplied, wondering whether the fish she bought for tonight's meal from the shop at the top of Fish Strand Quay had prompted her.

'Precisely,' Polly agreed. 'And after all, materials might be expensive, but we are having them cost price and we don't have to pay someone to make them.'

'No. It won't come to such a lot. I suppose you would regard the line in footwear and evening-bags rather like the millinery idea,' Lottie said. 'Available to the customers if they want to place a special order?'

'Exactly,' Polly said. 'It's a marvellous arrangement. And we can look on ourselves as guinea-pigs and find out whether it works well.'

Lottie grinned and nodded.

Before the morning was over both had decided on dress styles, and Polly hurried to the Post Office to place an order for shoes and evening-bags, Lottie's plain and Polly's beaded style . . . a unique idea, at least in local shops. Polly was excited at the prospect of how well they would look at the party. How foolish she had been to fear that meeting Joss again could change anything.

On the Sunday prior to the party, after morning service was over and the congregation were leaving church, the wives of two of Joss's old friends paused to chat.

'Are you and Edwin going to the party, Polly?'

Polly, dressed in her plum coloured coat and velvet hat, smiled. 'Yes, we're going. Are you?'

'I'd just love to,' Ada replied, 'so would Jane Ann here.' She indicated her companion who stood next to her. ' 'Tis our husbands!'

The two men hovered in the background.

'Oh dear,' Polly said, guessing the cause of the trouble.

' 'Tis a dressy affair and they haven't got the right suits. And it wouldn't be any good trying to get suits either. Even if somebody gave them suits they'd complain that they wouldn't be seen dead in them.'

'They're both afraid they'll be laughed at,' contributed Jane Ann.

One husband shuffled from one foot to the other; both looked uncomfortable.

'Come as you are,' Edwin addressed the men. 'You know it won't make any difference to Joss what you wear.'

One spoke up. 'No, we know it won't make no difference to Joss, but it might to his wife. And anyway, we'd stick out like Marcus Treloar's bull's . . . '

'Don't dare say it!' his wife interrupted fiercely.

The man bit his lip to prevent himself saying something coarse involving the anatomy of Marcus Treloar's bull, then said, 'We'd both look proper out-of-place if we dressed different.'

'Yes.' The other husband spoke at last. 'And we'd feel proper out-of-place if we dressed like they do. So we *ain't* going!'

'After a couple of whiskies you won't worry about what you're wearing or what other people think.' Edwin said with a grin. Polly nudged him warningly.

'True,' said the husband who first spoke, then jerked his stumpy thumb in the direction of the two wives. 'But we'd have these two to live with after, and we'd never hear the last of it.'

When they parted company, Ada and Jane Ann, the two aggrieved wives, could be heard arguing with their husbands as they walked away.

'Going to church seems not to have done them much good,' Edwin remarked to Polly, with a laugh. 'You wouldn't expect an invitation to cause anyone trouble, would you?' His words suddenly filled Polly with a feeling of unease.

Chapter Eleven

At the entrance to Manor Withiel a man dressed like a butler greeted arrivals to the party and directed them to bedrooms where the ladies could leave their capes and coats, likewise the men. Theodore, who seemed to enjoy scampering up and down the stairs, took it upon himself to escort Polly, Lottie, Edwin and George to the allotted rooms.

'I suppose we shall see our parents when we get inside the party room,' Polly said as she removed her coat.

'Oh yes, Joss would have driven them here this afternoon,' Lottie confirmed.

'I imagine they've engaged extra staff, there are so many flitting about,' Polly observed.

'It looks like it,' Lottie agreed. 'You do look fetching in that gown, Polly. To have the skirt and lower part of the bodice in plain material and the sleeves and yoke in the variegated was a good idea. And wild silk falls so beautifully,' she went on. 'You just reek of quality.'

'I feel good in it,' Polly replied. 'Edwin said I looked good enough to eat.' She grinned at this admission. 'But you look absolutely gorgeous in that lovely blue voile, Lottie. The little streaks of muted purple make it look rich. I bet George liked it.'

Lottie nodded. 'He did say I look "striking" which, coming from him, is a compliment indeed. And,' Lottie went on but lowered her voice at the sounds of approaching guests, 'don't the shoes and evening bags just set the whole thing off?'

'Absolutely,' Polly enthused. 'And I thought our two husbands looked quite splendid in their black tailcoats and trousers with white waistcoats and white bow ties.'

'George had to borrow his,' Lottie admitted in a low voice.

Polly and Lottie both turned to a mirror to check every hair was still in place. As they finished, two sedate elderly ladies, friends of Clementine's parents, Polly surmised, entered the room. The four exchanged greetings and a few pleasantries, then Lottie said, 'Shall we go down?'

'I'm ready,' Polly replied.

They found their husbands awaiting them at the foot of the stairs, and a young woman dressed like a waitress directed them. Clementine, looking impressive in a creamy silk taffeta gown embroidered in tiny gold beads and trimmings, welcomed them at the entrance to the room chosen for the event. Her face cracked into the toothy smile Polly remembered from way back in her childhood. But Joss was nowhere to be seen. Instead, at her side and taking the part of host was her brother, Rupert, tall, fair, slim, handsome and ever so slightly supercilious. He was a partner in a London firm of solicitors and had come down to Manor Withiel especially for the occasion.

'Here's my dear sister-in-law, Lottie.' Clementine took Lottie's hand and gave her a perfunctory kiss on the cheek. 'How lovely to see you my dear. And how elegant you look in that divine gown.'

'Lovely to see you again, Clementine,' Lottie replied. She was going to compliment her sister-in-law on her dress, but Clementine's attention now rested on George.

'Lovely to see you, George.' A handshake and kiss. 'What a smart pair you both make.'

'And this is . . . it's never Polly! Why bless my soul it is. Welcome, my dear.' Again a handshake and kiss. 'And this handsome man must be your husband.'

'Yes, this is Edwin,' Polly confirmed, as Clementine's eyes swept approvingly over Edwin.

'I'm so pleased to meet you at last . . . Well, I've kissed everyone else so I think I should include you too,' she said as she took his hand, and kissed his cheek.

Lottie, Polly and George were chatting and shaking hands with Rupert.

'Now, I must tell you all before I get caught up with other guests,' Clementine's voice interrupted. 'Joss will be here later.'

Lottie, who intended to ask as soon as the handshakes were over, spun round. 'What's happened?' she said.

91

'Your father had a peculiar turn late this morning,' Clementine said.

'Oh heavens! What was it?' Some of the colour had drained from Lottie's face.

'It's nothing to worry about. Joss is over-protective, but there is no danger. He's recovering quietly at home. Your mother is there too, of course. And I'm afraid Polly's mother stayed behind with her . . . You both look terrifically smart. Oh, here's Hugo and Madelaine Bassett. I'm afraid you'll have to excuse me.'

The folding wood partition which divided the large drawing-room from an even larger adjoining reception room, had been opened to allow ample space. In something of a daze Polly and Lottie moved to a distant corner and sat on a rose-coloured velvet sofa, their husbands both joined them.

'I didn't expect this to happen,' Lottie said. 'I hope it isn't serious.'

'Here, drink this,' Edwin took two glasses of sherry from a waiter who was circulating with a tray of drinks, and whiskies for himself and George. Lottie sipped the sherry.

'Thanks, Edwin,' she said.

Polly saw her brother approaching. 'Here's Jack . . . Jack, do you know how Mr Renfree is?'

'He's all right. There's really no need for alarm. The doctor has been and said he's in no danger, but he advised rest in bed for the next twenty-four hours, and if he seems well and recovered he can then get up, but must take things quietly for a while.'

Lottie gave a sigh of relief. 'Thank goodness for that,' she said, then added. 'If he's all right why is Joss still with him?'

'It was a shock for your mother, too.'

'Oh yes, of course.'

'He's staying on until she's had time to calm down, I think he's just extra anxious because he's been away so long. I believe he somehow expected to come home and find everything, including your parents, just as he left them.'

'And now he's come home and found two old fogies,' Lottie supplied.

Jack laughed, 'In a way.'

Lottie was now reassured. 'Well, I'm glad it doesn't seem serious. And we mustn't let it spoil the evening, they wouldn't want that . . . My goodness,' Lottie gazed about her, now able to

92

absorb something of what was going on, 'the place is filling up.'

Polly took her brother's hand and squeezed it. 'I'm glad you decided to come,' she said. 'It'll do you good to get out and enjoy yourself.'

Jack tilted his head to one side and smiled down at his sister. He bent and said in almost a whisper, 'Lottie looks wonderful and you are the best looking woman here.'

Polly laughed and pushed him away.

'What did he say to you?' Lottie was curious.

'He said we are the two best looking women here,' Polly replied.

'We intended to be,' Lottie replied. Then they all laughed.

While they were laughing the strains of a tea dance type band began playing on a small dais next to the grand piano, but the music was almost drowned by the ever increasing buzz of conversation.

'Look,' Polly said. 'There's Colonel Banks and his wife.'

'There are at least three sea captains,' Jack said. 'Two of them have houses along Greenbank.'

'Mr and Mrs Du Cane are busy circulating . . . but of course, there must be several of their old friends here,' Lottie observed. 'I believe they are coming across the room to us.'

Clementine's mother, upright and stately, looked impressive in a flowing lilac gown with panels hanging from her shoulders. Albert Du Cane, tall, with a drooping grey moustache and thinning hair accompanied her and he also looked quite impressive. The Du Canes came towards them.

'Lottie, my dear, and George . . . and this must be Polly, how charming you all look. And this must be Edwin and . . . ' she seemed to find difficulty in remembering.

'This is my brother, Jack,' Polly said.

'Oh, yes, of course.' The Du Canes shook hands with them all and were solicitous in enquiring for Lottie's father. So you should be. Lottie privately thought. Neither of you would be here lording it round if it were not for my brother. However, she did not let her feelings show, but smiled and was equally pleasant.

'Thankfully it does not seem to be too serious,' Margaret Du Cane smiled. 'They will be so disappointed to have missed the party. My dear friend, Alexandra Prescott was coming, but she too is unwell . . . I fear the weather has not been kind to us older ones.'

The ladies wittered on for a few minutes, then Clementine's parents moved to welcome a couple who had arrived from Mawnan Smith.

'How do you think Clementine looked?' Polly asked.

Neither Edwin nor George answered, but Lottie said, 'Very much in command, as usual. Very elegant, still very striking-looking. But even in this lovely soft gas-light she does look . . . older.'

'I thought so too,' Polly agreed.

As they were talking Clementine left her post near the door and walked across the room to the small dais where the band sat, with a grand piano close by. She spoke to the man who seemed to be leader, then went to sit with a nearby group.

'My Lords, ladies and gentlemen,' the band-leader said. The buzz of conversation ceased.

Lottie whispered, '*Do* we have any Lords here?'

The band-leader continued: 'Your hostess, Mrs Renfree, has asked me to make the announcement that we shall be having dancing interspersed with musical renderings . . . a sort of soirée-cum-ball. Mrs Renfree apologises that Mr Renfree was not here to greet you as planned, but you will all know the reason and I'm sure one and all wish Mr Renfree's father a speedy recovery.'

A ripple of genteel clapping followed this announcement.

'Mrs Renfree tells me she has persuaded Miss Ellen Cardew, soprano, to sing for you, and Mr Wallace Brice, the well-known baritone.'

There was another ripple of clapping.

'Mr Brice will now entertain you with two well-known and well-loved ballads.'

The guests sat in groups around small tables and half-circles of chairs arranged around the perimeter of the room, leaving a good space in the centre for dancing.

Being tucked away at the far end of the room and with all the talk and concern for Lottie's father, a number of guests were present Polly and the others had not yet seen.

Mr Brice, a tall, slim, balding man of around fifty, had brought his own accompanist, who had taken his place at the grand piano. Mr Brice rose from his seat near the dais and stood a few feet from the piano.

94

He had a pleasing, tuneful voice, and after each song there was appreciative clapping. Mr Brice bowed smiling to the guests, then to his accompanist, and again took his seat.

The band-leader thanked him, announced there would be a waltz, and exhorted the guests to all join in.

'May I ask our hostess, Mrs Renfree, to lead the dance?'

Clementine gave a toothy smile and nodded consent. In the absence of Joss, Polly expected Clementine to dance with Rupert. The band-leader picked up his instrument, a violin, and the band struck up a popular tune. Polly gasped in amazement. The handsome, tall, fair-haired man who sprang forward to partner Joss's wife was not Rupert, it was none other than . . . what was his name . . . Customs Officer Charles Brendon Copeland!

How does she know him, Polly thought. She hasn't been back from America five minutes!

'Shall we dance? . . . Polly! . . . you're never falling asleep!'

'Sorry Edwin. I was miles away.'

Polly rose from her seat as she spoke and Edwin slid his hand round her back, and with his other hand took hers. As they stood waiting to commence dancing at the appropriate beat of the music, he pulled her close to him. Lottie and George were already on the floor.

'Polly, you look sensational . . . you feel sensational!'

They were dancing now, and Polly felt her husband's fingers almost clasp her back. The texture of the material along with the whisky is causing him to have ideas, she thought. But this was quickly dismissed from her mind. She could not get over the unexpected sight of Officer Copeland, here at this party and, in a sense, taking Joss's place. If she ever thought Officer Copeland flirtatious, now she was sure of it.

She had completely forgotten the man. Although she spent so much time in Falmouth working on preparing the shop, helping Lottie with straight-forward stitch-work, and painting and papering, she had never seen him again. But of course, she wouldn't. The windows were covered with a powdery substance which let in light, but could not be seen through either from the inside or the outside.

As they waltzed around the room she heard the unmistakably cultured yet easy voice.

'Hello, Polly.' Polly and Edwin brushed against Clementine

95

and Charles Copeland. Polly felt shaken, though she did not know why. Before she could reply the two had gone.

'Who was that?' There was a strong note of demand in Edwin's voice.

'I'll tell you later,' Polly replied.

She glanced up at Edwin and saw his face was set. Surely he didn't suspect her of anything . . . untoward! Had Mrs Bray and Mrs Mason been spreading rumours about seeing them together that time she went on the bus to Falmouth; the time she met Lottie when she suddenly had the idea of jointly opening a dress shop. Surely not! Though innocent, she felt inexplicably guilty and a flush spread over her face.

The dance ended and they silently made their way to where the four sat.

'Who was he?' Edwin demanded.

'His name, if I remember it correctly, is Charles Copeland. I met him once by accident. That is all.'

Edwin was silent. Lottie and George had now joined them, breathless from exertion but happy. Lottie almost flopped onto the rose velvet sofa and would have done so had she not been conscious of Polly's and her role as advertisements for their shop. George needed to sit, but had clearly enjoyed the dancing.

'I'm out of practice,' he said, breathlessly, 'but I enjoyed it.'

There was a slight pause, then Lottie said in a half whisper which was loud enough for the four to hear, 'Did you notice Clementine dancing with . . . that Customs Officer . . . what was his name . . . Charles something or other?'

'I think it was Copeland,' Polly supplied. She now looked straight at her husband. 'I met him once. Lottie met him too . . . she was there at the time.'

This was the truth, but not quite the whole truth. Still it had the desired effect. Edwin, who had been staring fixedly at Polly, lowered his gaze and his set expression relaxed. Now she had made *him* feel guilty. Well let him. She now felt annoyed with him. Serve him right.

Another dance was announced and Polly was surprised to find herself relieved when George asked her to dance. She did not remember ever feeling so irritated with Edwin. Edwin partnered Lottie. George was an expert, smooth yet lively dancer. Polly wondered whether his condition was as serious as Lottie believed.

96

An explanation was soon forthcoming.

'That glass of whisky has done me a power of good. I feel so much better. In future we'll keep a bottle in the house!'

It was during this dance that Polly noticed Jack talking to a small group . . . Who were they? Why, they were the two aggrieved wives whose husbands would not take them to the party. All four were there. The men had evidently reached a kind of compromise and wore black suits. As she and George twirled around the room close to where they sat, Polly waved and the ladies waved in return while the two men raised their glasses. Polly chided herself for not noticing them during the first dance, but she had been in something of a daze, especially when Charles Copeland spoke to her, obviously arousing suspicions in Edwin's mind. She hadn't thought him capable of suspecting her of anything like that and it hurt.

The dance ended and Polly and George rejoined Lottie and Edwin, George telling her as they walked along, how much he enjoyed the dance. Polly admitted she was surprised how well he could dance. 'I'm not too bad on level ground,' he explained. 'It's hills, even a slight one, that rob me of breath. I'm really enjoying this, Polly.'

Polly did not take her seat. Instead she said she was going to speak to Ada Pearce and Jane Ann Phillips.

'Are they here?' Edwin asked.

'Yes, they're sitting near the other end on this side,' Polly said.

'I'll come with you.'

Polly knew he was trying to make amends.

He walked along at her side and Polly felt quite a few pairs of eyes surveying her. She held her head high. This could be good for business.

On the way she was hailed by a regal, elderly lady with a diamond and pearl choker.

'My dear, would you think me terribly rude if I tell you I've been admiring your gown?'

Polly's smile was reassuring. 'Of course not. I must admit I'm very pleased with it, and it's nice to have my opinion confirmed.'

The old but clearly once beautiful lady caught Polly's hand in hers.

'It can't have come from around here, I've not seen anything like it outside London and the really big cities.'

e

'Ah, but it did,' Polly laughed, and with her free hand patted the back of the hand that held hers. 'It came from Falmouth, just a few short miles from here.'

'Falmouth!' The old lady's voice rose to near disbelief. 'Surely not!' She had a rather imperious voice, which carried well.

'My partner made it.'

'The one wearing the beautiful blue voile?' the lady asked.

Polly sensed all nearby female ears were listening.

'That's the one. She's very clever. We're opening a dress shop in Falmouth quite soon.'

'*Do* let me know when.' The old lady fumbled in her evening bag. 'My name is Elizabeth Endersby-Harman. Here, take my card and let me know when you do open your establishment.'

'We might be having a Preview, so I'll let you know in case you care to come,' Polly said.

The other ladies sitting nearby all produced cards from their bags and pressed them upon Polly. She promised to be in touch with all, put the cards into her pink evening bag, and with a smile moved away.

What had possessed her to say there might be a Preview? Where did the idea and the word come from? She had not heard of a shop doing that! Had she read it somewhere? What on earth would Lottie say! What was coming over her . . . had the sherry gone to *her* head? She had drunk two glasses. She would not have any more. A Preview! Help! What did that entail? She couldn't think now. She would do that tomorrow. Thank goodness she only said '*might*' have a Preview.

The two aggrieved ladies, as she had come into the habit of calling them, welcomed her and Edwin with beaming faces.

'So you came after all,' Polly said, accepting the seat offered by Fred Phillips.

'Yes. 'Twas Ada's idea. She said, "We'll have their navy blue Sundays, Weddings and Christenings suits died black!" ' Mary Jane explained.

'Except mine shrunk,' said Ada's husband, who stood to reveal his slightly short trousers, also his sleeves. 'Ada had to move the buttons, too.'

' 'Tis you, getting too fat,' Ada laughed.

'We're really sorry to hear about Joss's father,' Wilf Pearce commiserated. 'And he'll be sorry to be missing this grand affair.'

But discussion was cut short. The band-leader announced that Miss Cardew would sing two songs.

There was a ripple of clapping, and the circulating wine-waiters retreated to the rear of the room, Wilf Pearce hailing one as he was about to pass by.

Though not particularly strong, Miss Cardew had a sweet voice. She used it to good effect and her renderings were warmly received.

The next dance was announced. 'Do you mind if I dance with my sister?' Jack who had just joined them, asked Edwin.

'Of course not, go ahead,' Edwin replied.

Jack and Polly took the floor and Edwin was left with little choice but to ask if one of the ladies would like to dance.

'I can't dance,' Ada said. 'But Jane Ann can.'

Edwin turned to the plump Jane Ann, who rose to her feet. She seemed delighted and with good reason. It was soon revealed the staid-looking Jane Ann was quite a good dancer, not a stolid heavy lump, but light and responsive to her partner's every move. Edwin was glad he had Jane Ann to partner him.

It was during this dance that Joss, unnoticed by most of the dancers, entered the room. He was immediately hailed by those sitting and standing nearby, and there were greetings, handshakes and enquiries.

He looked at the partners on the floor and noticed Edwin dance by, performing an intricate sequence of steps. But Edwin's partner was not Polly.

'Where's Polly?' he said to the old friend standing next to him.

'Haven't you seen Polly?' Jim Paull said. 'She's there somewhere, looking pretty as a picture and dancing with her brother. He's coming now. Look, there's Jack.'

'Polly . . . Little Friend,' Joss called, as Jack commenced a spin.

Polly heard the familiar name and her spine became goose-pimply at this deeper, more resonant sound of the voice from the past. Jack and Polly stopped dancing, and Polly at last came face to face with Joss!

Chapter Twelve

As she caught sight of Joss, Polly felt her heart judder and miss a couple of beats, then commence hammering wildly, causing a pounding in her ears.

He stood there, older, broader, handsomer, mellowed and for Polly, perfected. The pendulum on the Grandfather clock in the hall must have hung still as time halted and past and present merged. Joss's arms were slightly extended, as though from old habit, as though he still expected her to take a flying leap into his arms. He smiled, but in the velvet brown eyes which gazed into hers came a fleeting expression of pain, and his arms fell to his sides.

'Polly! My "little friend" is no longer the skinny scrap of a small girl who used to plague me,' he said.

Polly was unaware the band was still playing; her head throbbed from the pounding and hammering of her heartbeats, and she wondered if Joss could hear it too.

'Aren't you going to speak to me?' he said.

She took a step towards him . . . 'Joss.'

Joss moved towards her and stretched out his hand. Automatically Polly responded, and he grasped her slender white hand with both his, encasing it in his large, strong, brown ones, sending shock waves up her arm and paralysing her capacity for speech.

She wanted him to let go of her, and never to let go. This moment must last for ever, must suffice for the rest of her life. With an effort she forced her mouth to form a smile.

'Joss . . . it's lovely to see you . . . How are you?'

'Stunned by all the changes I'm finding . . . the latest and biggest is you. I was expecting to see the same little girl I left behind, only taller. Instead, it's the other way round. I find a composed beautiful woman who makes me feel like an awkward callow boy again.'

Composed! Didn't he know she was anything but composed? And Callow! Wasn't he aware he was the handsomest, most desirable man in the whole wide world?

He smiled, and though he still held her hand in his, her paralysed body relaxed and the hammering heartbeats slowed enough to allow her almost to breathe normally.

'How is your father, Joss?' Polly asked at last.

'Comfortable now . . . He'll make it!' Then added, 'This time.'

Polly nodded gravely.

'Mother never told me in her letters.'

'She couldn't have known, but would you have expected her to?' Polly asked.

Joss paused before answering. 'No,' he said.

Polly tried to withdraw her hand from his. He increased the pressure, then let go.

Joss continued to gaze at her, drinking with his eyes the vision before him.

'Polly . . . there's been a metamorphosis since I last saw you . . . the same little girl transformed into such a beautiful woman . . . I can't take it in . . . I can't . . .'

'Joss . . . don't,' Polly whispered, suddenly *aware* of people who stood nearby, of the band which was crescendoing to a halt, of Clementine coming towards them and of the band-leader speaking.

'Ladies and gentlemen . . . I hope you all enjoyed the dance. You will be pleased to know that your host, Mr Joss Renfree, is now with us . . . Would you care to say something to us, sir?'

Joss, regaining his composure, responded: 'I'm pleased to be able to tell everyone my father is now comfortable, and should be quite well again in a few days. Please, everyone, carry on with the party and enjoy yourselves.'

By the time Joss had finished speaking, as well as Clementine, Lottie and George and Clementine's parents had joined them. Lottie and Clementine bombarded Joss with questions and the rest listened intently.

When all the queries were answered Clementine said, 'You'd better change your suit, Joss.'

'I suppose so,' Joss said grudgingly, and disappeared.

Mr Wallace Brice again contributed two songs which brought all conversation to a halt. But Polly did not hear them. Joss was not like she expected. The tall, slim, good-natured young man who had been her number one playmate, had matured into a bigger, quieter, more authoritative giant, the hero of every dream she had never allowed herself to dream, of every desire that she had fought so hard to repress. Now, in one single prolonged moment, they all had burst from within her locked heart where they lay trapped, stifled, for so many years.

Her mouth had become suddenly dry and she tried to lick her lips.

The band-leader announced refreshments were waiting in the corridor outside.

'Are you all right, Polly,' Edwin asked.

'I'd like a drink . . . No, thank you . . . not sherry . . . ' she said, as her attentive husband passed her a glass from somewhere she did not even notice.

Everyone drifted to the corridor where yards of narrow abutting tables, covered in starched white linen cloths supported a mountain of assorted delicacies.

Edwin, who had briefly left Polly's side, appeared with a glass of water, and Polly gratefully drank and felt a measure of revival.

'Let's get something to eat,' she said to Edwin, not wishing anyone to notice her sudden strange 'indisposition'.

There was such a variety of dainty meats, and a plethora of assorted croûtes and croustades, canapés, barquettes, bouchées, timbales in aspic jelly and other savouries, to be followed by a variety of small decorated cakes, mousses, parfaits and bombes. iced fruit creams of all kinds and ice cream which had been kept in what was known as an ice-house.

By now the guests, warm, entertained and pleasantly mellowed with drink were relaxed, and chatter and bursts of laughter reverberated throughout the broad long corridor. The Pearces and the Phillips's were not far away and Ada and Jane Ann could be heard extolling the wonderful spread, marvelling at all the washing-up someone would have to do afterwards, and best of all, congratulating one another that it would not be themselves.

Theodore, who had been sent to bed, came creeping down the stairs in his pyjamas to get himself a share of the goodies and

Clementine said, 'Oh well, just this once, darling, but go upstairs and put on your dressing-gown.'

'Joss had to dig deep in his pocket for this "do",' Lottie remarked to Polly, as she tucked in to a plateful of savouries.

'Yes,' Polly said.

'Polly! Do you feel all right?' Lottie asked.

At this remark both Edwin and George shot a look in Polly's direction.

'Of course I do . . . I'm fine,' Polly came back, quickly.

'You look a little tired.'

'I'm really all right, Lottie,' Polly insisted.

'Oh, look,' Lottie said. 'Here's Joss coming.'

Polly looked up and saw Joss descending the broad, curved staircase, looking, if possible, even more handsome in black trousers with cut-away coat, and the white waistcoat and bow tie.

Once more the hammering started within Polly's breast. But Joss was immediately waylaid by the guests who crowded round him, vying with one another to converse and to question him. Even the most autocratic gentlemen, with Joss's fine whisky and food inside them, became remarkably cordial and 'hail fellow, well met'.

What money can do, Polly thought. Half the people here would not have favoured him with a glance had he remained poor and continued to live in the humble background from which he originated. But it occurred to her some of the ladies might . . . for though he looked eye-catchingly handsome in his dress suit, Joss had the looks, the easy bearing and the personality which would have singled him out from the crowd, no matter what his background or the clothes he wore.

Polly was aware that in the last half hour a chapter in her life had closed and another awesome, if not momentous chapter had begun.

Life would never be the same again.

Her heart had been wiser than her head; no matter how hard she had tried to silence what her heart said, the truth of its message, ignored by the logic in her head, had now hit her with massive force, for the truth was . . . she was in love with Joss! She always had been, always would be, then, now and for ever.

Madly, desperately and against her own will, she loved him, here or far away, rich or poor, young, old or as now, in his magnificent prime, Polly loved him, Polly lived for him and would not flinch to die for him.

And she felt his feelings were the same. Just one look into his eyes, the betraying flash of pain, the stunned hesitancy brought about by the realisation that she was his real love, that the two were meant for one another. Fate cannot be tricked or fobbed off. And it was their fate to love each other all their lives, from the beginning to the very end and hopefully beyond.

Yet they would never be able to give to each other the physical expression that love demands, craves. For they were imprisoned and separated one from the other by a prison without bars; shackled by the chains of the solemn vows each had made to another.

Their love for one another was a true and genuine love, and could not be tainted by betrayal of those partners they were pledged to honour.

'God, give us strength,' she said, silently inside herself.

At that moment Rupert joined the group, along with Customs Officer Copeland. Clementine had moved away to chat and mingle, as a good hostess must. Lottie stood nearest to them and with characteristic openness said, 'Ah, you two know each other.'

'We do, indeed,' Rupert concurred, smiling and looking very handsome.

'We were at school together,' Charles Copeland put in, and before anyone could remark said, 'Didn't expect to see you here, Polly . . . and this must be the lucky husband . . . Edgar, wasn't it?'

'Edwin,' Edwin corrected, all trace of annoyance banished. 'And yes, as Polly's husband I am exceedingly lucky.'

Dear Edwin, his moment of uncharacteristic distrust had gone. Many wives would be glad to know their husbands were capable of jealousy. And Polly loved him too. Not like she loved Joss, more like a close beloved member of the family. Oh dear, what a way to think of one's husband!

'I must say my brother-in-law's sister,' Rupert said, and Lottie grinned expectantly, 'and my brother-in-law's very charming and dear friend,' he looked in Polly's direction, 'are the two most gorgeous guests at the party.'

'Don't let Clemmie hear you say that,' Charles Copeland quickly commented.

104

They all laughed, including Rupert.

'I very carefully qualified that statement by saying "guests",' he pointed out.

Another ripple of laughter.

Charles Copeland spoke jointly to the two husbands.

'I hope you gentlemen won't mind if I plead with your lovely wives to allow me one dance with each before the party ends?'

'I think that's a very sound suggestion,' said George, who was now in party mood. 'It will leave Edwin and me free to cast our eyes about.'

The four men laughed and Lottie protested, feigning shock at such an agreement.

'Polly eats like a sparrow,' Charles Copeland observed. 'You will need more than that to fortify you for all the dancing that's yet to come. It's always in the second half of the evening that these house parties really get lively.'

At this remark Polly's eyes became downcast. Her meeting with Joss, seeing him standing there before her with eyes for nothing and no one but her, had shocked her deeply. For what seemed ages she had been both excited and fearful for the inevitable moment, and was high strung to near breaking point. Even so, she was unprepared for the impact of their coming face to face, the effect on her senses and on her physical being, causing the hammerings and poundings, the paralysis and at the same time light-headedness, the contradictory sensations of insecurity at feeling her cosy world was about to collapse about her, yet the security of knowing where and to whom she really belonged and who owned her heart.

Polly was aware of a long silence as the others waited for her response to Charles Copeland's remark. She must have swayed, for Edwin's arms were suddenly about her.

'Polly, you're not well. I'm taking you home.'

Polly did not resist. 'I think I've got a cold coming on,' she murmured.

Chapter Thirteen

Although Polly's 'turn' . . . which lasted only seconds . . . did not merit alarm, Edwin insisted they should return home.

'Stay here the night,' Joss said to Edwin.

'Yes,' Clementine agreed. 'You can have the room Joss's parents were going to have.'

But both Polly, and Edwin, though for differing reasons, insisted this was not necessary.

Polly remembered little of the homeward journey, only that she was swathed in a travelling blanket with her feet toasting against a Carriage Foot Warmer. Her head was heavy and congested with shock and jumbled contradictory thoughts of how she felt for the two men in her life, what would happen between her and Joss, between her and Edwin.

'I'll bring you some hot milk and whisky,' Edwin said, when he ensured Polly was safely tucked up in bed with hot water bottles.

'Please don't put any whisky in it, it will make my head worse,' Polly pleaded.

But Polly, weary and her brain totally overwhelmed by the complexities and emotional wrestlings which she felt sure were now and for the rest of the future to be her lot, fell into a deep and merciful sleep before the milk arrived.

She awoke late, with the mother and father of all headaches. What was wrong, she thought. What is this weight on my head? Her heart jolted as she remembered the party, the meeting with Joss. She saw again his intent dark brown eyes gazing down at her, his dear face, older, handsomer, quieter; his smile. She mentally raised her hand to caress his cheek. What a muddle! What a situation! Small wonder she felt this weight upon her.

Edwin brought her a cup of tea. The hot drink eased her head a little. Sneezing and aching limbs confirmed Polly really did have a 'flu-y' cold, and for once she was glad of this. At least it would be an explanation for her sudden indisposition last night, when she alone knew, and knew without a doubt, that the real cause was seeing Joss, her one true love.

She did love Edwin, she truly did. Only it was a different kind of love. But what she felt for Joss was a love which shook and electrified her to the core. And it wasn't a sudden love, a love for someone new which erupts into flame then burns out and dies away. She had known Joss all her life, as long as she had known her own parents. She had always loved him . . . Joss, her own true love. And like a fish needs water, she needed Joss. Like day and night formed one whole unit of time, so she and Joss were part of one another. Wherever Joss was, there would her heart be. This time the passage of years would not, could not, dim the intensity of her love, for whereas before she loved him as a child, this time she loved him as a woman, with all that vital, intense force that only a certain woman feels, and for only a certain man; a love with passion, with fire and with ecstasy, for each belonged to the other, not just for now, but for ever.

How could she endure it? Not to have a child was bad enough. To have Joss so near and yet so out of reach was a torture too harrowing to contemplate. Could she hide it from Edwin, from Lottie, from Clementine and most of all from Joss?

Or did Joss already know? Had he read it in her eyes as she felt she had read love in his. She half believed he had. Would he guess what was really the matter with her. If he suspected he'd not be sure because she did have a 'flu-y' cold. Would it happen again? It would be too awful, too embarrassing. She would have to exert all her strength to hide and to overcome her emotions, to be strong. She must not hurt Edwin, nor anybody, but especially not dear Edwin. She could not avoid being hurt herself.

Polly kept turning it all over in her mind. I didn't want this to happen, she silently told herself. Had she said this aloud there would have been a sob in her voice.

A solitary tear prickled under each eyelid. Don't cry, your headache will get worse. Try not to think about anything, but if you must think, then think about the shop. Don't even think about Edwin, that will lead to thoughts of Joss. Think about the shop, the shop, the shop . . .

Polly dressed and came downstairs in the afternoon to sit on the sofa by the fire. Shortly after there was a rap on the front door. Edwin rose from his sprung arm chair and went to answer.

'Joss, come in old chap,' she heard Edwin say, and once again her heart leapt, as she heard Joss's distinctive voice.

'I had to call and find out how Polly is.'

'It's a 'flu-y' cold. She's in here.' Edwin was speaking as the two entered the sitting-room.

Joss entered and the room seemed filled with his presence. 'Polly, how are you now?' He took her hand and pressed it in his, then released it. The warmth of his large hand which had encased hers for a few seconds, seemed to spread up her arm and pervaded her throat and head. She hoped neither of the two men noticed her suddenly flushed cheeks.

'It's only a heavy cold . . . I don't know what came over me,' Polly said dismissively.

Joss, looking smart in a casual fawn jacket and trousers of what must have been American origin, sat beside her in the chair, cornerwise to the sofa where Polly sat.

'Would you like a whisky?' Edwin asked Joss.

'Not really thanks, Ed. I don't normally drink in the daytime.'

'Nor I,' Edwin said, and sat on the sofa beside Polly.

'I didn't think I would find you up,' Joss said to Polly.

'I'm not sure she should be,' Edwin replied. 'But Polly insisted.'

Joss grinned.

'It was a lovely party,' Polly said. 'I was so disappointed to have missed the rest of it . . . But never mind me, how is your father?'

'I've just come from there, and he is feeling better, but drained,' Joss said. 'After you left last night, as Nora was staying with her cousin Madge, Lottie and George decided to stay the night. I've just driven them to visit mother and father.'

'They are there now?' Edwin queried.

'Yes. I came down to Penryn to enquire how Polly is . . . Lottie is very concerned . . . I shall be driving them home this evening and they'll call in to see you on the way, if that's all right with you.'

'That'll be fine,' Polly said.

'Clemmie would have come,' he said apologetically. 'But she has quite a bit to do, after the party, and I've not had time to help.'

'Of course,' Polly and Edwin agreed.

'She's hoping to come in and see father in a day or two,' Joss said, and Polly got the impression he was trying in some way to make excuses for her.

'I shall be better by then,' Polly's voice was steady and seemingly normal-sounding, belying the agitation within her at the nearness of Joss, the one man who made her weak at the knees, the man who should have been hers.

Edwin and Joss did not agree with her, and Polly, changing the subject, enquired for Theodore and Clementine's parents.

This topic dispensed with, Edwin rose and said he would make tea.

'I'm really glad Lottie and you are in partnership,' Joss said as Edwin left the room.

'Yes, we get along well together,' Polly agreed. 'And we seem to share the same ideas, usually.'

She looked away from Joss's steady gaze, and neither spoke. The fluttering inside Polly's breast increased to a pounding. Being left alone with Joss, the atmosphere seemed charged with their suppressed awareness the one of the other. Again she was lost for words, an experience new to Polly. Without looking, she felt Joss's eyes upon her, and was compelled to look up into his face. As if against her will she looked into his eyes, searching for answers to unspoken questions. And she knew that was what he too, was doing.

'You'll never know how surprised I was to see you last night, Polly,' he said in a soft low voice.

She did not speak but, as though mesmerised, kept her gaze into his deep brown eyes.

'How unprepared I was to find *my* "Little Friend" . . .' she noticed his accent on the possessive word 'my' ' . . . grown up and transformed into someone so beautiful, so different and yet someone I have always known and . . .'

His voice broke off. Was he going to say 'loved'?

'I was bowled over, Polly,' he said with a disbelieving shake of his head. 'I still am.'

Polly blew her nose, noisily, then said, 'Seeing me today should dispel all that.'

Joss did not speak, but in the split second Polly cast her eyes in his direction she saw his tiny involuntary head-shake of denial.

Her dark long hair hung loose about her shoulders, instead of pinned up in its customary coils. Evidently Joss did not see her as the mess she felt herself to be. At last she spoke of her own reactions.

'Seeing you was a surprise to me too, Joss.'

'What sort of a surprise?' he said quickly, staring intently into her face as he waited for her reply.

Polly hesitated, searching for non-existent words to interpret what she was trying to say.

'You look different.'

'I *am* older.'

'And handsomer.'

Joss dismissed this remark with a slight shrug of the shoulders and an 'I take that with a pinch of salt' grin.

'It confirmed my . . .'

What did it confirm? Was it hopes or was it fears, because for her the two amounted to the same thing. She didn't want the hero she remembered to be diminished, neither did she want her old admiration of him to be confirmed, for that would confirm her old love for him, a love that could never be and must forever remain unrequited.

An awkward silence was relieved by the rattle of teacups, as Edwin approached from the kitchen with a tray of tea and biscuits.

'Thanks, Edwin, I'm really ready for that,' Polly said as he entered.

'I think we're getting a bit low on biscuits, dear,' Edwin remarked, and conversation continued briefly upon lighter lines, when Joss, having drained his cup, declared he must leave, saying he would return with Lottie and George in the evening, if that wasn't too much for Polly.

No sooner had Polly and Edwin finished their Sunday tea, which they ate informally sitting by the fire, than Lottie, George and Joss arrived.

110

'We're early,' Lottie explained, after enquiring how Polly was. 'But I expect you will want to get back to bed soon and we don't want to keep you up.'

As if to confirm Lottie's reasoning Polly sneezed and blew her nose.

'It was such a pity you had to leave the party early last night. Lots of people enquired for you *and* remarked how attractive you looked.'

'I have the lovely dress you made to thank for that . . . Oh, Lottie!' Polly put her hand to her mouth as she remembered.

'What is it, Polly?'

'I did something awful . . . I didn't mean to . . . I didn't know I was going to, I must have had too much to drink!'

'It can't be that terrible . . . you only had two sherries . . . whatever did you do?' Lottie said.

'I didn't say we would . . . I only said we might, but I shouldn't have.'

'Shouldn't have what, for goodness sake?' Lottie said.

'An elderly lady . . . Mrs Endersby-Harman, said how much she liked my dress and thought it must have come from London, or one of the big cities . . .'

'Did she?' Lottie said, beaming.

'I told her you made it and that we are opening a shop.'

'Fine,' Lottie said.

'But I said we might have a Preview and if we did she would be invited.'

'A Preview,' Lottie repeated. 'You mean like people who paint pictures . . . artists?'

Polly nodded. 'I'm sorry, Lottie. I can't think what made me say it. I must have got carried away with the fine surroundings and the atmosphere and the drink . . .'

Lottie was silent, still assimilating what Polly had said.

'I only said "might". We don't *have* to do it,' Polly tried to placate.

'I'm not sure that's such a bad idea,' Lottie said after a long pause to consider.

'Mrs Endersby-Harman gave you her card, didn't she?' Edwin recalled.

'Yes. So did the ladies sitting nearby,' Polly said. 'The cards are all in my evening bag.'

111

'There are a lot of people we could invite. It would be good publicity,' Lottie said, then added, 'But the shop isn't big enough for so many people all at once.'

'That's true, forget it, Lottie. I'm sorry,' Polly said.

'Wait a minute,' Joss said. The men had been listening. 'It's a good idea. If you kept the invitation open from, say 10 a.m. to 4 o'clock or 4.30 they could come and go as they liked. Spread over the day you would be able to manage.'

They all started talking animatedly, and in this atmosphere Polly lost some of the dis-ease she felt in Joss's presence. With the exception of Joss, whose demeanour appeared quite normal, no one paid particular attention to her.

All had involved themselves in the 'goings on' with the shop. Polly and Lottie were quietly smug as well as pleased. The men were really treating their business venture seriously, now. That in itself was a little victory.

'It sounds a bit snobby, only inviting prominent or well-to-do people,' Lottie observed.

'I don't see it like that,' Edwin said. 'You knew when you set out you were not catering for the bottom end of the market,' he said. 'And it would be pointless to ask poorer people to view clothes they would not be able to afford, even if many of them are our friends.'

'Yes, you are right, of course,' Lottie agreed. '*Especially* if they are our friends really. They would feel uncomfortable at not wishing to buy anything.'

They talked over the details. The Preview would take place from, as Joss suggested, 10 a.m. to 4 p.m. and Ed Trevelyan who, amongst other things, printed the *Pen-Fal Advertiser*, would be approached to arrange the printing of the invitation cards.

It was decided not to open on a Monday, which for almost all shops was a very quiet day, but to open on a Friday and to have the Preview on a Thursday, the day prior to the opening.

The opening would take place the first week in December . . . just a few weeks away.

The invitations to attend the Preview would be sent out ten days in advance.

Extra display dummies would be required. Joss thought they might be able to hire some.

While Polly, Edwin and George discussed the likelihood of

cashing in on the Christmas trade, Joss spoke to his sister.

'Lottie,' he said, a note of concern in his voice. 'I think you are undertaking more than you will be able to cope with. You'll need help.'

'Polly helps me with straight-forward stitching in her spare time,' Lottie said.

'But if you become very busy, as well you might, opening so near to Christmas, Polly won't have much spare time and you will have more work than ever. If you needed extra help, would you be able to get it?'

'I'm sure I could,' Lottie said. 'I know quite a few who were in the trade and who would be glad of a little extra money. And I know the ones who were good and who were not so good.'

With a nod Joss smiled at his sister and was assured. Lottie gave him an affectionate pat, 'Don't you worry about me, little brother. I'll cope.'

'Heavens, Polly!' Lottie said. 'All this excitement and discussion will surely make your head swim. I didn't come here with the intention of talking business.'

'I was the cause of it,' Polly said. 'If I hadn't told Mrs Endersby-Harman we might have a Preview, we'd not have had all this discussion.'

'Don't let it keep you awake, Polly,' George advised.

Good-byes were said and Lottie and her husband and brother departed, leaving Polly suddenly exhausted.

'You must get to bed as soon as I have the hot-water bottles ready,' Edwin said.

Hot and perspiring, Polly took a long time to get to sleep. She struggled to suppress her thoughts and feelings for Joss by endeavouring to concentrate on the shop . . . perhaps with this event in the offing, they should have an even wider selection of clothes? Would Lottie be able to keep up with the demand? If the Preview resulted in heavy initial sales could Lottie get help? She had not heard the brief conversation between Joss and his older sister. If she had help could they afford to pay for it? What would it be like if Joss kissed her . . ?

Eventually she sank into a hot and sticky sleep, from which she awoke next morning feeling better.

*   *   *   *

113

Joss drove home in a daze from where Lottie and George lived in Falmouth. He had felt stunned, almost punch-drunk from the instant he beheld Polly before him, standing with her brother midway of the dance at the party at Manor Withiel, and so different from the child he remembered. Yet in that instant he knew without a shadow of doubt, that Polly was the woman who was meant for him. Polly was the woman he loved. He had never forgotten his 'Little Friend' nor lost his affection for her. He had always known he would never stop loving her. That would be taken for granted, for Penryn people were clannish and friendships made early in life lasted a lifetime come what may. But now he knew he would never now stop being *in love* with her!

The thought of the merest touch of her fingertips made his pulse race. To hold her in his arms would be transportation to paradise.

His Polly, the little child he cuddled and played with as a toddler, and hoisted unceremoniously onto his shoulder as a child, who rushed to meet him on his return from school. Polly always behaved as though she owned him and that anyone else who held his attention was an intruder.

How right Polly had been! He too, had felt he was her rightful protector, ordering off bigger children when they tried to intimidate, even though in his heart he knew Polly to be well equipped to stand up for herself.

Polly had been a small scrap of a thing, and he had no way of knowing he would return home from his long absence in America to find her literally the belle of the ball. He wasn't some callow, mooning youth! And he had no way of knowing that he, an established married man and father of an almost eight years old boy, would be love-struck, and in a way and with such force he never thought possible.

All he knew was he wanted to be with Polly, every minute, every day. To feel her fingertips touch his as she passed him a teacup, to look into her eyes when her gaze met his. Yet he knew to do this was courting danger. For in his heart he desired her, and warning bells told him seeing and brushing fingertips could inflame rather than satisfy his need for her.

And Polly was married to Edwin. It was a happy marriage, anyone could see that. Joss didn't know a happier man than Edwin, and clearly Polly loved her husband.

114

Yet Joss could swear Polly felt something for him. The look in her eyes when, in the middle of dancing and taken off guard, those large brown shining orbs, wide open with surprise, drank in the sight of him with an expression which was not just friendship but something more, something so deep. Surely it could only be love?

She did not rush to his arms as in times past, and as he thoughtlessly, foolishly assumed would happen again. His waiting arms had dropped to his sides, empty, for to hold in them a gangling, rangy, boisterous child was one thing, to enfold a beautiful, poised and elegant woman was another, and Joss had been rocked, shocked and totally unprepared for the blossoming forth into womanhood of the spindly young girl he remembered with such affection.

Joss turned the motor, a Minerva, into the tree-lined drive. After a couple of hundred yards the approach road curved right into more open, grassy slopes and shrubberies and gently ascended to the house.

Driving across the front of the manor he noticed a light in the drawing-room. Clementine's brother, Rupert, would have left early in the evening to travel back to London on the overnight train, and his Customs Officer friend, who had stayed the night after the party, at Clementine's invitation warmly encouraged by Rupert, would no doubt have also departed.

He drove the motor into one of the coach-houses, then entered the house and walked along the wide corridor to the drawing-room. As he approached he heard a shrill giggle. It was Clementine. He had heard that giggle before and it would not have been provoked by the company of Albert or Margaret Du Cane.

Quickening his steps he reached the drawing-room and turned the door handle, whereupon there was an instant scuffing sound. He entered to find Clementine draped on the sofa and Charles Copeland, hair and tie slightly awry, on his feet nearby.

'What's going on?' Joss glanced at Charles Copeland. 'I thought you were leaving the same time as Rupert,' he said, unceremoniously. The officer straightened his tie and cleared his throat to speak but Clementine forestalled. With a casual tone she explained.

'Charles was, darling. But I persuaded him to stay. He and

Rupert worked so hard helping to put the rooms to right. I don't know how I would have managed without them, with you deserting me at my time of need.'

Joss took a decanter and began to pour himself a drink. Clementine continued, 'After we both saw Rupert off at Redruth Station it was really far too late for me to allow Charles to make his way back to Falmouth, so I positively *insisted* he stay one more night.'

Joss still had the decanter in his hand. 'Do you two want one?' he said.

'That would be lovely, darling.'

Without speaking Joss looked questioningly at Charles Copeland.

'Oh, yes please,' came the eager reply, and Joss detected Charles Copeland breathed a suppressed sigh of relief. He passed them both a glass and Clementine listed all the things she, Rupert and Charles had done, which were mostly supervisory, telling the staff what to do.

'How was your father darling?' she remembered to enquire.

'He's recovering,' was Joss's brief reply.

'I'm so glad,' Clementine said with a toothy smile.

'Er, yes . . . yes indeed,' Charles Copeland said with an ingratiating smile.

'Well, I'm going to bed,' Joss said when he had finished his drink. 'And since you have had such a strenuous day, I suggest you both do the same.'

'We were saying that just before you came in,' Charles contributed.

'Were you,' Joss replied in a flat tone, and left the room.

A short time later Clementine entered the bedroom. Joss was about to get into bed.

'I see you're up to your old games again,' he said, sitting on the edge of the bed and pulling off his socks.

'Darling! I don't know what you're talking about,' Clementine replied. 'Mother and father were with us until just two minutes before you arrived. The four of us played Bridge.'

Chapter Fourteen

Polly recovered quickly from the heavy cold . . . at least, that was what she told Edwin. To a certain extent this was true. The weakness and lethargy had left her and despite the runny nose and developing chestiness she longed to get back to work at the shop and to helping Lottie with stitching. It was the only way she knew of occupying her thoughts with something which did not include Joss, the thoughts she could not prevent herself from thinking, the feelings, the wishes, the imaginings, the desires . . . what would it be like if Joss were hers, which in her heart she felt, no, knew he was.

It was so wrong of her. Yet how could she help herself. This was what she feared ever since the arrival of that fateful letter, the letter telling her Joss was coming home.

She loved Edwin. She truly, truly did. She wanted, she tried to be a good wife and mother. And Edwin was so happy with her. The only cloud was the lack, so far, of a child; a lack for which Polly blamed herself, and felt she had failed the husband she so desired to please.

But Edwin understood this. He not only was patient, he was downright indulgent. How many husbands would consider a silly whim to set up in business of all things, *and* supply the money for a wife to possibly fritter away.

And she was sinful to think the thoughts she had been thinking. Edwin had not the slightest inkling of her disloyalty; he liked Joss, always had done. They were good friends. Joss was married to Clementine. She *must* stop thinking of him.

But how do you stop being in love? How? There had never been a time when Polly didn't love Joss . . . further back than she could remember . . . long before she had any awareness of male

117

and female. The feeling of belonging was never extinguished with the passage of time. Joss had always been her own special person. And now he was more special than before. He was rightfully hers, they were always meant for each other, yet it was wrong. This was too cruel to bear, but what was she to do?

At all costs she must not hurt Edwin. She'd rather die than do that. Dear Edwin. He was closer than a brother, and she loved him in a gentle tender way. *But* she was not *in* love with him. Her heart didn't flutter at the sound of his voice, she didn't thrill at the merest brush of his fingers against her hand, never felt her legs weaken when his eyes gazed down into hers, never felt her breath quicken, her nostrils expand with the intake of extra oxygen necessary to stop her from feeling swoony, never felt her eyes become glassy with wonder at what his kisses would feel like, never felt the need in the core of her . . . 'Don't think it! It's wrong!' Aloud she commanded herself.

A couple of seconds later the door to the sitting-room opened and Mary came in.

'You called, Mrs Pendleton?'

'No, Mary.'

'I thought I heard someone call out.'

'Perhaps I coughed,' Polly said, lamely.

'You're letting the fire get low,' Mary crossed the room and picked up the tongs in the grate.

'You won't throw off that cold if you sit in a cold room,' she said, as she strategically placed several lumps of coal on the fire, then gave a couple of deep prods with a poker to let air through and encourage the embers underneath to flame.

Mary surveyed her efforts with dissatisfaction. 'I think I should have put a small piece of wood on first,' she said. 'That fire's going to take a while to get going again.'

'It'll be fine, Mary. And I don't feel at all cold,' Polly assured her.

After Mary had left the room Polly rose and went to the chiffonier, took out a writing pad and commenced drafting a specimen invitation to the Preview of the shop opening, telling herself she must think of something other than Joss, and work on the shop, no matter what; was the only solution.

But Polly's thoughts and attempt at drafting invitations were interrupted by a knock at the front door. Was it Joss? Her heart thumped violently. She heard Mary's voice greeting someone . . . a man, but not Joss. The pounding subsided, and the sitting-room door opened.

'The Rev. Shaw to see you, Mrs Pendleton,' Mary said. Rev. Shaw, hat in hand and smiling, entered and Polly rose to greet him.

'Mrs Pendleton . . I heard you were ill,' he said as he shook her hand.

'The story was exaggerated I'm afraid,' Polly smiled, gesturing to him to be seated, while she took the chair close by. 'I think I can guess who told you,' she said. 'Am I right?'

'Quite right,' he beamed.

'I think I was overcome by the heat,' Polly said.

'Their account did sound a little alarming. They were greatly impressed by the occasion,' the Rev. Shaw went on.

He accepted her offer of coffee and seemed glad to talk. He had heard Polly was embarking on some kind of business venture and was curious. In a round-about way he pointed out a wife's duty was to her husband and children.

In an equally oblique way Polly, after pointing out she had not been blessed with children, and that although the Reverend gentleman's cook was a single lady, the woman who did all the 'rough' work and the laundry was a married woman with eight children. She had to work to support her family, her husband being a labouring man who drank away half his meagre weekly wage, leaving his wife and children to survive any way they could. The Rev. Shaw smiled and nodded. 'Quite so, quite so.'

Polly admitted she loved the thrill and the creativity of her work and subtly reminded him the devil finds work for idle hands, but omitted to tell the danger she and her marriage were in right now if she allowed her own hands and thoughts to remain idle.

That night Polly had a dream, another horrible dream about having a baby and losing it. She was frantic; even Edwin was not there to comfort her . . . only the clergyman, who gave no comfort at all. She woke up, briefly, then was asleep again. Next she was holding a baby swathed in a huge lacy shawl. She was happy; she could actually see herself smiling, for she was looking down on both herself and the baby. Edwin was there, and her mother, and Joss. All were clustered about her and the baby, as though they were posing to have a photograph taken.

Next she felt Edwin getting up from bed and she awoke. It was only a dream, but such a vivid dream! She felt the familiar disappointment, but at the same time a ray of hope.

The dream was fresh in her mind all day. It seemed to have a promise of reality about it, or was that just wishful thinking? All day and for the first time in what seemed an age she felt a measure of serenity.

The next day was mild, balmy even, and Polly determined to go out for a walk. She kept in mind Mary's strictures to 'dress up warm'. It also occurred to her that now both she and Lottie would always be an advertisement, a shop window, just like at the party. She and Lottie had been aware that at the party there would be quite a number of dress-conscious 'well-heeled' ladies. But the same could apply every time she or Lottie went out of the house. You never knew who might see you, even if you didn't see them. It was sensible to make a point of always being 'well turned out'.

With this thought Polly fingered through her wardrobe which, in her first year of marriage she thought quite extravagant and excessive. Now she regarded this from a different angle. It didn't take Polly long to select and don a dark grey suit. The skirt had inverted pleats which commenced just at the hem of the long half-belted warm jacket. Her blouse was also grey with a narrow cerise coloured stripe. A high boned collar afforded protection for her throat. Matching gloves and grey hat with a darker grey band just above the brim, from which arose two long deep red feathers set the outfit off to Polly's satisfaction.

What happened to the tomboy she used to be, the girl who scarcely cared at all about fashion? Polly silently supplied the answer to her own question . . . 'She's turned into a business woman who is also Mrs Polly Pendleton, wife of Edwin Pendleton, Esq., Granite Merchant.'

Polly briefly surveyed her image in the mirror. A little pale but otherwise good, was the verdict. She walked downhill towards the Station, then down Helston Road to Upper Market Street.

Noisy traction engines transporting granite were passing through the streets but this drew little attention in Penryn. They were a common sight and a large proportion of Penryn families

120

were reliant on the granite business for their livelihood.

In Market Street one person was standing watching. It was Joss! He saw Polly at the same moment she saw him, and a smile lit his face as he raised his Homburg and waited for an engine to pass by to dart across the road to where she stood.

'Polly! How are you? You look so much better.'

'I am better, thank you Joss,' Polly's heart again pounded, and she knew the slight pallor had been replaced with a feint flush. But although the sight of Joss's velvet brown eyes smiling down into hers caused thrills to race through her body, she did not altogether lose command of herself.

'I was going to call on you, to see how you are,' Joss said. 'Then, sometime before I go home I want to see my parents.'

'Of course, how is your father?' Polly asked.

'We can't talk here,' Joss said. 'Unless my memory is playing tricks, there is a little room behind the cake shop over the road.' He nodded towards the baker's shop on the opposite side of the street. 'We could go and have a coffee and cake . . . unless, of course, you've got an appointment or something.'

'I'd love to,' Polly said, and they both waited for an opportunity to cross the street, Polly deliciously aware of Joss's protective guiding hand holding her elbow.

It was customary to tell the shop assistant at the counter what you wished to order and Joss did this before they moved into the small room which accommodated five or six tables and a number of hoop-backed chairs. No one else was in the room and Polly and Joss sat at a table by the window which overlooked the steep valley behind the shop buildings and the hotchpotch clusters of small granite cottages below which, at almost river-level was the busy Commercial Road where there were warehouses, forges and farriers and a variety of commercial properties.

'How is your father?' Polly asked again.

'He's recovered but he's not the same,' Joss said. 'Perhaps it's early days, but he seems so weak though he doesn't complain. You get the feeling that just lifting a cup to his lips is almost too heavy for him.'

'His strength will come back with time, I expect,' Polly said.

'I hope so. I can see mother is so anxious, though she won't admit it,' Joss said, concern showing in his eyes.

Polly nodded sympathetically. 'And how are Clementine

f

and Theodore?'

Joss, who had both elbows on the table as he leant forward talking to Polly, promptly removed them as a shop assistant-cum-waitress appeared with coffees and cakes.

'Theodore is settling in at school,' Joss said, when the waitress had gone, then added, 'more or less, and Clementine is well enough.' With a slightly ironic smile he said, 'I think she'd be jealous if she could see you now!' His eyes twinkled as he smilingly looked into Polly's face. Under his steady gaze her heart pounded again.

'She'd object to us having a coffee together?' Polly asked in some alarm and painfully aware of the deepening flush spreading over her face.

Joss's smile broadened. 'No,' he said. 'Jealous of the way you look. You look really stunning in that outfit, Polly.'

Polly relaxed and tilted her head back a little as she laughed.

'It's quite deliberate,' she admitted. 'Lottie and I must try to be our own advertisements and always wear something that looks good; that is, if we can remember.'

'I'm very impressed,' Joss grinned.

'That's what I want people to be,' Polly replied with a laugh. 'Then they'll come and buy our clothes, when we get started . . . perhaps Clementine will patronise us sometimes.'

'That's quite likely. She takes the Minerva to Truro to "do" the shops.'

Polly was incredulous. 'Does she drive a motor?' she gasped.

'People drive much more in America,' Joss answered. 'She's used to it, though she might find the winding roads and the hedges a bit tricky.'

'Aren't you going with her?'

'She said she prefers to go alone, so that I won't get bored standing around waiting for her to inspect the dress-shops.'

'That was thoughtful of her,' Polly said.

It did not go unnoticed by Polly that Joss made no reply to this observation.

Joss again leant over the table to look closer into Polly's face. 'Let's talk about you,' he said.

And again Polly felt herself turn trembly inside. She longed to raise her hand and stroke the dark, handsome face which was now so close to hers; to feel his cheeks with her fingertips, to . . .

Polly's hand was not caressing Joss's face though, it was resting on the table and Joss covered it with his large warm one as he spoke.

'I believe you and Edwin make a very happy couple.'

Polly, embarrassed by her thoughts which Joss could only guess at, lowered her gaze.

'Yes. Edwin and I are very happy.'

Her arm was tingling as currents generated by Joss's touch ran tantalisingly up and down her arm and beyond.

Joss continued to let his hand rest on hers, and his eyes continued to gaze into her face.

'You deserve it, Polly,' he said at last. Then added, 'I hope Edwin knows what a lucky man he is.' He removed his hand from hers.

'I'm the lucky one,' Polly said, at last raising her face.

Joss just gazed, not answering. Could she read the message in his eyes. Did he really envy Edwin? With all his fortune, his adventures abroad, his motor, his manor, his beautiful upper-class wife . . . were his eyes telling her it was she, Polly, that he desired more than all these things? Could *he* read in *her* eyes that she envied Clementine? He was trying to fathom what he saw in her face, she could tell. She had allowed his hand to rest on hers longer than was proper, though it was not exactly improper, and he had clearly desired to keep it there. What else did he desire? Did he truly feel more than the affection which was normal for a very old and cherished friend? She thought he did feel more, but was she deceiving herself? Was it just that in her heart she wanted him to feel more? But she must not think these thoughts, she must not admit to deeper desires by herself or Joss. One thing was sure. Joss was honourable. If he was attracted to her as more than a friend, if he desired her, she was in no danger from him. Was she in danger from herself? Well, she was honourable too. She had made vows to Edwin and those vows would be kept.

'Could I ask you to take a little drive around the seafront at Falmouth,' Joss asked, as at last they rose to leave. 'The fresh sea air might be good for you.'

At Penryn there was just the Penryn River which widened towards Falmouth and became Falmouth Harbour. Here at Penryn the river narrowed further into a mere stream. Polly loved the sea and Falmouth's deep, sheltered and busy harbour, with the jutting, almost island headland, topped with Pendennis Castle, and the beaches and open sea on the far side of the headland. Joss chose not to drive through Falmouth's town centre, with its narrow streets, thronging with people, and vehicles of all types. Congestion so often caused a hold-up, to deviate would be quicker.

Together they walked the short distance to Broad Street where the Minerva was waiting, and Joss took Polly's hand to assist her into the vehicle.

She felt luxuriously pampered sitting in the modern horseless carriage. Joss jumped effortlessly into the seat beside her and the vehicle was set in motion. Polly saw a Penryn doctor with a gentleman companion stand and stare in undisguised admiration, as the motor moved away. Polly knew they were looking at the motor, but she had the distinct impression the companion was giving more of his attention to her than to the vehicle. Shows what a smart outfit can do, she thought to herself.

To Joss she said, 'You'll be giving me a taste for high-living.'

'Not you, Polly,' came the swift reply. 'Your feet are too firmly planted on the ground.' Then he added, 'It wouldn't surprise me though, if you owned your own motor one day.'

Polly laughed outright. 'What an outrageous thought,' she retorted. Now, in a strange way, Polly was more at ease in Joss's presence. The attraction was undiminished, so was the desire, but Polly was coping . . . thankfully. It had been the initial shock, after wondering what he would be like, and of finding him matured into someone even more handsome than she remembered, so desirable, so loveable, which so intensely shook Polly. And the instant split second knowledge that she was head-over-heels in love with Joss, and the instant knowledge that her love would never abate, *and* that it could be catastrophic for her and Edwin if she were not scrupulously vigilant.

She *would* be careful. Today was not an ordinary day. It seemed providential that the business of running the shop had come about. The business would not only fill her thoughts, it would keep her away and out of reach. And Joss would probably not have been here today were it not for his father being unwell. The manor was some distance away and it was unlikely, in the ordinary way of things, they would come across each other in Penryn Streets. Today was unlikely to be repeated. She would enjoy this time with Joss, and live on it in the months and years to come.

Thus quelling both her fears and her conscience, she drank in the passing scenes and the joy of Joss's nearness.

As well as the imposing Falmouth Hotel, built many years before further development had taken place, there were a number of impressive buildings, all with glorious views of Pendennis Headland and Castle, the bay, the beaches and the surrounding cliffs and sloping green fields. Joss pointed out one beautiful property, the home of another well-known granite merchant, whose name she had frequently heard Edwin mention.

Polly wondered whether she might write to hotel proprietors, including invitations for guests to attend the Preview.

'What are you thinking,' Joss said.

Polly told him.

'Little Friend has undoubtedly grown into a business woman,' he chuckled, then added: 'If you carry on like that you'll be making it faster than Clemmie spends it!'

Was Clementine so expensive, Polly wondered, but did not like to ask.

'We'd better be getting back,' she said, after they traversed the seafront area. 'Mary is cooking for 12.45 and Edwin will be there then. Would you like to join us, I'm sure there'll be enough.'

But Joss declined, saying his mother would probably be expecting him. In spite of her trepidation, Polly had enjoyed her morning with Joss. She knew she would relive every moment again and again and again, especially the time when, over coffee and cake, Joss's hand rested on hers.

It was about ten minutes before Edwin was due home that Joss stopped the Minerva outside Villa Gwidden. Swiftly Joss jumped from his seat and went round the bonnet of the motor to open the passenger door and help Polly alight.

Polly stared up into his face as she held out her hand for his to shake. The smile she expected was not there. His expression was . . . solemn, almost grim.

'I'm glad you are feeling better, Polly,' he said. 'And I enjoyed your company this morning, very much.'

Polly smiled. 'I've enjoyed it too, and I really do feel better for the unexpected outing. Good-bye, Joss. And thank you.'

Joss did not then drop her hand or speak. Again Polly looked

125

into his face, questioningly this time.

'Polly . . . ' he said.

Polly waited, trembling inwardly.

Joss's eyes bore into hers. She waited. Joss's chest visibly expanded with a deep intake of breath which caused his nostrils to flare.

'Nothing,' he said, letting go her hand as he spoke. He jumped into the motor and drove off.

Chapter Fifteen

It was the morning after the chance meeting in Penryn of Joss and Polly that Myrtle, who spent much of her time helping cook and the remainder helping Mrs Harvey and Mrs Soloman, found Theodore unwilling to get out of bed. His excuse was that he was unwell. Not knowing whether to rouse the sleeping Clementine, she went in search of Joss to ask him what she should do.

'Leave it to me, Myrtle,' Joss said, and made his way to his son's bedroom, his thoughts of Polly temporarily pushed to the background.

'What's all this about, not wanting to get up?' he said as he entered the room.

Theodore, curled up and face almost hidden in the pillows, made a whimpering sound.

'Poorly, are you. Where does it hurt?'

'My tummy,' came the reply, and Theodore effected a couple of sobs but Joss noted no tears had dampened his cheeks.

'I'm sure it will go when you get up and dressed. I'll help you to get washed.' Joss pulled back the bedclothes as he spoke and Theodore, with a howl of anguish, rushed from the room.

'I want my mummy,' he cried and dashed to the adjoining room, followed by his father.

Clementine awoke with a start, and the boy clung to her.

'Darling, whatever's the matter? Did mama's little boy have a bad dream?'

By now a couple of tears actually did roll down the boy's cheeks.

'Daddy wants me to go to school and I've got a pain in my tummy,' he blurted between sobs. This time his distress seemed real.

127

'Then you needn't go to school my precious,' his mother soothed. Holding the boy to her she turned to Joss. 'He can't go to school like this.'

'He didn't seem that bad when I saw him,' Joss replied. 'Perhaps I was mistaken.' He didn't want to be harsh with the boy.

'I'm sure you were,' Clementine retorted.

Theodore snuggled in her arms, still shuddering an occasional sob.

'Does it still hurt, darling?' Clementine asked.

He nodded. 'Yes, Mummy.'

'There you are,' she said to Joss, her tone accusatory. The boy snuggled closer. 'Tell Myrtle to bring us both up a drink, would you Joss.'

'Right,' Joss said and moved to the door.

'Tell me a story, Mummy,' he heard Theodore say.

'All right, darling. Which one would you like?'

'Tell me about the boy who grew up too fast.'

Myrtle was not in the kitchen. Probably taking tea to Clementine's parents, Joss thought. It was high time those two left Manor Withiel and took up residence in the new home he had built for them.

Joss prepared the drinks and took them himself. As he mounted the stairs he could hear Theodore shrieking with laughter at the story. Hmmm . . . a quick recovery.

After Clementine's parents had breakfasted, Joss told them as he did not have to take Theodore to school he would make use of the time saved by moving the remainder of their belongings to the house they were to now inhabit. They had little choice but to take the hint.

After an early lunch he planned to go to Falmouth to see Lottie. He wanted to talk to her. Perhaps, as Theodore clearly was now perfectly well, he would take his son with him.

'Are you going in the motor?' Theodore asked, excitedly.

'Yes, I am,' Joss confirmed. 'Are you coming Clem?'

'Yes, I think I will. But I'll get off at Greenbank and pay a call on Jane McBride. Captain McBride, her husband, is away at sea and Jane didn't want to come to the party without him . . . she's such a shrinking violet. I told her, Charles . . . Charles Copeland of course, would have been quite pleased to act as escort . . .'

'Wouldn't you like to stop off at Penryn and call on Polly?'

'But you've already called to see Polly, so has Lottie and George, and after all, as far as she and Edwin Pendleton are concerned, *you* are the one they want to see. Jane McBride is *my* friend and she *missed* the party.'

'So did my parents,' Joss said, pointedly.

Clementine gave a long-suffering sigh.

'*You* are the one who matters to them, and they see you all the time. *I* had all the work of organising the party *and* putting Withiel back in order afterwards. I can't be in six places at once!'

'All right, I'll drop you off at Greenbank and call for you on our return,' Joss agreed.

Clementine's excuse that she had been busy was a valid one and he knew neither his parents nor Polly would actually be expecting her.

'And I'd like the Minerva on Friday. I want to go to Truro,' she announced.

'Would you like me to come?' Joss asked.

'No. I want to do some shopping. You'd only get bored,' came the crisp reply.

Joss privately thought all eyes would be on Clementine . . . a woman driving a newfangled motor! But Clementine would not be averse to attention, and she was accustomed to driving in America.

The houses at Greenbank stood in a row on a high wide terrace. The gardens which fronted them were tiny, but big enough to allow a colourful floral entrance. Every house had a glorious view across the harbour to the little village of Flushing opposite, and the protective green hills surrounding this pretty waterside village.

The McBride's house stood opposite to Greenbank Gardens. The gardens were perhaps mis-named, being a long narrow strip of ground above beach-level. There were shelters and paths at different levels and a good supply of garden seats. The seats provided were not so much for the customary reason of enjoying the beauty of the flowers and shrubs, which were almost non-existent, as for enjoying the beauty of the view across the harbour to Flushing where the houses nestled close to the water, and beyond the small village to Trefusis Point on the opposite side, and to Falmouth Docks, plus all the activity of the variety of craft and the excitement and good-natured rivalry of races between local and visiting yachts and owners of smaller boats.

The gardens were below the level of the road, and Theodore wanted to explore.

'Can we go in there, Daddy?' he asked, as Joss slowed the motor.

'What would Mr Christopher's answer be to that question?' Clementine asked, adjusting a stray, fair curl, as the vehicle came to a halt.

Theodore pouted.

'Well, what would he say, darling?' his mother insisted, glancing sideways at two approaching gentlemen, then, as no reply was forthcoming from the boy, herself supplied the answer. 'You *can* but you *may* not. Now ask again, correctly, my precious.'

'May we go in?'

'What else?'

'Please, Daddy,' came the reluctant response.

'Yes, all right,' Joss agreed. 'But only for a little while or we shan't have time to visit Aunt Lottie.'

'See you around four-thirty,' Clementine said, and kissed Theodore before crossing the road to ascend the steps set-in the high wide terrace, her ascent coinciding with the arrival close to the steps of the two well-dressed gentlemen, who both raised their hats to Clementine and nodded appreciative smiles of approval. Joss saw but was unaffected. He had discovered long ago that Clementine could no more stop herself flirting than a cat could stop itself liking fish.

He and Theodore crossed the road and entered the gardens at the main gate. Theodore ran about and dabbled his hand in the water of a raised ornamental fountain. Gradually they moved to the opposite end where the ground had been flattened, and a small boy and girl played with a ball on the green lawn. Two ladies, presumably their mothers, sat knitting in a nearby shelter. The children stopped playing and the boy ran towards Theodore.

'Hello,' the boy said as he came to a halt close by. Theodore

130

did not reply but poked out his tongue.

Joss frowned with annoyance. 'Say "Hello",' he commanded. Theodore withdrew his tongue but defiantly tightened his lips.

'Did you hear me?' Joss's tone was threatening. With a sullen expression Theodore said a grudging hello. Joss grabbed Theodore's arm and twisted his son towards the nearby second exit.

'We're leaving now,' he said. 'And don't you ever poke your tongue out at anyone again.' Joss then turned and waved good-bye to the two watching small children, who silently waved in return.

With Theodore struggling all the way in Joss's unrelenting grip, they returned to the Minerva watched by a small cluster of people who stood admiring the motor. They climbed in, Joss exchanging a few comments with the onlookers before he drove away. It didn't take long to get to Lottie's house. Fortunately she was working at her stitching at home and not at the shop.

Lottie greeted them both with delight and Joss said he hoped his unexpected arrival wasn't interfering with her work.

'It's just the excuse I needed to stop and have a cup of tea,' she laughed.

Over tea and a plate of heavy cake Joss came to the main point of his visit.

'Father seems to be making a good recovery,' he said. 'But how do you think mother looks these days, Lottie?'

'The shock has upset her,' Lottie replied. 'But then, that's only to be expected, isn't it?'

'Yes, it is,' Joss agreed. But I wondered if there was something more. Her colour isn't what it was.'

'You just haven't got used to seeing her grown old,' Lottie reasoned.

'You're right there. But she does look frail.'

The conversation passed to other things, mainly about the party which Lottie enjoyed relating and reliving, and Polly's unfortunate early departure. Joss felt himself tense at the mention of Polly. This feeling of being lost for words was new to him and he was thankful Lottie prattled on, thinking it would not appear odd, as for quite some time he had not been present at the party. Slanting the same topic to a different angle Joss said, 'I was very glad George came. He seemed to be enjoying it.'

'He thoroughly enjoyed it,' Lottie confirmed. 'It was so good to have *my* family all on friendly terms again.'

'You never said a truer word, Lottie,' he agreed, then asked if anyone had been aware that their father's condition was deteriorating? But Lottie, although she knew they were growing older and looking older and that her father had slowed down quite a lot, was not so aware of the changes which had gradually crept up on him. Most of his problems were attributed to stiffness from rheumatics. This attack had come out of the blue and Lottie was as surprised as Joss.

'And how is your tummy now?' Lottie had turned to Theodore.

'Better,' he shouted, and with a grin stretched out his hand for another square of heavy cake.

Joss took a heavy gold watch attached to a gold chain from his waistcoat pocket.

'We'd better leave when you've finished your cake,' he said to Theodore, then looked at his sister. 'We said we'd meet Clem at four-thirty. She's at Greenbank visiting her friend, Jane McBride, who was unable to come to the party.'

'Oh, I see. Well, they'll have a lot to talk about,' Lottie said.

Lottie went out of the house with them to the gate at the end of the tiny garden. A couple of men and three children were standing admiring Joss's motor. The men chatted amiably for a few minutes before they left, Joss waved to Lottie as they moved away but Theodore, unseen by his father, was busily poking out his tongue at the three silent, wide-eyed children who somewhat enviously watched their departure.

Next morning the performance of Theodore's tummy ache was repeated. Again Clementine was full of indulgence, but Joss would have none of it.

'He has *not* got a pain and he *is* going to school,' he insisted, and washed and dressed the protesting boy himself. Theodore, realising his efforts were to no avail, stopped crying and under his father's stern gaze, toyed with his breakfast.

They arrived early at Cresby and Joss asked to see Theodore's form-master. Several minutes before the boys were due to assemble, Mr Christophers appeared and bade them both, 'Good Morning.' He ushered Joss into a small study. Theodore remained seated outside in the corridor. The form-master, a small, balding man with wispy light-coloured hair, indicated a chair in front of the desk and himself took the seat behind it. His head looked rather too large for his small, compact body.

'How can I help you, Mr Renfree?' he asked.

Joss told him he thought Theodore didn't want to come to school because he was scared of something. Either he himself had misbehaved or he was frightened of somebody.

'What makes you think that?' Mr Christophers asked.

Joss explained and Mr Christophers listened, hands extended in front of him with fingers and thumb tips pressed together in contemplation.

'Yes. You've guessed correctly, Mr Renfree. I'm afraid it is the former.'

Joss sighed inwardly; he had a feeling it would be.

'What's he done?' he asked, resignedly.

'Nothing serious,' Mr Christophers replied. 'He sits next to Harvey Prescott who is one of the brighter boys, and seems to be a little jealous of him, or perhaps there is a personality clash.'

'What has he done to make you think that?'

'Petty little things, like scribbling over young Prescott's exercise books and altering the figures in his sums book.'

'I see.'

'Prescott enjoys lessons, he's quick and neat for his age. Theodore seems bent on spoiling it. At first I was lenient with him, being new, and coming from another country where teaching methods are probably somewhat different, but I can't overlook this behaviour ad infinitum, and young Prescott, understandably, is growing impatient. He's a boarder, you know.'

'You're sure Theodore is the culprit?'

'The scribbles are in an unusually bright red. No one but Theodore has a pencil or crayon in that distinctive colour. Apart from that, Prescott's missing Spellings Book was found at the bottom of the books in your son's desk.'

Joss nodded. He knew the bright red pencil to which Mr Christophers referred.

'What do you propose doing about it?' Joss asked.

'He knows that I told him he would get a caning if he did this sort of thing again.'

'If that's what you told him, that's what you must do,' Joss said.

Mr Christophers smiled and nodded. 'Then, when he is composed I will call Prescott in, Theodore will apologise and the two will shake hands. At his age the anticipation will be much worse than the punishment, I can assure you.'

'Fair enough,' Joss agreed.

'I'll ask him in here first and give him a chance to speak for himself.' Mr Christophers rose and opened the door.

'Come inside, Renfree.'

'Yes, sir.' Theodore's eyes were downcast, and he did not look in his father's direction.

At first he hotly denied he was the culprit, but in the light of the evidence started to cry and nodded admittance of his guilt.

'I'll leave you to it, Mr Christophers,' Joss said, glumly. 'And I'll call for you after school, Theodore,' he added, closing the door behind him.

A few yards along the corridor Joss slowed and waited. Three yells told him punishment had been administered, and he hurried away, thankful he had taken Theodore to school and not Clementine. His son deserved his punishment.

The matter was now at an end and thoughts of this minor incident were replaced with thoughts of Polly, Polly Pendleton, wife of Edwin Pendleton, who should and would have been Polly Renfree, his wife, his own Polly, mother of his children . . . had he not been such a blind, naïve, dolt, Joss told himself.

Chapter Sixteen

'Good morning, Polly. Good gracious, you do look smart!'

'Good morning, Lottie. Gosh, it's good to be back,' Polly greeted her partner.

'I hope you haven't returned to work too soon, but from the way you look and what you just said, I take it you are feeling better?' Lottie asked, questioningly.

'Nothing left but a tickly cough, and that will soon go,' Polly said.

'I suppose you take that cough mixture our mothers used to give us, the one with wine and treacle.'

'That's it,' Polly said. 'It's a solution of acetate of ammonia, Ipecacuanha wine, Antimony wine, muriate of morphine, treacle and water, only I can't remember the measures.'

'Anyway, it's good to have you back, Polly,' Lottie said

'What do you think of my outfit – do you approve?' said Polly.

Polly was wearing the same grey suit which she had worn when she met Joss a few days earlier.

'Of course I approve. It's lovely . . . smart and "good-looking",' answered Lottie. 'It's just that it doesn't look very . . . '
She paused, searching in her mind for a suitable word or phrase. 'It doesn't look as though you came out to go to work.'

'I know,' Polly replied.

'But you mustn't work if you don't feel up to it,' Lottie hastily added, as she put an overall over her skirt and jumper. 'You just take it quietly and I'll go upstairs and get on with the stitching.'

'Wait a minute, Lottie. I've had an idea.'

'What's coming now,' Lottie said under her breath, and sat at the small table in the kitchen.

Polly grinned. 'We're feeling our way, Lottie,' she said, and sat beside Lottie. 'Learning as we go.'

Lottie silently waited.

'Now you know we had special smart dresses made for the party . . .'

'Yes,' Lottie said.

'And it was a success . . . the effort promises to pay dividends.'

'It certainly does,' Lottie agreed. 'You had a real brainwave there, Polly.'

'We could go on doing it,' Polly said.

'We can't keep going to parties!' was Lottie's incredulous reply. 'Who'd invite us?'

'Not parties, Lottie. When I got off the bus this morning I couldn't help noticing several women eyed me and a very smartly dressed gentleman looked me over appreciatively. He raised his hat and said, "Good Morning".'

'You're not suggesting we try to get off with men are you?' Lottie giggled!

'What I'm saying is, if we look smart when we are out we shall get noticed. If our shop is the success we hope it will be, people will get to know who we are; and when we are out in town . . . or anywhere . . . you never know who might see us. People notice. We've got to do all we can to publicise our clothes and ourselves as best we know how!' Still Lottie looked dubious.

'What impression do you get of all the others you see going to work?' Polly said.

'By golly, you're right, Polly,' Lottie said. 'Most look downright dowdy . . .'

'Yes, work-a-day,' Polly agreed. 'But we're not dealing in work-a-day clothes, Lottie,' Polly went on. 'Shut in here at the moment, no one can see us through the window or door, so it doesn't matter what we work in, but I think we should try to ensure, once we open, we look smart all the time for work *and* in our private lives whenever we are *out* anywhere. I don't mean over-dressed, and we mustn't be in competition with our clients . . . just quiet good taste!'

'I'm with you there. Why didn't I see that,' Lottie chided herself.

'It's because we've both been brought up to look good for church or chapel on Sundays and Bank Holidays and the rest of the time we've worn second and third best . . . working clothes.

136

Marrying Edwin, I've raised my requirements in that line a little, really in order not to let Edwin down. I wanted to be a credit to him, and his mother always looks so, so lady-like and smart, and Lottie, at times it has made me feel really guilty spending Edwin's money on clothes I don't absolutely need. But now we've got to think differently. The business and good style must be our priorities. Looking smart is a necessity . . . a duty, if you like, part of the business.'

'Agreed!' Lottie said, emphatically.

'I hope you've got plenty of machining for me to do, Lottie,' Polly said, ready to get started.

'I certainly have, but hold on a minute,' Lottie said.

'Yes?'

'Now I've got a proposition,' Lottie went on. 'We really do need a good stock . . . a good selection . . . to open and for the Preview. Especially with all the clients you intend to attract,' she added grinning mischievously.

'Yes, I've been thinking about that,' Polly agreed. 'I want to help all I can with sewing. I'd have a machine at home and do some in the evenings but I did assure Edwin at the start that I'd work only in the daytime and that it wouldn't interfere with his home-life.'

'I told George something similar,' Lottie said. 'And with that in mind, and if you're agreeable, I'd like to ask May Bascombe to do some machining for us at home . . . or here, if she prefers.'

'I think that's an excellent idea?' Polly agreed.

'I know May well, she's an old friend from way back,' Lottie said. 'I think if I asked her she'd be willing to sew for us and have payment when the items she has stitched sell. So much for every dress, skirt, or whatever and payment when sold . . . at least until we get established and start getting some money back into the business.'

'There's no need for that. I've still got most of the £165 Edwin let me have until Great Aunt Elizabeth's legacy comes through.'

'But Edwin's already made your savings up to mine so that we could invest equal shares in the business,' Lottie protested.

'Yes, but see all the money we've saved from that wonderful gift from *your brother*. That would have cost us much more than paying for temporary help from your friend,' Polly reasoned.

They argued a little, then came to a compromise. Polly would supply the first twelve pounds of wages, which would take several weeks – months, in fact. Anything over that must eventually come out of the business.

'I am excited,' Lottie said.

'I'm excited too,' Polly laughed, and suddenly realised she had not thought of either her inability to become a mother or Joss for at least half an hour, apart from Joss's great help with the equipment.

'I'll see May this evening,' Lottie said and jumped to her feet, saying, 'Come on, let's get on with it. We've got work to do.'

'Too right,' Polly agreed, and they both made their way upstairs to the workroom.

'Have you seen it, Lottie?' Polly's animated face betrayed her excitement, as she greeted her partner a few short weeks later.

'Good morning, Polly,' Lottie said as she closed the door behind her and commenced to remove her smart navy coat and the matching hat with an Egret plume. In the few weeks since Polly's return to work dressed in her eye-catching grey outfit, Lottie had paid more attention to her 'going out' clothes, and in some strange way it actually changed her feelings about herself. In a small way, she really was somebody. 'Have I seen what?' she queried.

'The *Pen-Fal Advertiser*.'

'Have you got it?' Lottie eagerly demanded. 'Let me see.'

Polly thrust the paper into Lottie's outstretched hand. Lottie read aloud: Opening of Ladies' Fashion Establishment . . . Mrs Charlotte Simpson and Mrs Polly Pendleton wish to announce the opening of their Exclusive Fashion Establishment . . . The Lady . . . Market Street, Falmouth, on Friday, 1st December. Dresses and Gowns, Suits, Jackets, Blouses, Skirts, etc. Model Garments ready to wear, or made to measure in styles of client's own choice. Choose from our selection of Silks, Satins, Laces, Voiles, Chiffons, Tulle, Lawn, Velvets, Taffetas, Cashmeres, Tweeds, etc. Matching gloves available. Matching hats made to order by Madam Delia, Milliner. Matching Evening Bags and Footwear also available to order.

'That's fine, Polly,' Lottie smiled, looking into Polly's excited but anxious face.

138

'You're sure you approve the wording?'

'I couldn't improve on it,' Lottie affirmed.

'Mr Trevelyan, the printer, said Mrs Trevelyan was very interested.'

'Let's hope she'll be a customer,' Lottie laughed. 'It's going to be in the *Advertiser* again, isn't it?'

'Oh yes, three weeks running, then we'll be opening.'

'Which is really in just over two weeks,' Lottie said.

The thought sent a frisson of excitement mingled with fear up Polly's spine, and she knew Lottie was in the same high strung condition and had been so for some time.

'Thank goodness May Bascombe agreed to help us. It's making a lot of difference, Polly. We really shall have quite a lot of dresses and outfits to put on show.'

'Having her help has lifted a weight from your shoulders, hasn't it?' Polly said.

'Don't get me wrong, Polly,' Lottie swiftly replied. 'You've been a marvellous help and you've got the hang of it wonderfully well. But May can do anything I can, and with her husband away mining in South Africa and the children grown up except for Betty, she can get on at home without interruption anytime she feels like it, which seems to be most of the time.'

'Don't worry Lottie, I didn't take anything amiss. My side is the sales and paperwork, etcetera, and help in between with straightforward plain stitching. You've got the real work on which the whole venture rests . . . actually making the clothes and making them better than any other shop around. I could never do that, but I am happy to do hems, seams, and suchlike!'

'We're a partnership,' Lottie agreed. 'I couldn't function without you, nor you without me.'

Chapter Seventeen

During the final stages of preparation for the opening of the shop, Joss had become increasingly sceptical about Clementine's now regular shopping expeditions to Truro, but had not bothered to do anything about it. After the first few spending sprees, Clementine came home laden with expensive purchases, plus novelties or chocolates for Theodore. Recently she had uncharacteristically returned home without any new clothes, not even inexpensive items. The last time she didn't have even a bag of sweets for the boy, which promptly resulted in a flood of tears.

'Oh darling, I'm so sorry, I completely forgot! But I promise you next week I'll get you a new toy *and* a lovely box of chocolates.'

'Will you get me a clockwork motor?' Theodore stopped crying as he waited for her reply.

'I'll search all the shops for a clockwork motor,' Clementine promised.

'You go with her, Daddy, and make sure she doesn't forget,' Theodore said. Joss was about to agree to this but before he could speak Clementine quickly replied for him.

'Daddy will get bored standing around while I look at dress shops.'

'Yes. I would get bored if I went shopping with Mummy,' Joss agreed.

On the day Clementine was again going in the Minerva to Truro, Joss was out early. This would have been no surprise to Clementine. Joss was invariably out and about before her.

On this occasion he rode the nut-brown mare, Tess, cross

country to Perranwell where he left her at William Parnell's farm, the farmer handing over care of the mare to one of his farm lads. The mare ambled along with the lad to where the stables were; she was familiar with the surroundings having been left there on several occasions.

Joss and William chatted a while, then Joss left and walked the rest of the way to the pretty Perranwell Station where he caught the branch-line train to Truro.

At Truro Station he made his way down Richmond Hill, along Ferris Town then River Street, to Victoria Square where a gathering of people waited to board a horse-bus and the passengers on another were alighting and forming a small crowd outside a baker's and confectioner's shop. Joss made his way along the wide Boscawen Street to where three placid horses in the shafts of hansom cabs stood, middle of the road, lined up one behind the other waiting for fares. Behind the cabs was a granite trough where the magnificent creatures could drink, a tall gas lamp, a fountain and a little further along, a pump.

Before long, somewhere around here Clementine would put in an appearance, and a motor driven by a woman, especially a woman like Clementine, was guaranteed to attract attention.

Joss idled the minutes away looking in the window of a large draper's shop. He did not notice what was on display, his thoughts were not on shopping. Suddenly, something did catch his attention. It was not inside the window, it was a reflection. And what, or rather who was it? None other than that bloody customs officer, Charles Brendon Copeland. He was not in uniform but wore a black top hat, morning coat and waistcoat, and trousers of light grey cashmere with a dark grey stripe. White drill-cloth spats were worn over his black shoes and he carried gloves and a cane. Definitely handsome, definitely suave and definitely the sort of dandy a certain type of woman would find attractive.

Joss remained where he was, keeping his eyes fixed on the image reflected in the window. And just how friendly was he with Clementine? I'll soon be finding out, Joss thought. The quarter hourly chimes of a clock told him it was quarter past eleven.

Charles Copeland strolled past. At a distance Joss followed, but when Copeland paused, Joss ducked into the doorway of the Red Lion, almost opposite to where Lemon Street fed into Boscawen Street. Copeland moved on to where a bank stood cornerwise to where Boscawen and King Street merged, and Joss moved forward to Cathedral Lane, a narrow pedestrian alley, lined with assorted small shops which ran parallel with King Street, and on the other side of which stood the massive Cathedral. Copeland stood waiting, his eyes fixed on the Lemon Street junction. Joss waited, his eyes fixed on Copeland.

About ten minutes passed when several people turned to look in the direction of where Lemon Street opened into Boscawen Street. Joss followed their gaze and saw the Minerva, hood down, rounding into Boscawen Street with Clementine driving, 'dressed to kill' in a sky-blue jacket and a large-brimmed hat held in place with a wide chiffon scarf. Joss's eyes darted to where Charles Copeland had stood and saw Copeland was crossing the street to stand outside Robert's draper's shop. Clementine had slowed the motor, giving interested onlookers a close view, while her eyes searched the watching bystanders. Charles Copeland walked forward from his position by the shop door, and reached the kerbside as Clementine brought the Minerva to a halt beside him. Smiling, he deftly opened the passenger door and entered. It evidently looked quite romantic to the ladies out shopping, who smiled to see what seemed to be a happy handsome pair, while the men absorbed details of the motor. The Minerva moved forward and after covering a short distance, turned right into King Street.

Joss moved speedily through Cathedral Lane and came out at the other end in time to look along the street known as High Cross and saw the Minerva continuing along King Street. He covered the distance swiftly but when he reached the junction the Minerva was nowhere to be seen! The motor couldn't have covered the whole cobbled street in that time, it must have turned into a side street. Cautiously he moved along and in a few seconds ducked swiftly into an ironmonger's shop as he caught sight of the two coming out from a wide opening which led into the rear of a sizeable hotel. He could hear Clementine's high-pitched laugh as the two drew nearer.

'Can I help you, sir?' asked a grey-haired man in shirt sleeves over which was a grey waistcoat and a hessian type apron.

'A small box of three-quarter-inch screws, please,' Joss said.

'These all right?' asked the man, holding up a box he had taken from the shelf behind him.

'They're fine.' Joss hadn't even bothered to look.

142

'That'll be tuppence, please,' said the man, handing over the box which Joss took and gave him two pennies.

'Thank you, sir.'

'Thank you,' replied Joss, and left.

Clementine and Charles Copeland were some distance ahead now, and walking towards Boscawen Street. Joss followed, quickening his pace as the two neared the junction. Clementine, followed by Copeland, went into a draper's shop. This will probably take some time, Joss thought. But no, ten minutes later the two emerged, Charles Copeland carrying a paper bag. This was out of character, Clementine usually spent ages looking around clothes shops.

Joss was obliged to take refuge inside the entrance to a bank when the two retraced their steps, this time going in the direction of Victoria Square. In the square Clementine made a purchase in both a sweet shop and a toy shop.

Charles Copeland was talking animatedly, and Clementine's shrill laughter carried clearly to Joss's ears. The two made their way back to the hotel where Clementine had left the Minerva, and went inside.

Standing out of sight but easily within earshot of Clementine's high-pitched voice Joss learned they were going to the dining-room. At this, Joss entered the saloon by a side door, where the likes of Clementine never entered, but where the lower orders drank their beer and a few, such as smallholders on market days, bought sandwiches, though most were too poor to buy these . . . their wives or mothers made them at the essential saving of a few pennies.

Joss ordered a cheese and pickle sandwich and a pint of beer, and sat where a locked door to the interior of the main entrance to the hotel gave glimpses of the reception area and entrance to the dining-room. The glass in this door was not clear, but there were clear chinks and patches where there was a pattern in the glass and where the word 'Saloon' was in clear glass, large enough for Joss to see all he needed.

An hour passed and Clementine had not emerged. Joss began to wonder whether there was another door leading from the dining-room. He waited. After a little longer the two came through the dining-room door and went to the reception desk. A youngish man took a key from a row of hooks and handed it over.

Joss could not see whether Clementine or Charles Copeland took it, but that was irrelevant. They did not go up the staircase but along a passage at the rear of the dining-room.

I'll give them a few minutes, Joss thought. Enough rope to hang themselves. After a short wait he rose from his seat and left the saloon by the side-door, rc-entering the hotel via the front entrance. He made his way to the reception desk. The man greeted him.

'Good afternoon, sir.'

'Good afternoon. I believe you have a lady booked in here . . . ' Joss gave Clementine's description. The young man knew at once.

'Oh, yes, sir. Mrs North, Room GF3. She is not *staying* here, but she is *booked* in here.'

'She is not staying here but she is booked in here?' Joss repeated, in a questioning tone. He stared unblinking into the man's face, awaiting an explanation.

'Mrs North is a business lady. She comes here occasionally for a business conference.'

'You have conference rooms?' Joss asked, sceptically.

'Well, actually it's a sitting-room, sir. Quite suitable for the purpose if the number is small.'

'Quite so,' agreed Joss. 'I also have business with Mrs North. Perhaps you would be good enough to take me to her.'

The young man hesitated. 'I don't know,' he said. 'Mrs North said she was not to be disturbed until she rang for tea to be brought.'

'I wish to see her.' Joss's tone was quiet but insistent.

'I'm afraid I'll have to ask the manager,' the young man replied. 'Fetch Mr Harris, would you, please.' The young blue-uniformed page-boy to whom he spoke hurried away and a few moments later the man Joss had earlier seen speaking to Clementine and Charles Copeland, appeared from the door to the rear of the reception desk.

'There is some query?' He smiled ingratiatingly. 'How can I help?' The young man explained the situation and the smile disappeared from Mr Harris's face.

'I am sorry, sir, but I have explicit instructions from Mrs North that she must not be disturbed. She is conferring on a business matter.'

144

'She will see me,' Joss insisted.

The manager stood firm. 'I cannot go against her express orders,' he said. But Joss knew the manager had guessed what sort of business Clementine and Copeland were up to.

'Mrs North is not Mrs North, neither is she a business woman. She is Mrs Clementine Renfree and she is my wife! Now . . . Are you going to accompany me to room GF3 or am I going to have to knock the door down?' Joss's voice was low and intense.

The manager stared for a couple of seconds, summing up the situation. Joss's fine physique plus his fixed, unnerving look of grim determination were clearly not lost to him. 'Come this way, sir,' he said, wisely.

Joss followed closely beside Mr Harris, along the long passage, Mr Harris taking a key from an inner pocket of his cut-away coat. On passing rooms one and two, Joss snatched the master key from the manager's hand, swiftly inserted it in the lock of number three, and threw open the door!

Joss noticed no furniture in the room nor their outer clothing draped over the backs of chairs, only the settee on which was a view of Charles Copeland's white rutting buttocks encircled about by Clementine's legs and over his shoulder the top of Clementine's head and her blue eyes, wide with fright. Striding across the floor on which their inside garments were strewn, he hauled the astonished and terrified-looking Copeland off his wife, aiming a punch to his face which sent him hurtling over the back of the settee and out of sight behind it, from where Copeland slowly arose holding a blood covered hand to his nose.

g

Chapter Eighteen

The week prior to the Preview flew past. Polly had written the wording for the cards of Invitation to attend the Preview and Ed Trevelyan had them delivered in good time for Polly to address and despatch in their matching envelopes, to recipients in and around both Penryn and Falmouth, including Flushing, Mylor, Stithians, Mawnan Smith, Budock, Constantine, Treverva, Devoran and Mabe. Included in the list were the Mayoresses of both boroughs along with the wives of all Aldermen and Parish and Town Councillors, Town Clerks wives, etc., and wives of all prominent businessmen in the area.

On the Monday of that momentous week a meeting was arranged behind the closed doors of the soon to be opened shop, with Mrs Dora Bates, a relatively comfortably off widow otherwise known as Madam Delia, the milliner, and May Bascombe. Delia and May, knowing extra help would be welcome on the day of the Preview, had both already offered their services. Polly and Lottie were grateful for this suggestion and both were especially keen to have Madam Delia so that prospective clients might talk to her about hats if they wished, and Delia could talk to them and get more fully acquainted and a better insight into what might be required of her.

All four were excited and felt personally involved in the new and somewhat unusual enterprise. Polly, wearing a black silk dress which Lottie had made specially for her to wear in the shop, would be on duty in the ground floor showroom. May, who was shortish, round-faced with gingery-brown hair greying at the front, would likewise be attired in her own well-cut black dress, and on duty in the first floor showroom. Lottie, not being strictly speaking a saleslady, would wear a specially made soft

146

Wedgwood blue blouse with matching skirt. Madam Delia, tall, angular her dark hair streaked at the front with silver-grey, had a steel grey, satin trimmed Bolero Suit with a matching blouse of the same material as the trimming.

Some time previously Polly and Lottie thought it would be rather pleasant to get in a supply of tea, coffee and a selection of the tiniest biscuits available. The ladies could cope standing up with these, seating being limited.

Polly concluded all four would have enough to do without having to leave possible clients in order to make drinks. She would arrange for Mary to come for the day and attend to this. They could all then be free to chat to the ladies without distraction.

At last everything was coming together. Lottie confessed she would breathe a sigh of relief when Friday the first of December was over. Madam Delia, who had been more than a little taken aback by the elegance of the premises, pooh-poohed Lottie's fears. 'It will all go famously, you'll see,' she assured.

All were to contribute their bone china tea-sets for the occasion and, heady with enthusiasm, fears about chips and breakages were brushed aside.

'I really think we've covered everything,' concluded Polly at last, and laughing and bidding each other cheerful good-byes, they went their separate ways.

Am I late, what time is it! In the weak light of the moon, Polly peered at the clock. Five a.m! She hadn't overslept. She lay back, relaxing a little. How the few days since the meeting in the shop had flown by. Neither Edwin nor George raised objection to their wives staying late at the shop the special evening before the Preview, and Polly and Lottie as well as May Bascombe had worked until quite late ensuring every garment and item on display was arranged to perfection, every guilt edged mirror had been polished, not one speck of dust sullied the chairs and fitments, not a fleck of fluff on the carpets. Mary had been warned she would be needed to help, and she arrived too to acquaint herself with the kitchen and its contents.

Edwin and George both called at the shop to escort their wives home, in Edwin's case Mary as well. George and Lottie accompanied May Bascombe and Madam Delia had ordered a cab. Mary was amazed at the lavishness of the shop, she had never seen anything the least bit like it; the elegance of the thick carpets, the layout of the showrooms and fitments AND the wonderful gowns! In spite of insisting she was lost for words, she babbled all the way back to Penryn. She was also surprised at the number of public-houses in Falmouth . . . even more than in Penryn . . . and at that time of the evening some of the imbibers were beginning to get lively, you could tell from the sounds of chatter, singing and raucous laughter which assailed the ears as they passed through Falmouth streets to where they were to get the horse bus. Some shops stayed open late, especially the ones with perishable goods. It was really fairly safe to walk along, but it was not the done thing when the evenings were dark, for a lady to be out walking about without the company of a male protector, and Edwin was a very protective male.

When Polly tumbled into bed she was now so excited and at the same time exhausted that even thoughts of Joss were arrested. It was with surprise she realised she had slept soundly for several hours. Now she was ready for the day ahead. She forced herself to stay in bed so that Edwin would not be disturbed and complain she was wearing herself out.

Polly breakfasted in her dressing-gown, leaving toilet preparations and dressing until last, with plenty of time to ensure her clothes and every hair were just right. Without being asked, Edwin washed the breakfast dishes, then enquired if he could do anything else to help.

'No, thanks, Edwin,' Polly put her arms around his neck, pulled him close, and kissed him. 'You've been wonderful, just by being so understanding,' she said, gratefully and lovingly, for she did love him; she loved him too much to ever hurt him.

'I think I'll be off and make an early start, if you're quite sure there's nothing more I can do.'

'No. You go ahead, dear,' Polly answered . . . 'Edwin . . .'

Edwin, with one arm in his coat-sleeve, paused, 'Yes, dear.' He waited.

'It was nothing,' Polly said.

'Sure?'

'Positive.'

'Good-bye then, Polly my darling, and good luck.' With coat

now on and buttoned he kissed her, winked, put on his bowler hat, and left.

Alone with thoughts of the enormity of the undertaking she had initiated, Polly felt suddenly alarmed at how it would all turn out. Would it be a success? Polly had been sure it would be but now her mind was suddenly flooded with doubts. Why on earth should she, a country girl with just a basic education, imagine she could start and run a business; compete with old established highly experienced and relatively well-off people. How did she ever have the audacity, the check, to think she, Polly Pascoe that was, could do this. Marrying Edwin must have gone to her head! How could she look Lottie, dear trusting Lottie, in the face if it was all a dismal flop. Fright took hold!

With shaking hand Polly put water to heat in the kettle and made yet another cup of tea. She looked out through the window as she waited for the tea to draw. It was a dry day and not too cold, but she still shivered. A thought struck her; she hesitated, then went to the little cupboard where Edwin kept the whisky. She'd put some in her tea. Hastily she picked up the bottle and trembling, removed the stopper. With the neck of the bottle poised over the steaming teacup she suddenly paused.

Don't be such a fool! She spoke to herself inside her head. Don't be such a stupid coward. And how dare you let Lottie down, turning up at the Preview with all those hoity-toity women . . . ladies . . . and your breath whiffing of whisky! So much for your quality, your good taste. The Preview was your idea . . . remember? You'll be the talk of all the posh drawing-rooms . . . a joke, something for the old moneyed fossils to snigger at, something to make Clementine sneer – the lower classes not knowing how to behave . . . they always let you down in the end . . . don't know any better . . . no backbone.

And what would Joss think of her. She'd let him down. He'd be disappointed. He'd be sad. He'd be ashamed of her!

Oh, no! Not that.

Decisively she replaced the stopper in the bottle and returned it to its place noticing as she did so that her hands were now suddenly steady. Hastily she drank half the tea in the cup and threw the rest away. Then she marched upstairs and quickly but carefully prepared herself, went out at the front door, locked it and walked purposefully towards Penryn town centre.

Mary was at the bus stop waiting for her and they exchanged greetings. The young housemaid was clearly pent-up. 'Isn't it exciting!' She said as they boarded the horse-bus.

'I must admit it is,' Polly agreed. 'Have you got your starched apron, cap and cuffs?'

'Yes,' Mary answered and indicated a small shopping bag.

'The ones with the lace trimming?'

'Yes. And I've brought a spare pair of cuffs . . . just in case, and I'm wearing the black dress.'

'I'm sure you'll look very smart and capable,' Polly said.

'I feel quite nervous,' Mary confided. 'I wish I could be more . . . oh, what's the word?' Mary hesitated! 'More . . . '

'Composed?' Polly queried.

'Yes, I think that's it. More composed, like you are.'

Polly gave a wry smile. If only Mary knew. But Polly was feeling steadier now, and for that she was thankful.

The horse-bus was almost full but the two miles to Falmouth were soon covered. It was not often Mary went to Falmouth and she stared about her at the bustling, jostling narrow streets, the shop-keepers and their staff putting out their wares for display, taking deliveries of stock, humping all manner of boxes and baskets hither and thither. Also it was not lost to Mary how many people glanced appreciatively at her smartly dressed mistress. In some way she felt this reflected on her and she enjoyed basking in the reflected approbation.

Lottie had already arrived at the shop. 'How are you, Polly?' she said, after the 'Good-morning' greetings had been dispensed with. 'I haven't slept a wink,' she went on without waiting for Polly to reply. 'I'm that strung up, now it's come to it, I'll be glad when the day is over, I can tell you. Whichever way it goes, good or bad, I'll be glad when the day's over! How do you feel?' she asked Polly again.

'Not too bad,' came the reply.

'Did you sleep?'

'Yes, better than I expected.'

'I wish I could be like you,' Lottie said, enviously and looked at Mary. 'Cool as a cucumber,' she said nodding her head in Polly's direction.

Polly did not admit to them that less than two hours before she had been in a real funk!

150

They were about to troop up to the workroom to deposit hats, coats, gloves, etc. When Madam Delia and May Bascombe arrived. Staff for the day's big event was now assembled.

Shortly after, an ample supply of miniature fancy biscuits which Polly had ordered arrived from Edwards Confectioner's Shop. They were delivered by Mr Edwards son, the errand boy on this occasion, not being trusted with them.

Mary squealed with delight as she unpacked them from their layered boxes. She had never seen such dainty biscuits. They were so tiny and so varied . . . shortbreads, ginger — hard outside and tacky within, Almond, Imperial, Shrewsbury biscuits tasting of lemon, etc., in rounds, star-shapes, diamonds, half-moons, each topped with either a pink sugar-flower, crystallised fruit, violets, etc., flowers and leaves made with almond paste or almond nuts. They were all so tiny you could, unless you were on your best behaviour of course, cram several into your mouth at once. None had chocolate. Polly feared the remote possibility of the chocolate melting and causing a stain on something. The biscuits were to be put on plates and in dainty bowls, and placed at strategic places. A gallon and a half of milk was left outside the kitchen in the small courtyard, where it would keep cool and fresh.

Mary was beginning to feel she had a real role to play in the venture. A good cup of tea or coffee in a dainty bone china cup, with the tempting tiny biscuits, served with a smile in plush surroundings could, as her mistress said, and she now clearly saw, make such a good impression. In nervous yet eager anticipation, Mary put the kettles of water to heat.

Chapter Nineteen

At one minute before 10 a.m. the roller-blinds which covered the window and the glass section of the door, were raised. 'The Lady' was ready for launching into the world of business and awaiting selected prospective clients.

At 10 o'clock precisely Cordelia Pendleton, Edwin's mother, arrived.

'I've come very early,' she said to Polly and Lottie. 'Nobody likes to be the first to arrive, so I thought I'd be here sharp on time so that the one who is really first will not know she is.'

'How very thoughtful,' both Polly and Lottie said, and Polly proceeded to show Cordelia over the premises.

How elegant Cordelia always looked. A soft-hued misty blue dress was visible under her grey fur-trimmed coat. Sitting on top of Cordelia's immaculately waved and upswept grey hair was a matching hat with a splash of deeper blue feathers. Even in old age Cordelia's face was beautiful. But now . . . how delicate she looked. And again, how elegant. It was not only thoughtful it was downright kind of Cordelia to make the effort to be here, and at such an early hour. And she was such an asset . . . she graced the shop. 'The Lady' was just the right name where Cordelia was concerned.

'I wish Edwin's father could come and see it,' Cordelia said to Polly when she had been shown over the premises. 'He would be so proud of his daughter-in-law.'

This was praise indeed. Edwin's father was of a generation when such an enterprise by a married woman was out of the question, unthinkable.

Polly told Mary to bring a cup of coffee. Mary brought the coffee and presented the plate of dainty biscuits and Cordelia

152

smiled with pleasure and approval. The minutes dragged by, but no one else came.

Polly and Lottie grew tense with suspense. This waiting was far worse than the dentist's waiting-room. Madam Delia, whose short Bolero jacket showed to advantage her tiny waist and the expert cut of her matching skirt, was unperturbed.

'It's early yet. They'll come, you'll see,' she said. And she was right.

At 10.25 two Falmouth Councillor's wives arrived. 'We're not the first, are we?' one said, a note of anxiety in her voice. Polly guessed this was a little outside their sphere of experience. Little did they know Polly and Lottie were in that same situation.

'Oh no,' assured Polly, and inclined her head in Cordelia's direction. 'Would you like me to show you around or would you prefer to browse . . . there is another showroom upstairs?' As she was speaking, Agnes, Edwin's sister, arrived and was eager to see everything.

'I'll show you around,' Cordelia volunteered, Agnes confessing herself quite bowled over by the stylish surroundings.

Soon another lady arrived. Polly allowed several minutes to elapse before offering tea or coffee.

By now a steady stream of ladies began arriving. Most already knew someone who was present and there was such a buzz of conversation it became like a social occasion.

The higher up the social scale, the more questioning the ladies were in their demands to know exactly how the system of making the garments worked. They wished to see the bolts of materials and to feel and inspect the quality. Who did the designing? . . . They pored over Polly's portfolio and she frequently explained that except for basic classic skirts and some blouses such as button-front with collar, shirt-style blouses, garments were unique, that was . . . no two exactly alike. A dress or less severe blouse could have different yokes or yokes in different material, a variety of sleeves — not just long, short or somewhere in between, but cut, styled and embellished in dozens of different ways, and sometimes using diaphanous material. Neck-lines could vary enormously, with or without collars . . . the choice in collars being wide including the popular throat-band style stiffened with whalebone, celluloid or wires, and decorated in a variety of ways. There was an assortment of fichu or chemisettes for a low décolletage. The number of ways in which a bodice could be treated seemed endless, likewise skirts and overskirts. Making garments original and to suit every individual client was no problem.

The ladies were also interested to know who did the cutting? Who made them up? Where did the matching hats come from? Madam Delia coped well with questions about millinery, styles, embellishments, etc. Many were intrigued by the prospect of matching shoes for evening wear. Sample handbags, shoes and hats were on display, and they carried a variety of gloves. Almost all remarked on the fitting-room. 'Usually it is so dowdy, sometimes resembling a junk-room,' Lottie was told by one old lady. 'But this is quite remarkable, my dear.' Her querulous voice rose to a higher wavering pitch. 'I must congratulate you. Quite remarkable.'

Lottie smiled. 'Thank you, madam,' she replied, and assisted the lady down the stairs.

'My name is Lady Florence Marchbury, and you will be seeing me again,' the voice rang out. By now they had reached the Ground Floor Showroom. 'Your coffee was quite delicious and very welcome,' she said as an afterthought, and paused to look towards the door to the kitchen where Mary, who had overheard, stood with a beaming smile.

'Thank you, young woman.'

'You're very welcome, Your Ladyship,' Mary replied, with unflinching new-found composure.

'Very nice, very nice,' Lady Marchbury muttered. She nodded graciously to Agnes who was now enjoying coffee and biscuits and Cordelia who couldn't resist a second cup. A manservant was at the door to accompany her and Lottie concluded that not too far away a carriage awaited her ladyship.

Agnes was about to ask Polly how she managed to attract so many posh ladies, when the deputy mayoress of Penryn arrived, and the three were soon deep in conversation.

Later in the morning Clementine, who had not visited the shop premises in the preparation stages, put in an appearance. Dressed in a russet-coloured coat and matching hat swathed about the brim in creamy curling feathers which were almost the same shade as her hair, she made a striking appearance.

'Well . . . Polly . . . Polly Pendleton!' Her voice shrilled above the buzz of conversation. 'My, how you have grown into a smart young woman, haven't you. And after such a poor unenviable start in life! Congratulations, my dear. Your window display looks very chic . . . Ah . . . it's Elizabeth Scott-Barfield.' She walked to a small group of ladies of roughly her own age. 'Imagine bumping into you here . . . how are you, my dear . . .'

Polly was left fuming, but glad Clementine moved away before she said something she would be sorry for. Thank goodness she didn't rise to the bait.

Clementine's voice still shrilled above everyone else's. Eventually she and it drifted upstairs to the first floor showroom.

Lottie heard her coming, and though she had not heard what Clementine said to Polly, she felt a sudden unease. Why did she feel so? Clementine could be a good client. It was something in the tone and pitch of her voice which gave Lottie this feeling of foreboding. From what snatches she could hear, Clementine seemed to be inspecting the contents of the upper showroom.

A Sea Captain's wife who had been looking at the fitting-room departed, complimenting Lottie as she went.

'Ah! There you are.' Clementine had spotted Lottie and came towards her. 'What is this?' she demanded.

'It's the fitting-room, Clementine,' Lottie answered. 'Would you like to come in and have a look?'

Clementine stepped inside and gazed down at the small two-seater blue-grey plush French directoire style settee and the matching carpet, the guilt-edged mirror, the white freshly-painted woodwork.

'I hope you and that girl . . . Polly . . . are not too deeply in debt!' Her hostile voice was even louder.

Tight-lipped, Lottie replied, 'We are not one penny in debt Clementine.'

'Then it must be a very good thing you've got *my husband* to foot the bills for your little venture!'

Lottie stepped towards the fitting-room door and closed it.

'I'll remind you you're referring to *my brother*, and I think *your* family would know more about debts and him footing bills than I do,' Lottie retorted, trembling with anger.

'Well . . . ' Clementine snorted, lost for words.

'I would also remind you that Polly has come into a recent substantial legacy but in any case Mr Pendleton, the husband of my partner . . "that girl", as you call her . . . is quite wealthy enough to stand any costs involved in setting up this business. He is very well-off and so is his family, which is more than can be said for someone who is standing not two yards from where I now stand!'

The instant the words were out of her mouth, Lottie knew she had said too much. She didn't know how she managed to think of such cutting remarks.

'Why you . . . you . . . you little bitch!' Clementine spat the words from between clenched teeth and pulled the door open to leave, bumping into two ladies who were standing listening outside.

It was fortunate no one was mounting the stairs or, as Lottie later described, they would have been sent flying.

Clementine barged through the ground floor showroom and left without a word, leaving Polly momentarily open-mouthed with astonishment.

It was now clear to Polly that Clementine arrived in a raging temper and that she and Lottie were on the receiving end of her venom. Swiftly she left her post to go upstairs and see if Lottie was all right. Madam Delia did not appear to be engaged in conversation and Polly signalled to her to go down to the lower showroom.

She found Lottie alone in the fitting-room, quivering with both rage and fear. Lottie briefly explained to Polly what took place. 'I wish I hadn't said all those things,' she said, tears brimming around her eyes. 'But, Polly, I could not stop myself. I don't know where the words came from . . . I just seemed to be out of control.'

Polly put an arm around Lottie's shoulder. 'No one would blame you, Lottie. She came in spoiling for a fight only she got just a little bit more than she bargained for, that's all.'

'I'm glad you understand,' Lottie said. 'Though I don't really understand myself. But I've been so strung up today. It's the total unfairness of her.' Lottie muttered, as though to herself.

'We've both been pretty strung up, and her behaviour was the last straw,' Polly said. 'Now, you just sit there and I'll nip down and tell Mary to bring us both up a cup of strong sweet tea with a couple of Aspros from the First Aid Box.'

In a few seconds Polly was back in the fitting-room again.

156

Lottie was dabbing her eyes. 'Poor Joss,' she said. 'He must have a terrible time with her, not to mention that family of hers.'

Polly remained silent. There was nothing anyone could say to sublimate that thought.

'And whatever will all these people think?' Lottie went on. 'She's ruined the whole thing.'

'I don't think so,' Polly soothed. 'There was so much chattering going on, I doubt anyone heard what she said, and you said you shut the door before you said anything.'

'Yes,' Lottie agreed. 'But not before she said *her husband*, if you please, footed the bill, loud enough for *all* to hear.'

'But there was so much noise and conversation, it probably went unnoticed,' Polly said. 'We must carry on as though nothing has happened . . . If anyone heard, I doubt they will remember.'

'Two of them will,' Lottie said emphatically. 'They were listening outside the door.'

'I expect they were the only two. Lots of people have come and gone, and new ones will be coming later who won't know a thing about it. Don't worry, Lottie.'

'You're right,' Lottie said. 'At least, I hope you are. And I was saying to Joss only the last time he visited me, how lovely it was that the family were all friendly again.' Then she added, 'George mustn't know about this.'

'He won't,' Polly assured her.

They sat in silence for a few minutes.

'Feeling a bit better now, love?' Polly asked.

Lottie smiled weakly. 'Yes, thank you. I think so,' she said.

During the slack lunch-time period, all talked together of what happened and everyone was of the opinion that no real harm had been done to the business. Polly requested that the incident be kept secret and not mentioned to anyone outside themselves. All agreed, and Lottie began to feel less worried.

At ten minutes to 4 o'clock the last ladies entered the shop and by 4.30 p.m. all had departed, leaving the five tired but delighted with the success of the Preview, apart from the visit from Clementine which Lottie swore she would never forget. But 'least said soonest mended' was Lottie's motto and all agreed not to repeat to anyone what happened.

Chapter Twenty

On the way home Polly was debating in her mind. They had all agreed to tell no one about the awful episode with Clementine. But surely she should tell Edwin. She was certain a few ladies overheard part if not all that took place. There was nothing to stop them from gossiping. Suppose it reached Edwin's ears from some other source! Someone could speak of it to him. Cordelia and his sister Agnes left shortly after Clementine arrived but did they hear any of it? She was not sure. How hurt Edwin would be if he found out she had not confided in him.

Lottie was not going to let George know anything about it. But that was understandable. The rift between George and Joss's family had at last been healed. She didn't want it opened up again. Joss was the one who would pay the penalty; Joss and Lottie. Polly had the impression Lottie didn't care whether she ever saw Clementine again. She didn't seem over-fond of her nephew Theodore either, and once confided she thought he had a sly streak.

All these thoughts went through Polly's head at lightning speed whilst engaged in chat with Mary about the assorted ladies who had come to view the new establishment, turning it into something of a social event – a grand event, according to Mary.

Mary was going straight home and Polly, who didn't feel like cooking, was tempted by the smell coming from the fish and chip shop on The Terrace and bought some to take home. She hurried up Helston Road, telling herself she would not make a habit of not having a home-cooked meal waiting for Edwin. But he did like fish and chips, so it wouldn't matter just this one time.

By the time the meal was over, the few dishes washed and the fire burning brightly, Polly at last collapsed into a chair beside it. Edwin was keen to hear all about the Preview, and over the fish and chips and tinned peaches and custard, Polly told him about the events of the day and the possible clientele. Edwin thought they were off to a very promising start.

'You look whacked, dear,' he said as Polly sank deeper into the cushions. 'Why not go straight to bed. I can bring you up another hot drink later, if you're still awake.'

'Thanks Edwin, but I don't want to go to bed yet. You're right ... I am tired, but I'm bodily tired. My mind is still buzzing with all that's happened and I know that if I go to bed I won't be able to sleep. I'd rather just sit here a little while and wind down.'

'You know best, my dear.'

Edwin picked up the local newspaper and sat in a chair close to Polly.

'I haven't told you everything!' Polly blurted out suddenly, as Edwin started to unfold his paper.

He refolded the paper, placed it on a small nearby table, then looked at Polly.

'What haven't you told me, Polly?' he said quietly, his hazel eyes fixed on her face.

'Clementine came in,' she said, after a pause.

'Yes,' Edwin waited.

Polly drew a deep breath, then the whole story came tumbling out.

'You mustn't breathe it,' Polly said. 'Lottie doesn't want George to know, and you can understand that, can't you Edwin?'

For a couple of seconds he didn't answer, mentally weighing up the circumstances.

'Yes,' he said at last. 'I think on this occasion she has good reason to withhold this from George, and he *has* got a bad heart.'

'They will all carry on, inside the family and out, as though nothing had happened. Least said, soonest mended Lottie said, and at least she had the satisfaction of putting that Clementine in her place. Other than Clementine's visit the day was a resounding success,' Polly went on. 'Several ladies insisted appointments for fittings be made there and then, including Mrs Endersby-Harman. Do you remember Edwin, the lady who admired my dress at the party and I said we might be having a Preview?'

'Oh yes, I remember, she was the unwitting instigator of all this,' Edwin said.

'Yes, she's the one. Lottie has agreed to visit the homes of some of the less able. Those who live any distance away are going to send a carriage to fetch her, and of course, she will include a small charge for the time she spends travelling. We've got a bumper order book. If it hadn't been for Clementine it would have been a wonderful day for us . . . all of us, in fact.'

Edwin sat with his chin cupped in his hand, mulling over the situation.

'Well Polly, darling it looks as though your business is off to a good start,' he said. 'The bother you had with Clementine shouldn't affect it. And you and Lottie handled it all extremely well. Lottie did hit back at Clementine harder than I would have expected her to do, but no one could blame her for saying what she did – the woman asked for it. Lottie must have been tense and anxious, but she did have the presence of mind to close the door before she spoke. If you all, like you said, treat the whole thing as though it never happened, it shouldn't make any difference to your business. You don't know whether or not Clementine will say anything to Joss?'

Polly shook her head.

'Let's hope not, and that the episode will be ignored,' Edwin continued. 'Just you and Lottie keep your heads down where Joss's wife is concerned, and wait and see. I think you could be better off without her as a client.'

There was a pause in the discussion, then Edwin said, 'They don't seem too happy together do they?'

'Clementine and Joss?' Polly asked.

'Yes.'

'Perhaps not.' Polly realised she herself had been thinking this on some lower level of consciousness.

'Joss has been a lucky man in so many ways.' Edwin took her hand in his. 'But he's not as lucky as I am. If I didn't have a penny, Polly, I'd still be the richest man in the world.'

Polly leant forward, stretched her arms around his neck and kissed him. Dear Edwin. She loved him truly, but he must never know who really owned her heart.

The next day was to be another memorable one; the day the shop opened its doors to the public.

Lottie and Polly were on their own now. Madam Delia would only be contacted when a hat was required, and May was at home getting on with the sewing, though she sometimes preferred to come to the workroom when a garment was nearing completion. Lottie was busy in the workroom, but on hand should anyone require a fitting. In the first hour after opening a number of passing townsfolk peered with interest through the window, and Polly could hear the complimentary remarks on the three lovely dresses displayed on models, two complete with hat and gloves and an evening dress with long gloves, a bag and matching shoes. There were a few of Madam Delia's hats for display and effect.

Then a well-dressed lady came in to look around. She looked at everything, saying little except that she was staying at a hotel on the seafront. Before leaving, and after going through Polly's portfolio, she placed an order for a skirt and jacket in cashmere with a matching high necked blouse, and an evening dress with tulle-lace over taffeta and all the matching accessories.

Lottie showed the lady, Mrs Dora Etherington, into the fitting-room to take measurements, and once again was congratulated on the charming little room.

'Thank the Lord May is helping me,' Lottie said after Mrs Etherington departed.

Another lady came in and bought a skirt and blouse off the rail, after first trying them on.

In ones and twos, ladies, some with escorts, drifted in and out throughout the day. Polly was glad of the reduced pace after the frenetic activities of the previous day. Even so, with two showrooms to watch over and order books to keep record there was little spare time. It was decided a little hand bell be purchased to stand on the small counter, which was close to the entrance, so that a client could ring for attention if Polly was in the upstairs showroom. Lottie took a break from sewing to keep her eye on the showrooms, whilst Polly went out to buy it.

'Any customers?' she asked Lottie when she returned a short while later.

'A lady bought a pair of cream-coloured elbow length evening gloves,' Lottie answered. 'Did you get the bell?'

'Yes,' Polly said, and produced from a royal blue coloured box a silver bell shaped like a lady in a crinoline dress.

'Like it?' Polly asked as she gently swayed the bell, which made a pleasant tinkling sound.

'Very nice.' Lottie stretched out her hand for the bell to

161

examine it more closely.

'Hey, Lottie, who do you think I saw in Church Street?' Polly said.

'I don't know. Who did you see?' Lottie replied somewhat indifferently, still examining the crinoline lady.

'Clementine!'

'You didn't!' The bell forgotten Lottie instantly turned a shade paler.

'And who do you think was with her?'

'Not Joss?' Increased anxiety was obvious in Lottie's voice and facial expression.

'No, not Joss. That Customs Officer . . . Copeland!'

'Well . . . ' Lottie drew a long breath, as all sorts of implications flashed through her mind. 'Did they see you?'

'She did,' Polly replied. 'I looked out of the shop window at the same time she looked in and for a second we just stared at one another, then she just passed by and was gone.'

'I hope she won't come here,' Lottie said.

'I don't think she will . . . not after yesterday.'

'I'll bet Joss doesn't know about this.' Lottie looked thoughtful.

'That's what I was thinking,' Polly replied, 'but I think it's a good thing one of us saw her.'

'Why?' asked Lottie.

'If she wants us to keep quiet she'd better do the same.'

'By golly, you're right there.' A brief smile of relief flitted across Lottie's face, but quickly disappeared. 'Poor Joss. I shouldn't say it but I can't help wondering just what she and that Copeland are up to!'

In the afternoon Polly was pleased to find several ladies had come from Truro to see what the new shop, 'The Lady', had to offer. The word certainly has got around, Polly thought, surprised by their joint achievement. As a dream to toy with and speculate over, the idea seemed marvellous, but in reality it didn't seem possible that she and Lottie could have achieved so much. But it wasn't a dream, it was reality. Today the shop was here, yesterday seemed like a dream, and tomorrow the shop and Polly and Lottie would be here, and the days and weeks and, with luck, the years after. Surely it wasn't possible. But it was, *and* it was occupying her mind, except in quiet moments when Joss's image, his eyes, his mouth, the remembered touch of his hand blanked out all else. Dear, darling Joss . . . Joss . . . The shop door opened and a tall elegant lady in a topaz coloured outfit sailed in . . .

162

Chapter Twenty-one

With the build-up to Christmas getting closer business at 'The Lady' continued to be brisk. Lottie consulted Polly over the situation. Orders were being taken faster than she and May could complete them, and the stock of ready-made wear in the shop must not be allowed to run down at this time of year, quite the reverse. Polly agreed with this.

'Could we get some temporary help?' Polly suggested.

'I've been thinking about that. I do know someone who might help us,' Lottie said.

'She is good?' Polly asked.

'I wouldn't suggest her if she wasn't!' Lottie retorted. 'Our clothes and our success are based on good material, good cut and good finish.' Lottie's growing pride in 'The Lady' and in her reputation were evident in this remark.

'Agreed,' Polly said.

'I'll ask her, I'll tell her it's temporary, to help us out during the busy period.'

The lady, Mrs Ethel Angove, eagerly seized the opportunity and became part of the workforce two days later.

Polly's and Lottie's leisure time and their time at home was now vastly reduced. Neither had seen anything of Joss and his family since 'The Lady' commenced business. Both Polly and Lottie made a point of seeing parents and parents-in-law at some time during either weekends or their early closing day on Wednesdays. One morning Lottie announced that Joss had been to see her and George the previous evening.

'Anything said?' Polly asked.

They both knew to what she was referring. Clementine's unforgettable visit to the Preview.

'No,' Lottie replied. 'I don't think Clementine could have told him anything.'

'How was he?' Polly asked, hoping Lottie wouldn't notice the tremble in her voice, and the sudden pink tone of her face and throat.

'Very interested in hearing all about "The Lady", Lottie said. 'And he wanted to know how you are . . . Edwin too of course.'

Polly pretended to be looking for an invoice as she felt her colour deepen.

'I thought he seemed a little subdued,' Lottie went on. 'I had the feeling he had something on his mind, but he didn't say, and I couldn't ask. I do hope he's all right.' She spoke as though to herself. 'What's the use of all that money if you're not happy at home. Still, we all know someone who'll find a use for it . . . '

John Renfree was now well enough to accept Joss's and Clementine's invitation to spend Christmas at Manor Withiel. He still had not visited his son's home and Joss called for his parents on Christmas Eve and drove them in the Minerva while Polly was still busy at 'The Lady'.

Polly and Lottie were both adamant that in addition to Christmas Day and Boxing Day, they all take the day after Boxing Day off work. They needed the break. Both felt no one would be shopping for clothes immediately after Christmas, and on the first of January everyone who wanted new things would be endeavouring to buy them in the January sales. Having so recently opened they had no old stock to off-load. They doubted if there was any point in opening at all, but they were feeling their way and had to be ready, willing and able at all times.

The day after Boxing Day Joss drove his parents home to their cottage. Before returning to Manor Withiel he called at Villa Gwidden. Polly opened the door in response to a rap on the knocker, and was briefly taken off guard seeing Joss standing there before her. As she opened the door Joss removed his Homburg hat, at the same time a smile spread across his handsome features, causing Polly's heart to somersault.

'Good afternoon, Polly. How are you?'

164

'Why Joss, I'm fine . . . oh dear, how nice to see you. Come in,' she said, covered with confusion and annoyed with herself for being so.

'Have I come at an inconvenient time?'

'Not at all,' Polly led the way from the hall, which was bedecked with holly and other greenery, into the sitting-room where Christmas decorations and a blazing fire in the grate created a festive atmosphere.

'Please have a seat, Joss. I'm afraid Edwin's gone to his office at the quarries for a couple of hours, and most of the men are working.'

'And do you have to be busy with something else?' he asked, uncertain.

'Oh no. Lottie and I have both agreed . . . the day after Boxing Day we would have a rest, a complete break.'

'Did you have a good Christmas?' Joss asked.

'Lovely. Edwin and I went to mother's. Jack was there, and she enjoyed us all being around the table . . . like old times,' she said. 'Edwin's father was not up to leaving home, but Agnes, Caleb and Mary Jane went there on Christmas Day, and we visited them on Boxing Day.'

'I've heard all about the successful Preview and the opening of your business venture from Lottie. Congratulations Polly,' Joss said.

Polly was calmer now. 'Thank you, Joss, but without your sister's expertise it could not have happened.' Polly looked at Joss who was sitting in a comfortable chair cornerwise to the sofa where she sat, his chin resting between thumb and forefinger, a tiny smile curling the corners of his mouth upwards as he gazed towards Polly in apparent contemplation.

'And how have you been faring, Joss?'

Joss shifted his gaze and did not immediately answer. He seemed to be silently debating what to say. Then he looked up at her and said with a wry grin, 'Perhaps I'm a little bored with a gentleman's style of living.'

Polly laughed and Joss laughed too.

'It's so good to see you Polly,' he said.

'You too, Joss. And Edwin will be sorry he wasn't here. Would you like some tea?' she asked, 'or something stronger?'

'As it's the Festive Season . . . ' Joss started to say.

'Sherry, whisky, port, Madeira?'

'Sherry will be fine.'

Polly's heightened awareness in his presence caused her to tingle at the slight brush of Joss's fingers against her hand as she passed him the sherry glass. The resultant tingling made her heartbeats quicken and she could not meet Joss's gaze.

'How was your father over the Christmas?' she asked, her eyes averted.

'He seemed to enjoy it. Didn't join in the conversation as much as he once did, but he seemed happy to be with us and to just sit and watch all that went on and, of course, to have time with Theodore.' Joss paused, then added, 'But I don't think he really feels "at home" at the Manor, nor mother for that matter. But they were both glad they were able to come.'

They sat and chatted, mostly now about Theodore and Joss's parents as they sipped the sherry. Neither seemed keen to talk about Clementine, but Joss did mention Rupert stayed at Withiel Cottage where Clementine's parents now lived, and they all spent Christmas Day together at the Manor.

These subjects exhausted, Joss said it was time to go, and Polly led the way to the front door with Joss close behind her. Between the staircase and the front door Joss's head brushed against something and he and Polly both looked up. It was a bunch of mistletoe which Edwin had hung there, as was customary in most households at Christmas. It remained unnoticed when Joss came into the house and Polly had forgotten it was there. They just had to kiss, in fact, not to do so would have been unmannerly.

Silently and with gentle firmness Joss pulled Polly to him and his warm lips descended upon hers . . . softly . . . smoothly, as a tender caress; then with gradually increasing pressure Joss pulled her slender body close to his. Slow delicious seconds passed. Did they become minutes? Then, with growing urgency, the kiss took on a deeper intensity. Polly knew this was too much but she was powerless to bring it to an end, for she wanted to stay locked in his arms. Oh Joss, my Joss, my love . . . The words were in her head, unspoken.

Suddenly, almost roughly, Joss released her and his lips were removed from hers. She stumbled, slightly intoxicated, with delicious sensations which raced through her body. Joss put out a hand to steady her.

'Polly . . . I'm sorry . . . ' he was gazing earnestly down into Polly's eyes. 'I didn't mean to . . . oh Polly, I am so sorry.'

As he finished the words he reached for the front door and opened it.

'Good-bye, Polly,' he said, and without looking round closed the door and was gone from Polly's sight.

Chapter Twenty-two

Polly and Lottie were amazed to discover that business did not slacken in the way they expected when Christmas was over. Clients were mainly those at the upper end of the market. At the lower end people were wondering if they could afford to buy anything at all, and those in between including the wives of owners of small shops, some councillors wives, etc., were only looking for January bargains. The ladies who came into the shop were mostly interested in evening wear and, of course, the New Year was a party season. Polly's portfolio was much in demand and she kept a record of each dress ordered to be made and of how variations in the basic style were achieved, so that no two were identical. Lottie was thankful for May's expertise in appliqué work. Lottie could do it equally well but whereas Lottie found the work slow and tedious May enjoyed this . . . to her it was an art form. However, the clients lessened by the third week in January.

'I expect February will be quiet and we can all take things a bit easier and dispense with Ethel's services for a time,' Polly said.

'Oh no we can't,' Lottie answered. 'As soon as the orders are completed we must get started on the Easter stock, and we'll need a portfolio of Easter outfits, don't forget.'

'Sorry Lottie. I wasn't thinking,' said Polly ruefully.

Absolutely everyone but the very poorest had a new outfit for Easter, including children. It was the done thing.

It was true Polly wasn't thinking about business. As so often in slack moments, she was thinking of Joss, picturing his face, his velvet-brown eyes gazing down into hers, remembering his smile, his handsome profile when she stole glances at him the time he drove her in the motor along Falmouth seafront, the dark single-breasted high buttoned jacket which showed to advantage his broad chest and shoulders, the way he sometimes said her name. She wondered what he was doing, did he often kiss Clementine the way he kissed her beneath the mistletoe? Did his hands often caress Clementine? What would it be like if those masculine yet lovely hands caressed her? If, as he kissed her, one hand rested on her slender white throat, then slid slowly over her filmy sundown-coloured dress along to her shoulder, then down to where . . . shut up, Polly! You mustn't, it's wrong. Though she was now alone in the showroom she blushed at her own thoughts.

Polly's current portfolio was in the showroom but fashion news and pictures of the latest styles and trends along with sheets of paper with ideas for new outfits were in the kitchen where Polly would sit and study or draw when there were no clients. With the door ajar she could easily hear when someone entered the showroom and the crinoline-lady bell was on the counter for anyone to summon assistance. No one had time to be idle.

A few days later Lottie arrived at 'The Lady' a little late. A client was waiting to see her for a fitting, but as she had not previously made an appointment she could not, and for that matter did not, complain.

On finding the lady sitting drinking a cup of tea which Polly had made for her whilst she awaited Lottie's arrival, Lottie became somewhat flustered, and apologised profusely. The lady assured her she was quite glad she had to wait . . . she really welcomed the hot drink.

After the client had left Lottie came downstairs from the fitting room and asked Polly to come into the kitchen with her, and the kettle was again put on the stove to make tea.

'What's wrong?' Polly asked

'Couldn't get to sleep for ages and then I slept late,' Lottie said.

'Any particular reason?'

'Yes, I went round to May Bascombe's last evening and between us we finished the outfit for Mrs Chard to wear to her nephew's wedding.'

'Problems?' Polly asked.

'Oh no. It's all finished and ready, and looking very nice,' Lottie said. 'But when I got home George said Joss had called

h

round . . . '

'Yes.' Polly said, her heart suddenly thudding.

'He wasn't drunk . . . nothing like that . . . but George said it was obvious he'd had a few drinks, and he told George how he'd been to Truro and caught Clementine and that Customs Officer, you know, Charles Copeland, redhanded if that can describe it, together in a hotel room!'

'Oh, no,' Polly said, astonished. 'Was this recently?'

'Apparently not. It was sometime before Christmas. George said he thinks he only opened his heart and told him about it because he had been drinking.'

'I suppose he doesn't have anyone but you two to confide in. He wouldn't upset his mother and father by telling them,' Polly said.

'No, he wouldn't do that,' Lottie agreed, 'and he told George not to tell me, but he accidentally let the cat out of the bag with one odd-sounding remark and I pestered him until he told me. I know it's safe with you. Apparently he won't allow her the use of the motor any more, and he now has a separate room.'

'Poor Joss,' Polly was genuinely sorry. 'I wonder if it was before or after I saw them together when I went out to buy that bell?'

Lottie tried to work it out. 'I think it was before you saw them, because I'm pretty sure George said it happened just before we had the Preview . . . prior to opening.'

'That might account for the foul mood she was in,' Polly said.

Lottie's eyes widened. 'You're right, and that means the brazen hussy's still seeing him! Come to think of it,' Lottie went on, 'mother did mention to me that Clementine was particularly pleasant and anxious to please when they were there at Christmas . . . gracious was how mother described her. And she was agreeable to Joss too, but apparently he took no notice and was brusque at times.'

'That's not like him,' Polly said. 'You couldn't find a more good-natured person than Joss. And if his temper is a little quick on occasions, he never bears a grudge. It's up and over with Joss.'

Polly was conscious of the deepening flush on her face as she praised Lottie's brother.

'I know,' Lottie agreed. Thankfully she appeared not to notice. 'It would take a very strong reason indeed to make Joss turn

170

against anyone. But if he ever did . . . ' Lottie sucked in a long breath. 'Polly, what can I do?' she beseeched.

'I don't know, Lottie,' Polly said, her heart heavy with sympathy for Joss and Lottie and their parents. 'You have to keep quiet about it, it would only make Joss more miserable and more angry if you don't.'

'I know,' Lottie said, and took a couple of Aspros from the cupboard to swallow with the tea Polly had poured.

'What did George have to say about it?' Polly asked.

'Only that he was sorry for Joss. He said it would serve Clementine right if Joss divorced her!'

'Divorce! That's unthinkable. It would break your parent's hearts!' was Polly's reaction.

'I know,' Lottie agreed. 'Everyone would say the bed you make is the bed you have to lie on. I felt there was something wrong, the last time he came to see us.'

There was a tinkle from someone shaking the crinoline-lady bell, and Polly hastened into the showroom. Lottie made her way up the stairs into the workroom.

Polly assumed she could, in confidence, tell Edwin.

'Somehow I'm shocked,' he said. 'And somehow I'm not.'

'I think that's how both Lottie and I feel,' Polly agreed.

By the end of February clients, including several who ordered evening gowns for the New Year Parties, came to choose new Easter outfits, either from stock or made-to-measure from styles in Polly's portfolio and some from patterns which they themselves had acquired. Lottie's fitting's diary was filling up. Many seemed to be aware there would be plenty of orders and did not wish to be at the end of the queue. These were executed in date sequence except for emergency outfits, like funeral-wear.

It became clear to Lottie, Polly and May Bascombe that Ethel Angove was likely to become a permanent member of staff, as May had now become. Madam Delia was also kept comfortably busy, and for Easter was likely to be more so. She followed closely the latest trends in ladies' headgear.

The stock of bolts of materials was also enlarged and Jack was asked to erect more shelving in what had been considered a most spacious work-room, to accommodate the new impressive stock of materials, short sample lengths being kept in one of the showrooms.

There was no longer time for Polly to entertain thoughts of helping with stitching. Keeping an eye on two showrooms, dealing with clients except when they required Lottie's service for measuring and fitting, making portfolios and keeping records both of stocks, purchases, sundry expenses, wages, including an equal wage paid weekly to Polly and Lottie along with the two seamstresses and somewhat irregular payments to the milliner, and a record of sales and income, filled Polly's working day. Lottie, on the other hand, kept a record of each client who had made-to-measure garments and of clients' measurements, and fittings at various stages were almost always essential. Both she and Lottie thoroughly enjoyed and took pride in the business side of life.

Apart from Lottie's concern about members of her family, and Polly's concern that she and Edwin were childless and her secret and abiding love for Joss, everything in both their worlds was blooming as far as the very important business was concerned. They both had such dreams about setting up a ladies' top-quality fashion shop; they both gave it so much thought and worked so hard, and had made the comparatively small shop more elegant and luxurious than anything they had seen before. Now 'The Lady' was open and flourishing. Already in a few short weeks they had 'regulars' . . . clients who were sufficiently pleased with their purchases to come back for more. The business was already thriving, and the future was rosy. Their dream had come true.

After only three months, discounting the money laid out to acquire and set up 'The Lady' they not only 'broke even' but had made a substantial profit. In one section of Polly's records this was offset against the cost of buying and setting up the premises. This showed that if they had borrowed all the money involved in this outlay they would have been able to pay back three months' instalments on a twenty years loan including interest with wages and running expenses already paid, and still have a fair sum of money left over.

Polly discussed this with Edwin and showed him the books. He was impressed and genuinely proud of his astute wife. He asked if he could show the books to his father, who, although he had not said in so many words, disapproved of Edwin allowing his wife to work and to set up in business. But George Pendleton had to admit he was impressed.

Weeks became months and at the end of the first year Polly and Lottie were in the fortunate position of being able to each take £100 out of net profit which they could set against their original investments in the venture. The remaining profit was retained for ploughing back into the business, running expenses, etc. The situation was healthy and promising.

One year drifted into two. The business continued to make steady and sustained progress and Ethel Angove had also become permanently engaged. The reputation of 'The Lady' was spreading, with clients coming from as far away as Penzance.

Twice a year Polly and Lottie went together to Plymouth to keep abreast of what the Fashion Houses there had to offer. This was always on a Monday, when clients were usually fewer, and Madam Delia obliged by being 'on duty' in the showroom. hobble skirts had been in vogue and some ladies wore fetters on the lower parts of their legs to keep their steps very short in the narrow restricting skirts. Some skirts, to make walking easier, had slits. This was a somewhat daring deviation from what was customary. Some ladies, of course, refused to wear this style of skirt. Mostly they were in the older age group. 'The Lady' ensured clients were able to obtain whichever style they preferred.

Polly and Edwin rarely saw Joss, and on those occasions when they did see him the meeting was brief. Some of the spontaneity had gone from his smile, and Polly longed to throw her arms about him and hold him close. Someone heard a rumour that Joss was drinking too heavily.

It was when Theodore was approaching his eleventh birthday that old John Renfree died. He had not been particularly unwell, or so it seemed; he just suddenly collapsed with a heart attack and died shortly after without regaining consciousness.

Joss and his mother were with him at the time, and Joss was thankful for that. After taking Theodore to school, he now frequently went straight to the cottage where his mother continued to live, not returning to Manor Withiel until he called at Cresby to drive Theodore home after school. Lately he did not

173

always do that. The boy was old enough to make his own way home, and these days what Joss said 'went'. Humouring Clementine was something with which he no longer bothered himself.

Nell Pascoe, Polly's mother, also spent most of her spare time with Emily, cooking meals, making tea for the numerous visitors who called to express their sympathy, and often just to be with her old friend in her sadness.

Joss was so thankful he had returned from America when he did. Although he could never replace his father . . . no one could . . . his mother saw him as a replica of John Renfree. And Nell Pascoe was a great comfort, just as Emily had been when Daniel Pascoe died and left Nell with two children to rear.

Madam Delia was called upon to 'stand in' so that Polly, accompanied by Edwin, could attend the funeral. Both Lottie's sons Eric and Oliver attended the funeral, staying two nights with their parents. Edwin allowed more than half his workforce time off also to go to the funeral and pay their last respects to an old work-mate. Both Clementine and Theodore were present and seemed appropriately subdued. Clementine was not effusive with Lottie or Polly but at least they were polite to one another and Clementine expressed her sympathy to Lottie, which Lottie politely accepted.

Lottie took a week off work to be with her mother and Joss. But before the week ended her mother was insisting there was no need for Lottie to be away from work and from George and Nora. Joss was often with his mother and her dear friend, Nell Pascoe, was next door. She would be all right.

174

Chapter Twenty-three

A year of successful business passed with little change taking place. 'The Lady' was prospering, with a growing clientele. May Bascombe and Ethel Angove worked almost as hard as Lottie and Polly and they too felt a sense of pride and accomplishment in the success of the business. They enjoyed the work and the interest, and their families were benefiting markedly from the extra cash.

Nora had begun to take more interest in 'The Lady', and to become conscious of her mother's prowess in the fashion trade. At home Lottie showed her how to use the sewing machine and was surprised to find how quickly her daughter became adept at using it.

'I'd like to help in the workroom when I'm a bit bigger,' Nora told her mother. 'And in the shop,' she added.

'So you shall, my love, if you still want to,' Lottie answered.

'Oh, I shall want to; I know I shall,' Nora said emphatically.

Lottie smiled with satisfaction.

Visits from Joss were rare and contact with Clementine even rarer. It was one Saturday evening, about eight o'clock, that there was a rap on the door of Villa Gwidden. Polly was in the kitchen, her hands messy with rubbing lard and butter into flour to make pastry in advance for a pie she intended to make next day.

'Could you see who it is, Edwin?' she called from the kitchen.

'I'm on my way,' came the reply.

She heard the distant tones of a male voice. Her heartbeats quickened. Though indistinct, it sounded like Joss's voice. Edwin came almost crashing into the kitchen, one arm through his overcoat sleeve.

'I've got to go at once, Polly! Father's been taken ill! Someone has dashed from Long Downs to Emily's to see if Joss was there,

175

to ask him to drive here for me.'

'Shall I come too?' Polly asked.

'No. You stay here. Joss will return and let you know more as soon as I know myself. Bye love,' he said, giving Polly a quick peck on the cheek before dashing out.

Polly, scraping the pastry mixture from her fingers, tried to hurry to the front door, but too late, the two had left and she heard the motor being driven away. By now Joss had acquired a four cylinder thirty horse power Rolls Royce, already noted for its silent running and beautifully upholstered bodywork by the famous Barker Coachbuilders.

Polly waited anxiously, but it was over an hour before Joss returned. On hearing the sound of the motor stop outside the Villa she went to the door to let Joss in.

'Polly,' he said, his face sombre. 'I'd better not stay, it's getting late.'

'It's only half past eight,' Polly said. 'And we can't talk out here on the doorstep. Come on in, I want to know what's happening.' She led the way into the sitting-room where a fire burned in the grate.

'Phew, it's hot in here,' Joss said, hat in hand.

'Take your coat off,' Polly advised. 'Just drop it there on a chair.' She indicated a rarely sat in chair in the corner.

Joss did so, and sat sideways to both the fire and to the sofa, where Polly sat facing the fire.

'How is Edwin's father?' she asked.

'Pretty ill. He's surrounded with Nelson's Inhalers, a copper bronchitis kettle, bottles, jars, medicine glasses and invalid feeding cups. The doctor was there and I don't think Edwin will return.'

'As bad as that?' Polly said, gravely.

'It looks that way,' Joss said, leaning forward, elbows on knees. 'But you can never tell. While there's life there's hope.'

'Yes,' Polly agreed. 'I think Edwin's grandfather had a bad heart for many years, but he lived to a ripe old age.'

Joss tilted his head sideways, looking into Polly's face as he spoke. He nodded as she finished speaking, gazing into her eyes, causing her heart to pound.

'And how are *you*, Polly?' he asked.

Again Polly was thankful for the shop . . . something different, and an easy topic to talk about.

'Lottie and I are both very busy, but we enjoy it,' she said and, warming to the subject so important to her, chatted on at some length.

'I'm sure you must have heard all this before from Lottie,' she said, after prattling on so long and suddenly aware that her enthusiasm was running away with her. Joss was gazing intently into her face. Her heartbeats quickened and she lowered her eyes.

'It's interesting hearing it from your viewpoint,' he said, with a little smile which pulled at Polly's heartstrings.

'And how are you Joss?' she said without looking at him, no longer able to bear his steady gaze, afraid her eyes would betray her feelings, her desires.

'You probably know Clementine and I are not on good terms?' she heard him say.

'Yes . . . I did hear,' Polly said, her eyes still averted.

'In fact, we no longer live as man and wife,' he added.

'Joss . . . I'm so sorry,' she again raised her eyes to his face. There was a pause, their faces close.

'You're very happy with Edwin, aren't you Polly?' Joss said.

'Yes, I am. I love Edwin,' Polly said, her voice soft.

'Lucky man,' Joss commented, a hint of wistfulness in his voice. For a brief few moments there was silence. Joss rose to his feet and moved to where his coat lay.

'But I'm not in love with him,' Polly suddenly blurted out. 'Joss . . . I've always been in love with you . . . Oh Joss . . . I love you so much!'

Joss, who was bending to take his coat, swivelled around, startled. With an anguished expression she looked up into his dark brown eyes. His face was serious, unsmiling. The coat fell from his hand, and instantly his arms were about her as he smothered her face with kisses. Polly flung her arms about his neck, her fingers stretching up the back of his head, into the locks of black hair sprigged with grey, holding him close. 'Polly . . . my little one . . . my Polly,' he murmured between kisses. Joss was now kissing her mouth while her fingers were caressing his cheek. His hand reached for her throat as he once had done in her fantasy, and after a while his hand moved gradually towards her arm, then slowly, slowly, so slowly downwards until it reached her breast, which he cradled in the palm of his hand, and they remained for

177

long silent minutes, his mouth clamping hers. She felt his arousal hard against her.

'Polly . . . dearest Polly, I must go; I don't think I can control myself much longer,' he whispered against her ear.

Suddenly Polly knew what she must do. She wanted it, Joss wanted it, her Joss, her own Joss. She couldn't deny him; she didn't want to deny him; she wanted to give him love, to give him joy, and she would. Pushing him gently away, she reached for his hand, saying, 'Come upstairs with me, Joss,' hearing while she did so Joss's sharp intake of breath.

Sleep came easily to Polly after her rapturous oneness with Joss, the man who was the one real love of her life for as long as she could remember and for as long as life might last, Joss was her love, her man. And they had yielded, they had stolen one hour out of that lifetime, to experience the wonder that should have been theirs all along.

But though sleep came easily it did not last. In the small hours Polly awoke with the weight of guilt heavy upon her. She had betrayed Edwin, the kind loving man she married after years of coming to terms with the fact that Joss could never be hers. To Joss she had been as a little sister . . . much loved but nevertheless a little sister, and that was not the same. But for Joss, how could it have been otherwise? How could it have been more? When she was a child, not yet even adolescent, and he was a handsome young male with all the stirrings, the desires, and thoughts and instincts natural to a young man. And along came Clementine, smart, beautifully dressed, an entertaining and witty conversationalist whose eye-catching good looks with her challenging blue eyes, haughty yet inviting smile which he must have found so intriguing, so fascinating. And she must have found him different. No namby-pamby young blade from a wealthy family with all his needs catered for and attended to, but a handsome, rugged country boy who by a fluke, had been well schooled and who had prospects. Capturing and enslaving him would have been both a challenge and an amusement Clementine would have found hard to resist. Where men were concerned she had the instincts of a big-game hunter. And Joss, young, simple in the ways of the world, inexperienced and transparently honest would

178

not have been too difficult a target. The scene was set for disaster, and Joss's mother, Emily, had sensed it all along.

And now that disaster was threatening Polly too. Her thoughts were a turmoil of mixed emotions. For the first time she was glad she was alone that night. To have Edwin with her would have paralysed her with guilt. She had been unfaithful to him, she would never be able to forgive herself for that, and at such a time, while Edwin's father lay on his sick-bed, possibly dying, possibly dead.

But Joss loved her, Polly. He had long since come to his senses where Clementine was concerned. As a young man he had made a mistake and was now the proverbial sadder, wiser man.

As soon as his eyes beheld Polly *the woman* he knew as surely as he knew night must follow day, that she was *his* woman, his love, his other half and should have been his partner through life. And last night Joss had made love to her, was one with her, reached indescribable heights with her. They had no lawful right to make love, no moral right. But each knew in their own heart that they belonged to one another, they were the two sides of the same coin, there were invisible chains which bound them one to the other. These chains had always been there, they always would be. Polly was full of guilt and remorse for her unfaithfulness to Edwin, a selfless, loving husband. Yet at the same time, having her beloved Joss make love to her was a fulfilment she could never regret. Her head seemed to be spinning and she was glad to be alone with her violently conflicting emotions. Her love for Joss and what took place last night, and her loyalty, and her different love and deep respect for Edwin, left her in a delirium of combined ecstasy and hell.

At six o'clock she got up from bed to make a cup of well-sweetened tea to steady herself. As she sipped it she tried to gather her thoughts before Edwin returned. For the first time she dreaded Edwin's key in the lock, his kiss of greeting. She must get her priorities in order. She had wronged Edwin and now she wanted what was best for him. Think in an orderly way, Polly, she silently instructed herself.

She loved Joss and wanted to be with him always. *But* . . . He was married, unhappily, but married nevertheless, *and* he had a child. She was married, and to a good, kind husband whom she genuinely loved.

179

In these circumstances it was not possible for her and Joss to have any kind of deep relationship. And neither would want a furtive, deceptive 'hole-in-the-corner' affair.

Also, her vow never to hurt Edwin was as important as ever. No matter what pain it caused her, she did not want dear, loyal, blameless Edwin to be hurt.

But she had been unfaithful to Edwin. To deceive him in this would make her behaviour even more derisory. Yet to tell him would break his heart.

Was that fair? It would ease *her* conscience, but leave *Edwin* in permanent torment. Should she, therefore, keep her guilty secret to herself? She must keep away from temptation, from Joss, dear, dear Joss, her one and only all-time love. He was so near, yet must remain out of sight and out of reach. What a punishment! What a price to pay! She had tasted ecstasy, but now it was to be withdrawn, like a bowl of water just out of reach of a shackled prisoner dying of thirst.

I am not strong enough, she told herself. I can't give Joss up! You have no choice, came the voice of reason from some place inside her head. And Polly knew this was true. Nothing must change, no cleansing confessions. She must bear her own burdens, and her own hopeless yearnings and her own guilt. She and Joss, dear Joss, could never be together in this life. Perhaps there was a place in another world, on another plane, where they could be one together. But in this world they must go their ways separately, must learn to live on memories . . . memories of that one time when their love was consummated and they were one. At least no one could ever now take that away from either of them.

At around 11.30 a.m. Edwin arrived home in a wagonette driven by Will Triggs a neighbour. Polly, by now dressed, hurried to greet him, her face anxious. Edwin immediately put his arms about her and kissed her.

'It's all right,' he whispered, with a sigh of relief. 'He's over the worst.'

'Come and sit down,' Polly took his hand and led him to the sitting-room. 'I'll make you a cup of coffee and you can tell me about it.'

A few minutes later, with coffee and biscuits on a small table beside them, Edwin told Polly that after what he described as a

180

'rough' night, his father improved and at about 6 a.m. fell into a restful sleep. He was still sleeping peacefully when Edwin left, and Cordelia, his mother, and his sister Agnes had both gone to bed. The doctor had visited him but did not disturb his sleep, saying the worst was past and he now needed rest.

'And you must do the same, and get to bed,' Polly said.

'I'm certainly ready for it,' Edwin told her.

'Would you like some breakfast first?' Polly asked.

'I've had some . . . porridge and a boiled egg,' he replied.

They sat talking for a few minutes longer, then Edwin made his way upstairs to their bedroom and was asleep almost as soon as he got into bed.

That evening both Polly and Edwin went to his parents' home, and while they were there Edwin's father awoke and was able to take some strengthening beef-tea. Agnes and Caleb were also present and Agnes intended to stay with her parents for the coming week.

Every day George Pendleton seemed to improve, and by the end of the week everybody in the Pendleton family had relaxed, no longer living on a knife-edge . . . all was now back to normal; Agnes was returning home and back to the usual routine of life, that weekend.

On the following Saturday afternoon Edwin visited his parents and returned in time for his meal with Polly and told her that his father was as jovial as he had ever been. The doctor had advised he be fed poached fish or a little chicken for the first few days after his recovery, then told Cordelia to let him have a little of whatever he fancied. He fancied roast-beef and was looking forward to his Sunday roast the following weekend.

When Polly and Edwin went to bed on Saturday night, Edwin appeared not in the least tired or ready for sleep. Their love-making had been reduced to a once-a-week Saturday night routine. A week of anxiety about his father and mother had weighed in varying degrees on Edwin's mind. But his father had survived and tonight Edwin, now free from worry, had only one thought on his mind.

The brief kissing and caressing with which Edwin routinely preceded copulation was prolonged, heightening his desire. Polly, with guilt weighing heavily upon her, tried to feign enthusiasm. As Edwin's extended member entered her, she wondered just how

Edwin would react if he knew the last person to make that entry was not himself, but Joss. All Polly could do was imagine the scene. Would there be blows? If he struck Joss, Joss would just stand and let him; though he had the strength and ability to swiftly floor Edwin, he would just let his arms hang limply at his sides and not even try to fend him off. Would Edwin strike her? No, she knew he would not. He would just turn, hurt stricken eyes upon her, staring in disbelief.

But Edwin was blissfully unaware that with Polly anything was amiss. Groans and gasps of ecstasy escaped him. He was really making up for last weekend's lost time, Polly thought. Having climaxed, Edwin fell exhausted, sated and deliciously relaxed beside her.

'Polly, that was lovely,' he murmured, then made the supreme effort to rise on his elbow sufficiently to briefly kiss her before falling back, asleep seemingly before his head even reached the pillow.

Edwin slept long and soundly. Polly, who took hours to get to sleep, also awoke late. They breakfasted around coffee-time and concluded they were too late to attend the church service. They had barely finished when there was a loud rapping at the door. Edwin went to open it. There stood the solemn-faced neighbour who had brought Edwin home with his pony and wagonette the previous week.

'Why Will, come on in,' Polly heard Edwin say.

With a sudden qualm she hastened to hear what news Will Triggs had brought. The three just stood inside the sitting-room. Will rotated the brim of his hat which he held in both hands in front of him. He seemed unable to find the words. 'Er . . . er . . . sit down both of you,' he stammered.

Polly lowered herself into a chair, but Edwin remained standing, his eyes fixed on Will's solemn, ruddy face. They waited.

'Is it father? Out with it, Will,' Edwin demanded, unable to bear the suspense.

'Your father's dead, Edwin . . . died in his sleep,' Will said.

Chapter Twenty-four

Joss returned in a daze to Manor Withiel after his call on Polly at Villa Gwidden. He felt tremendously guilty that he had taken advantage of Polly, but at the same time exhilarated that Polly loved him . . . she loved him as much as he loved her. Actually offering herself to him was the ultimate proof, if proof were needed which it was not, for Polly was a moral person, on top of which she was a married woman with a thoroughly respectable husband for whom she had great affection. But Joss always knew that to Polly he was a special person, as she was to him; long before reaching the age when it was in the natural order of things to start falling in love.

Joss felt profoundly for the anguish Polly must, he was sure, be now enduring at betraying Edwin. In this Joss shared in her suffering. Dear Polly must be in torment, and because of him. If only he could bear this burden for her . . . instead of her.

On the other hand, where Clementine was concerned he felt no such qualms. The vows he had made on their wedding day he had every intention of keeping. But those vows applied to them both. When he first discovered her infidelity, it was with a handsome and apparently wealthy businessman of dubious repute and Italian origins. This was in the United States. He tried to make allowances. The man had Italian good looks and a fine physique. His wife had been bowled over, lost her head, and she had had too much to drink. She didn't know what she was doing. He would be generous. What else could he do? His suspicions had been aroused on other occasions but he had told himself Clementine wouldn't behave like that . . . no respectable woman, whether married or single, would. But he was wrong, he had been naïve, a simple country lad. By this time he was no longer in love with

Clementine. That had been eroded long since, and he soon realised that the boyish infatuation he had for Clementine was not love.

When Joss met her Clementine had been full of wiles and girlish charms. He must have been flattered by her attention. Almost all the chaps at the School of Mines were fawning over her, vying for her attention. But Joss did not. He was the one from a working-class background. He didn't stand a chance and didn't want to anyway. He hadn't realised his very reticence would have been a challenge to Clementine's predatory instincts, nor did he realise he was the handsomest young man amongst them. For Clementine his indifference to her and his good-looks were a combination she found impossible to resist. It was the perfect challenge and she had to test her mettle.

Her friends watched with girlish giggles and squawks, her overtures to Joss at the Party at Camborne. He could not know that his certain awkwardness and slight ill-ease at the grand party, wearing a suit a mite too small which he borrowed from a mining student friend, and his limited knowledge of dancing, were short-comings most of the giggly young ladies present would have been delighted to assist him remedy. And Clementine had made up her mind to do just that. Joss learned fast, for he was not unduly shy and his sense of humour soon came bubbling to the surface. He found it was fun, and they laughed together. He had no thought of it going further, but Clementine amused herself and entertained him all evening, the pretext for her insistence being that she would not leave him alone until she made sure he had mastered all the dance steps. This was a very full evening's work.

When the last dance ended and the party broke up, Joss thanked her for her help and patience with a clumsy oaf.

Clementine, still standing close after the dance had smiled up at him, her head tilted back to look into his face.

'I think I am entitled to a reward,' she said, still smiling. Joss was at a loss. What did she mean? What reward had he to give her? With ease she read his thoughts, stretched her head up and closed her eyes confidently awaiting his kiss.

Joss hesitated a second, then kissed her waiting lips. Instantly her arms slid around his neck, holding him fast and prolonging the reward. This behaviour was new territory to Joss. He could hear giggles from onlooking young ladies and cheers from fellow students. Gently but firmly he pulled her arms downwards and they bid each other goodnight, again with Joss's thanks for the dancing lessons.

But on the way back to the friend's home in Camborne, where he was staying the night, Joss's mind dwelt on the kiss. He knew nothing of that type of long-lasting kiss, and he liked it, it aroused certain feelings deep inside him. Although it wasn't proper, at least, Joss didn't think it was, he'd like to do it again. But that was hardly likely, he didn't expect to see the young lady again.

But a week later Joss received an invitation to attend a party at Manor Withiel, along with all the other young men who were fellow-students in his group at Camborne School of Mines. It was then Clementine started to get her tentacles stealthily around Joss, with wiles and sweet charms which prevented him from discovering what type of person, unfamiliar in his limited experience of women, this outwardly entrancing young lady really was.

Joss's thoughts again turned to Polly, and to Edwin. How could he have taken another man's wife, and Edwin's of all people? He was certain Edwin had never done an immoral act of any sort in his whole life. Yet how could he regret making love with Polly, the real and only genuine love of his life, when she felt exactly the same way about him, making it clear she wanted to give herself to him.

One thing was certain, he and Polly must avoid seeing one another in future; the strain would be too much. Holding Polly in his arms, kissing her, making such exquisite love to her not only fed his need, it increased it to an almost unbearable degree. To see her in just the casual and relaxed way old friends do would be more than he could endure. He knew Polly's feelings would be the same. Perhaps it would be better if he went away? But he had bought Manor Withiel, and his mother needed him. After his father's death he couldn't leave her.

Clementine declined to go to the funeral, saying she had no appropriate sombre clothes and did not wish to buy any.

Joss wrote a letter of sympathy to Cordelia and the family, saying that he, with his mother would be attending the Church Service but that he would not be able to come to the house afterwards with family and friends. He had to meet Theodore at

Cresby Boys' School, etc.

Joss could tell by his mother's expression that she was a little surprised at this but the Pendleton family would have too many more pressing things on their minds to wonder at Joss's need to now collect his growing son from school.

Six of the older men employed at the quarries, who had worked under George Pendleton bore his coffin into the Church, followed by Cordelia and her family. Joss was surprised at how pale Polly looked. Twice his heart thumped violently, and he held his breath as he saw her walk up the aisle behind the coffin with Edwin and the other family mourners. Perhaps it was the black clothes in which she was dressed. But no, he was sure it was not. He lowered his head. Oh, Lord, please let her be all right, he silently entreated.

As he expected, the service was touching, and the hymn-singing beautiful and reverent. Cordelia, although frail-looking, was marvellously composed throughout. After the burial under one of the few trees in the open, wind-blown cemetery which surrounded the church, Joss and his mother departed. After leaving his mother at the cottage Joss headed for Cresby Boys' School.

As the few day-boys came running out from the side door near to the day-boys' cloakroom, Theodore was the only one dawdling, as though reluctant to see his father.

'The Head wants to see you,' the one other day-boy in Theodore's age group said to Joss.

A swift glance told Joss that Theodore had been in a fight, one darkening eye was swollen and there were signs of a bloodied nose.

'How did you get in this state?' he asked his son.

The other boy answered for him. 'He shut Harvey Prescott's younger brother in the gardener's shed, and everybody was looking for him last evening, and . . . '

'Shut up,' Theodore interrupted, the words half spoken, half sobbed.

The boy gleefully enlarged, '. . . and Timothy's big brother, Harvey, laid in wait when he arrived this morning and beat him up!'

Theodore glared at the boy. 'I said shut up!'

The boy did not shut up, ' . . . and everyone said serve him

186

right,' the boy smirked. 'Good-bye, Mr Renfree, good-bye Theo.' He ran off towards the other departing boys shouting, 'Wait for me.'

Theodore was reluctant to accompany his father to the Headmaster's study but had no choice.

'Come in,' came the reply in response to Joss's rap on the study door.

'Ah, Mr Renfree.' The Headmaster, Mr Anderson, rose and came forward to shake Joss's hand. 'I was expecting you . . . and Theodore here.' He shot a brief, unsmiling glance in Theodore's direction.

'Good afternoon, Headmaster,' Joss said. 'You know why I'm here'.

'Yes, you want to know how young Theodore came to be in this state.'

'I've already received a version from one of the boys,' Joss replied.

A fleeting I might have known smile crossed the Headmaster's face. 'I will enlarge,' he said. 'Timothy Prescott started at Cresby as a boarder at the beginning of this term. He is a rather timid boy who is taking a while to adjust to living away from his home and parents. It seems that Theodore, who has often been somewhat antagonistic towards Harvey Prescott, Timothy's brother . . . you might remember a previous minor incident when he was in Mr Christopher's form.'

Joss nodded.

'Theodore,' Mr Anderson went on, 'pretended to befriend young Timothy during break-time yesterday and said he would show him a puppy in the gardener's shed. The shed is on the perimeter of the grounds and is surrounded by shrubs, etc. There was no puppy. I'm afraid it was a ruse Theodore thought up to get young Timothy into the shed to see the non-existent animal, then locked the door on him. Young Prescott's absence became apparent at meal-time. Someone was sent to see whether he was in the dormitory or other likely places, and when he was not found a search was immediately started.'

'Is all this correct, Theodore?' Joss interrupted and turned his attention to his son, who stood looking down at the floor. Theodore did not reply. Grimly Joss turned to Mr Anderson. 'I have no doubt all was as you said, Headmaster.'

187

'I'm afraid Harvey Prescott seemed to have made up his mind to punish your son for what he did to his smaller brother, and for this I can assure you he has been punished and severely reprimanded.'

'You needn't be concerned on account of that, Headmaster,' Joss said. 'If Harvey hadn't done it I'd have thrashed him myself!'

Joss noted the upward curl of the Head's mouth who, with a flicker of a smile replied, 'That is also why we spared him a caning, Mr Renfree. But he will be given three weeks extra homework in mathematics, which is his weak subject. Prescott is here waiting in the adjoining room.'

The Headmaster opened a door and called for Prescott to enter. Again he addressed Joss. 'I have told Prescott that his brother received an apology from Renfree earlier today and he is therefore willing to make an apology to your son . . . Go ahead, Prescott.'

'I'm sorry for what I did, Renfree,' the solemn-faced boy said.

'That's all right,' the equally solemn-faced Theodore replied.

'Shake hands,' the Headmaster prompted. The two boys shook hands.

'You may leave, Prescott,' the Headmaster said.

As he moved to go Joss thrust out his hand. 'Shake,' he said. Harvey Prescott put his hand into Joss's large one, and glanced up at Joss, his deep blue eyes engaging Joss's gaze as he did so and, seeing his smile, the taut muscles of the boy's face relaxed into a returning smile, then he left. Joss noted the Headmaster's expression of satisfaction.

'You may wait outside, Renfree,' he commanded.

'Thank you, Sir.' Theodore instantly strode to the door and left the room with a scowl on his face which only Joss could see.

'This all seems like a storm in a teacup, Mr Renfree,' the Headmaster said when Theodore had shut the door. 'But young Timothy Prescott was extremely distressed. It seems he has a phobia about spiders, and to be shut in a dark shed, where undoubtedly these creatures are likely to be, terrified him. He had previously complained of feeling unwell, and his teacher assumed he had gone to see Matron. In the first few weeks the more sensitive ones, who are homesick, sometimes complain of feeling unwell until they have adjusted to their new surroundings and new friends.'

'The thing I don't like,' Joss admitted, 'is that Theodore picked on a much smaller, vulnerable boy.'

'Yes,' agreed Mr Anderson. 'Prescott was kept in the sick-room until mid-morning, but he came to my study this afternoon, when your son was obliged to apologise to him.'

'I'm glad about that,' Joss said. 'And I can only apologise too . . . I am sorry and disappointed about his behaviour. Boys have scraps, but you don't pick on younger ones,' he added, speaking more to himself than the Headmaster. 'Please be in touch if you have any more trouble with him,' Joss said.

'I will,' came the reply.

The two shook hands and Joss departed. He and Theodore left the school building in silence. Once outside, Joss, with a grim expression, spoke to Theodore. 'Don't you ever behave like that again!'

The scowl on Theodore's face deepened. There was a developing side to his son which Joss definitely disliked.

Chapter Twenty-five

'You look pale,' Lottie said.

Polly pretended to be absorbed in her Accounts Books.

'In fact you've been looking *wisht for quite a while. Are you sure you feel well, Polly?'

'Yes, I'm all right, Lottie, thank you,' Polly said.

Lottie eyed her with disbelief. 'Well you don't look it, and I'm going to make you a cup of tea.'

'Lottie . . . please don't.'

Lottie waited for an explanation.

'I just couldn't face a cup of tea,' Polly insisted.

'Neither could I when I was carrying my three babies,' came Lottie's swift reply. 'Is that what's wrong with you?'

'It's just a bit of digestive trouble. It'll wear off,' Polly answered.

Lottie still eyed her in silent disbelief.

'Lottie, you know I can't have children,' Polly insisted.

'I'm not sure that I do,' Lottie replied. 'Look Polly, have you missed a month?'

Polly hesitated. 'Well, yes,' she admitted, 'but I've been late before. It doesn't signify anything. Lottie don't get my hopes up, or yours. I don't want to wish for the moon. You know I wouldn't have thought of starting this business if I thought I could have children.'

'Sorry, Polly. If it's not that, I expect you've been overdoing it with one thing and another,' Lottie said. 'Why don't you have a few days off, and ask Madam Delia to look after the showrooms?'

Polly was non-committal. 'I'll think about it,' she said.

But Polly did not improve and Lottie had put into words what

*Weak, poorly, not well.

she had been wondering during the last few days. She had heard of someone who had all the signs of being pregnant . . . morning sickness and weird food fads and preferences, followed by increasing girth, only to find it was a false-alarm, all in her head, there was no baby at all.

Could that be happening to her?

If not, if she really was going to have a baby it surely meant one thing . . . Edwin, not Polly, was the cause of her childless condition. The father was Joss! She would have to be honest and tell Edwin that he was not the father of her child, that she had been unfaithful.

This weighed heavily on Polly's mind. The joy of anticipating a baby had turned to dread. She delayed seeing the doctor in case her fears were confirmed. She had managed to conceal from Edwin that she was sick each morning on rising. But he *had* noticed that she was pale and so much quieter. He attributed this to overwork, and believed 'The Lady' was too much for her. But in the last two weeks the sickness had begun to abate, nor did she feel quite so weary.

By now, Polly had to know for certain and she decided to see her doctor on the way home from the shop, on a day it was Mary's turn to cook the evening meal. The diagnosis was positive!

Polly received the news with mixed feelings. Dread of having to hurt Edwin with the news that he was probably not the father of the baby she was carrying far outweighed the delight of at last becoming a mother. Until recently, to have a baby, to share with Edwin the joy of parenthood had been the zenith of all her desires. The shop had merely been something to take her mind off her disappointment, to fill in time . . . a replacement baby.

Edwin had arrived home a couple of minutes ahead of Polly. He came forward to greet her with a kiss. But Polly pushed him away and sobbing, dashed upstairs to the bedroom. Edwin followed close behind her. She sat on the edge of the bed, weeping.

'Polly, darling, whatever's the matter?' He put his arms about her; but again she pushed him away. He wouldn't want to touch her when he knew the truth.

'I'm expecting a baby,' she blurted out.

There was a moment's silence as Edwin struggled to comprehend the news.

'But that's marvellous, Polly. It's the best news I've ever had in my life, apart from the time you said "Yes" to me.'

Polly reached for her handkerchief to wipe a long drip hanging from her nose. Edwin's arms were about her and he buried his face in her hair, kissing her head.

'You're overcome, my love, but you'll never know how happy you've just made me.'

Polly, all tensed up to tell Edwin the worst, suddenly decided not to inflict this further cruelty on him, not now. Susan Chapman's baby was stillborn, Ethel Evans' baby died soon after birth, so too did Olive Martin's: She'd postpone the news until the baby was born, just in case it didn't survive. Then Edwin could at least be spared the pain.

She let him embrace and comfort her. She was too weak, too drained to resist. And in any case, she either had to behave as before, or tell Edwin the truth. She couldn't stand somewhere in the middle.

At last she put her arms about him and rested her head against his chest.

They sat on the edge of the bed silently clinging to one another. After a few minutes Mary shouted up from the bottom of the stairs.

'Do you want me to dish up now, Mrs Pendleton?'

Edwin replied, 'You have yours Mary. Mrs Pendleton is over-tired. We'll be down when she's had a little rest.'

'Very well, Mr Pendleton,' came the reply.

'You do still want a baby, don't you?' Edwin softly asked Polly.

'Oh yes, yes I do, Edwin.'

Silently Edwin wondered whether Polly was scared of the ordeal of birth which lay ahead of her. But he didn't think Polly was the type to be unduly alarmed about that. Or was she worried about the shop? He would deal with these things later. Now was definitely not the time.

It was not long before the nausea Polly experienced in the early weeks of pregnancy completely petered out, and she started to feel well again. A cup of tea tasted like nectar and she tackled the shop-work with renewed vigour. The time for the baby's birth

192

was still some way off and seemed more like fantasy than fact.

For much of the time this enabled Polly to push thoughts of confessing to Edwin into the background. For one thing, she had to plan for the time when her condition started to show. It was not the done thing for her to work in the showroom then. Polly discussed the situation with Lottie, who could not quite hide an 'I told you so' expression. She could carry on doing simple machining in the workroom for a while. Then she would have to stop work altogether. Edwin would have preferred her to stop work right away but conceded she had Lottie and the staff to consider.

Madam Delia agreed to work in the showroom part-time and either Lottie, May or Ethel could be called upon when and if necessary. Nora would also work at 'The Lady' on Saturdays. Payment to Madam Delia, young Nora, and extra for time worked by Lottie, May and Ethel would come pro-rata from the wages Polly would have received for the job had she been working. This, of course, had no effect on the net profit which looked likely to accrue by the end of the financial year. Polly's and Lottie's payments for the work they did in the business was a business expense just like the wages paid to staff they engaged. Whether Polly worked or did not work for 'The Lady' made no difference to her share of profit, it only affected her wages.

This was Polly's pre-birth plan. For after the birth she made no plans whatsoever. All would depend on Edwin's reaction to learning he was not the baby's father. If the worst happened, she could support herself and the baby with the income from the shop, and her mother would stand by her. She knew Edwin would never see her go hungry, but if he took the news that badly she would want to be independent.

Nine months to the day, after the death of Edwin's father. Polly's baby, with a final mighty push, was thrust into the world weighing in at seven and three-quarter pounds. The infant cried lustily.

Polly, exhausted, sank into the pillows. The midwife held the baby on a white towel for Polly to see and Polly with a great surge of love, beheld her son.

'A fine healthy boy,' the midwife said. Tears trickled down

j

Polly's face as she stretched forth her hand and took his tiny fist, stroked his soft cheek and dark hair. Then the midwife whisked him away.

When the afterbirth had been expelled Polly drifted into a kind of doze, a relaxed floating sensation. She looked up and saw Edwin advancing towards her, smiling. He bent over and kissed her damp forehead.

'You've been marvellous, darling,' he said tenderly, and kissed her again.

'Edwin . . . Edwin . . . ' Polly tried to rise from the pillows . . . 'there's something I must tell you . . . '

'Would the proud father like to see his son?'

Polly's agitated words were interrupted by the entry of the midwife, carrying the bathed baby swathed in a shawl.

Edwin moved from her bedside and tip-toed to where the midwife stood holding the new-born infant. Polly saw him gaze down at the baby, saw the look of indescribable joy on his face, saw his eyes suddenly brim and a lump in his throat move as he involuntarily swallowed when he held the tiny fist as though he feared to crush it.

The midwife placed the baby in his arms for him to hold, and Polly watched him gaze in wonder at what he believed to be *his* precious long awaited son. He bent to touch with his lips the tiny dark head, and as he raised his head she saw the tears of joy rolling down his cheeks.

Oh God, what have I done! She struggled to stifle a sob, but Edwin heard the sound and looked up. He passed the baby to the midwife and rushed to Polly's side.

'Darling! What's the matter?'

She struggled to sit up and swiftly but gently his arms encircled her, his tears of joy mingling with her tears of horror at the enormity of the hurt she was about to inflict on him.

'Edwin, Edwin,' she gave a great sob as she said the words 'The baby's not . . . '

'I think you'd better leave for a little while Mr Pendleton.' It was the midwife's voice. She had put the baby into the cradle and was standing at Edwin's side.

Edwin looked up at her. 'Yes,' he said, then gently lowered Polly onto the pillows. 'See you in a little while, dearest,' he said, his lips brushing her damp brow.

Drained, Polly sank deep down into the pillows as Edwin silently moved away, pausing to glance into the cradle as he went, and turning to smile at her before closing the door.

With a great shuddering sigh Polly felt all the strength and all the pent-up tension ebbing from her. She couldn't do it. It had to be here and now, or never. It was too late. Now Edwin would never know.

Chapter Twenty-six

Though Jonathan Guy Pendleton flourished, Polly remained languid. For a time Edwin accepted this as normal for a woman during and for a short time after confinement. A new mother needed time to rest and renew her strength, to recuperate.

Nell Pascoe, Polly's mother, was staying with them, helping to look after Polly and the baby, but even she was also beginning to show concern.

Both doctor and midwife told Edwin women sometimes go through a patch like this, but they soon get over it. Edwin must be patient. It was Polly's first baby. The baby was thriving. All would be well.

Edwin was patient, but he worried. He knew of only one thing which could be responsible for Polly's condition . . . the shop. She had been doing too much! Later he would broach the matter with her. It would do no good to speak of it now, Polly burst into tears for the slightest reason and no reason. It was so unlike her.

But Polly knew the cause, and guilt weighed upon her like a slab of granite. She loved her baby son but she had no right to such love and it served to make her depressed. Yet she must break its strangle-hold; there was the baby to consider, the innocent baby. She had intended to tell Edwin the truth, but each time something intervened and the opportunity was lost. Suddenly she had seen a bigger dilemma than her own burden of guilt, Edwin's great love, great joy, in the little baby which he believed was his son and which she, his wife, had delivered into the world. To tell him he was not the father would be a cruelty she was not strong enough to inflict on him.

And it was *possible* that Edwin really was the father! She remembered his ardent love-making exactly one week after she had given herself to Joss. That was the night George Pendleton, unbeknown to them, had died peacefully in his sleep. From the beginning Edwin had attributed the baby's conception to that night, but she was convinced the baby was not Edwin's.

Polly had spared Edwin and at the same time spared herself the punishment, the rejection, she deserved. But she had to bear alone the burden of guilt and deceit. Polly regarded being unfaithful to her husband as an unpardonable violation of marriage vows. She felt she should, she needed, to be punished. Yet by some strange logic, she was not sorry she and Joss had made love, been one together. Deep inside she was convinced they were meant for each other, they belonged to one another, from the beginning to the end, together or apart, they were one. It was confusing, and her head ached with the complexity of the situation. Since the birth she was always on the brink of tears which now, for the umpteenth time, she wiped away.

One Sunday afternoon just over a week later, Polly again had a bout of weeping. Neil offered to bath the baby, but Polly would not hear of it.

'You have enough to do cooking the Sunday roast. I will do it,' she replied in a way which both Nell and Edwin recognised as final. To argue with Polly when she used that tone would have been useless and only serve to irritate.

Edwin watched, fascinated, as Polly lowered the baby into the warm water, which baby Jonathan seemed to enjoy. Polly seemed calmer now, and when the bathing was over he ventured to ask to be allowed to dry his son.

'All right,' Polly agreed. 'Take the towel.'

Edwin picked up the waiting large, snow-white towel and she passed the dripping, slippery, kicking baby to him. Gently Edwin patted the infant dry, handling him as though he were made of Dresden china.

'Look!' he exclaimed suddenly, anxiety in his tone. 'He's got a red mark!'

Polly was quickly at Edwin's side. 'Oh, the mark on his hip,' she said. 'It's nothing to worry about. The nurse said it's not at all uncommon. Sometimes it runs in families apparently, but not always.'

Edwin's face relaxed. 'It's shaped like a crescent moon,' he said, now with a smile. By this time Jonathan Guy had begun to bawl loudly.

'He's impatient for his feed,' Polly said, and dressed him as fast as flailing arms and legs would allow, while the baby endeavoured to turn his head towards 'the milk supply'.

Nell had prepared the meal in as tempting a way as she knew how, and while they were eating Edwin had endeavoured to conceal that he was watching to see Polly ate a reasonably good amount. She must keep up her strength. After all, she was still 'eating for two'.

When the table was cleared Nell and Edwin banished Polly from the kitchen, Nell insisting she would wash the dishes and Edwin insisting he would dry.

It was on this day the turning point came. Polly was checking that Jonathan was still asleep when there was a rap on the front door. Edwin quickly emerged from the kitchen to answer it. It was Lottie accompanied by May Bascombe, come to visit, bringing flowers for Polly, tiny baby clothes for little Jonathan Guy and a box of cigars for the proud father.

Edwin hid a slight feeling of annoyance. He did not feel Polly was up to receiving visitors. Lottie had heard Polly was 'low' and, contrary to Edwin's expectations, her cheerful presence along with May had a tonic effect, a much needed breath of fresh air.

Lottie and May spent the first minutes looking at and admiring the still sleeping new member of the family.

Towards the end of this discussion Edwin left them to their feminine chat, but walked into the adjoining dining-room anxiously keeping his ears alert as he heard snatches of the conversation.

They talked of the ordeal of birth pangs and the struggles and 'the great push' . . . no wonder it was called labour!

But then Polly wanted to know about 'The Lady'. How was Madam Delia managing in the showrooms? Who had been in with orders? Were there many new clients? They all talked so animatedly that Edwin could not hear what they were saying. What he did hear though was Polly . . . laughing!

Nell, who was standing near the kitchen door, watching Edwin standing in the dining-room, straining to hear what was going on, saw him smiling with relief. Their eyes met and they grinned at each other, each knowing what the other was thinking . . . Polly was 'on the mend'.

'I'll make tea,' Nell said, and Edwin nodded. The talk and laughter going on in the sitting-room all seemed to indicate one thing to Edwin though . . . work at the shop was *not* responsible for Polly's low state. The reverse was the case. The business, and the people she worked with lifted her spirits. Perhaps it would be unwise to try to persuade Polly not to return to work at the shop. What strange unfathomable creatures women were.

'Lottie will be coming here on Wednesday evening,' Polly told Edwin and her mother over their Sunday tea. 'We need to discuss arrangements for the shop.'

'What thoughts have you on it?' Edwin asked, after a slight pause.

'Up to the baby's birth I didn't have any thoughts on it,' Polly said. 'I didn't want to tempt fate.'

'You mean you didn't want any more disappointments?' Nell said remembering clearly her own first baby, Joseph, who died two days after birth.

'That's right, mother,' Polly answered, not letting on what had really been on her mind.

'I rather hoped you'd give up work, after the baby was born,' Edwin said.

'Well, let me tell you what I thought and then see what you think,' Polly said.

She is better Edwin thought. Before Lottie and May Bascombe's visit she would have been in floods of tears by now.

'What do you think?' Edwin asked.

'If the staff at the shop are willing to carry on as now for six months, I thought I would stay at home with Jonathan until he is six-months old and well into being weaned, and then I'd go back to the shop, perhaps part-time at first.'

'And who would look after the baby?' Edwin asked.

'That can be arranged,' Polly said . . . she had been giving this some thought. 'First, would you be interested in giving up your part-time job at the Vicarage and coming here to stay or live with us, Mother?'

Polly's mother hesitated. 'It's nice of you to think of me, Polly, but . . . '

Polly interrupted, 'But you don't want to leave Emily

199

Renfree,' she said.

'Emily and I have lived so close to each other all these years, Polly. She was marvellous to me when little Joseph died, *and* when I lost your father, and now she is without John . . . We're as close as sisters . . . closer than some.'

'I know exactly what you mean, mother, and I did think you might see it like that. I have an alternative suggestion . . . we ask Mary to live in, help with some of the meals and look after Jonathan when I'm not here . . . already she loves him. We can engage a woman to do the housework and washing which Mary now does. I'm sure Mary will look after Jonathan well.'

'Yes, yes she would,' Edwin and Nell both agreed.

'She could have Sundays off, and the shop is not busy on Mondays. I could leave 'The Lady' for Mary to have a half-day off then, in fact.'

'I'm free on Mondays. I could come in time for lunch and Mary would be free to leave as soon as we have eaten,' Nell volunteered. 'I'd enjoy looking after little Jonathan.'

'That would be wonderful,' Polly smiled, pleased with this suggestion.

Neither Edwin nor Nell could fault the arrangement, and Polly's income from the business made it financially workable.

'What do you think?' Polly asked Edwin.

'It sounds feasible, but I'd like to sleep on it,' Edwin answered.

'Fine,' Polly replied. She looked towards her mother. 'What do you think mother?'

'Like Edwin, it sounds workable, but I've been brought up to think it natural for a mother to be at home looking after the children.'

Polly had no reply to that.

'But I know you'll make sure Jonathan is well looked after, and Mary is used to children and babies. She'll be good with him,' Nell added, trying to placate Polly for speaking her opinion in such a forthright way.

'That's what I think, Mother. And I'd never have thought of starting a business if I thought I could have a baby,' Polly added defensively. 'Now that it's done I can't wash my hands of Lottie and the others.'

'No that's true,' Nell said. 'I'm sure, like I said, that you will make the right decision, Polly.'

Edwin slept on the situation. It made no difference to his feelings, which were identical to those of his mother-in-law. But he had no argument against it, provided Mary was agreeable, which he felt sure she would be. All Polly said made sense. And there was no doubt the shop had been a great success.

As anticipated, Mary was delighted and felt honoured that she was considered capable of caring for the precious baby.

When Lottie came on the Wednesday evening she was happy with the arrangement and confessed she had a terrible fear Polly might want, or be persuaded to 'pull out' of the business and stay at home with the baby. Polly had flair and just the right touch with the clients, and more than that the two, like their mothers, had become close friends. Lottie felt she could guarantee Madam Delia and the others would be happy to agree to the arrangement.

With this settled, Polly's next thoughts turned to the Christening. She wanted it to be before she went back to work at the shop, and thought when Jonathan reached about three or four months would be a suitable time.

Chapter Twenty-seven

Polly was adamant she wanted Lottie to be Jonathan Guy's Godmother. She had always known Lottie, though as a small child Lottie, being older, was not such a vivid recollection, and Lottie had married and gone to live in Falmouth when Polly was still a child. But now a deep affection had grown between the two.

When it came to Godfathers Polly had no definite preferences but she thought someone from Edwin's family should be included. Edwin suggested Caleb and Joss as the two Godfathers.

At the mention of Joss, Polly felt the skin on her face tighten. 'We've already decided on Lottie for Godmother. I think we should have someone else to be Godfather.'

'Jack then,' Edwin suggested.

'I don't think he's yet reached the stage of being interested in babies. Let's think about it,' Polly said.

But when Polly went to bed that night she pondered the matter. She was scared of seeing Joss again, scared of her own emotions, that in some way . . . she knew not what . . . she would say or do something to reveal her feelings, or the secret of who had fathered her baby.

But this was hysterical nonsense. Nothing like that need happen. They would both keep a tight rein on their emotions. Although he didn't know it, Polly had become convinced the baby was as much Joss's as hers. Surely that meant he deserved a little share in Jonathan. To be his Godfather was the one way in which Joss could be entitled to an interest in the baby's progress, his growing-up, his life. Yes, Joss was entitled to that.

And Jonathan was not only the baby she had longed for so very much, he was a little bit of Joss which would always belong to her. Nothing could now ever take that away from her . . . nothing.

Also, the baby had brought Edwin the joy and ultimate fulfilment of his life. He had whispered to Polly the night after the baby's birth that his cup of happiness was overflowing. The change in him since the baby's arrival in the household had been amazing. Some men grumbled that their spouses talked about nothing but babies. Every evening over their meal, Edwin wanted to hear details of what had been happening during the day. Who had been to visit? What did they think of Jonathan? He went into ecstasies over Jonathan's first real smile, and seemed to wear a permanent smile himself. Edwin's delight in his son knew no bounds.

Jonathan was fifteen weeks old when the Christening was arranged to take place. Emily Renfree was pleased and flattered that both Lottie and Joss had been asked to be Godparents. She had only been to Villa Gwidden once to see 'little Jonathan' as everyone called him, and on that occasion he was fast asleep and so swathed in shawls she really didn't get a good look at his face. Arrangements were made for her to come again with Nell to have tea and see more of Master Jonathan. But on that occasion she developed a heavy cold which she could not risk passing on to the baby, and didn't feel well enough to leave the cottage in any event. So Emily was looking forward to getting her first really good look at Polly's long-awaited baby.

Joss had not seen Polly since that very special night. He had kept his resolve that, for both their sakes but especially for Polly, it would be courting trouble and adding to their anguish to see one another.

On learning from Lottie that Polly was at last expecting a baby, he felt glad for her, yet just a little wistful. The baby would surely cement her marriage to Edwin Pendleton. Any vague and foolish hope which occasionally came unbidden to Joss's mind that one day they might be free to . . . any such illogical dream was now completely crushed. Polly never, never could be his.

He was laying himself open to further heartache . . . going to the Christening, seeing Polly again, this time with Edwin and their baby. But it was clearly what Polly wanted, for he could imagine Edwin being so elated to now have both Polly and their baby he would agree to anything Polly wanted . . . well, almost anything. Yes. he would be Godfather to Polly's baby, though he knew he would pay dearly.

Polly, though still as she always would be, bearing the burden of guilt, had things more in perspective, and with the lifting of the depression and lethargy, took pleasure in organising the Christening arrangements. After the actual Christening in church, the party would return to Villa Gwidden for the customary refreshments, Christening Cake, etc. Edwin had insisted their home, the 'White Villa' should be freshly painted for this extra special occasion. Her mother would stay a couple of nights and, apart from feeding of course, would look after Jonathan while she and Mary got on with preparing, baking, and finally making sandwiches. Emily Renfree had volunteered to make tiny finger-pasties, and Belbins Confectioners would make the Christening cake and an ample variety of small cream cakes, iced and other dainty cakes.

Mary assumed she would stay at Villa Gwidden, having kettles 'on the boil' ready to see to the tea and making sure pre-cooked pasties, sausage rolls and tiny pies were properly heated in the oven. But Polly would have none of it.

'No Mary,' she said. 'You are going to be the one who is going to take care of Jonathan and you are coming to the Christening as a guest. I'll get Ada Pearce and Jane Ann Phillips to see to the tea, etc.' Mary was delighted and felt that in some way she was 'going up in the world', well . . . in Penryn.

After breakfast on the Christening day, Edwin put Bessie in the shafts and went to collect Emily Renfree.

Everybody was busy, for a morning service did not leave much time for all the last minute preparations, including getting dressed and smartened up.

Emily, wearing her best navy suit and hat, arrived carrying a large basket of pasties covered in grease-proof paper and several layers of white linen cloths.

'I've been up since before five o'clock baking these,' she told Polly. 'And if you put the basket somewhere warm they'll keep their heat and won't need warming.'

'Fine,' Polly said. 'And thank you Mrs Renfree. They smell delicious.' She handed the basket to Mary to put near the Cornish Range.

'Now where's that dear little baby?' Emily demanded. 'I haven't properly seen him yet.'

'Mother's giving him his bath. Come and see,' Polly said and led the way. Jonathan had been taken out of the bath when Polly and Emily entered, and was swathed in a large white bath towel.

Nell greeted Emily, laid the baby down, and pulled back the towel for Emily to see and admire him. An expression of shock banished the smile from Emily's face, and her jaw dropped. With mouth agape she shot a fleeting glance at Polly, one pair of brown eyes meeting another. Polly was certain she read both astonishment and knowledge in Emily's wide-eyed gaze! It happened for only an instant, then Emily's composure was immediately regained and the smile reappeared.

'Oh, what a little dear,' she cooed as Jonathan gurgled and blew a few bubbles while his feet, legs and arms moved vigorously, enjoying his freedom from clothes and shawl. 'May I hold him, Polly?'

'Y . . . yes, of course,' Polly stuttered.

'He's a lovely baby, Polly. I'm so glad for you.' Emily Renfree smiled and kissed Polly, and when they moved apart Polly noticed Emily Renfree's eyelids fluttering as though blinking away tears. Polly silently let out a long breath which she had unwittingly been holding since Emily's momentary look of . . . of what? Recognition?

'Thanks, Mrs Renfree,' Polly said. 'I'll . . . I'll leave you to it, Mother,' she said to Nell, then left the room and darted to the privacy of her bedroom where she held onto the bedpost, panting as though she had just run for her life.

Panicking, Polly dimly realised there wasn't time to waste. She went downstairs into the kitchen where Mary was putting out cups and saucers, now that the table was arranged, apart from the savouries which needed to be served warm.

'Did you see the Christening cake on the sideboard, Mrs Pendleton? . . . Are you all right . . . you're white as a sheet!'

'Am I? I'm a bit shaky. Don't tell Mr Pendleton Mary, I'm not ill, it's something different.'

'But Mrs Pendleton . . . ' Mary protested.

'No Mary!' Polly interrupted, her voice loud and sharp. 'I'll have a cup of tea and some aspirins, and then I'll be all right.'

Mary, who was wearing a brand new suit bought specially for the occasion, silently put tea into the pot and took it to the steaming kettle on top of the range.

'Have a cup yourself,' Polly commanded, pinching her cheeks in an endeavour to bring back some colour. 'And please say nothing to Mr Pendleton. I am definitely not ill and he will only worry that I am.'

'Very well, Mrs Pendleton,' Mary replied, and poured two cups of tea.

As Polly drained her teacup Jack arrived, looking smart in his dark 'Sunday suit' and bowler hat. The pinched look had gone from his lean face and he looked his old happy self.

'You're both looking very smart,' he said.

'Thank you, you are too,' Mary replied.

Ada Pearce and Jane Ann Phillips came next and were made familiar with what to do and where to find things.

They were closely followed by Cordelia, dressed in a black mourning outfit. She was accompanied by Caleb, in morning suit and silk top hat, and Mary Jane, now a plump round-faced young woman wearing a navy suit and hat. She was planning to follow in her father's footsteps, and hoped to soon teach at an infant school. Caleb apologised for Agnes's absence. She was feeling unwell, a tummy upset. Cordelia was concerned and Edwin and everyone expressed sympathy.

Polly was still shaken by the look she saw on Emily Renfree's face. Nell and Emily chatted, and all appeared normal. Perhaps she had imagined it. Perhaps her guilty conscience was playing tricks on her. Or was that wishful thinking? She could see so clearly Emily Renfree's shocked expression.

Two hired cabs arrived and the group piled into them, Polly dressed in a new marmalade-coloured suit and a matching toque hat and baby Jonathan still asleep and resplendent in the Pendleton family's antique Christening robe. The Godparents and other guests at the Christening were outside the church awaiting their arrival. The ladies were all so smartly dressed they could have been attending a wedding, as Lottie whispered to May Bascombe, Ethel Angove and the elegant Madam Delia. Those men not in morning suits and silk top hats, wore dark suits and bowler hats.

Polly's heart hammered violently when she saw Joss, standing next to Clementine and Theodore and looking particularly handsome. The hammering intensified when their eyes met. Joss's behaviour was impeccable, just the way any good long-

206

standing friend would behave. He shook Edwin's hand, giving Edwin's arm a slap with his free hand and heartily congratulated him, then he shook hands with Polly, giving her a brief peck of a kiss on the cheek as he did so. His attention then turned to the sleeping baby. He gently touched the tiny fist, and turning to Clementine and Theodore, mouthed an invitation to come and see. Everyone clustered around Polly and the baby until the vicar joined them and said the service could commence any time they were ready.

Little Jonathan slept through the start of the service but protested when the Holy Water was sprinkled on his head. His protests were short-lived though, and with eyes wide open, he stared around at everyone as though puzzled by the proceedings. Both Grandmothers dabbed their eyes, but Polly had an iron control on all her emotions and no tears came to her eyes, although she noticed Edwin swallowed noisily.

After the service the gathering moved to Villa Gwidden which, although moderately spacious, seemed full to capacity.

By this time everyone was ready for refreshments and justice was done and compliments paid to Polly for the splendid buffet-spread. Lottie's daughter Nora tugged at her Uncle Joss's arm to show him she was wearing the bracelet he brought home from America for her. He smiled and told her he thought she looked very pretty wearing her new dress. When it was time for the toast and Christening cake Edwin ensured that glasses were filled and ready, while Ada Pearce cut and plated pieces of cake. The glasses and plates were passed around. Mary's heart swelled with pride as, standing next to the mistress's brother, Jack, she, like the other guests, was waited upon.

Outwardly calm but inwardly a turmoil of emotions, Polly watched as Joss lifted little Jonathan and gently kissed his dribbly-wet cheek, while Edwin called for silence.

'Ladies and Gentlemen,' Joss said. 'It is my honour to propose a toast to Polly's and Edwin's little son, Jonathan Guy. May he enjoy good health, good fortune and the fine characteristics of both his parents . . . strength, loyalty, kindliness and . . . with a bit of luck . . . his mother's good looks . . . '

Here there was a pause for much laughter, and Edwin laughed louder and longer than anyone.

Joss, with his free hand raised his glass . . . 'To Jonathan . . .

God bless him.'

'To Jonathan, God bless him,' they all repeated and tipped their glasses.

By the time the drinks were consumed and refills about to be poured Jonathan began to whimper, then bawl. Polly moved to where Joss was holding him.

'He's hungry,' Polly said.

Joss kissed the baby's dark head and passed him to Polly. As he did so their eyes met and Polly's suddenly brimmed. Unable to speak, and not daring to glance in the direction of Emily Renfree, Polly took the baby and with weakening knees fled upstairs to the privacy of the bedroom.

Chapter Twenty-eight

On the day following the Christening, Edwin, after their evening meal, left Polly and the baby to visit Agnes and Caleb and enquire about his sister's health. He came home with a sombre face.

'Isn't Agnes any better?' Polly asked.

'No. It's stomach trouble . . . she always did have a delicate digestion. I can't help wondering whether she's got an ulcer,' Edwin said.

'She does like pasties and heavy cake,' Polly recalled. 'People with digestive trouble usually have to cut down on those.'

'Well she's not had anything like that lately,' Edwin replied. 'All she seems to want is porridge without any milk . . . '

'Yuk!' Polly exclaimed.

' . . . and boiled greens and potatoes,' Edwin continued.

'That doesn't sound like Agnes,' Polly mused. 'I always got the impression that she and Caleb were hearty eaters; and as for Mary Jane . . . '

Polly's mind went back to their wedding anniversary party when Mary Jane sneaked into the dining-room and started gobbling up the refreshments while the adults were chatting in the sitting-room.

'Of course, she must be close to "the change",' Edwin reasoned. Since Polly had become pregnant and more so after the baby's birth, Edwin had become far less reticent about personal and delicate female matters.

'I didn't think that caused digestive troubles,' Polly replied.

'It can give you severe stomach pains,' Edwin said, knowledgeably. 'Bert Williams told me his wife had such terrible abdominal pains, she didn't know where to put herself!'

Baby Jonathan began to howl and attention to his loud

demands put thoughts of Agnes and her digestive troubles right out of both their minds.

It was about three weeks later that Edwin came home from work with a broad grin on his face.

'You're looking pleased with yourself. Had a good day, dear?' Polly said after Edwin kissed her.

'There must be something in the air where the Pendletons are concerned,' he replied, still with a self-satisfied grin.

'Why . . . What's happened?'

'You'll never guess,' he went on.

Polly laughed, then impatiently demanded, 'Then tell me!'

'Agnes is expecting!'

'A baby?'

'What else?'

'Never!'

'It's true. I left work early to call and see them on the way home. They were told the good news this morning.'

'Are they pleased?'

'Oh yes, but Caleb confided in me when I was leaving, he is concerned . . . Agnes is not young.'

'I'm sure she'll be all right,' Polly soothed.

Edwin's sister was expecting a baby! Could it be possible Jonathan was Edwin's baby, she wondered. No, she was convinced Joss was the father or was it, in some contradictory way, that she wanted Joss to be the father! No, no of course she didn't . . . well, in one way she didn't, but in another way . . .

The week after Jonathan reached six months, had four teeth with two more about to come through the gums, and was sitting up and taking notice of everything, Polly returned to work at 'The Lady'. Being Monday, her mother would arrive around coffee-time so that Mary could take her half-day off from around 1 p.m. or as soon as they had both eaten. Jack had also become a fairly regular caller and liked to play with his little nephew, who roared with laughter at his uncle's antics. Polly always enjoyed a chat over the pot of tea Mary always made them, and when Jack's packed lunch was a pasty, Mary always warmed it for him. Mary was fully installed at Villa Gwidden a week before the Christening, and didn't mind that she 'mucked in' and helped when needed irrespective of time. There were no strictly set hours for 'live-in' servants. It was customary for Mary to have evenings off, Sundays and one half-day each week, and she usually spent this time with her own family, as well as frequent evening visits.

Mary counted herself fortunate indeed to work for Mr and Mrs Pendleton. She felt almost like one of the family and ate the same food. Her friend Mabel Ferris, worked for a stingy couple, who bought cheap cuts of meat. Mabel was never allowed more than one slice, and had to have watery porridge every morning. The lady of the house bought half-price stale bread for Mabel to eat, and one stale loaf was expected to last most of the week. Cleaning materials were doled out in small amounts, tablets of household soap being cut in half as a dubious saving. Poor Mabel hated her job, but with a large family, there was no room for her at home.

Ada Pearce, now the cleaning help, arrived at Villa Gwidden as Polly was about to leave. As usual for a Monday, the shop was fairly quiet, and to celebrate her return, Lottie, May, and Ethel had organised a special mid-morning coffee break with cream cakes delivered from Edwards Bakery and Confectioners.

Of course, over coffee Lottie was anxious to hear about 'little Jonathan's' progress, and told Polly that Joss was delighted to be a Godparent.

Polly smiled. 'He's been around to see him a couple of times,' she said. She did not mention Joss was careful to come at times when he knew Edwin would be at home. And Polly was glad of this. To be alone together would have been electrifying, and far too much of a strain for both. But it tugged at her heart-strings to see Joss play with Jonathan, and pick him up and make him shriek with dribbly laughter, not knowing that the infant he made so much fuss of was almost certainly his own little son! What emotions of sadness and great joy the innocent baby caused Polly! She had no one to blame but herself. Joss would never have *initiated* what happened, no matter how great his desire. But what delight had come from it, especially for Edwin . . . Polly continued to ponder this when the coffee break was over.

'How very nice to see you back here again, Mrs Pendleton!'

Polly's mind was jolted out of her abstractedness and the subject which so often occupied her thoughts.

'Good morning, Mrs Endersby-Harman. It's lovely to be back, and to see you on the first day of my return.'

'Thank you, my dear. And how is your little . . . a girl wasn't it?'

'A boy. We've called him Jonathan. and he's very well, thank you . . . positively thriving.'

Mrs Endersby-Harman had come about a three-quarter jacket which was being made. She had decided to have fur trimming instead of velvet.

At the end of what seemed a very long day, Polly could hardly wait to get home to Jonathan. Had he missed her? Did he take his first feed well . . . he didn't care for milk in a bottle, which a month before Polly had started him on for one or two feeds a day to accustom him gradually to different feeding. But he now enjoyed gruel, bread dipped in egg yolk or a little bread or potato mashed in broth with marrowbone or chicken jelly. She just hoped he hadn't fretted for her.

Once home, Polly found Jonathan contentedly bashing a toy rabbit with his rattle. He gave her a broad welcoming grin and a long thin dribble dangled from his mouth, then dropped onto the rabbit. He had been quite happy with Mary and with Polly's mother. Both Polly and Edwin, who arrived home close on Polly's heels, wanted to know details of how Jonathan's day was spent. After giving this information, avidly listened to by doting parents, Nell insisted she must rescue from the oven the cottage pie, made from the minced remains of the Sunday joint; it was in danger of drying up.

Ada Pearce had done the washing. Tomorrow she would wash the kitchen floor and do the ironing. The rest of the week up to Friday would be filled with routine housework and small oddments of washing. All would work out well.

After the first week, which seemed endless, Polly fell back into the routine of work at the shop. Throughout her pregnancy and after, she had kept the accounts and all paperwork up to date. The business was now well and truly established. The continual feeling of guilt and remorse over her act of unfaithfulness, and the dubious fatherhood of her son, which weighed so heavily upon her during her pregnancy and up to the time she returned to work at 'The Lady', now began to be more bearable. She was convinced Joss was the father of the little dark-haired baby, but it no longer completely clouded her life. She adored little Jonathan and Edwin worshipped him; his joy in the baby was boundless.

Weeks turned into months. At ten and a half months Jonathan took his first wobbly steps. It was the age at which Polly started walking. Edwin drew comparisons.

'He has dark hair like Polly, and he started walking at the same age as Polly,' he would tell people. 'He's got the same colouring as the Pascoe's side, but I can see a little bit of Pendleton in him!'

Polly, however, imagined she saw a few, to her, unmistakable resemblances to the Renfrees.

Chapter Twenty-nine

Lottie and George were sitting by the fireside one evening, while Nora was in the sitting-room chatting and giggling with her cousin Madge and another school friend.

'I think I heard someone at the door,' Lottie said, rising to her feet to see who was there.

'It's Joss,' she cried, welcoming her brother with a hug. 'Come in, lovely to see you.'

'Am I interrupting anything?' Joss asked as they entered what was known as 'the middle room', for Lottie was sometimes busy sewing in the evening.

'Lottie's not doing anything and neither am I,' George replied for her, as he pulled up a chair before the fire. 'Have a seat Joss. Nice to see you, boy.' George had become on good terms with his brother-in-law. He had learned to greatly respect the man.

'Thanks George,' Joss said, lowering himself into the chair.

'We haven't seen much of you lately, my handsome,' Lottie said. 'Not at all since the Christening.'

'How is Polly's baby?' Joss enquired.

'He's walking and getting on fine,' Lottie replied, as she settled into her chair.

'And Polly and Edwin?'

'Polly is coping marvellously. She's back at the shop now, you know. She's a good organiser. And Edwin . . . talk about the cat that got the cream . . . Little Jonathan is really the light of his life.'

'And you and George?'

'We're fine,' Lottie went on. 'I sometimes can't believe my good fortune. The money we're getting from the shop, in addition to George's pay, is really setting us up.'

'As you know, Joss,' George said, 'people like us just live from week to week. But some of them think if you are in an office and go to work in a suit, you are better off than they are. But we're not. Like I said, all of us live from week to week. It's just that we can't go to work in a scruffy old jacket and trousers like a craftsman might, or a labourer.'

'True.' Joss agreed.

'Until Lottie and Polly joined up to open a shop, my suit for work had such a shiny backside you could almost see your face in it. We just had to struggle to keep up appearances.'

Joss laughed and agreed. 'It seems to me that's the way it is with all classes of people, George,' he said.

A disbelieving expression crossed George's face. He, like Lottie, found the extra money coming into the house a great comfort and a blessing. They could save a bit for an emergency and it gave a secure feeling. But Lottie noticed the grim expression on her brother's face.

'What's up, Joss? Is there something wrong?'

George laughed. He saw no cause for concern. 'Don't tell me *you're* feeling the pinch,' he said, turning with a grin to look into Joss's unexpectedly solemn face.

'Not really, but you're not too far off the mark, George,' Joss replied grimly.

Lottie's mind instantly turned to Clementine.

'Don't tell me that wife of yours has been throwing it around,' she said, unable to hide her dislike of Clementine.

Joss remained silent.

'I thought you curbed her spending,' Lottie said, questioningly.

'It's *my* problem, Lottie. No need for you to bother your head with it.'

'I *am* bothered. You're my brother, and she's a conniving . . . ' Lottie bit her lip to prevent her tongue from running away with her.

'It seems she has persuaded certain establishments to allow her to open accounts and to send me the bill on a half-yearly basis,' he explained.

'How much?' Lottie demanded.

'Around two hundred pounds!'

George whistled, looking in astonishment towards Lottie. Two hundred pounds was considerably more than he earned in a whole year!

Lottie's eyes were downcast as she silently and swiftly did a few calculations. Joss had helped her when setting up the shop with almost that amount of money and thought nothing of it.

'What else?' she persisted.

George looked at his wife in astonishment; Wasn't two hundred pounds enough to make any man exasperated?

Still Joss remained silent.

'Joss, I am your sister and I care. I shall imagine all sorts if you don't tell me,' Lottie pleaded.

'I can see I shall have to, though I don't know how the conversation turned the way it did,' Joss paused again.

'Go on,' Lottie said.

'It's Clementine's brother,' Joss pressed his lips together in exasperation.

'Rupert?' Lottie was clearly puzzled. 'But he's out of harm's way in London. How could *he* get his hands on *your* money?'

'It seems he was "carrying on" with the wife of the senior partner in the firm of solicitors . . . '

'But he's an old man, isn't he?' Lottie interrupted.

'Yes, but his wife is quite young, and apparently attractive . . . 'flighty' according to Clementine's mother . . . '

'*They* can talk,' Lottie interrupted again, then swiftly put her hand to her mouth as though to suppress her tongue. Joss appeared not to notice.

'It's his second wife,' he went on. 'His first wife died. Anyway, it seems someone knew about it and threatened to tell the husband unless Rupert paid him a thousand pounds.'

'That's blackmail!' George said incredulously.

'Yes, it is. But Rupert couldn't risk being dismissed and the scandal. Instead he apparently took the money from an account for clients' funds, then borrowed more from the same source to back a "cert" horse at the races, and lost, and has been repeating both the gambling and the losing.'

'Bloody fool,' George said under his breath. He was not in the habit of swearing.

Joss continued, 'It escalated until he had only three weeks to put back all the money, or he would have been found out, when the amount of clients' money shown in the books was due to be balanced with the account held by the bank.'

'Then the deficiency would show up,' George said.

'And you gave him all that money,' Lottie said in disbelief.

'I gave it a great deal of thought before agreeing,' Joss said to Lottie.

Lottie loudly sucked in her breath in shock and disapproval.

'If I didn't, Lottie, he would not only have been dismissed, he would have been taken to court, found guilty, there would have been a public scandal, he would have been sent to prison, his family would have been disgraced. All this would have made no difference to my friends, but Clementine and her parents would lose all theirs. They would be ostracised and at school Theodore would probably be baited by the other boys, especially since he's not himself been a shining example.'

There was silence while Lottie and George pondered the situation. At last George spoke.

'I don't suppose you could have done any other,' he said in a dubious tone.

'But you've already bought that great rabbit warren of a Manor,' Lottie said, 'and had all the work done on it, just to bail out Clementine's parents . . . now you've got all this . . . '

Lottie saw the droop of Joss's broad shoulders. She rushed to put her arms about him. 'Sorry love,' she said, hugging him. 'I'm sounding as though it's your fault . . . but I get so mad, the way they take you and everything for granted.'

'I know,' Joss said softly, and put his arm around his sister.

'You keep them all going, yet with it all they look down on us!' Lottie said with a catch in her voice. Again there was silence, while Lottie held on to her brother's hand.

Still in a quiet tone, Joss broke the silence. 'You haven't seen what they've been like, Lottie,' he said. 'Clementine and her mother have wept for hours, since they found out. Margaret is forever crying or on the brink of tears. She actually put her hands together and went down on her knees before me and begged me to help Rupert. Albert has hit the bottle . . . '

'Your bottle I take it,' Lottie said.

'Yes,' Joss agreed with a wry smile. 'He drinks, weeps and gabbles incoherently. They know I've put my foot down with Clementine's spending and other things,' he said, meaningfully. 'But I've let them know this is the last straw. If there's any more trouble with any of them then as far as I'm concerned they've had it.'

k

Again there was silence. This bombshell shattered them all.

'I'll make us a cup of tea,' George said at last.

'I'll do it, dear,' Lottie half rose from her chair.

'No. You sit there with Joss,' George replied, and went into the kitchen.

'Is Rupert going to pay you back?' Lottie asked after a couple of minutes.

'No,' Joss said. 'Oh, he said he would, swore he would. And he might make a token gesture or two, but he won't . . . he won't be able to. They all have a way of living and spending beyond their means. And it's all to impress their friends, so called. No, I don't expect to ever get it back. Frankly Lottie, we're going to have to make a few economies. We won't have to watch the pennies, but I'll certainly be watching the pounds.'

George came in with three mugs of tea. Lottie glanced at the clock.

'Look at the time!' she exclaimed. 'I forgot about those girls.' She went out of the room, leaving the door open. 'Time to go home girls, your mothers will be wondering what's happened to you,' she said to Nora's friends.

Joss heard them all wishing each other 'Goodnight' and the front door being closed. Nora came into the room.

'Hello, Uncle Joss,' she smiled.

'Hello Nora. You look more grown-up every time I see you,' Joss said, thinking what a pretty young girl she was growing into.

'There's a cup of tea in the pot you can have,' Lottie said to her daughter. 'Then you'd better get to bed.'

'Thanks mum,' Nora answered as she moved towards the kitchen.

'Does anyone else know about all this?' George asked Joss, again returning to the subject of Rupert Du Cane and the money.

'No. I haven't spoken to anyone else,' Joss said. 'And I don't want it to get out. You know how upset and angry mother would be, and it wouldn't do her any good.'

'You're right there,' Lottie agreed. 'She never did like Clementine or the Du Cane family.'

'I know,' Joss grinned wryly. 'She never pretended to me or to Nell Pascoe that she did. Mother was no fool.'

'Talking of Polly's mother, shall I tell Polly? Do you want her to know, or not to tell her?'

'Yes, if you want,' Joss replied. 'Tell her it mustn't go further than her and Edwin, but you can tell Polly if you want to.'

'I'm glad you don't mind her knowing,' Lottie said. 'The Pascoes have always been like family. And working so closely with Polly it would be difficult. She sometimes asks how you are.'

Joss's face briefly softened a little at this last remark.

After Nora had gone to bed they continued to talk the subject over until well past Lottie's and George's customary bedtime, which made little difference, neither would have been able to sleep. Joss drove back to Manor Withiel, feeling better for having discussed the matter with his sister and brother-in-law, though it had not been his intention. Mentally he totted up his assets and deducted the amount needed to get Rupert clear of trouble. He still was well off . . . compared to his contemporaries he was rich. Provided his wife and her family were not allowed to burden him in the future with financial catastrophes all would be well. It was just the crass stupidity of the way these people behaved which rankled with him. Still, he'd hardly been white as the driven snow, he conceded to himself, remembering his lapse with Polly.

Joss arrived at Manor Withiel with a lighter heart and the situation more in perspective. He realised that in dipping so deeply into the funds for the Du Cane family, he had felt that he could not control the wealth he had been fortunate enough to acquire, and that the old saying about fools and their money being soon parted was seeming to prove true for him. But he held the reins; he was still able to maintain the manor and the staff. He had already dealt with Clementine and this was the last time he would 'stump up' for any of them!

Chapter Thirty

Agnes and Caleb became parents for the second time late one July evening. The birth had been prolonged, and left Agnes quite exhausted. Early in the pregnancy she had suffered badly with sickness. Then, as her girth, arms and legs all expanded the hot summer days wearied her. Caleb fussed around her a lot and was, as Agnes put it, a 'bundle of nerves' but of little practical help.

Despite all this the baby, a girl, was fine and healthy, arriving two weeks early and weighing-in at six and three-quarter pounds. Her head had a covering of short fine fair hair. Laura Ann Collins was lovely and perfect.

The nurse held the bathed infant close for Agnes to see and she viewed her baby with a smile of both relief and delight. With some effort she raised herself sufficiently to touch the tiny forehead with her lips, then sank back onto the pillows and fell fast asleep. The ordeal was over. Mother and baby had been safely delivered.

Edwin, who had recently become a daily visitor to his sister and now considered himself something of an expert on the subject of ladies being in an 'interesting condition', brought the joyous news home to Polly, who was happy and relieved for Agnes. She rather hoped the baby would be a boy, a future companion for Jonathan, but the baby girl was delivered safe and sound. That was what mattered.

Edwin seemed to think it a happy if not significant coincidence that Laura Ann was born eleven months after his own precious Jonathan. They would be celebrating Jonathan's birthday in a few weeks with a special birthday tea and a cake with a candle. Only the two grandmothers were invited, and Mary Jane, to give her a change from the somewhat frantic and chaotic activity which

220

goes on in a household when a baby is born.

Mary and Nell arranged the Birthday tea except Polly had ordered the cake from Belbins. When she arrived home everything was ready, with Cordelia and Nell clucking and cooing over their grandson.

After tea the presents were opened. Jonathan soon mastered how to tear off the wrappers, which he enjoyed doing more than discovering what was inside . . . that is, until he came to a present which Nell has been asked to bring from Emily Renfree.

'How kind!' Polly exclaimed.

The gift was a toy, a coloured tin box with a hinged lid . . . a Jack-in-the-Box! Edwin showed Jonathan how to open the lid, and Jack, with a large nose and pointed hat, shot out on a coiled spring. Jonathan jumped with surprise, then roared with laughter and wanted to repeat the trick himself again and again. He had no further interest in tearing wrappers and seeing the presents inside. All he wanted was to play with Jack-in-the-Box!

This made everyone, including Cordelia, laugh. But Polly felt a wave of guilt. The present which gave her son so much pleasure could be from his grandmother! Next year, when Jonathan could better understand, there would be a bigger party. The Godparents and the new member of the family, Laura Ann, would be invited and Emily would in future always be included in any little celebration.

It was not until after the baby's birthday that Lottie confided in Polly the latest problem Joss had been called upon by the Du Cane family to remedy. Polly felt her eyes brim at this latest unexpected burden which had been heaped on Joss's shoulders. When Lottie berated the moral standards of her sister-in-law's brother and Clementine too, Polly agreed with her, upheld her opinions, and inwardly felt both guilty and deceitful. Was she any better than they were? She had been unfaithful to her husband. She was pointing a finger of condemnation, but had she the right?

Nevertheless, she did feel Rupert was wrong, as she had been wrong. And she did feel sorry for Joss. He deserved better.

That evening she told a sombre-faced Edwin, but she could not look him in the face as she did so. Edwin expressed disgust at Clementine and Rupert. Poor Joss . . . what a load his broad shoulders had to bear.

Polly expected Edwin to be his normal agreeable self next

morning, but he was still sombre. Jonathan brought a smile to his face, but nothing else did. He's really taken Joss's troubles to heart, Polly thought.

But as a week turned into two, then three weeks, the spontaneity had gone from his smile. On leaving for the quarries and arriving home in the evenings his kisses seemed almost perfunctory.

Polly began to worry. Surely Edwin didn't hanker for some other woman . . . not Edwin! But what else could bring about this change in him? He still adored Jonathan. But it was only with Jonathan that he became animated, cheerful.

Another thought struck Polly . . . was Edwin ill? That must surely be it. He must see the doctor! Oh, Lord, had he already done so! Was it that he didn't want to tell her the bad news?

Polly worried and turned the matter over in her mind all day. She would tackle him that evening. She couldn't go on in this suspense. And that was just what she did. When the meal was over, Jonathan fed and asleep, and Mary out . . . presumably seeing her parents . . . Edwin seated himself in his customary chair and was about to read the paper, but Polly forestalled him.

'Edwin . . . I want to talk to you.'

He looked in her direction. 'What is it, dear?'

'You've not been yourself lately. Are you unwell?'

'Of course I'm not unwell, dear,' was Edwin's immediate reply. Polly hesitated, then questioned him again.

'You're not . . . ' she searched in her mind for a suitable expression, 'not as carefree as you used to be. I can't help wondering if there is something on your mind. If there is, I wish you'd tell me.'

Edwin removed his gaze from her face for a few seconds, then looked straight at her.

'You're right, Polly . . . I can't keep anything from you, can I? And I mustn't . . . I think I'm going to have to lay some men off!'

This was an answer Polly was not expecting. 'Lay men off! Whatever for? The granite business is so prosperous.'

'For a very long time it was . . . but not any more, at least, not to the same extent,' Edwin said. 'I just hate the thought of putting men out of work, but if I don't we won't break even this year.'

Polly sucked in a long breath of surprise and dismay.

'The trouble is concrete,' Edwin went on. 'Builders now are finding it cheaper to build with concrete blocks. Granite will still be needed for some things . . . for large public buildings they might still use granite, and for bridges etc. There is still a demand from abroad for granite for new ports, bridges, important buildings. Headstones are still likely to be made with granite. But for houses and suchlike, which is a big slice of business, the outlook is not very rosy.'

There was silence as Polly assimilated the new situation.

'But surely quite a number of houses are already made with cob walls,' she said at last.

'Well, whatever they were made from in the past concrete seems to be the building material of the future,' Edwin said, resignedly.

'Could this all be a flash-in-the-pan?' Polly asked, ' . . . a temporary situation, a bad patch?'

'I think not,' Edwin replied.

'Then surely the other granite merchants must be in a similar situation,' Polly argued.

'They are,' Edwin answered. 'At the moment we're all hoping for something to happen, something to save the day, but it's no good keeping our eyes blinkered. The granite business is in decline. I've lost several contracts, not to other granite merchants, but to concrete. The last biggest one was the day you told me about Joss's problems. The business is not quite dying, but it is definitely dwindling. Some of us will go out of business. Some will carry on . . . in a much smaller way.'

'Do the other quarry owners think like you do?' Polly asked after a long pause.

'They can be a bit cagey about what they really think,' Edwin replied. 'But as far as I can tell, not all do. Some don't think people will buy concrete buildings. They will buy what they know they can trust, they say. But it doesn't look that way to me.'

Polly tried to think of something comforting to say. 'I know you're astute, Edwin, but let's hope this time you are wrong, dear. Let's not cross our bridges before we come to them. But whatever happens the three of us have still got each other, that's all that really matters,' she added, and put an arm around him.

'What a comfort you are to me, Polly!' he murmured. 'I feel better already for having talked it over with you. Whatever would I do without you, my love.' He heaved a long sigh of relief and smiled down into her eyes, then lowered his head to kiss her.

Edwin's forecast proved correct. Business did not improve and men had to be dismissed. Edwin expressed his sorrow at this and though the men were only entitled to a week's notice, he gave them a month in which to look for alternative employment. The men took it stoically . . . they had seen it coming, as one remarked. A few grumbled, but at the situation not at Edwin. It deeply saddened Edwin to see skilled men, such as monumental masons, lose employment and have to take what they could get . . . labouring or other unfamiliar, unskilled work.

Not only the granite business was in difficulty, a woollen cloth manufacturer was rumoured to be closing and his staff would have to look elsewhere for work.

Practically all the men thrown out of work had families to support, some very large families, and most received low wages, but it did come at regular weekly intervals. Some made the reluctant decision to emigrate, the United States, South Africa, Australia and Canada being the countries likely to be considered.

Strangely enough, 'The Lady' did not suffer any noticeable degree of business loss. Edwin attributed this to the shop catering mainly for the upper end of the market, the well cushioned and the few idle or otherwise rich. The businessmen, the people who kept the wheels of trade turning, *and* their employees were the people who were the backbone of the country. Trade was what counted, not the minority of very rich people, nor to a lesser degree the professionals, nor the poor wretches at the bottom end of the scale, but the middle and working classes between them carried the country on its busy hard-working back.

Even so, Edwin recognised that change is always taking place. Sometimes it seemed to happen in fits and starts. In the early years of marriage, when he was hoping for a son, Edwin cherished the dream of leaving a thriving granite business and a good, trained workforce for his son, or sons, to inherit. Now at last he had his beloved son, but the dream of continuity, of handing down the business yet again from father to son, had crumbled.

Edwin felt sure his son, his Jonathan, would be good and successful at something. But it would not be the granite business. The thought made him sad.

Joss called on Lottie, his sister, fairly regularly. His visits to Polly and his Godson were less frequent and always at times when Edwin was likely to be present. Polly was not the only one to feel shame and guilt, and both were aware of this.

His latest call on Lottie and George brought the news that he and Clementine had decided it was time for Theodore to go away to a larger school in Hampshire more suited to older boys in the pre-university age group.

Theodore was not keen to go but on the other hand he did not raise any great objection because he was less than popular with the boys at Crosby, though he was quite 'thick', as Lottie put it, with a boy with a reputation for being 'slippery', who was known as 'Greaseball'.

'I think Clementine and Joss are hoping he will eventually go to university,' Lottie told Polly as they discussed Joss's latest call on his sister and brother-in-law.

'I suppose so,' Polly replied, and confessed she knew little about the upper realms of education, though she was sure a good education was an advantage. But it was her opinion that a Grammar School education was perfectly suitable for any young man who aspired to do well in business. She knew of no university-educated man who was successful in trade and running his own business. She had not considered the dizzy heights of university education. People with her humble background would be truly 'out of place' in a university! Lottie agreed, though conceded Clementine's family had a distinct advantage over them in this and the social sphere . . . but what good came of it?

Theodore, accompanied by Joss, did the rounds of visiting relatives and friends before being taken to Hampshire to start in his new school. As 'Greaseball' was going too, Theodore had begun to look forward to the new adventure.

The evening when Theodore and Joss called on Polly and Edwin, Polly was getting Jonathan ready for bed. Jonathan instantly recognised his Uncle 'Dos' and ran with outstretched arms to greet him. The little boy had formed a natural attachment to Joss, which pleased both Polly and Edwin, though for differing reasons.

How Joss would treasure these moments if only he knew the happy, laughing small child he played semi-rough games with, was his own son! She was grieved that he would never know. A lump rose in Polly's throat. How sad! What happiness, what much needed and certainly well deserved happiness Joss was missing out on in not knowing the little boy they all loved was his own son, his flesh and blood. Poor Joss, he had won such big prizes in life's lottery, yet had lost the biggest ones . . . his unfortunate choice of a wife, Clementine, his life-time partner, and in never knowing Edwin's precious boy was really his. How she would love to tell him! But how could even Joss be strong enough to behave as though the little boy was only his friends' child. He would be overwhelmed with emotion and pride in Jonathan, and sooner or later it would show. She *must* keep her guilty secret. Joss's loss was Edwin's gain, and what joy Jonathan had brought to Edwin. The decline and possible eventual loss, if the worst happened to the granite business, would count as nothing compared to the loss Edwin would suffer if he knew Jonathan was not his. It would surely kill the kind, the loyal, innocent Edwin. Polly felt she could count on the fingers of one hand the number of nights she had gone to bed and to sleep without pondering and fretting over the situation.

Two days later Theodore, accompanied by Clementine and Joss, departed on the train from Redruth Station on their journey to Hampshire and the Harcourt School for Young Gentlemen.

They had to change trains several times en-route, and on one station Theodore spotted 'Greaseball' and his parents: The two managed to chat briefly at a chocolate bar vending machine. 'Greaseball' told Theodore he must call him Silas in future. He had been given strict instructions by his parents, particularly his mother, that on no account must anyone learn he was ever known as 'Greaseball'. The nickname was not nice, and the impression it gave was detrimental.

After an overnight stay in Hampshire, Joss and Clementine went to London for a few days, Joss making sure Clementine did not have carte-blanche to spend as she pleased in dress and other shops, though he did allow her what he considered, and she did not, to be a very reasonable sum of 'spending money'.

Clementine paid a visit to Rupert, but Joss did not accompany her, he had business matters which he said needed his attention, and privately thought he didn't care if he never saw Rupert Du Cane again.

A couple of weeks after Joss and Clementine returned to

Manor Withiel, Lottie told Polly she needed to leave the work-room at 'The Lady' for half an hour to do some shopping.

'Take as long as you like,' was Polly's reply. 'We're not rushed in the shop this morning.'

In less than half an hour Lottie returned, red-faced and puffing with exasperation. There were no clients and Polly looked up from an invoice she was checking.

'Are you all right, Lottie?' she asked. Lottie answered her question with another.

'Who do you think I saw in town?'

Polly paused. Who could make Lottie this hot and bothered, no one . . . except . . .

'Clementine?' she said.

'Right first time,' Lottie said. 'Nose in air, dressed to kill and looking like she'd lost sixpence and found a gold sovereign. And who do you think was with her?'

Polly felt her jaw drop slightly. 'Not . . . '

'Yes,' Lottie interrupted, quivering. 'Charles Brendon Copeland!'

'Oh, no . . .' Polly murmured. Poor Lottie! Poor Joss!

'I'd just bought some fish and was coming up the steep opening down to Fish Strand Quay, when who do I see but Madam, mincing out of The Royal Hotel, with him holding her elbow and dancing attendance. They stopped to look at advertise-ments outside the Grand Theatre next door to The Royal Hotel. I scurried past on the opposite side of the street.'

'Did they see you?' Polly asked.

'I don't think so,' Lottie said. 'It makes me so mad, Polly. If I tell Joss it will upset him, though in one sense I think he's past caring. And if I don't tell him . . . '

'Oh dear,' Polly sighed, suddenly wearied by the apparently insoluble problem of Clementine. 'What a way to repay all he's done for her and her family.'

'Don't I know it,' Lottie answered, her lips pursed.

Two ladies came into the shop 'just to browse' and Lottie made her way upstairs to the attic workroom.

Chapter Thirty-one

One evening Polly arrived home from work to find Jack there, apparently amusing Jonathan. Mary was in the kitchen busy with the meal.

Polly warmly greeted her brother.

'How are you, Jack?' she asked, gazing up into his candid blue eyes.

'I'm fine and I've got something to tell you,' he was smiling a genuinely happy smile. 'Can you come here a minute Mary?' he called to Mary in the kitchen. Mary appeared in the doorway looking somewhat ill at ease. This was curious. She greeted Polly and said the under-roast was almost ready.

'That's fine, Mary,' Polly said, then turned to her brother. 'Will you stay and eat with us, Jack?' she asked.

'No. Mother is expecting me,' Jack said. 'But first I've got news for you.'

'What is it?' Polly asked eagerly.

'It might be a surprise,' Jack warned. Then the bombshell burst. 'Mary and I are engaged to be married.'

'Engaged!' Polly shrieked delightedly and kissed both Jack and Mary. 'You dark old horse,' she chided her brother. 'How long have you known?'

'Only since today,' Mary interjected, not wanting it to be thought she had been secretive about a relationship with her employer's brother.

'Since 1.15 p.m., to be exact,' Jack said. 'And you're the first to know.'

As he spoke Polly heard the front door open; Edwin had returned home.

'What's all the excitement?' Edwin demanded as he came into

the dining-room, gathering Jonathan up in his arms as he did so. 'I could hear Polly shrieking even before I opened the front door! What's going on dear?'

'Jack will tell you,' Polly said, and Edwin turned to Jack.

Jack beamed. 'It's good news,' he said.

'I'm listening,' Edwin replied.

'Mary and I are engaged to be married!' Jack told Edwin, who promptly congratulated them both, put Jonathan down on the floor, kissed Mary and shook hands with Jack.

By now a snag had occurred to Polly, and delight turned to partial dismay.

'My goodness, you're a deep pair,' Edwin said to Jack and Mary.

'Exactly what I just told them,' Polly said.

'This calls for a drink?' Edwin took out glasses as he spoke.

'It's a bit sudden,' Edwin remarked as he filled the glasses.

'Yes and no,' Jack said. 'I occasionally used to call in, middle of the day to see Polly and Jonathan and have my pasty or sandwiches at the same time.'

'I know you always call in on Mondays when mother is here,' Polly said.

'Oh, yes, I came home a couple of times and found you here, but I thought you called to see Jonathan,' Edwin laughed.

'I did call to see Jonathan, at least that was how it started,' Jack agreed. 'But now I've realised that for some time I'd been coming oftener and not just to see Jonathan, but to see *Mary*. Then it suddenly hit me!'

'And I've *always* had a soft spot for Jack,' Mary admitted, blushing crimson as she spoke.

Edwin handed the glasses round. 'Well, here's to your future happiness,' he said. 'To Mary and Jack.'

'To Mary and Jack,' Polly echoed.

They sipped their wine while Jonathan held up his hands for a taste of what they were having, demanding, 'D'ink, d'ink' and Edwin lifted him up while Mary fetched a small glass of home-made lemonade.

'I must be going,' Jack insisted when the glasses were drained. 'Mother will be wondering where I am.'

'She'll be pleased,' Polly told him.

'I'm sure she will,' Jack agreed, then kissed the still blushing

229

Mary, kissed his sister and baby Jonathan, shook hands with Edwin and departed.

After the meal, Polly helped Mary clear away the dishes and washed while Mary dried them.

'Jack's gain will be our loss, Mary,' Polly said.

'How do you mean, Mrs Pendleton?' Mary asked.

'You must call me Polly now,' Polly said. 'I mean when you and Jack marry, Jonathan is going to miss you terribly, and so shall I . . . and Edwin, of course.'

The smile disappeared from Mary's face. 'Well, I know we can't live here,' she said haltingly, 'but I thought I could still work here the same hours.'

There was a pause. Polly made no reply.

'You're married,' Mary pointed out in a small voice, 'but you go out to work.'

'Bless my soul, you're right,' Polly said. 'Why didn't I see it like that?' Then she added, 'But what if babies come along quickly?'

'A lot of people have more than one baby to look after. They manage,' Mary said.

'Why yes, you're right there, Mary. You haven't had time to talk about this with Jack, I suppose?' Polly asked.

'No. But I think he'll be agreeable. After all, you are his sister,' Mary ventured.

Polly nodded. 'Yes, that's right too. I think everything will work out,' she chided herself.

Why on earth did she think Mary would have to leave because of marriage. She hadn't applied any such rules to herself. She had assumed, just like everyone assumed, a wife would stay at home looking after the home and the husband and eventual family. She had done so herself for a time. It was because no babies came along that she needed to fill the gap.

It was when Polly went to bed that ideas came unbidden into her head. This always occurred when she had something on her mind, pleasing or otherwise. Edwin was asleep and gently snoring. The idea which came to her that night must keep until tomorrow evening. She hoped Edwin would approve.

Next day at the shop, Polly told Lottie about her brother's engagement to Mary. As expected, Lottie enthusiastically approved. 'They'll make a lovely match,' she said. 'Mary is such

230

a nice girl and so capable. Strong too, unlike that poor little Milly Bartlet.'

'Yes, that was so sad, and it hit Jack hard. But that's life I'm afraid,' Polly said with a long sigh, for Joss's image came suddenly into her mind with her final remark.

Over the meal that evening there was the usual exchange of news of the days happenings. Edwin didn't say much about work at the quarry. He was still sad about the reduced workforce and hoping no more dismissals would be necessary but feared a further decline in trade was inevitable. Polly waited for the main dish to be consumed before broaching her idea.

'Edwin . . . I've been thinking . . . '

Polly felt Edwin stiffen slightly, and he carefully placed his spoon in his pudding bowl and waited. When Polly had been thinking it was usually something he needed time and thought to come to grips with.

'Yes, dear.'

'You know Mary and Jack are getting married.'

'Yes.'

'And she said she would still like to continue working here, the same hours and everything, but not sleeping in, like now.'

'Yes.'

'Well, they'll have to have somewhere to live.'

'Let's hope it's somewhere not too far away,' Edwin said.

'I asked her this morning if they had a place in mind to rent and she said they hadn't had time to think about it, which was what I thought, but wanted to make sure.'

'What's this leading up to?' Edwin said.

'We own the field at the back of the house which used to belong to Valley View Farm.'

'Yes.'

'There's an access lane to our field and the farm at the side of this house.'

'Yes.'

'With the granite from your quarries, couldn't we use some of it to build a cottage in the field for Jack and Mary to live in and, at the same time, build a lovely house for Jonathan to have one day?'

Edwin sat silent, his mouth slightly open, as he tried to grasp not only the idea, but some of its many implications.

'Well?' Polly said at last when Edwin did not answer.

'We can't assume Jonathan will want to live there,' Edwin said. 'For a start, I don't think he'll be in the granite business. He might not live in Penryn. We can't map out his future for him, we can only try to give him a good start.'

'Owning a nice house is a good start, even if he doesn't want to live in it,' Polly said. 'But it wasn't for Jonathan the idea came to me. It would also be so nice for Jack and Mary, and so close by. It would be almost the same as now with Mary living-in. And we'd have rent coming from it. Property is always an asset. Bessie's getting older. You might not want a horse and wagonette when she's past it.'

Edwin saw the split-second smile on Polly's face.

'You mean I might want a motor?'

Polly didn't answer.

'You can forget that, Polly,' Edwin said. 'With business the way it is, and me having to get rid of men. The idea is out of the question.'

'I didn't say a word,' Polly said, and managed to look straight-faced.

'It's the cottage for Jack and Mary that I'd like you to consider first and foremost. And possibly a nice house for Jonathan if you think it feasible. That's all.'

'And that's quite enough,' Edwin retorted.

After a short silence, he said, 'I'll think about it.' Promptly, and to indicate the discussion was closed, he picked up his spoon and finished his now cold pudding.

Three days later, after fully weighing up the pros and cons, Edwin decided he approved the idea of having a cottage built for Mary and Jack; that is, if they wanted to rent a cottage from them. He felt sure Mary would, but they had not yet had the idea put to them. He was not agreeable to the suggestion to build a bigger, grander home for Jonathan.

That evening he told Polly his decision about the cottage and she was delighted. Jack would be calling for Mary shortly, and when he arrived they would put the suggestion to him and Mary.

But when Polly heard Edwin did not wish at this stage to build a grander house for Jonathan, her face fell. She couldn't believe

Edwin would build a house for Jack and Mary, who was in actual fact their servant, but not for his own son.

Edwin saw the dismay in her face. 'You said that first and foremost you wanted a cottage for Jack and Mary,' he gently reminded her.

'I know I did,' she admitted.

'Darling, in the present uncertain situation I can't afford to have too much capital tied up. Don't you think it would be a delight to me to build a lovely house for my son, to plan and with your help design a home for him, built under my direction, with granite from our own quarries for him to live in, for my grandsons to be born in. If it were not for the decline in the granite trade, nothing would please me more.' There was a strong hint of passion in his voice. 'But neither I nor anybody else in the granite business, knows what the future holds in store. I'll build the cottage first, if Mary and Jack would like it, but that is all.'

Unshed tears had gathered in Polly's eyes, and she blew her nose.

'Bear in mind, Polly, trades-people don't earn much. Most of the people who rent those tiny granite cottages in Helston Road and all over Penryn pay two shillings or half-a-crown a week. With buildings now being made with concrete blocks, they have no choice but to take the cheapest. Every penny counts to so many of them. *You* should know that.'

'Yes, I do know that, but if you build a really nice house for Jonathan won't it provide some work at the quarries?' she argued.

'It will provide some short-term work, but merely put off the evil day. It won't be making money, it will just diminish my capital with absolutely no return at a time when I don't know what the future holds in store. You realise Polly, by the time Jonathan is old enough to occupy the house, I might not have a granite business.'

'You're looking on the black side,' Polly said. 'Surely it's not as bad as that!'

'Not at the moment. But the outlook is not good. Concrete and 'artificial stone' look like being here to stay. It could be a flash-in-the-pan but for some time its sale to the builders has been expanding with a corresponding fall in the need for granite.'

Polly put a comforting arm around her husband, but said

nothing. She did now understand Edwin's reluctance.

'I've been so full of my own little business I hadn't fully appreciated the difficulties you've been wrestling with,' Polly sighed. 'I see now, it's really good of you to bother your head with a cottage for my brother.'

Polly turned her face up to his and kissed him. Edwin was about to put an arm about his wife and return her kiss when they heard Jack at the front door, followed by the sound of Mary hurrying down the stairs from her bedroom.

A couple of minutes later Jack, his hand clasping Mary's, entered the sitting-room to have a few words with his sister and Edwin before they both went out

'Sit down, sit down, we want to talk to you,' Polly said after greeting her brother.

'Just for a little while,' Jack said. 'We're meeting Jack Trewin and his wife.'

Jack sat next to Mary, who took a chair next to the fire.

'We've got a proposition to put to you both,' Edwin said. 'We don't need an answer now. But if you can spare a few minutes for us to tell you, you can think about it . . . turn it over in your minds for a week or so.'

'What is it?' Jack said.

Edwin turned to Polly. 'You tell them, darling. It was your idea.'

'I understand from Mary you haven't made any decision about where you will live when you are married,' she said to Jack.

'No, not really,' Jack answered. 'There hasn't been time, but I suppose we shall rent a little place somewhere in Penryn.'

'You know we've got a field at the back of the house?'

'Yes,' they both said.

'There is a lane at the side of our house for joint access to the farm and to our field,' Polly said. Neither Mary nor Jack spoke. They appeared not to see what this had to do with them.

'How would you like it if we built a cottage in the field near to the lane, for you to rent and live in?' she asked.

A new cottage to rent! Mary and Jack were dumbstruck at their unexpected good fortune.

'Mary said she wants to carry on working for us,' Polly added.

'I know,' Jack answered. 'That would be wonderful! It's really good of you both. I don't know what to say . . . it's wonderful news!' Jack's face beamed and Mary was overwhelmed.

'Mrs Pendleton . . . !'

'Polly,' Polly corrected.

'Polly . . . How can I thank you . . . oh, I can't believe it, a cottage of our own . . . all to ourselves. I never expected to be so lucky . . . so blessed. Oh dear, oh . . . '

A tear suddenly welled and began to run down Mary's cheek. She hastily wiped it away with the back of her hand.

Polly rose to her feet. 'I'll make us all a quick cup of tea,' she said and disappeared into the kitchen.

Mistress waited upon maid. Mary blew her nose and took a grip on herself, simultaneously smiling at her own thoughts. She was going to marry Jack Pascoe, she was going to be a sister-in-law to the master and mistress and she was going to live in a brand-new cottage. What a momentous week!

Chapter Thirty-two

Edwin wasted no time in putting into operation the plan for Mary and Jack to have a cottage in the field behind the rear of Villa Gwidden. The wedding would take place to coincide with the completion of the building.

The layout of the cottage had been planned by Polly and Edwin, but mostly by Polly; then the plans were put to Mary and Jack for suggested improvements, only they could think of none. The cottage sounded heavenly. Work on building commenced and was completed a year later. Jack helped with woodwork in his spare time, making doors, windows, fitments etc. He also made some of the furniture.

There were three bedrooms, a sitting-room, a large 'live-in' type kitchen, a scullery *and* a bathroom with a wash-basin and a large cast-iron bath. How modern! How elegant! How luxurious, posh, swanky! Mary extended greatly her list of normally used adjectives to describe the splendour and convenience of such an expensive and unusual, for working-class people, addition to the home.

Edwin did not entirely agree with Polly's idea to include a bathroom in the plans. It was an unnecessary extravagance in which only middle and upper class families indulged. But Polly was sure times would change, and said she would pay for the bathroom and all the expenses that went with its installation. Edwin did not labour the point, for Polly was aware that for a time Edwin thought her plans to make the dress shop so plush and luxurious were extravagant and he had been quietly astonished at the success of the venture, and at the wealthy and elevated ladies who patronised his wife's business; not to mention the distance some had to travel to be dressed in clothes by 'The Lady'. He did

236

not want Polly to think him penny wise and pound foolish.

Then there was the W.C. which was an additional delight to Mary. It was not at the end of a long garden. It was not on the opposite side of a back yard like at home. It was not in a lean-to at the back of the house. Nor was it necessary to fill a bucket from an outside tap to flush it. All one had to do was go out at the back of the house via the scullery door . . . it would not be healthy or proper to have the door to a W C. inside the house . . . walk a few steps to open another door, and there it was, all incorporated in the cottage and beneath where the bathroom was internally located but with entry from the outside. It had an overhead cistern and a chain-pull for flushing, just like the gentry now had.

All was brand-new and Mary was delirious with delight. *And* she was marrying Jack, the man she loved. Mary considered herself to be the luckiest girl in the world.

The wedding was a low-key affair. They didn't have money to spend on a big wedding and Mary's parents had little money to spare for anything. Looking presentable at the wedding and getting a small wedding present, a set of saucepans and a clock which had belonged to Mary's granny, was all her parents could manage apart from some home-made cakes and sandwiches to eat after the ceremony. Mary herself made a single-tier wedding cake. Her older brother provided a bottle of Sandimans port for the toast.

Mr & Mrs Bastian didn't have a lot to say, being quite overawed by the whole thing – their eldest daughter going up in the world – and by the unbelievable good fortune of having a lovely home built specially for her to live in, with a *bathroom* and a *flush privy* just like 'the gentry' had. It just didn't seem possible, nor did it seem quite right.

With scant success Polly tried to put them at ease, understanding how they felt. But she didn't share their unspoken conviction that everyone should know 'their station in life'. Just where in life would she have been if she hadn't married Edwin? Probably no better off than Mary's parents. How lucky, how blessed she had been!

Joss continued to call occasionally at Villa Gwidden, but still always when Edwin was there. Polly was glad of this; it lessened the inevitable tension there would have been between them had they been alone together. Without Edwin's presence the atmosphere would have been charged with pent-up emotions, rising desires. Nevertheless she knew that if Joss had the slightest inkling Jonathan was his son, his own flesh and blood, the product of his and Polly's union, he would have been a very frequent visitor. Clearly Joss was blissfully ignorant . . . well, ignorant. Poor dear Joss! He would have been so proud of his good-tempered fun-loving boy who was always delighted to see him. It was as though some invisible cord drew the small boy to the man he knew as 'Uncle Joss'.

But something did happen to Joss. There were days and weeks when no one except his mother saw him. On one such occasion not even Emily saw him, though she received a letter telling her he would be busy with business for several days.

Edwin heard it, Polly heard it, and Lottie had heard it too – that Joss had been seen by somebody – nobody quite knew who, with a 'shiner', a black eye!

Was it coincidence that about the same time Charles Brendon Copeland had been picked up one dark night by a waterfront man, on North Quay, Falmouth, with two black eyes, a cut lip and what seemed to be bruised ribs? He was also wet through, having dragged himself up a flight of quay steps from where, he said, he had fallen into the harbour. But clearly he had been in a fight.

The waterfront man reckoned a boatman or men, caught with a cargo of contraband, had taken revenge.

Lottie grinned as she related this to Polly. 'More like Joss threw him in,' she said. 'I can just see my placid brother picking Copeland up by the scruff of his neck and the seat of his pants and throwing him in the water,' she chuckled. 'And if he did you can bet he had his reasons.'

Some time later news filtered through that Customs Officer Charles Brendon Copeland had transferred to a port in the South East. Whether he applied to transfer or was ordered to do so no one seemed to know.

When Jonathan was nearing school age Polly and Edwin agreed it would be beneficial if he attended kindergarten for one term before starting at the Council School where Caleb taught.

This, they thought, would break him in gently to the routine of school-life and being with other children. Then, after a few years at the local Council School, he would go to Falmouth Grammar School.

So when the new term commenced Jonathan was taken by Polly to the kindergarten of a small private school run by the Misses Emmaline and Charity Jelbart. Lottie volunteered to look after the shop until Polly was able to get there.

The school building was the home in which the Misses Jelbart has been brought up. The two maiden ladies, from a genteel but impecunious background, had apparently fallen on lean times when their parents died and set up the school which took in a few boarders, catering for girls up to the age of around eleven. The boarders were all girls, and were of school, not kindergarten age.

Another good reason for Jonathan having a term at kindergarten was that Mary was expecting a baby.

Jonathan, on the first morning of this new experience, did not seem at all shy or concerned that he was to be left for three hours until he was collected by Mary, but ran to join the other small children. It was a group of five girls and three boys, Jonathan making the number of boys up to four.

The school term had started a week before the kindergarten and as she was leaving Polly caught a glimpse of the boarders in the hall as they made their way to the school-room. They were a quiet group, almost woeful compared with her lively, talkative boy. Their faces were pale too, and Polly thought they looked as though they did not get enough time out in the fresh air.

A few weeks later Mary told Polly that she was glad Jonathan's time at the Misses Jelbart's school was only temporary. She had told her sister who worked in a baker's shop, that Jonathan was going to the kindergarten. Her sister had confided it was well known to the shop assistants that the Misses Jelbart bought cheap stale bread, and sometimes stale cakes for Sunday tea for the boarders and apparently for themselves and the one feeble-minded poor woman who cleaned and cooked and lived in the basement.

Mary and Jack were happy about the forthcoming addition to their wedded state, but not in the ecstatic way Edwin had been. But to Mary marriage, then children, was the natural and expected progression. To Edwin and Polly it was the fulfilment of a cherished dream and a blessing which, it seemed for a time, fate was determined to deny them.

The ecstasy for Mary and Jack, apart from the joy in belonging to one another, was the cottage, and Jack was amused that Mary was slightly but noticeably speaking 'more posh'.

Chapter Thirty-three

Theodore's school reports were something of a disappointment to Joss. His school work was never hopeless, and rarely bad, just average, but with a liberal sprinkling of 'could do better', 'disappointing work', 'slovenly work', 'does not seem interested'. His behaviour left more to be desired: 'Unreliable', 'Has been a frequent source of concern', 'Has been found untruthful on occasions, for which he has always been punished. It is difficult to make him realise that, as in any worthwhile society, in this school mendacity is regarded as one of the more serious offences.'

Joss hated the last criticism, because it was correct, not the reverse. Lying, for that is what it was, was a particularly loathsome fault. Nobody, himself included, had any respect for a liar.

Clementine though, treated the reports as normal, only to be expected of a lively young lad away from home and missing his mama and her benign influence.

Joss kept his thoughts on character traits to himself. It would be useless to talk to Clementine of such things. She did not like or dislike a person because of their character or their integrity.

Several times, when home on school holidays, Joss had serious talks with Theodore; not complaining, not laying down the law, but discussing and pointing out how much Theodore had to lose . . . in friends, in the respect of others, particularly of people he would eventually have to work with, and most of all, in happiness. Joss allowed for youthful high spirits, though he did not voice his opinion that youthful high spirits had nothing to do with, cheating or untruthfulness.

Theodore had outgrown the tantrums of earlier years and was

241

more subtle, more composed. He now always listened to all his father said, agreed with all his father said, and smiled engagingly, leaving Joss with the hope that the boy, now almost as tall as himself, would mend his ways. But always his hopes seemed doomed to disappointment.

Now, when he thought of his son, his spirits were depressed rather than uplifted, and he experienced a feeling of apprehension about the future.

About once a month the most senior boys at Harcourt School for Young Gentlemen would gather with several of the masters, including the Head, in a small assembly hall in a hut, separate from the main school building and sited near the Gymnasium, for a relaxed grown-up type of social evening. Masters and students apparently chatted and laughed together, almost on equal terms.

Theodore had noticed quite a number of these seniors subsequently stopped behaving as other boys – no more larking about, no whispering smutty jokes and sniggering, no pushing one another and laughing at nothing in particular. They suddenly began to ape the masters, made a point of using long obscure words when a short one would have sufficed, made jokes which were 'over the heads' of the younger boys and instead of giggling, snorting and shoving each other, laughed, 'ho ho ho'. Becoming one of the seniors who attended these evenings was rather like becoming a member of an exclusive club. They were a set apart.

It was when Theodore was nearing seventeen, that once a week, for one hour after their evening meal, the boys in his age group were to learn how to dance and to perform the social niceties a lady would expect from a gentleman in the ballroom, at afternoon tea, etc., etc. This instruction was to take place in the hut when the masters and seniors gathered for their special evenings.

On the allotted night Theodore's form-master conducted the group to the hall and introduced them to Madam Elmeira, a buxom lady of around fifty, who was to instruct them in this completely different aspect of their education.

The boys – Madam Elmeira addressed them as 'young gentlemen' – were awkward and gauche. They were instructed to line up at one end of the small hall, then walk – more of a glide –

242

to the other end of the hall, their steps to be in time with the beats of the music played on the piano by Madam Elmeira's pianist.

The 'young gentlemen', always sure-footed and composed on the sports-field, seemed suddenly to lose control of both their feet and legs. They wobbled and stumbled, and bumped into each other, collapsing in uncontrollable laughter without even getting to the other end of the hall.

Madam Elmeira was not in the least perturbed by this behaviour. She had seen in all before.

'Move to the side of the hall, young gentlemen,' her voice rose above the noise. 'I shall have to give you individual tuition,' she said as she strode purposefully to where they stood, her body erect, head up, bosom thrust forward under her voluminous, flowing robes.

Without ado, she selected the two most clumsy boys, and took each by the hand as though they were two-year-olds.

The onlookers giggled and stared expectantly. This was a new and amusing experience.

'Now . . . stand tall, listen to the music, and walk with me, starting with the left foot.' She addressed the pianist, 'Ready!' The music started and the three moved forward.

'One, two, three . . . stop! Don't you know your left foot from your right?' She glared at the boy she held tightly with her left hand, who grinned and turned pink. There was a burst of laughter from the onlooking group standing along the side of the hut.

'Again,' she announced, 'Ready . . . *one*, two, three, four, one, two, three four. Stop!'

Once more she addressed the boy on her left. 'You are learning the rudiments of dancing, young man, not going on an army route march! Walk in a smooth manner, almost a glide. Now start once more, with back straight. *No!* Not stiff as a board. Stupid boy,' she muttered to herself. 'A good natural stance, *if you please!*'

The boy's face turned an even deeper pink. The others had not yet stopped laughing. This was great fun.

By the time they reached the opposite end of the hall the boys were keeping time, more or less, with the music.

'That's better,' she announced with a condescending smile, as the music and steps ended.

'You two young gentlemen on the end nearest the piano, come here please.' No one moved.

'Now come along,' she ordered.

The next two boys reluctantly ambled to where Madam Elmeira stood at the end of the hall, conscious that although they and the others sniggered at the first two boys who tried with small success to glide the length of the hall in time with the beats of the music, it was now their turn to be the objects of scrutiny and ridicule.

The process continued until each boy had performed at Madam Elmeira's side, one wrist firmly grasped in her hot podgy hand. Then they were all ordered to the end of the hall again, and after a few more walks up and down Madam Elmeira declared the lesson over.

'It might not seem to you that you have learned much,' she said. 'But I can assure you, until you have learned to walk in time with the music, you will never be able to dance. Moving to the beats is absolutely basic. Thank you young gentlemen, you may now leave.'

She stood by the door and shook hands with each boy in turn as they were about to pass through, and wished each one, 'Goodnight,' to which they reciprocated . . .

'Thank you, Madam Elmeira, Goodnight.'

Laughing, the boys returned to the main school building to complete their prep., but most did not have their minds on studies. Instead they minced about imitating walking to non-existent music, several performing a caricature of Madam Elmeira and mimicking her way of saying 'Forward on heels, backward on toes', even though they were not sufficiently advanced to walk backwards.

Some looked forward to the next lesson, some dreaded it and vowed they wouldn't be seen dead on a dance floor. Most were entertained by watching and laughing at their companions' efforts, but were scared of being laughed at themselves. Some were overawed by the commanding, loud-voiced female.

As the weeks progressed, so too did the boys . . . but painfully slowly. They had learned to waltz – some boys found it necessary to say aloud the change in beat counting to one, two, three. They were told by Madam Elmeira to try dancing with a partner – they would have to partner each other. This was a fiasco! They fell over each other's feet, pushed, shoved and collided with other 'couples'. Two 'couples' ended up on the floor and all collapsed with laughter.

But a few weeks later the laughter and near chaos which occurred in the hall each Monday night was replaced by stunned silence when Madam Elmeira made an announcement!

'Young Gentlemen . . . may I have your attention, please.' The boys became silent.

'As you all no doubt know, St. Anne's School for Young Ladies is about three miles from here, and I also teach the more senior young ladies there. Your Headmaster has given me permission to tell you that there is to be a dance here in this hall two weeks from tonight, and the young ladies from St. Anne's who are in your age group will be coming here to partner you.'

Madam Elmeira's words were interrupted by a concerted gasp of horror which arose from the listening boys.

'I hope you young gentlemen will not show any displeasure at having these young ladies as your guests,' Madam Elmeira said, a warning note in her voice. 'Remember they will be here at the invitation of this school for and of, *I hope* . . .' she emphasised, as though she doubted the accuracy of this, 'young gentlemen. You will be polite and courteous at all times.' Here she paused again for the instruction to register, then continued, 'You know the procedure for asking a young lady to dance. Remember also you will be guiding your partner. It is up to you to look where you are both going, to guide and to avoid colliding with other couples. At times in the past the scene in this hall has seemed more like a rugby scrum. There must not be anything remotely resembling *that sort of behaviour!*' Madam Elmeira's voice rose. 'Do you understand?' The silence which followed her words was almost tangible.

'*Do you understand?*' she thundered, her face fierce and threatening.

'Yes, Madam Elmeira,' they chorused. Their voices, uncommonly subdued, incorporated a tone resembling a groan.

Madam Elmeira appeared satisfied. 'The young ladies will be accompanied by one or two mistresses, and will arrive in a hired omnibus,' she added. 'Once again, remember your manners *and* that you must live up to your designation which is *gentlemen.*'

The boys appeared completely stunned. They hadn't given any real thought to what the lessons were leading up to. School was to prepare them for the far off future, not for the here and now.

Some boys seemed to have shrunk and shrivelled at the fearful prospect. One timid boy actually became white-faced. There was no laughing. The lesson progressed, some boys making a greater effort to perform well, a few seemed to have completely lost what little ability they had formerly acquired.

But as the days passed it was obvious a few were actually beginning to look forward to having an evening with the girls. Some, who never previously bothered to look in a mirror, were doing so at every opportunity, feeling and viewing above their upper lip for downy areas, and inspecting and squeezing pimples. Included in this was Silas Latimer, formerly known as 'Greaseball'.

Theodore took stock of his own appearance — tall, slim, fair hair slightly waved, blue eyes, a longish but otherwise neat nose rather like his mother's except his was now developing a slight bump or bridge, and this seemed to enhance rather than detract from his appearance. His lips were neither too thin nor yet too thick, and he had a chin and jaw-line that was just right. Theodore felt pleased with what he saw. He was really quite good looking!

Chapter Thirty-four

Except for the continuing worrying decline in the granite industry, life for Polly had carried on in a calm trouble free way. All the people who really mattered to her were well; there were no particular problems.

'The Lady' continued to flourish. Jonathan had left the Kindergarten and was enjoying school, Polly's mother was well and Emily Renfree seemed to have adjusted to the loss of her husband, John Renfree. Jack and Mary were blissfully happy and their son, little 'Jack Junior' was walking, talking a little, and had a sunny disposition. Clementine she rarely saw, but Joss looked relaxed and seemed to be his old easygoing self. Edwin noted with satisfaction and pride, Joss's growing fondness for Jonathan, and his pleasure in seeing and chatting to him.

Lottie had persuaded George to take early retirement. He had been getting very tired, but with the income from the shop they had no problems about where the money was to come from. Nora now worked at 'The Lady', in the showrooms on Thursdays, Fridays and Saturdays which were the busiest days, and in the workroom the rest of the week. She was popular with her contemporaries – especially the young men, and prettier than ever.

Agnes and Caleb were well, though Cordelia was more frail-looking than ever. Mary Jane had a young man, and Laura Ann was a delightful child and looked as though she was going to be a replica of her lovely grandmother. She was also Jonathan's favourite playmate, and any child who dared to annoy or pester Laura found, to their sorrow, they had Jonathan to deal with. His liking for his cousin was reciprocated – Laura was always happiest when playing with Jonathan, and Jonathan had tea with his cousin every week, alternating at Villa Gwidden and his Aunt

Agnes's home.

But all good things come to an end. The forerunner of a series of misfortunes, though a shock and a sadness, was to be expected before much longer. Agnes had taken her mother her customary cup of early-morning tea in bed and found Cordelia dead, having passed peacefully away in her sleep.

The funeral service and the burial under the tree in the same grave as George Pendleton seemed like a re-run of what happened at Edwin's father's funeral.

Whenever Clementine met or became involved with a male whose attentions she desired and was attracted by, a change came over her. It was as though she functioned on a battery which had suddenly been charged. She became vibrantly alive, energetic in the pursuit of pleasurable social intercourse, her eyes sparkled and she smiled, joked and seemed to almost crackle with inner vitality. She was like a frisky racehorse waiting for starter's orders. Not that Joss benefited from her apparent *joie de vivre*, for deep inside, despite buying and repairing the Manor, building a house for her parents and paying a minor fortune to get her brother out of a hole of his own digging, she still nourished a grievance over the way he had curtailed her spending and the loss of and humiliating way in which he treated dear Charles Copeland, who now, alas, was far away and who had not bothered to get in touch with her. No doubt he feared repercussions if Joss intercepted a communication.

Joss recognised the all too familiar signs, not that he now cared that his wife had a penchant for other men. He was not attracted by her and was both amazed and exasperated with himself that he ever had been. There were a few occasions when, having drowned his sorrows too thoroughly, he had bought the services of a certain 'lady' though she had admitted that for Joss she was available free. The only woman Joss loved was Polly, dear dear Polly, the only girl he had *always* really loved. If only he had the sense to wait. But the road trod by youth is full of pitfalls, and at a certain age it becomes the sole aim and occupation of each young woman to have her trap well baited until a certain young man, the too often *eager* young man, has fallen into it.

Well Clementine wasn't going to get away with this. Joss held the whip-hand and he knew how to crack the whip, only most of the time he was too indifferent to be bothered . . . past caring.

On a particular morning, included in the post which arrived for Joss, was a letter for Clementine's parents delivered to the Manor instead of 'Little Withiel Cottage'. Joss recognised the writing as Rupert's, and asked Myrtle to take the letter to Mr and Mrs Du Cane when breakfast was over. Myrtle now prepared breakfast, Miss Trembath having been instructed by Joss to get up later at her leisure, for she was now stiff with rheumatism, and Joss saw to it that she had sufficient help in the kitchen not to work at all unless she really felt like it.

As soon as Clementine's breakfast was served, Myrtle delivered the letter, only to be called back by a screaming hysterical Margaret Du Cane, who told her to tell Mr and Mrs Renfree to come to the cottage right away. Clementine finished her egg and bacon and swallowed the remains of a cup of coffee, patted her mouth with a napkin and rose from the table, leaving the toast and marmalade untouched. Joss had waited for her and in silence they made their way to the cottage. He was out of temper this morning because of the certain knowledge that Clementine was up to her old tricks with yet another man.

They could hear Clementine's mother noisily weeping before they reached the front door which was already open to receive them.

'Mother! Whatever is it?' Clementine said in alarm as she entered the sitting-room and found her mother slumped on the sofa, a crumpled handkerchief clutched in one hand while Albert Du Cane, whose height was now diminished by a permanent stoop, and who now seemed to stand with legs permanently bent at the knees, hovered hopelessly in the background. Clementine moved to put an arm around her mother, but Margaret Du Cane rose and ignoring her daughter's comforting embrace, ran to Joss. Joss instantly knew she was about to ask for something . . . something big . . . again!

'Joss, Joss please help us . . . you've got to help,' she cried. Firmly Joss took her wrists and removed her arms from around him.

'What's he done this time?' he demanded.

'Rupert's got to have £750 within ten days or he will be found out and dismissed,' she sobbed. '*And* sent to gaol,' she added.

'His name in the papers . . . dragged through the mud!'

'It seems that's the only thing that will teach him,' Joss said coldly. A flood of tears followed this statement, and Clementine succeeded in putting her arm around her mother.

'But you know he'll pay you back,' Margaret wheedled.

'I know he will *not* pay me back,' Joss retorted. 'But don't worry, he won't have to, because I'm not lending nor giving him the money.'

Here Clementine intervened, while her father continued to look on helplessly.

'You'll *have* to lend him the money,' she said. 'It's a family debt and you'll have to lend the money to him.'

'I'll *have* to do no such thing,' Joss replied. 'And it would not be lending, it would be giving, throwing the money away. I've done far too much already for this worthless family!'

'Worthless!' Clementine spat the word. 'You say that! Coming from your background, your father no better than a common labourer!'

'My father was a monumental mason, which is a skilled if low paid job. What little money he did have he got by sweat, by hard work. At least he was not a common thief!'

'Don't you use the word "common" to refer to *my* family, nor *thief*, you jumped-up nobody!' Clementine snarled.

'A nobody you thought worth setting your cap at I seem to remember,' Joss said with a shrug of his broad shoulders; then added as though to himself, 'To my sorrow.'

'To your sorrow,' Clementine repeated in a tone of incredulity. She believed no man could ever be sorry to have been the recipient of her favours. 'Well that accounts for it. I hear you have a preference for your own low types . . . common tarts!'

'Yes I must have,' was Joss's instant reply. 'I married you didn't I!' Clementine's jaw dropped and her face turned white with rage.

'I hope the one currently servicing you is well off, and that you don't have to pay for his services.' Joss went on. 'After all, you must have spent a pretty penny of my money being "hospitable" as you call it, to that Copeland fop.'

Clementine's fingers began to wind themselves slowly around a small heavy bronze figure of a woman which stood on a nearby small table.

'The way you carry on you could easily earn enough to replace the money your brother took from the firm, just by lying on your back and opening your legs! But you should know that better than I do.'

Joss moved to leave, which was fortunate for him, as the heavy bronze figure whizzed past his ear, missing his head – the intended target – and crashed into a framed picture which hung on the wall. Margaret screamed as broken glass flew in all directions. A second crash instantly followed as Joss left, slamming the front door and leaving two bawling females behind him.

He had covered but a few yards when he heard the front door being opened and Clementine shouting, 'It's your fault.' Her voice took on a whining tone, 'Theodore has been sent away and you don't love me, you hardly speak to me, you don't even share our marital bed. What do you expect me to do?'

But Joss's expression was like the stone by which his father and grandfathers had earned their livings – granite.

Within a week Joss received a pleading self-pitying letter from Rupert, requesting a loan and that Joss reply right away. Joss complied with the latter request by telegram, containing a terse one-word, one-syllable message – 'No'.

Much correspondence took place between Clementine's parents and Rupert, also Clementine and her brother. Then nothing. A fortnight passed but despite letters and requests no one heard a word from Rupert. A letter from the senior partner in the firm of solicitors came next. It was addressed to Clementine's and Rupert's parents. They had been unable to contact Rupert Du Cane and there had been no word, no message from him to account for his absence from the office. Was he ill, and did they know? They had to admit they did not know his whereabouts, or if he was ill. They were extremely worried. They did not, however, mention that he owed the firm money, which he had 'borrowed' without their knowledge.

A few days later another letter arrived from the senior partner. A check had been carried out and £2,000 was missing from funds. A total of £750 withdrawn in a series of smaller amounts, had been withdrawn eight weeks previously. Three weeks ago a further £1,500 had been removed from their Clients' Account at the bank, £100 of which had been in American Dollars. It seemed Rupert Du Cane had absconded to America. Did they know his address? If not, they were requested to get in touch immediately should they hear from him. A representative of the firm would be calling on them in the near future, with a view to retrieving, if at all possible, the money which Du Cane had fraudulently removed from their accounts. Failure to achieve this would result in the usual official procedures.

Margaret ran screaming to her daughter, and between sobs blurted out the latest news. Joss accompanied them back to the cottage. They found Albert Du Cane seated and leaning forward over the arm of a chair, grey-faced and gasping painfully.

Against his better judgement Joss knew his heart was melting. 'I'll go into Penryn and speak to my bank manager about coming to some arrangement with them,' he said – a 'cover up' now being out of the question, too late.

On hearing Joss make this pronouncement, Albert Du Cane turned his eyes upwards to look into Joss's face. A smile which expressed both thanks and relief began to spread across his grey face but was swiftly obliterated as an excruciating pain seized him. A strangled groan escaped his throat, while his fists were so fiercely clenched all the knuckles showed white as they were pressed against his chest. Two long agonising seconds passed, then Clementine's father relaxed . . . dead!

Chapter Thirty-five

Manor Withiel was not a happy place. Margaret Du Cane, who was living in the Manor temporarily to have company, was distressed at the loss of her husband Albert, in addition to the disappearance of her son Rupert. Clementine was tight-lipped and wore a haughty, grim expression, having conveyed to Joss that she considered he was to blame for her father's death. And Joss himself was in low spirits. What a life! What a family! What a marriage!

It was all so different from what, in his naïve youth, he thought being married and having a family would be like. He just assumed it would be the way it was in the home in which he grew up. They were short of money, just like everyone else from his background – that was taken for granted – but they were a happy family, kind to each other, they laughed together, occasionally were sad together, sometimes had differences – what family didn't. But they never stopped loving and caring for one another. It was a way of living he just took for granted. He couldn't have been more wrong. If only he'd waited . . . he and Polly would have had a life just like that.

Joss had come to an arrangement with the firm from which Rupert had absconded after embezzling around £2,250. The firm stood the loss of £1,000 and Joss paid the remainder to let the matter rest, thereby keeping the whole disgraceful business and its attendant stigma out of the newspapers, so that neither the firm nor, therefore, the Du Cane family, suffered adverse publicity. If Rupert was known to ever return to this country he was not sure whether or what action the firm might then take, neither did he care.

He opened another letter. It was from the Harcourt School for

Young Gentlemen and was signed by Mr Brightman the Headmaster. The Headmaster was seriously disturbed by Theodore's behaviour. He would prefer to talk to his parents concerning this as it was a delicate matter, not suited to written correspondence. Would they please get in touch to arrange an early meeting. Joss heaved a sigh. What now?

Half an hour later, when Clementine appeared, he silently passed the letter to her. Her expression did not alter as she read then handed back the letter to him, saying, 'Well, I shan't be going to Hampshire. I can't leave mother in the state she's in.'

'Please yourself,' was Joss's indifferent reply.

A few days later Joss, his face grim, boarded the train on his way to Hampshire. He stayed the night at the village nearest the school and made arrangements for a cab to be waiting for him at 9 o'clock the next morning.

The latest events at Manor Withiel had wearied him and he went to bed earlier than usual but was unable to sleep. What on earth can the boy have got up to this time, he wondered. Joss took a final swig from his silver mounted brandy flask and drifted at last into a fitful sleep.

Next morning, at 9.30 a.m. precisely, he was ushered into Mr Brightman's study. The tall, thin, balding, long-nosed Headmaster rose from his seat at a large polished desk, on which were piles of neatly arranged papers, and came forward to greet Joss, his hand extended.

'Good morning, Mr Renfree, I'm so pleased you are here. Please take a seat.'

'Good morning, Headmaster,' Joss replied as the two shook hands. Joss took a seat on one of the two chairs in front of the desk, and apologised that his wife was unable to be there. 'What's he done this time?' he asked weakly and without ceremony, as he sank into the chair.

The Headmaster, however, took his time. He was not to be hurried nor hustled. Slowly he made himself comfortable in the chair behind the desk, crossed his legs and, elbows on chair-arms, raised both hands to press his fingertips together in a contemplative pose.

'This, as I indicated, is a rather delicate matter,' the Headmaster said.

Joss waited.

'The boys in his form have been taking instruction in how to behave in social situations, as is proper at their age.' He paused.

'Quite,' Joss agreed.

'This . . . ' the Headmaster went on, 'included lessons in dancing.' Another pause.

'Yes!' Joss said, trying to hide his impatience.

'When the boys reach a certain stage, Madam Elmeira, who instructs them and who also gives similar instruction at a nearby prestigious girls' school, St. Anne's School for Young Ladies, arranges for the well-chaperoned girls to come here to partner the boys for their mutual benefit from the point of view of improving their dancing techniques.'

'Sounds sensible,' Joss commented, wishing the man would get to the point.

'In return,' the Headmaster continued, 'the boys get an invitation, arranged between the Headmistress of St. Anne's and me, of course, to attend a similar function at St. Anne's School; and so it continues every fortnight at alternate venues.'

The Headmaster shuffled some papers around.

'The only time the girls and boys are allowed to leave the hall where the dancing is practised, is to visit the "Cloakroom" . . . the girls have separate facilities, of course.'

Joss made an almost imperceptible nod of his head.

'On the last occasion your son visited St. Anne's it was noticed he absented himself for longer than seemed necessary. It was then also noticed that the young lady who partnered him was also absent for, again, quite some time. It was subsequently discovered neither were in their respective cloakrooms. A search was commenced, discreetly of course, and they were found together in the girl's study-cum-bedroom.'

'Not . . . ' Joss said.

'No,' the Headmaster quickly interjected, 'not like that! That would have merited instant expulsion. But the young lady's clothing was in disarray, apparently to an embarrassing degree . . . '

'You don't mean she . . . '

'No,' the Headmaster quickly interjected. 'It was only her outer clothing.' He paused. 'Where this would have led had they not been interrupted, no one can say.'

'Do you know who caused her clothes to be in disarray?'

Mr Brightman gave a slight shrug of his shoulders. 'I understand they were questioned, but neither would say.'

Joss lowered his gaze in silent contemplation.

'Was there anything improper about Theodore's clothing?'

'He had a certain button undone,' the Headmaster replied.

Joss gave an exasperated sigh, knowing to which button the Headmaster referred. 'It might have been accidental,' he said.

'It might, it might not,' the Head replied. 'In either event your son had got himself into a perilous situation, and I can only repeat, were they not interrupted the result could have jeopardised your son's whole future.'

'I can see that and I am disturbed to hear what happened,' Joss said. There was again silence for a few moments as the implications registered.

'I'm not trying to blame the young lady for Theodore's behaviour, but I can't help feeling the fault cannot all be on one side. After all, they were in the *girl's* room. He could not have taken her there if she didn't wish it, he wouldn't know where it was.'

'The Headmistress of St. Anne's and I have also come to that conclusion, Mr Renfree,' the Headmaster said. 'We have both taken the following steps. Both are banned from dancing instruction. I might add Madam Elmeira is quite upset. Your son is also banned from visiting St. Anne's School and the young lady is banned from visiting this school. They are warned not to see each other again, on pain of expulsion if they do. You will understand these young people are at a very difficult time and to thoughtlessly behave in the way they have could ruin the rest of their lives . . . in many ways.'

'I do realise that only too well, Headmaster, and I thank you for the way you have handled the situation,' Joss said, only too aware how easy it could be to make a mistake or wrong choice and never to stop paying for it.

'Normally boys leave here at around eighteen and most go on to University,' the Head continued, now in a more relaxed way. 'If young Renfree behaves himself he can still complete his schooling with his character and record intact, which will serve him well for the future. If not . . . ' the Headmaster shrugged, 'who knows what he might lose by it?'

'Thank you. I see very well,' Joss said.

'We shall be keeping a watchful eye on him, and this he will not like. But frankly, I will tolerate no more misconduct of any kind,' the Headmaster added.

'I wouldn't expect you to,' Joss replied.

'Would you like to see your son, Mr Renfree?'

'Yes, for a few minutes.'

Theodore was summoned to the Headmaster's study.

'Come in,' called the Headmaster, when there was a knock on the door. Theodore entered, looking pale but composed, and Joss noticed with a jolt, Theodore no longer looked like a boy, but a tall self-possessed young man with all the attributes that he had learned a certain type of flighty young lady found attractive. Though clearly subdued, his calm composure in the face of being caught out in such an embarrassing and improper situation, somehow reminded Joss of Clementine's suave, worthless brother Rupert and of that Copeland peacock.

'Ah, Renfree,' the Headmaster said, 'your father has come all the way to Hampshire, at my request, to discuss your most improper and ungentlemanly recent behaviour. Now I will leave you here in my study for as long as Mr Renfree wishes. He shifted his gaze to Joss. 'I shall be in the adjoining room should you require me, Mr Renfree.'

'Thank you, Headmaster,' Joss said, and the Head, picking up a pile of papers from his desk, left the study.

Joss and Theodore stared at each other for a brief second, then Theodore lowered his gaze.

'Well . . . what have you to say for yourself?' Joss said.

'Sorry, father,' Theodore replied.

'Of course you're sorry . . . you behaved disgracefully and you were caught,' Joss said angrily. 'How could you have contemplated such behaviour in the first place?'

'I didn't actually.'

'Don't tell me you're cowardly enough to blame the girl,' Joss felt his anger rising.

'I'm not doing that,' Theodore defended.

'Then just who are you blaming?' Joss demanded.

'You asked who thought of it . . . contemplated you said. The answer is Greaseball . . . sorry, Silas Latimer.'

'Don't tell tales. You're the one who went to the girl's room not Silas Latimer!'

'The girl he asked wouldn't go. My partner was more than

willing.'

There was silence as Joss assimilated the situation.

'Look Theo,' he said at last, his tone more conciliatory, 'decent people . . . gentlemen . . . don't behave like that.'

At this remark Theodore stared unflinchingly into his father's dark eyes. Joss stared back into his son's defiant blue ones.

'Don't they?' Theodore's tone was slightly mocking.

'Whatever *you* might think, *decent* people don't,' Joss said. 'You know if you make one more mistake you'll be expelled, and that would be a considerable disadvantage to you and your career. You can at least manage to see that, I hope.'

'Yes, all right. I can see that, father,' Theodore replied.

'Theodore,' Joss's tone had softened, 'your mother and I only want what's best for you. She'd be very upset if you did something to spoil your future.'

Theodore pursed his lips and remained silent. Joss was aware that his son had always seemed to favour his mother, who spoiled him and made excuses for his every misdemeanour. His son's reply was not what he had expected.

'I expect she'd find consolation,' Theodore said, then added pointedly, 'with some gentleman, or whatever.'

'I think you've said enough,' Joss said quietly, then knocked on the door of the adjoining room. The Headmaster opened the door and Joss bid him and Theodore good-bye. He shook hands with both, issuing a final warning to Theodore as he did so.

With a heavy and guilty heart Joss strolled back to the village inn where he had stayed the night. Clearly Theodore was aware of his mother's peccadilloes, her carryings on. He was now old enough to understand certain things which, if he ever bothered to give it a thought, might previously have puzzled him. Joss doubted his son knew his own record was less than snowy white, but from the way Theodore seemed to view things he probably assumed his father had outside 'interests'. And Du Cane blood obviously ran in the boy's veins. What sort of man could he be expected to grow up into?

It was a hard thing for a man to begin to lose pride in his only son. But that, he realised, was what was happening. He tried not to make comparisons between Theodore and the sons of some of his contemporaries. None of them had Theodore's advantages, yet most were better young men than Theodore was ever likely to be. No, no. That wasn't fair. How could he think such thoughts about his own son. He loved the boy. Go into the bar and find some men to yarn with, he told himself when he arrived at the inn. It was too late to journey back to Manor Withiel. Somehow he didn't want to go back there, to Clementine and her fault-finding and long face, and Margaret Du Cane's tears. He could probably get a train to London today. He'd have a few days away from it all.

Chapter Thirty-six

Before leaving Hampshire Joss wrote to Clementine telling her he intended going on to London, that there was now no need for her to worry about Theodore, and that he would give her details on arrival home. He also wrote to his mother, Emily, who thought he was just paying Theodore a visit while on a business trip. No need to give her cause for concern.

But now that he was in London, in a hotel in the Rotten Row end of Park Lane, he found London was not the answer to his low spirits, neither was drink. The company or services of certain women he did not even consider. There was no substitute for love . . . real genuine love . . . and Polly was the only woman for Joss.

Being married to a woman he did not love, who turned out to be an entirely different person from the woman he thought he was marrying, was hard to bear. But when she deliberately made herself a constant thorn in the flesh, and a lot of everything, including men, was never enough was more than any man could tolerate. For how much longer could he stand this? He would not unburden himself to his mother. Joss knew she was aware he and Clementine were less than happy together, but she could have no idea how bad things really were. Lottie was doing well and she really was happy with life. Her business success had not had an adverse effect on her marriage, quite the reverse. It enabled George to retire early and in comfort instead of forcing him to work to support his wife and youngest child when he was not fit, and when to carry on would almost certainly ensure his early demise. George did not begrudge his wife her business success and when, before he retired some of his work colleagues joked about him having a working wife, he grinned and reminded them he earned exactly the same meagre wage they did, and not to be jealous of the extra income his family enjoyed. He was proud of his wife. It was a dream come true for Lottie, and Joss did not want to tarnish it with worry about his problems.

And dear Polly and Edwin must never know. Edwin had Polly's respect and her undoubted affection for his kindness, his generosity, and all his other admirable qualities. But Joss knew with absolute certainty that he and he alone owned Polly's heart. It was hard enough for her to hide her feelings *without* knowing how deeply unhappy he was. If she did know it was possible it would be too much for her not to fly to him. What heaven it would be if she did; if he could for a short while, feel the comfort of her arms about him, know once more the sensation of his lips upon hers. He must stop even thinking such thoughts, and not breathe his troubles to anyone. Have a drink, Joss, he told himself, and made his way downstairs to where half a dozen men were propped against the bar.

Next morning Joss awoke, unable to remember going to bed. He felt dreadful, and the thought of fried bacon and eggs made him want to vomit. This wouldn't do. Don't complain about your son and then set him the example of becoming a drunkard, he told himself. He splashed his face with cold water, decided to wash, shave, dress and go for a walk in Hyde Park. The fresh air might clear his head.

Joss spent the day walking around London, treading the paths of sight-seers in the City. He stared blankly at the usual sights, Buckingham Palace, Houses of Parliament, Westminster Abbey, St. Paul's Cathedral. The theatres and picture-houses held even less attraction as he glanced disinterestedly at the placards and posters. Joss strolled through St. James's Park, sat on a park bench, opened a newspaper and glanced at the headlines. A couple of tarty-looking young women walked towards him, giggling and nudging one-another.

'Fancy a good time, sir?' one of them said, and they both stood all teeth and giggles, awaiting his reaction. Joss did not react, but continued to stare disconsolately at the newspaper, scarcely aware of them or the news, lost in his own thoughts.

' 'orrible to be deaf ain't it?' the other one said, and the two moved off, still giggling and speculating that perhaps he could not raise the cash . . . or something.

Not for even an hour had he shed the unfamiliar despondency

which had taken a hold on him. He might as well not be in London. Apart from Theodore being at school his concerns and all he cared about were at home in Penryn, in Tiggy Lane where his mother lived, in Falmouth and, in some ways least of all and some ways most of all, at Manor Withiel. First thing tomorrow morning he'd go to Paddington Station and take the train . . . The Cornish Riviera . . . for home.

Late in the afternoon of the next day, Joss alighted at Redruth Station. A cold wind was blowing from the direction of the Atlantic. It was a grey day and under a lowering sky the light was already dimming. Joss felt a sudden chill of foreboding as he made his way to the rank of Hansom cabs and black-coated, top-hatted drivers. The man who drove the cab at the head of the line, came forward.

'Can I be of service, sir?'

'Yes, thank you,' Joss replied, and the driver took his case, while Joss got up into the cab, and opened a newspaper he had bought from a vendor on the platform. The news matched his mood – depressing. The German Kaiser, cousin to the King, was displeased with the Prime Minister and critical of this country, while the French thought Britain was too friendly with Germany which they seemed to see as some sort of threat to themselves. Joss folded the paper and placed it on the seat.

'Where to, sir?' the driver said, before himself climbing into his high driver's seat behind the massive Shire horse.

'Manor Withiel. Do you know where it is?' Joss said.

The driver's face took on a startled expression, combined with disbelief.

'Did you say Manor Withiel, sir ?'

'Yes . . . what's wrong?' Joss said, the feeling of foreboding, deepening.

'Haven't you heard about the fire, sir?'

'Fire! What fire?' Joss demanded and jumped down from the interior of the cab to speak to the man at close quarters.

'It's been the talk of Lanner and Redruth, sir. I only know what I've heard. But there's been a big fire there and it seems most of the Manor was burnt out!'

'When?' Joss demanded, feeling the colour drain from his face and his skin tighten.

'Late Monday night. Fire Brigades went from all around, sir, but it's a long way for horses to pull, and they had to use water from the lake.'

'Was everyone saved?' Joss said

'Yes, as far as I know sir. The servants' end of the building was practically undamaged, but an old lady was greatly distressed and a man was in a state about something, though apparently he was unharmed.'

'Man! What man?'

'Don't know, sir. Do you still want to go there?'

'Yes, right away,' Joss said, climbing back into the cab as he spoke.

The driver made a clicking sound out of the side of his mouth, and with a slight flick of the whip the powerful horse moved forward, the driver only partially releasing the brake as the cab moved downhill, then releasing it fully as they turned into the long stylish Albany Road. 'Gee up, Mary,' he called, flicking the whip as he did so. The cab went quicker, but slowed slightly when the road began a long ascent out of Redruth, then over the brow of the hill and down, more slowly and with the brake again partially on, through the village of Lanner with its long rows of miners' granite cottages, which lined each side of the road.

With Lanner behind them the road continued flat. After they curved right to ascend yet another hill, Joss began to notice a dank, acrid smoky smell. The smell grew stronger as they neared the turning right toward Manor Withiel.

Joss had been going over in his mind the procedure necessary to get a steam fire engine on the road even before it reached the fire. First the engineer and the bugler would have to be called and the bugler would have to run to where each fireman lived and ensure it was the right house by checking there was an enamel plate displayed, bearing the letters F.M., then blow on his bugle to awaken, hopefully, the sleeping fireman until all the crew were roused and making their assorted ways to the Fire Station. While the bugler was doing this someone had to go to the field where the horses were and round them up. Meanwhile, the Firebox would have to be lit to get a good head of steam. Doing all this could take almost an hour before the steam fire engine and the firemen started out. Other fire brigades called up would have to go through the same procedures.

'Whoa,' called the driver and the horse slowed to an

unscheduled stop.

'What are you stopping for?' Joss called, anxiously.

'Cow on the road,' came the reply.

Joss and the driver alighted simultaneously, Joss clucking with impatience. 'The hedge is very low a few yards back,' he said, being familiar with the road. 'She must have got out from there.' Together they drove the animal back along the road and without too much difficulty persuaded it to scramble over the hedge and into the ascending field.

'I'm surprised the farmer hadn't noticed she was missing,' Joss muttered impatiently, for it was well past milking time.

They returned to the cab, the horse having taken advantage of the stop to crop the grass growing at the base of the hedges which lined both sides of the road. It seemed reluctant to leave.

'Will you make that horse get a move on,' Joss shouted.

' 'es sir, sorry 'bout that,' replied the driver, cracking his whip and shouting, 'Gee up, Mary!'

A few long minutes later they turned into a narrow road, and after a quarter of a mile passed the lodge where Tom and Mrs Soloman lived, and along the driveway to Manor Withiel. By now the air was pungent with dank smells of sodden, burnt wood, etc. With a sinking feeling in his stomach Joss stared ahead as the cab was about to round a bend where Rhododendrons were blocking the view of the building.

Suddenly the Manor came into view! 'Oh, my God,' Joss uttered aloud as he saw the black voids where there had been richly draped windows. Much of the roof was open to the sky. No one seemed to be about. No lights. The place looked dead, and Joss felt, no knew, that it was. Then he noticed the far end, to the left of where he now was, seemed unharmed, likewise the old stables, outbuildings, etc.

The cab was nearing the massive front door, which miraculously still stood.

'Do you want me to stop here, sir?' the driver asked.

'Yes.' Joss spoke automatically. In a daze he paid and tipped the man.

'Would you like me to come with you, sir?' the driver asked, sensing his customer was profoundly shocked by what he saw.

'No, no. I'll be all right,' Joss answered without even looking at the man.

Dimly he heard the driver say, 'Goodnight then, sir,' and signal his horse to move off.

Joss turned towards Withiel Cottage which, from where he now stood, was hidden from view, when he heard Miss Trembath, the cook, call to him.

'Mr Renfree! Oh, sir, sir!'

Joss turned and Miss Trembath came hurrying towards him as fast as her rheumaticky legs would allow.

'Sir, the mistress has been trying to contact you.' The cook then burst into tears,

Joss, coming now to his normal senses, put a comforting arm about her heaving shoulders.

'You don't deserve this, sir,' she blurted out. 'There's never been a better master at Manor Withiel!'

'Where is Mrs Renfree?' Joss asked as her sobs subsided.

'She and Mrs Du Cane are staying at Withiel Cottage.'

'Is the cottage all right?' Joss asked.

'Yes, sir. The paint's blistered and two or three of the window-panes are cracked. That's all.'

By now Myrtle, cook's assistant, and the other 'live-in' servants had gathered, and Tom Soloman was running up the drive to join them.

'I believe we had a guest here on Monday . . . the night when there was a fire. Was he all right do you know?'

'Mr Farnell, sir,' said cook.

Instantly Joss recollected Clementine's friend Jane McBride who lived at Greenbank, in Falmouth, had a cousin called Farnell. He had a sick wife who, it was rumoured, never left her room at the back of the house where they lived in nearby Stratton Terrace.

'He escaped the fire, though I don't know that he was all right,' cook went on.

'What do you mean?' Joss said.

'He came out unharmed, though he was making a fuss about something he lost. It might have been this, it's got an engraving on it.'

Cook produced a gold watch and chain from her pocket, saying 'Young Fred found it.' Fred was now on the scene.

'I found it in the rubble, sir,' he said.

Joss turned to look at him. 'I'm glad you handed it over, Fred,' he said. 'You did right.'

m

'Thank you, sir . . . sir.'

'Yes.'

'Mrs Soloman ain't had her blanket back yet, and she told him she wanted it back.'

'What blanket?' Joss said.

'The man who stayed here was naked.' Incredulity caused the lad's voice to rise to a high pitched treble. 'Naked as the day he was born, he was. He wanted to leave and the firemen took him away and covered him up in one of Mrs Soloman's blankets, and she said she wants it back.'

Joss, his expression grim, nodded knowingly. 'I'll see Mrs Soloman has her blanket, or a replacement,' he said.

The rest of the staff had been standing silent and downcast, waiting their chance to express their sorrow. Tom Soloman had now joined them. Joss learned that while awaiting the fire-brigades all the staff including rheumaticky Miss Trembath, had formed a chain to pass buckets of water up to him in an attempt to quell the blaze. This they clearly did not succeed in doing, but they did slow its progress through the Manor, thus preventing it from reaching and destroying the kitchens and servants' quarters, except for a couple of attic bedrooms.

'Where did the fire start?' Joss asked.

'We thought it started in the blue sitting-room, sir, where Mrs Renfree and the family usually like to spend their time,' said Tom Soloman.

'Has anyone any idea what caused it?' Joss asked.

'Not for sure,' Tom said.

'Well I'm sure,' said Mrs Harvey, who assisted Mrs Soloman with the housework. 'I think It was the blue sofa.'

'I agree with that,' said Tom Soloman's wife who had now joined them.

'Not the fire in the grate?' Joss queried, surprised.

'I don't think so, sir. That Mr Farnell was always smoking cigars and he wasn't at all fussy about stubbing them out when he finished, or where he dropped them when he was smoking,' Mrs Harvey said.

Myrtle nodded her head in agreement. 'That's right sir,' she said.

'He burned the polish on one of the small tables when he was here before,' remembered Mrs Soloman. 'And singed the upholstery of a chair in the big room.'

The weariness of spirit which had beset Joss over the last few days, and which had for a long time been sapping his normally genial disposition, reached new depths. What good was it to row with Clementine? It would make no difference. She would never change and he knew in his bones his son was destined to follow in her footsteps. What was the point of it all? Why struggle, why bother to try? He'd tried, God knows he had. See where it got him. To hell with the lot of them.

'I'd like to thank you all for all you did . . . '

'I'm sure we all wish we could have done more, sir,' Cook emotionally interrupted, a sob in her voice.

'I know, I know,' Joss said. 'Thank you all, more than I can say . . . I'd better be getting to the cottage. Good night, all of you.' Joss turned to head for Withiel Cottage. Tom Soloman instantly picked up Joss's suitcase and walked silently behind. They made their way across the front of the burnt-out skeleton of the Manor, down the drive to where Withiel Cottage stood hidden behind a clump of Camellia trees. A light was showing in the sitting-room window.

At the path to the front door, Joss took the suitcase from Tom, bade him goodnight and went into the cottage. As he entered the sitting-room, Margaret Du Cane who sat close to the grate, burst into tears and Clementine rose to her feet, eyeing him with hostility.

'So, you're back at last.' Her tone was accusatory.

'Well, there's a fine welcome, and a fine mess to come home to,' Joss said in a quiet voice.

'If you returned straight home instead of living-it-up in London, this might not have happened,' Clementine said.

'Yes it would,' Joss said.

'What do you mean?'

'The fire started on Monday night, the night I spent in a village near Harcourt School, *before* my appointment with the Headmaster next morning.'

Clementine's jaw dropped slightly. Joss was not entirely ignorant of what happened, yet he didn't seem angry! She made no reply, not realising an ice cold temper was more dangerous than a fiery one.

'If you had taken the trouble to come with me to find out and sort out what was happening with your beloved son, then this would never have happened,' Joss said, still without raising his voice.

'I . . . I don't know what you mean,' Clementine said, the attack in her tone lessened.

'Yes you do. But since, as usual, you intend to lie about what took place, *I* will tell *you* what happened. You did not refuse to come to Hampshire because you wished to keep your mother company, you refused because you intended to have someone in the Manor to keep you company . . . a chap called Farnell, and cousin I believe to your friend Jane McBride. He kept *you* company in bed – not for the first time. And he burnt down the Manor by leaving a lighted cigar on the blue sofa. Again not for the first time. He's damaged furniture with cigars on his previous visits when the way was clear.'

Clementine uttered a cry . . . 'It's lies, all lies,' she shrieked.

'Lies is it?' he said, his voice steely cold. 'Then why was he taken from here without a stitch of clothes. And, by the way, Mrs Soloman wishes to have her blanket, which covered his nakedness, returned to her.'

'No, no . . . you've got it all wrong.' There was a note of desperation in Clementine's voice.

Joss put his hand in his pocket.

'Can you deny this was *his* gold watch and chain with an inscription on the watch with his father's name?' Joss read from the back of the watch, ' . . . Edward Bennett Farnell 1850, engraved on it.'

For once Clementine was lost for words.

Joss went to the kitchen to make himself a pot of tea. Clementine followed.

'Let me do that for you, darling.' Her voice was sugary sweet.

'Get out of my sight,' Joss said between clenched teeth, without bothering to look up from what he was doing.

'I did lie darling, I was scared. Darling, I'm so sorry. It would never have happened if I wasn't so lonely. You don't come near me, and I've wanted you so much,' she cajoled.

'Are you going to get out of my sight or do I have to throw you out?'

'Darling, listen. You'll have to sleep with me. There are only two beds and mother has to have one, so you'll have to sleep

268

with me.'

'No. You'll have to sleep with your mother,' Joss said coldly.

'But she weeps all night, and I wouldn't get any sleep. Please, darling. I know I've been bad, but I'm willing to try again.' She took his arm. 'Let's sleep together tonight.'

As she spoke Joss violently shook the arm Clementine held and she was sent reeling against the wall. 'Nothing would induce me to sleep with a bitch like you,' Joss snarled. 'Sleep in the gutter for all I care, that's where you belong!'

Clementine's face contorted with rage. 'Your precious mother's ill. She's been asking for you,' she said, gloating at the dismay on Joss's face.

Joss's brown eyes darkened. 'Why didn't you say so before?' he demanded, grabbing her upper arms in a vice like hold, his angry face looking close into hers.

A contorted toothy grin spread over Clementine's face. 'I hope she's bloody dead!' she sneered.

It was the first time Joss had ever raised his hand to a woman, and Clementine's grin was instantly removed as he smacked her hard across the face.

Chapter Thirty-seven

'Joss! Thank God you're here,' Lottie said in a low urgent voice as Joss entered the door of his mother's cottage. Nell Pascoe hovered anxiously in the background.

Joss kissed his sister and Nell. 'How is she?' he asked

'Not good. She's been asking for you Joss, but her voice is weak and she can't speak properly.' Lottie's face was pale and strained.

Swiftly and silently Joss mounted the stairs, Lottie followed behind. His mother lay in bed propped up on pillows, her face was a yellowy-grey colour in the light of an oil lamp. Her sunken half-closed eyes widened a little when Joss entered. She raised one shrivelled arm to reach out to him and struggled to say something but Joss couldn't understand. He took her hand in his and kissed her then sat in a waiting chair beside the head of her bed.

'What is it mother?' he asked. She was clearly agitated and he glanced at Lottie who was seated at the other side of the bed.

'Got to tell you . . . Got to tell you . . . ' she gasped.

'What have you got to tell me, mother?' Joss said tenderly, still holding her hand in his.

'It's . . . it's . . . it's yours. He's got the mark.'

'Tell me when you're stronger. Whatever is mine is not important now.' These words from Joss only increased her agitation.

'The mark . . . he's got it . . . ' Emily's head flopped against the pillow and her mouth was open, gasping from the effort. Again Joss looked at Lottie.

'Let her tell you,' Lottie whispered. 'That's what she wants.'

'What mark? What is it that's mine, mother?' Joss said, gently.

'The b . . . b . . . b . . . '

'The box?' Joss asked, thinking she might mean a wooden box where she kept her precious photographs.

Emily Renfree gave a small agitated shake of her head.

'The baw . . . '

'The boy,' Joss said. 'Yes, Theodore is my boy.' Joss's eyes stared into hers for a sign that she knew he understood what she was trying to say. But all he saw was a look of frustration.

'Do you mean Theo . . ?' The words froze on Joss's lips as his dying mother interrupted.

Summoning all her strength she said in a loud voice, 'The baw . . . Got the m . . . m . . . m . . . ' Suddenly her head fell to one side. For long seconds both Joss and Lottie held their breath, hoping and searching her face for the tiniest flicker of movement. But Emily was dead! Gently Joss closed her eyes and kissed her face and the hand which he continued to hold in his.

Lottie stroked her mother's face, kissed her and held her other hand. She dabbed her eyes with a handkerchief and brother and sister relinquished their hold on their mother and clung to each other as together they stood gazing down at her.

At last they went downstairs where Nell, who wept silently when she saw them descend the stairs together, was waiting with hot sweet tea.

The three spoke in low voices, as though Emily was still asleep and they feared to wake her.

'I wonder what she was trying to tell me?' Joss said as they sat at the table and sipped their tea.

'I've no idea,' Lottie said, then added, 'Joss, I know about the Manor. I can't tell you how sorry I am.' Tears tumbled down her cheeks, and Nell, putting her hand over Joss's which lay limp on the table, repeated her sorrow at this dreadful blow . . . and now his mother's death on top of everything else.

Joss admitted that he thought life really ended for his mother when his father died. Nell was her life-line, the one who helped her keep going. Yet at some stage it seemed to Joss a change came over her. It was not at the time of the birth of Polly's baby, but later. He noticed something different, something of her old sparkle when she was at Polly's baby's Christening 'do'.

'I didn't notice any change,' Lottie said.

'Perhaps I imagined it,' Joss replied.

'I noticed it,' Nell confirmed. 'I told her getting out and being with people was good for her. She agreed with me and seemed in some way to be more at ease.'

When at last Joss drove Lottie home after the doctor had been to certify their mother's death, she insisted he stay with her.

'I'd be so glad of your company,' she said. 'George is good to me, but after all, it's our mother.'

Joss, who had no intention of returning to Manor Withiel, was glad to accept. He could stand Clementine no longer. Her last words to him, 'I hope she's bloody dead', when she told him his mother was ill, were seared in red in his memory. More than her lies, her unfaithfulness, her deceit, those words had stung him beyond description. He did not bother to inform her that her wish had been fulfilled.

Telegrams were dispatched to the Headmaster of the Harcourt School for Young Gentlemen, requesting Theodore be allowed leave to attend the funeral, also to Lottie's sons Stanley and Eric.

Sleeping accommodation was offered for Lottie's two sons and their wives, by the neighbours who lived either side, but a telegram was received from Theodore's Headmaster, stating 'Theodore cannot travel. Influenza.'

In a way Joss was relieved his son was not coming. The funeral of the boy's grandmother would be enough. But to witness the sight of the blackened shell of the Manor, the acrid almost choking smell of sodden burnt ashes, to hear Clementine's mother, his other grandmother's demented babbling about Rupert and, worst of all, to discover the venomous bitterness between Clementine and himself would be a horrible shock for Theodore. Better he stayed in bed and suffered influenza – that he would get over and forget.

It was when Lottie and Joss went together next day to engage the undertaker and to register their mother's death that Joss met a man from Lanner who had helped put out the fire. The two shook hands and Joss introduced the man, Jim Truscott, to his sister.

'I hear that Farnell man was responsible for starting it,' he said. 'The bugger ought to be shot . . . oh, pardon me m'am,' he apologised to Lottie.

Joss tried to cut short the conversation, saying they had an appointment. The man turned to Lottie, 'You look after him m'dear. He's looking pretty wisht.' A strong hint that Clementine was a poor wife.

'What was that about?' Lottie demanded when they parted company with Jim Truscott.

Joss instantly realised it was now no use trying to keep the story from Lottie. The servants knew, the firemen knew, and the story would have spread through the whole of Lanner, and most of Redruth and Camborne. It wouldn't do for Lottie to learn about it from somebody else; this meeting with Jim Truscott was proof of that. 'I'll tell you and George when we get home,' he said. 'We've got mother's funeral to sort out first.'

Four days later Emily Renfree joined John Renfree in the windswept cemetery little more than a mile from the cottage where she had lived and raised her small family with her beloved John.

Alone in her cottage with Emily no longer in the adjoining home, Nell Pascoe felt lost. Joss had bought his parent's cottage, along with a few others which brought them in a little rent. Now they had reverted to him. He would install Miss Trembath, the cook at Manor Withiel, in his mother's home. She was a kindly soul and he felt sure she would get along with Nell, though for Nell it would never be the same. The now empty cottage would be somewhere for Miss Trembath to live out her remaining years, otherwise there would probably be nowhere for her but the dreaded workhouse.

Lottie and George insisted Joss continue to stay with them. Rebuilding the Manor was out of the question. The staff would be given reasonable time to find work elsewhere. The Solomans could carry on living in the Lodge if they wished, or move if work with accommodation could be found. He supposed Clementine and her mother could carry on living in Withiel Cottage, the home he had built for her parents. He now felt he didn't care what became of Clementine or the Du Canes.

Polly and Edwin had, of course, attended the funeral, and the funeral tea afterwards which, for convenience, was held in the schoolroom of the church, the catering being done by the baker in the nearest village. Edwin had warmly invited him to spend time with them, and Polly had echoed her husband's hospitable invitation. But to be with Polly at such a turbulent time would be more than his or her emotions could stand. He was certain Polly felt this but was merely repeating her husband's invitation because Edwin would expect this. Joss could accept his sister's love and be strengthened by it. But tenderness from Polly, which he knew she would find near impossible to conceal at such an emotive time, would completely bowl him over. He would crack and fall apart, and he had to keep an iron grip on himself.

Sleep was elusive. Lottie had assured him that his mother had known nothing of the fire at Manor Withiel, for which Joss was enormously grateful. To feel the shock of the fire was the cause of the attack which ended her life would have been more than he could bear. And he had not let her know there had been a request from Theodore's school for a discussion on the boy's behaviour. She thought he was on a business trip.

Where would he go from here? Also, what now was his financial situation? With his mother's illness and death coming on top of the destruction of the Manor, he had not had time to give it thought. Now he must work out where he stood, then reorganise his life both financially and domestically.

The welfare of the Du Cane family would no longer enter into his calculations apart from an amount adequate for Clementine to 'keep body and soul together' until such time as he decided whether or not to divorce her.

A discussion with his bank manager confirmed Joss's calculations that his finances were in a very different state to when he arrived home in Cornwall from America, a wealthy man. He should have, *if* they had all lived in reasonable comfort, moderate luxury, be now even wealthier. He was still by no means destitute, but definite cuts in spending must be made, as he had been realising for some time. The virtual rebuilding of the Manor would rob him of the means to employ the staff necessary to adequately run the place, not that he wanted to restore it. He had wasted a hefty amount once already on this folly. It was not even as though he ever wished to live there in the first place. He had no intention of repeating that expensive mistake.

Could he still comfortably afford a good home, a cook, a maid and help with rough work . . . yes. A part-time gardener, yes. Theodore's schooling, yes. Running a motor, yes. A reasonably well-dressed wife was included in the bank manager's calculations. Modest middle class living at neither the upper nor the lower end of the scale, but somewhere mid-way. Spending the sort of money Clementine and her family had got through would be impossible. The restoration, upkeep and staffing of a manorial home, no. A spendthrift wife, no.

He could still continue to be numbered among the idle rich, and Joss was physically weary, his energy drained by the unremitting strain of domestic upheavals. He'd like to work again, get his hands dirty, be with the men. But these were idle thoughts and a form of escapism, a hankering after times past when life was different, better.

If he could freely rush to Polly's arms, that would be balm to his wounded spirit. There he could rest and feel secure, at peace. If only . . . Meantime, a good swig or two from the whisky bottle wouldn't come amiss.

Though Lottie and George insisted Joss was welcome to stay in their home for as long as he liked, and George was genuinely glad to have Joss's company in the house now that he had retired and Lottie was usually at the shop all day, Joss, after a few weeks, insisted he must return to the near burnt-out Manor Withiel. On a less conscious level he noted surprise at how grown-up Nora now was, and how tall and really quite beautiful. She was no longer a school-girl but a working woman, and enjoyed being employed by Polly and her mother, doing both sales work and learning dressmaking. Nora was also being courted by a young Merchant Navy Officer who was studying for his Master's Certificate.

Joss had decided to sleep and live in the still habitable area of servants' quarters, and that Clementine and Margaret Du Cane would stay in the cottage . . . separate living, separate everything.

The acrid smell still hung about the place, which served to increase the gloom. Conversation between Joss and Clementine was almost non-existent, except for an occasion when she assailed him in the grounds and spoke . . . as though it were a foregone conclusion . . . of rebuilding.

'You'll be lucky,' Joss replied with a mirthless laugh, and continued on his way to the two rooms in the servants' area which now served as his bedroom and sitting-room.

A few days after returning to the Manor, Joss spoke individually to the staff members, who were obviously aware that changes must take place, and concerned to know what those changes were and how they would be affected. Although anxious for their own well-being, they were obviously in sympathy with Joss's problems. Their dislike and condemnation of the mistress of

Manor Withiel was barely concealed.

At the word 'retirement' Miss Trembath's face registered alarm, which changed to bafflement when Joss proposed she live in the cottage which had been his mother's home.

'You mean I can *live* in the cottage, sir?'

'Yes, Miss Trembath.'

'Who with?'

'Nobody . . . it will be your retirement home.'

The cook remained silent a few seconds, convinced she must have misunderstood.

'I'm to have the cottage all to myself?' This was too good to be possible.

'That's right.'

'But who would I be working for?'

'Nobody, Miss Trembath. Like I said, it will be your retirement home.'

Again cook paused, silent, pondering. 'You mean it, don't you sir? . . . You're going to let me live in the cottage all on my own,' she murmured and held her breath awaiting his reply.

'Of course I mean it,' Joss laughed for the first time since his return from London.

'Oh, sir . . . Oh, thank you, sir. Thank you . . . thank you,' she cried, unable to express herself in any other words, then suddenly lowered her head as tears of relief flowed without warning. 'I don't know what to say,' she blurted between sobs.

'There, there,' Joss patted her on the shoulder. 'You didn't think I'd put you out on the street, did you?'

'Not exactly,' Miss Trembath replied haltingly, gulping every few words. 'But plenty of masters would, and I didn't know what to think, and . . . '

'And all sorts of rumours have been going about,' Joss added, knowingly.

'Yes . . . all sorts of stories!'

Miss Trembath left the room which had now become Joss's sitting-room, walking on air. She, Ada Trembath, was going to stop work for the first time since she was twelve, and for the first time she would have a home of her very own and no one to fetch, carry, clean or cook for. She would be able to do as she liked, and with the new Old Age Pension she need not go hungry. Best of all, *she* was not going to end up in the Workhouse! 'Tis an ill wind that blows nobody good, she reflected sagely, and it's blowed me something wonderful!

Fred, the stable-boy-cum-gardener had secured work on a farm in the area. He did not want to leave the district because he was 'walking out' with a girl who lived in Lanner. With no one to look after Tess the one remaining mare, Joss, who did not intend to spend a great deal of time at the Manor, arranged with William Parnell to have the animal on his farm at Perranwell for a generous annual payment. Tess, the nut-brown mare was familiar with the farm and would be happy there.

It seemed providential that a few weeks later Joss received a letter from Jock MacClaren, a Scotsman with whom he had business dealings during his time in America. He and Jock had remained in occasional contact and now Jock had accumulated enough money to return to Scotland and set up in business as landlord of an Inn. Would Joss like to come and visit.

Lottie and George urged Joss to take the opportunity to get away from Manor Withiel. Joss promised to think about it and, after yet another row with Clementine, concluded it would be a good thing for them both to have a break from each other even though they lived in separate quarters. A week later he drove off on a leisurely journey to Scotland, intending to be away two or three weeks.

He was surprised to discover the Inn was not an established business, it was not even an 'Inn' as yet, but a large old house overlooking a loch, which Jock and his wife Ailsa were themselves converting into an Inn. Joss quickly became interested in the planned conversion and was busy helping knock down walls, install plumbing and all the dusty and physically demanding work which went with such a venture. Luckily usable cooking facilities were kept functioning and at the end of every hard-working day, Ailsa rewarded them with a hearty meal.

After two weeks, Joss was enjoying sharing in the challenge, and had forgotten his intention to stay only two weeks. Satisfaction with his work at the end of each day, mingled with healthy physical weariness ensured he no longer had to endure sleepless nights, when worries about his wife, his son, the fire, sadness at the loss of his mother and unfulfillable longings where Polly was concerned, all became magnified. In this remote but beautiful part of Scotland Joss found a measure of peace.

Chapter Thirty-eight

As well as the decline in the granite business, Edwin worried vaguely about the political situation. The German Kaiser seemed to be at loggerheads with the leaders of this as well as certain European countries. Of course, there wouldn't be a war, they lived in an advanced age, and war between civilised countries was unthinkable. But that didn't alter the fact that there was always the possibility *trade* between countries could be affected. He still exported granite and anything which curbed one section of business or industry, affected all. These things had a ripple effect. Money was round and made to go round, and the more it changed hands the more it prospered everyone. Anything which improved or even just halted the downward trend in the demand for granite was to be welcomed.

Meantime, the change of surroundings, away from things which bothered him, had a remedial effect on Joss, but after several weeks, thoughts of Theodore and of home caused Joss to leave Jock and Ailsa for a while and visit Theodore. The term and the school year would soon be ending; he would visit and find out how his son had been faring and behaving since his last visit and the distasteful reason which prompted it. Then he would return to Manor Withiel and to Penryn just to reassure himself all was well. How long he stayed would probably depend on how he felt when he was there.

Both the Headmaster and Theodore welcomed his visit. Theodore had been behaving well and there had been no further cause for complaint. Academically he did not shine but his work was reasonably good. The Headmaster thought Theodore was maturing, showing signs of growing up. Joss smiled and nodded. This was really good news.

278

After the interview Theodore and Joss were free to spend an hour together, which passed most agreeably. Theodore showed genuine concern about the fire and the state of the manor. Joss felt he was really becoming a responsible young man. He was anxious to return home and perhaps be able to himself do something helpful. This brought a smile to Joss's face and once again he noted what an attractive-looking young man his son was becoming.

'Try to do well,' Joss said when he was about to depart, a serious note in his voice. 'It will be important to you.'

'Yes, I'll do that, father.'

Joss left Theodore feeling reassured that all was well and that Theodore had become more sensible, more responsible. He was starting to really grow up.

A brief advance letter had given Myrtle and Clementine warning of Joss's return. On his arrival at Manor Withiel Clementine was out; Myrtle said she was visiting friends in Falmouth. Margaret, her mother, rushed to greet him, smiling expectantly, when he went to the cottage.

'Joss . . . you've been a long time. Have you seen him?'

'Hello, Margaret. Seen who?' he answered.

'Rupert. Have you seen Rupert. I know you went to see him.'

A pang of pity shot through him. Where Rupert was concerned, Margaret was completely deranged.

'He's fine,' Joss said. 'He sends you his love.'

A smile lit up Margaret's face. 'When is he coming home?'

'Soon,' Joss soothed. 'Shall I make you a cup of tea?'

'No, I'll do it,' Margaret was still smiling. 'Then you can tell me all about Rupert.'

Joss sat down and waited to see if Margaret was capable of making tea. He could hear the rattle of cups coming from the kitchen, and after a few minutes Margaret emerged, slowly moving towards him with a tray of tea and biscuits, which she placed on the table, then with a shaky hand poured milk and tea. She could evidently manage simple tasks.

'Does Myrtle still do the cooking for you?' Joss asked.

'Oh, yes. Sometimes she cooks in the kitchen here, and sometimes she brings it from the Manor.' Then added, 'She is going to cook at the Manor tonight because Rupert is coming . . .'

'Because I'm here now,' Joss gently corrected.

'Oh yes, I know you're here. But Rupert will come, you'll see.'

Joss sighed. Rupert was the one who had caused his mother so much grief, driven her out of her mind and probably precipitated his father's death. But Clementine blamed him, not her precious brother for this sorry state.

As these thoughts were going through his mind a hansom cab drew up and Clementine alighted. On entering the room she gave a brief, indifferent glance in his direction.

'You're back,' she said, peeling off her gloves.

'How are you, Clementine?' he asked.

Clementine did not deign to reply.

After one full day and two nights spent at Manor Withiel Joss concluded the situation was just ticking over, neither better nor worse than when he left for Scotland; they were not likely to get better but they would most certainly get worse if he stayed, because Clementine was unremittingly hostile. To hell with her, he would spend a day or two visiting his sister Lottie and George, and then return to Scotland. There seemed little point in fitting in a visit to Villa Gwidden. During the day Polly would be in Falmouth, Edwin at the quarries and Jonathan at Falmouth Grammar School. He longed to see Polly, yet at the same time dreaded seeing her – always fearing his composure would break.

But Joss's plan to return to Scotland was interrupted. A telegraph arrived. Hastily Joss tore it open. It must be a message, a request, from Rupert! No. The news was from America but not from Rupert, it was from Bill Boaden. 'Oil discovered at RR. Instructions? Bill.'

There was only one thing for it. He must return to America to see the situation for himself and make decisions then. Meanwhile he would keep the news to himself, with the exception of his sister Lottie. Oil was not really in Joss's sphere of experience, but he knew it could be short term surface oil or extremely profitable deep reservoirs.

Joss sent a telegraph to Bill to expect him as soon as possible, also a letter to Scotland telling Jock and Ailsa that a situation had arisen and that he intended returning to America. Then he visited the shipping agent's office in Falmouth, which was near to Custom House Quay and learned the first available passage was on a ship leaving Southampton for New York in a week's time. Joss booked his passage. He would say nothing to Clementine about his departure until nearer the time to leave. Meantime, he would acquaint Mr Borlace, his solicitor, of his impending departure. He did not know how long he would be absent. He would have to wait to assess the situation when he was there and knew more.

But the situation in Europe was worsening. Germany's ally, Austria, had declared war on Serbia. Before Joss left for Southampton there came news that was to rock the world!

Britain, which had recently been voicing its disapproval of Germany's aggression towards France, declared war on Germany! The unthinkable was happening! Could it be sorted? Surely decency if not common sense would prevail. Meantime, and Joss's brain was reacting on several levels at once, he would not leave the country. If the worst happened he must help where he could. There would be mechanised travel, as well as horses and foot-slogging. If there was fighting America might provide or sell Britain equipment. No one could be sure, though, that America would approve of Britain, or that to Americans it would make much difference what happened on this side of the great Atlantic Ocean. The American Government did not allow itself to become involved in Europe's internal squabbles. Reactions across the water could only be guessed at, but that did not alter the fact that America was faster at making motors, and ownership of motors in the U.S. was not exclusively for the rich few. The main supplier of fast-production vehicles was Henry Ford, in America . . . in Detroit. Detroit was in Michigan. The Ranch was in Michigan. In Joss's mind it seemed to form a link. He sent a second telegraph to Bill Boaden. 'Passage cancelled. If viable go ahead with production. Joss.'

Joss then instructed Mr Borlace, his solicitor, to write to Bill officially authorising him to temporarily act on Mr Renfree's behalf. If reasonably viable and profitable, to agree to let production of oil go ahead, to take a set percentage of the profit, to keep accurate records etc., etc., and to reply stating whether this arrangement was agreeable.

The declaration of war was the one topic of conversation in Penryn, Falmouth, the surrounding villages and no doubt throughout the entire country. What would happen? What did war between civilised countries actually entail? There would be soldiers . . . fighting each other, guns, bayonets. What else? How would it affect other people? Some would have to work in factories, making armaments. What else would happen? Lottie and Polly had no idea, they could not envisage it.

The buses which regularly ran between Falmouth and Penryn were crowded with people, all talking about the one subject – our peaceful country had declared war on the aggressor. 'One thing was sure though . . . It was *men* who started wars,' said a woman on the packed Penryn bus. Other women in the bus nodded knowingly and agreed. Male passengers who smoked, drew on their pipes, others shuffled their feet and some pretended to be looking out of the bus. All knew war as a possibility had lately been spoken of, but possibility and reality were two different things. Now it was actually happening everyone was stunned.

Polly had not been especially following the 'whys and where-fores' of the problems in Europe. Lottie was worried about whether Eric and Oliver would be affected and Nora who was still involved with the young Merchant Navy Officer, was uneasy about how he would fare if there really was a war.

Joss subsequently called and he and Edwin fell to discussing the situation. Polly gathered there had been a Treaty which Germany had signed, agreeing Belgium would be a neutral country. Germany then totally ignored the treaty they had agreed, in order to enable an attack on France to be made via Belgium. This violation of the Treaty incensed the British. War was declared against Germany. A prominent German complained that Britain was making war over just one word – 'neutrality'. 'Britain, he bitterly declared, 'would wage war "just over a scrap of paper!" '

The thousands of brave Belgians who resisted the unforeseen violation of the Treaty and the invasion of their country, suffered terrible slaughter, and on 20th August Germany captured Belgium's capital city, Brussels.

By now Lottie and George's two sons Eric and Oliver, had volunteered their services. Eric joined the Army and Oliver joined the Royal Navy. Lottie and Nora both had time off to go with George to their sons' respective homes, so that they did not have to lose precious hours from home, both now being family men, in order to travel to Cornwall. This presented no great problems for Polly and the staff. The outbreak of war, despite assurances it would soon be over, precipitated not a dive, but certainly a stumble in trade.

'At least we can all go,' George said to Lottie. 'If you and Polly had not set up in business we'd never have been able to afford to go away and visit.'

His opinion was further confirmed when, on Truro Station where they had to change trains, the porter wrongly assumed they were passengers who travelled first class!

Polly felt deeply for Lottie and her family, realising how the war service would worry them all, but shortly after learned Jack had also enlisted in the army. His mother's lined face betrayed her anxiety, but Mary wept uncontrollably. He had not consulted the womenfolk. He knew what their reactions would be. But he was still a young man, a fit young man. He couldn't leave it all to the others of his age to risk everything while he stayed safe and snug in Penryn. He'd never be able to look the returning young men in the face or, even worse, the eyes of the mothers and wives of those who did not return.

But Mary's distress deeply upset Jack, and had Mary known she was in the early stages of her second pregnancy, she might have been successful in prevailing upon him not to volunteer.

Contrary to initial general expectations, exactly one year later war with Germany still continued. In a few days after the capture of Brussels, German troops were in Northern France and heading towards Paris! In this they did not succeed but the youth of the country, the volunteer army, was suffering losses on a horrifying scale.

Joss, too old to serve in the armed forces, had made himself available for any work in which his mining expertise would be useful. He thought coal-mines would be the most likely area and attended an interview, more of a discussion, and was listed as available for inspection work, advising and/or supervising as, where and when required. At intervals between he was free to remain at home awaiting directions. This had a leisurely sound, but Joss soon found he was away most of the time.

Then, in May the following year, the British Liner *Lusitania*, the fastest ship on the Atlantic route, fell unexpected victim to German U-boats and was torpedoed, sinking with the loss of 1,250 passengers, Americans included. So much for civilised countries!

Joss endeavoured to be at home when Theodore was due to return at the end of his final year at Harcourt School. The next and final stage of his education would be at university. He returned to Manor Withiel the day before Theodore was expected to return but next day a telegram was received informing him and Clementine their son's return would be delayed by four days.

Clementine clucked with impatience while Joss hoped he would not be called upon to leave before his son's arrival. On the fourth day a further telegram arrived confirming Theodore's home-coming and the time he was due to arrive at Redruth Station. Clementine's temper slightly improved.

Joss was going to meet Theodore at the Station in his 30 hp Rolls-Royce and Clementine had decided to accompany him, the sooner to meet her 'darling Theodore'.

She and Joss arrived in advance of the time the train was due. Clementine, fetchingly attired in a French Ultramarine outfit, sat in the motor to await the train's arrival. But for once the motor and its eye-catching occupant received scant attention from the people around, mainly Redruth tinners who would normally gaze at the motor, and their wives who would admire Clementine's clothes and general superior looks. Young men in army uniform were 'milling about' with a sprinkling of sailors, but many ordinary folk wore preoccupied expressions. Their sons or sweethearts had either gone away or off to fight the Kaiser. What would become of them? Would they come home safe and sound, and the same as when they left home? Would they return at all?

When the train was almost due Clementine got out of the motor and she and Joss crossed the railway tracks via a wooden bridge to the platform where Theodore's train would pull in. At last a distant faint rumble announced its approach. The sound swiftly increased in volume and with a shrill whistle, a thundering of wheels and a cloud of smoke the train rattled noisily along the length of the platform before screeching to a halt. Before it had stopped, doors up and down the length of the train opened and people poured out. Amongst them were quite a preponderance of khaki and of navy uniformed men and a few women in nurses uniform.

Clementine's and Joss's eyes searched the arrivals. Where was Theodore? Some started closing the train doors, and passengers and those who had come to meet them began to mount the steps of the wooden bridge.

'He's not here,' Clementine said, alarm and disappointment in her voice.

Joss's eyes continued to rake the people still on the platform.

'Yes, he is,' he said. 'There.'

'Where?'

'There . . . by the child in a red coat.'

At that moment Theodore saw them and smiled.

'Oh . . . Oh, my God!' screeched Clementine. 'He's enlisted! . . . My boy is a soldier!'

Chapter Thirty-nine

Clementine was distressed to discover her precious and only child was risking life and limb by enlisting in the army of a country at war.

'They shouldn't have accepted you,' she wailed when the three were back at Withiel Cottage. Margaret was struggling to understand.

'All the other chaps are enlisting. I felt I had to. Can't let the side down, don't you know,' Theodore soothed.

'But don't they know it's interfering with your education? You will be going to university.'

'I can do that when the war's over, Mater,' Theodore replied.

Clementine looked accusingly at Joss. 'Don't stand there like a dummy! *You're* his father. *You* stop him!'

Joss sighed. 'If the boy has volunteered, that's that. It's his choice. He must do what he thinks right.'

'What a father!' Clementine flashed back.

'Don't squabble over it,' Theodore broke in, and reverting to more homely language, tried to reassure. 'And don't worry, mother, the war will soon be over.'

'People said that a year ago,' Clementine cried and dabbed eyes and nose with her handkerchief. 'Ah, well . . . ' She took her son's hand, held out his arm and stood back to survey him. The army officer's uniform was certainly flattering. Theodore looked so tall, so manly, so handsome! Clementine smiled and decided there was something to be said for wearing a uniform. She always knew Theodore would be handsome. He was no stocky, black-haired Cornishman. He was tall, fair haired, with a clear complexion, broad shouldered yet willowy and refined. His deep blue eyes would melt any female heart and the finely chiselled nose strangely enhanced now by a slight bridge, which stirred memories for Clementine of another handsome man, a good chin which neither receded nor jutted, and a well defined mouth which broke easily into a smile, displaying slightly prominent well-regulated teeth. Despite his winning smile there was a slight haughtiness about him, an air of superiority. He would be a challenge to any aspiring and mettlesome young lady.

What a son! What a charmer! She knew of no one who had a son as handsome and desirable as Theodore. How her friends would envy her. And how their daughters would fawn over him. Victoria Pope's dowdy daughter, Emma, would absolutely drool. Theodore was going to break so many girlish hearts . . . and she'd enjoy every minute of it!

Having her son in the army wasn't going to be too bad after all. Everyone said the war would soon be over. Meantime, she would make sure everyone saw her precious boy. She would show him off and dazzle all her friends, and have all their daughters vying for his attention, his favours. They would hang on his every word, flutter their eyelashes, laugh or more likely giggle, at his every witty remark.

And how he would tantalise them . . . a little attention, a little flattery, a lingering handshake when he would smile and gaze down at them, making their hearts pound, their hopes rise and their dreams run riot!

She must arrange a little party or something, so that as many as possible would have the opportunity to see her handsome Theodore. But it couldn't be held at the Manor. What a pity! She would have to think of somewhere else, and time was short.

Joss too, was proud of Theodore, and concerned but at the same time gratified that his son had volunteered to fight for King and Country. He was happy to go along with Clementine's suggestion for a 'get-together' with friends, a social evening. Clementine favoured the large Fal View Hotel, with its impressive views of Falmouth Bay, and she was happy to make all the arrangements. Joss was happy to let her, provided she did not arrange anything too opulent or lavish. War was a serious matter, not something to celebrate. He agreed to an evening with Theodore's contemporaries. Some drinks — not too much with young people — refreshments, some dancing and perhaps one or two of Theodore's age group would oblige with a song or monologue. It sounded fine to Joss, if that was what Theodore would like. The sort of thoughts Clementine had been entertaining never entered Joss's head. He was well aware Clementine seemed a little more affable, not that it would now normally concern Joss whether she was affable or not. But with Theodore at home for a few days it was good to have a more pleasant atmosphere.

Theodore was still shocked by how extensive was the fire damage at Manor Withiel, but youth, being resilient, and with so many things happening . . . leaving Harcourt School, war, enlisting in the Army, the party to be given in his honour, he was able to push the devastating fire damage etc. to the recesses of his mind. He had a vague feeling his mother was responsible; he knew she was devious and seemed always to be at the bottom of any trouble or row with his father. For him that was a fact of life. But it had never previously particularly bothered Theodore . . . his mother was always indulgent with him, so he didn't much mind the faults that did not affect him; in fact she had been extra indulgent when she and his father argued.

Lottie, George, Nora and Alec, the young Merchant Navy Officer, whose ship happened to be in dock at the time were invited along with about a dozen young men, several of Theodore's age group being already absent in the services, and a substantially larger number of ladies all of whom were accompanied by either a young gentlemen, their parents or a friend's parents. Both Theodore and Joss thought Margaret should be at the party, but a persistent tickly cough which followed a cold gave Clementine an excuse to keep her now embarrassingly dotty mother at home with Myrtle.

Clementine, Joss and Theodore, who was dressed in his Army Officer's uniform, shook hands with guests as they arrived at the hastily arranged party, and Clementine hugely enjoyed watching the effect on the young ladies of now seeing her grown-up and handsome son, no longer with the bored, petulant expression he so often wore as a child, but smiling, urbane, attentive and obviously very . . . what was the word . . . practised, yes, practised in the art of conducting himself in the company of ladies, young or otherwise. Clementine instinctively knew her son could ensnare a young lady more easily than a piece of cheese could trap a mouse. Several times when a budding young woman and her parents entered the party room she imagined she heard an intake of breath as the young female beheld and fell under the spell of her lovely son.

It also seemed that Joss, though proud of Theodore was barely aware of the effect his son was having on most of the young females, who simpered, giggled and stood with mouths agape as Theodore took each dainty hand and gazed down with appreciative blue eyes into those of each young woman. But of course, Joss wouldn't notice; it wasn't to be expected of a simple, unsophisticated country bumpkin who, when she married him, had few social graces. Looking back, she couldn't now think how it was so many of her friends seemed to find him so likeable. It must have been his looks . . . he was considered to be very handsome; and he seemed to make them and several of their parents laugh too. Probably they were just being polite. What a burden it was to be married to someone so much beneath one. She could congratulate herself on having suffered it stoically.

Then Joss's sister Lottie arrived, along with her twopenny ha'penny clerk of a husband and their daughter Nora, who was accompanied by a young Naval Officer. Joss kissed his sister and niece and was clearly delighted to see them; Theodore joined them and repeated the greetings. They all seemed so happy to see each other. Clementine felt a pang of annoyance. Nora did look so eye-catchingly attractive in the latest straight-cut, low-waisted style dress, with a matching headband decorated with tiny beads, and her escort was equally impressive. She fixed a toothy smile and joined them. Her 'So glad you could all come!' cut short all conversation and she felt Lottie recoil as she kissed her sister-in-law's cheek.

'Nora! You look absolutely charming,' she effused. 'But we've got a lot of attractive, delightful young ladies here.' She took hold of Alec's arm. 'You'll have to keep your eye on this handsome young man. He might be tempted to stray.'

Alec's grey eyes levelled with Clementine's. 'No fear of that, Mrs Renfree,' he replied smiling with his mouth but not with his eyes.

When all the guests were present and busily occupied in chatting to acquaintances and old friends, and some in making new ones, both Clementine and Theodore, and to a lesser degree Joss, dutifully circulated. Clementine loved such occasions when

n

she was in the limelight.

'What do you think of my Theodore?' she asked of Victoria Pope's deadly plain and less than bright daughter, Emma.

The shy Emma flushed uncomfortably, only too well aware she did not attract the attentions of young gentlemen. Emma's mother pursed her lips.

'I think he's very nice,' Emma stammered nervously.

'I'm glad,' Clementine said, her tone low and almost conspiratorial. 'Because he told me he liked you too,' she smiled broadly. The girl's eyes suddenly widened. ' "Charming," he said, and I think he used the expression "sweet-natured",' Clementine enlarged.

The girl's slight flush deepened but her mouth widened into a smile. She suddenly looked almost pretty. Clementine smiled in the direction of Emma's parents. Her father seemed to be paying more attention to his empty glass than the words Clementine had spoken but though Victoria Pope smiled, in her eyes was a look of distrust.

By now Miss Elizabeth Harding, who also wore a headband of blue velvet to match her eyes and her dress, had been prevailed upon to sing. The pianist in a four-piece band which was on a dais in the corner of the party-room vacated his music stool to allow Elizabeth's mother, Mrs Elsador Harding, to accompany her daughter. Theodore had acquired a seat nearby. The song was about the pain of unrequited love, and as the young lady sang the saddest words, she focussed on Theodore's upturned face. He gazed up at her in rapt attention, ignoring for a few seconds the fact that Emma had contrived to sit next to him. He seemed somewhat nonplussed by her persistence but, thoroughly enjoying being the centre of attention, continued to keep the charm turned on and caused poor Emma to misinterpret the reason.

But the moment the song ended Clementine rose from her seat and moved across the centre of the room, clapping her hands as she did so. 'That was delightful Elizabeth,' she said. 'I think a dance would be welcome for the young people now *and* some of us older ones, and *I* intend to be the first to dance with my dear son.'

Smugly aware of how the up-to-the-minute damson coloured narrow style gown she wore flattered her still youthful figure, she moved to where Theodore, now on his feet, awaited her. The band struck up and though the young men were quick to acquire partners, all waited for Theodore and Clementine to take the floor.

Clementine was in for another delightful surprise. Theodore was a superb dancer. He must have had plenty of practice to reach this standard, Clementine thought. Her son had undoubtedly grown into a man, a gentleman, a very polished and sophisticated gentleman, and without her even noticing! She told herself none of these things should be really surprising; she had always known he had it in him, it was in his blood.

'Come on, join in,' Theodore shouted to the young men. 'I'm not here to give an exhibition.'

'I think you should be,' Clementine whispered. 'I didn't know my darling son was such an expert in the art.'

By now a number of dancers were on the floor and Clementine noticed Victoria Pope and her husband were dancing. She smiled inwardly; from a rear view Victoria looked as though bustles were still in fashion. She glanced about at the ones who were not dancing but couldn't see Emma. Had they left their daughter alone on the perimeter of the dance floor? Then she saw Joss, he was on the dance floor partnering the girl. Wasn't it just like him! There were several quite pretty girls without partners, yet . . . he had to choose Emma, the plainest and the dowdiest. Typical, Clementine thought. He couldn't make the distinction.

She and Theodore brushed past Nora, who looked quite beautiful in her fashionably styled gown. Alec looked impressive, but not over-pleased. Clementine attributed his sombre expression to the fact that Theodore's friends were paying Nora quite a lot of attention. Come to think of it, Lottie was the recipient of much attention too, from the older ladies and a few of the men. Clementine's smile briefly deserted her. Lottie did look exceedingly smart in her flattering silver-grey dress and coatee.

By having a few 'Progressive' dances, Theodore was able to dutifully dance with all the young ladies and at least some of their mothers who had come to wish him well before his service in the Army commenced in earnest. Emma, who now seemed convinced Theodore was 'taken' with her, somehow managed to partner him several times.

During the break when refreshments were served, Major Clemens, Retired, made a little speech wishing Theodore well in his service in the Army, and Theodore's good health and safe deliverance were toasted.

When the band was about to announce another dance Theodore asked if they could play 'Ragtime'. To his delight the band could, but they only knew a couple of tunes.

But very few knew how to perform the latest dance crazes such as 'The Turkey Trot', 'Grizzly Bear' and 'Bunny Hug' which had spread throughout America and were now catching on in this country. The rhythm was fast and, some thought, downright unladylike. Theodore's partner, Miss Madelaine Squires, was fortunately quite expert, but for the other guests the dance was not a resounding success.

'Stay on the floor everyone,' Theodore commanded when the band stopped playing. 'Maddie and I will teach you how to do it.'

'You do it first,' Madelaine said.

'If you prefer, Maddie,' replied Theodore with a smile. 'Pay attention gentlemen . . . ' He gave directions for a few steps, demonstrating as he did so. 'Now I'll do it to the music.' He glanced in the direction of the band and Theodore and band performed together.

'Now you chaps, do the steps with me.' He repeated instructions and the young men obeyed, some a little self-consciously. At the second attempt Theodore seemed satisfied. This process was repeated with a couple more sequences. 'Will you instruct the ladies now, Maddie?'

Clementine's bosom heaved with pride. How masterful her Theodore was. All the young people present hung on his every word. It must be obvious to everyone he had leadership qualities.

Madelaine was adept at imitating her partner's teaching method. The girls quickly grasped how to perform to the new fast rhythm. Some parents appeared amused, some confused, and a few were downright disapproving of the new-fangled dancing. There was no grace in the movements. The music was raucous, the dancing so energetic and unbecoming . . . unladylike.

Theodore deemed all were ready to perform the new and exciting dance. The young ladies giggled excitedly, and the band struck up with a slightly slowed pace. There was much laughter as the young people attempted the new dance style with a partner, and one or two young ladies, accidentally of course, stumbled and toppled into their partner's eager arms, causing even louder shrieks of laughter. Then the dance was repeated at a faster speed. It couldn't be described as sedate, but by golly it was fun!

Those on the dance-floor all clapped loudly when the dance ended, several ladies breathless and pink-faced with exertion while the older onlookers clapped with less enthusiasm, a few quietly muttering they didn't know what the world was coming to.

Lottie and George quite enjoyed the evening though, except when briefly George was obliged to dance with Clementine. She turned on her most fetching smile and told him he danced divinely. George made no reply.

Chapter Forty

With the passage of time victory over the Kaiser and his troops seemed as far away as ever. The atmosphere of mixed emotions and nervous excitement mingled with apprehension which had enveloped Penryn as young men enlisted to serve their country, was frequently replaced with low, almost whispered voices, exchanged among sombre groups of townsfolk as news of the latest heavy casualties in France was related. Too many mothers, young wives and sweethearts had red-rimmed eyes set in white faces, while of the fathers of the young men who had made the supreme sacrifice, some were red-eyed while others, striving to contain their grief, were tight-lipped and taut, their expressions resembling the hard unyielding granite on which Penryn and the outlying villages stood. Rich and poor suffered alike.

Despite the grim facts and incredibly heavy losses, as boys reached the tender age at which they could volunteer to serve, they usually enlisted immediately.

Penryn was a small and ancient town. Generations upon generations had lived and died in continuity. The people all knew each other, their backgrounds, individual virtues, shortcomings and foibles, and the sorrows of one were shared by all. In hard times people helped one another. But so many were now suffering; not one family seemed to remain untouched by the previously unimagined brutality and carnage of war between civilised nations. Acts of heroism and gallantry by those on the field of battle and the high seas were legion.

But of the high-ranking top-nobs who sat behind desks and, safe from the dangers of the battleground, directed operations, a few ordinary people began to doubt their abilities and to suspect they didn't realise what they were doing. Being brave and being foolhardy were two different things. A stiff upper-lip without common sense was not much use, and a posh imperious accent didn't stop bullets as the cream of the country's youth obeyed orders to come out of their trenches and march forward in long spread-out lines. This made easy human targets for the relatively sheltered enemy troops entrenched within close shooting range, all in the vain hope of gaining a few feet of muddy bloody French ground. Small wonder the Germans seemed baffled by the tenacity of the British Tommies and their Officers at the battle-front.

But the Germans were not cowards. In situations of more equal danger they also fought tenaciously, and they also suffered heavy casualties and loss of life.

The seemingly endless time spent in wet muddy trenches, the horrific sights, the deprivations and scanty food and the atrocious weather, after so long and so much effort, sapped the remaining men's strength on both sides of the fighting. Those who were lucky enough to survive without serious wounds were cold, wet, footsore and utterly weary. God, how awful it was! The rare letter from home, provided news was not bad, was read avidly, treasured, and reread again and again and again. When a Tommy in possession of a cigarette lit it he would take a long comforting draw, fill his lungs and pass on the cigarette to the next Tommy to repeat the process, while he slowly and reluctantly expelled the stimulating yet soothing inhalation from his lungs. Then for a while all silently enjoyed the smoky smell which lingered on the damp air.

Theodore had been sent to France, but worked mostly some way behind the front lines. Frequently he would be sent to the 'front' to pass on instruction to the officer in charge of a Platoon or Company of men, or to take back the senior officer's assessment of the current situation to the senior officer he served. Apart from a slight graze from a bullet which whizzed past his shoulder and a twisted ankle from slipping on the muddy uneven ground up at the 'front' Theodore had been unscathed.

Less than a mile from where he was encamped was a village where the inhabitants endeavoured to live lives as normal as circumstances allowed. There was a tavern which was a popular meeting place for older French males, a few females and quite a lot of soldiers. Madame Lisette Dubois in the absence of the proprietaire, ran both the drinks and food side of the establishment, though there was precious little of either, especially food.

The plump dark-haired French woman was attractive in a brassy sort of way. She also appeared to be popular with all those who frequented the 'pub', but how genuine was the customers' regard could not be gauged as it did not pay to slight or get the wrong side of Madame Dubois. She had her favourites who fared relatively well and Theodore could not resist the challenge to become a favourite with the bold-eyed self-assured lady. She had a weakness for good-looking young officers. A small minority of the older male imbibers thought Theodore looked like a German. But others disagreed. He resembled the Hollanders, Danes or Swedes, and they were decent types, not like the heel-clicking, foot stamping, humourless, ruthless Germans.

Theodore became accepted by the locals. He was also accepted by Madame Dubois. She was at first attracted by his accent and he endeavoured to use his school French to good account. Then, when he smiled his winning smile and his blue eyes gazed down into her near black ones, something deep under her hard and brassy surface melted, and she felt a stirring, a need. Albert was away, had been for over three months. She had not heard from him for weeks. He could be dead. Theodore read the message in her eyes. Covert meetings were arranged. People began to whisper one to another but not a word did they speak to the two subjects of their surmises.

Time continued to drag. Despite unyielding efforts the war was not being won by either side. For both sides there were only losses in the form of the countries' youth. Then came a momentous announcement. The United States of America was joining the Allies in the fight against the Kaiser!

This was wonderful news for all, and Joss's spirits rose. Americans didn't do things by halves. Their troops would be well equipped; tanks, guns, every imaginable aid to beat the enemy would be provided.

Up to now, despite the two sides in battle being terrifically depleted and what troops remained exhausted, each remained in stubborn unyielding deadlock. Surely the entry of the Yanks would settle the matter once and for all. His spirits soared. Thus far Theodore had been practically unscathed. All would now soon be over and with a bit of luck his son would survive, little the worse for his experiences.

But next day, when he was far below ground and about half a mile from the shaft, he was informed someone was above asking to see him. The messenger was a young lad fresh from school who, like his father before him, planned to earn a living underground in the Yorkshire coal-mines.

'Be there in a few minutes.'

'It's an Army Officer, sir . . . Two Army Officers.'

Joss's stomach lurched. 'I'll come right away.' He left off inspecting the timber supports and transoms and hastily made his way to the shaft where the cage was waiting to take him and the lad upwards to where, even on a dull day the light seemed unbelievably bright after the benighted gloom of the 'pits'.

Joss had made his whereabouts known so that should there be a telegram, that dread bearer of bad news, Clementine and her near witless mother would not be alone at Withiel Cottage to receive it. Should the worst happen he would be the first to know and he would return home and break the news himself.

'You did say Army Officers, not a telegram?' he queried, mystified. Could it be Theodore? Surely he would go straight home to Cornwall. It could just be friends of Theodore's, but he doubted any of Theodore's friends would actually come here to his current wartime place of work, the coal-mines in a section of Yorkshire.

Blinking against the daylight, he quickly made his way to the shack which served as an office. The earth beneath his feet was mixed with black dust and small knobs of coal, but tufts of grass and weeds had managed to grow, cushioning the sound of his quick footsteps. As he neared the back of the shack he distinctly heard a young male voice.

'You're not going to tell him, are you?'

'Of course not you idiot!' came a low reply, but the words were clear and unmistakable.

Joss's foot stepped noisily onto the gravelled path around the sides of the shack and the voices were silent. The door faced away from the pithead and he rounded the side of the shack and entered the open door. The young army officers, a Captain and a Subaltern, both with grave expressions, stood awaiting him. As he entered the young Captain, who had a black eye-patch over his right eye, took a step towards him.

'Good day to you, Captain,' Joss said, holding out a hand which he forgot was grimy. There was something familiar in the candour of the officer's visible blue eye.

The Captain sombrely shook his hand, saying, 'Mr Renfree, sir.' Joss noticed he did not repeat the greeting 'good day to you', nor did the Subaltern as they shook hands.

'Sit down,' Joss said as he quickly opened two folding wooden chairs which were propped against the side of a rickety cupboard, and himself sat informally on the edge of the table. 'Have you news of Theodore?'

The Captain's face was serious, unsmiling. 'I'm afraid it's bad news, sir,' the Captain replied.

'Oh,' Joss's throat constricted, and he found himself unable to continue speaking.

'I'm due for a few days leave, and I offered to come and tell you myself, en route. I live in Yorkshire now . . . so does Vickery.' He inclined his head in the direction of the officer.

'Yes,' Joss rasped.

'I'm afraid . . . '

'He's dead?' Joss cut in.

The Captain nodded. 'Yes,' then added, 'The war, you know. He died in France.'

'How did it happen?'

The young Captain lowered his gaze.

'He was a victim of the fighting, the war.'

'He was shot?'

Silence.

'Was he blown up?'

The Captain hesitated. 'I wasn't there, sir.'

'But you know what happened,' Joss said. 'Look, I heard you both talking as I approached the hut. There is something you said you were not going to tell me.'

The Captain shot the Subaltern a grim look. The Subaltern lowered his gaze.

'I want to know what happened.'

Silence.

'Was he blown up?'

Still no reply. Joss could hardly bring himself to say the word,

'Bayoneted?'

Almost imperceptibly the Captain shook his head.

Then an even worse possibility. 'He wasn't shot and left hanging from barbed wires was he? . . . I'll come to terms with it when I can stop imagining how he might have died.'

Once more the Captain shook his head. 'None of those things, sir.'

'Thank God,' Joss breathed, then paused a moment. 'Then what?'

The Subaltern swallowed noisily but neither spoke.

'For God's sake what, man?' Joss was growing impatient.

'It was an accident.' The Captain was prevaricating.

'What sort of accident? I want the truth,' Joss insisted, now impatient, seeing again the soldiers' reluctance.

The Captain, who had been staring uncomfortably at the ground, looked up into Joss's eyes and without removing his gaze said, 'Wait for me outside, Vickery.'

Joss recognised the name which had been mentioned in Theodore's letters. The Subaltern left, placing a comforting hand on Joss's shoulder as he passed by.

Alone together, Joss stared unblinking into the candid blue eye of the Captain, who paused a moment, then drew a deep breath.

'It seems Theodore was in the habit of visiting a Tavern run by a Madame Dubois, whose husband was away on some kind of war work. He returned one night and . . . ' His voice trailed away.

'And what?' Joss demanded, rising to his feet.

'And found them together after the Tavern had closed,' came the reluctant reply. 'There was nothing untoward,' the Captain endeavoured to assure. 'But it seems the husband was suspicious of his wife, apparently not without reason, and there was a scrap.'

Joss, suddenly limp, sank into the wooden chair the Subaltern had vacated. 'Oh no,' he uttered. 'Oh my God!' He leant forward, his grimy hands covering his grimy face.

'The husband didn't mean to,' the Captain said quietly. 'He was jealous of his wife. Theodore fell and struck his head on an ornate brass fender. He appeared perfectly all right, but it seems a clot formed and . . . ' Again his voice trailed, then he added, 'The Frenchman was very upset.'

Joss dropped his hands from his face and, stunned, stared ahead seeing nothing, his breathing shallow and spasmodic.

'Let me get you some water, sir,' the young Captain said, his face white. He spied an enamel mug half buried under papers on the table, and poured into it some cold water from a kettle which stood on an unlit Primus stove, then passed it to Joss.

The cold water gave Joss a measure of revival. For a few minutes there was silence.

'I'm sorry to have to tell you this,' the Captain said at last.

'Don't be,' Joss answered. 'Thank you for having the guts to tell me the truth.'

'It wasn't my intention to sir, but I wanted to come myself, you see I met you some years ago at Cresby School . . . my name's Prescott. Harvey Prescott.'

Joss nodded. 'I remember.'

A small part of Joss's brain was beginning to function. 'I shall be going home to break the news to Theodore's mother,' he said. He couldn't help wondering whether Captain Prescott was correct in saying 'nothing untoward' happened, or whether he was sugaring the bitter pill.

'I'll tell her Theodore was killed in France. The rest I shall never tell anyone.' Then added, 'If she doesn't learn it from me she must never learn it from anyone else!'

'Of course not, sir,' Captain Prescott replied. 'Will you be all right, sir? Would you like me to stay?'

'No. You go, I'll be all right, thank you,' Joss replied, and got unsteadily to his feet. 'Thank you for coming in person.'

The two shook hands and Captain Harvey Prescott moved to go. Though numb, somehow Joss remembered the Officer's younger brother, the boy Theodore had locked in the gardener's shed.

'Harvey,' he called.

Captain Prescott, who was making his way towards a motor where the Subaltern waited, turned and paused.

'How is Timothy?'

'Dead I'm afraid, sir. He too was killed in France.'

Chapter Forty-one

'Get out! Get out of my sight! I don't want to see you. I want *my Theodore*, my beautiful boy.'

Joss dodged a heavy flying ashtray. The volatile Clementine had maintained totally hostile behaviour ever since he arrived at Manor Withiel, three days earlier. Margaret, her mother, wept *again*. Sometimes the old lady was aware it was Theodore who had died, sometimes she thought it was Rupert, which made her even more agitated and caused Clementine to shout abuse at her. Occasionally she forgot anyone had died and seemed to think Joss had returned from America.

The situation at Withiel Cottage was both impossible and tragic. Though Joss no longer had any love whatever for his wife, though he would never forgive her words about his mother, he did genuinely wish to comfort her in their shared sorrow. But if he came near her she vented her grief and rage by pounding both fists furiously against his chest.

At the end of the week he must leave and return to his work. He had paid a brief visit to Lottie's home and was thankful for both the sympathy and the sanity of his sister, George and Nora, though Nora seemed unnaturally quiet, and on leaving Joss remarked to Lottie that he thought she looked pale.

'She hasn't heard from Alec for a long time,' Lottie said in a whispered voice, not wanting her daughter to overhear. 'She's heard his ship was sunk. Some survivors could have been picked up but nothing is certain.' Joss nodded in silent understanding.

In some inexplicable way he could not bear the thought of seeing Polly and Edwin, nor Jonathan.

Once again Joss retreated from attempting to console Clementine and made his way back to his customary two rooms in the remains of the Manor. What was he to do? With elbows supported on the table he sat holding his head in his hands. Myrtle and the remaining servants were the soul of kindness. He learned with sorrow that Fred, the lad who found Farnells' inscribed gold watch and chain amongst the rubble after the fire, had a leg blown off and was suffering from shell-shock; farmer Marcus Treloar's eldest son had been blinded. Oh God, what a mess!

Myrtle knocked and entered the room and Joss let his hands drop to the table. 'I've made myself a cup of tea and I thought you might like a cup, sir,' she said, placing a tray on the table in front of him.

'Thanks, Myrtle. Pour me a cup would you?' Joss felt too weary to make the effort.

'Certainly, sir,' Myrtle obliged. 'Would you like me to cook dinner in the kitchen here tonight, instead of at the cottage?'

'I don't mind, wherever you like. But wherever you cook it, I'll have my meal here.'

'Mrs Renfree still upset then?' Myrtle ventured, having witnessed some of her violent behaviour.

'I'm afraid so,' Joss replied. 'I shall call at the cottage again after we've eaten.'

But Clementine's mood had not improved by the evening, and Joss believed his presence was aggravating rather than doing anything to alleviate his wife's suffering. He was due to travel north at the end of the week but contemplated leaving earlier. He wanted to do what was best for Clementine, and staying in this atmosphere wasn't good for either of them.

The next morning Joss packed his suitcase, made his way to the cottage and between Clementine's shouts of 'Get out', told her he *was* getting out. He was just leaving.

This seemed to take the bite out of Clementine's abusive words. Dimly Joss noticed she looked a mess, not yet washed or dressed, hair awry, white-faced with wrinkled skin beneath reddened swollen eyes.

'Is Margaret about? I'd like to say good-bye to her,' he said.

'I don't know. She's late waking up this morning.'

'Then let her sleep. Tell her I said good-bye.'

'Wait a moment.' Clementine's tone was more moderate. She went upstairs to her mother's room.

'Joss!' Clementine's voice sounded urgent. 'Joss come up here.'

Quickly Joss mounted the stairs. Margaret appeared to be asleep, one hand on the pillow near her blue-tinged face. Joss took her hand and found it to be very cold. He felt for a pulse but there was none.

'Margaret,' he said gently, but there was no response. Then with his thumb, he gently raised one eyelid. An unseeing eye stared up at him. He looked at Clementine.

'I think she's dead,' he said in a soft voice.

'Oh, no!' Clementine screamed, then threw herself at Joss, clasping him to her. 'Don't leave me now! I need you . . . I need you so much. Don't leave, don't leave me, don't leave me,' she was babbling now.

Joss, dumbfounded, automatically raised his arms and loosely, perfunctorily, they encircled her still slender form. 'Of course I'll stay . . . if you want me,' he said.

'I do, I do. You don't know how much,' she pleaded, then convulsed into uncontrollable weeping, her face pressed against his neck, soaking his shirt collar with the profusion of her tears.

Joss's one week of absence was extended. In that time he concluded he had a lot to do, which was as well for him as, though tired, he just had to keep busy. To be idle would be to crack up.

This confirmed his thoughts that it would be bad for Clementine to remain at Withiel Cottage alone and isolated. He could not regard Myrtle or any of the servants as 'company' for Clementine. She had always regarded them as a lesser species . . . necessary, useful, but not the sort of people a lady like herself would 'talk' to, and she certainly would not, could not, make a friend of any of them. She never understood why they so obviously liked Joss and were so willing, so anxious to please and to be friendly, but had long since concluded it was a case of birds of a feather . . .

No attempt was made to seek out Rupert. Even Clementine realised it would be hopeless. In less than a week Margaret's funeral would take place. Even if they knew of his whereabouts in America there would not be time.

George and Lottie were present at the funeral and Edwin attended the service, apologising for Polly's absence due, he said, to having a cold. Very few of Margaret's friends and contemporaries attended but a number sent letters of condolence and listed the assorted reasons which prevented their being present.

The funeral took place on a dull and misty day. Coupled with the shock of Theodore's death, the gloom was intense, almost tangible. For this occasion though, Clementine kept her feelings under control, walked erect, only her pale face betrayed her feelings, for which Joss was thankful.

As well as making the funeral arrangements, Joss enquired for properties in Penryn and Falmouth. In Penryn there was a rather elegant old town house close to that of a doctor, which, though not of manorial proportions, was quite spacious with semi-basement kitchens and a servants' sitting-room, as well as servants' attic bedrooms reached by a narrow stairway separate from the main staircase. The rear of the property could be reached from a lane, and there was stabling enough for two horses, though Joss considered hired transport would be simpler.

The house stood in a little square, Lowenna Square, off the main street but near to all the town facilities. Clementine would not be so lonely, so isolated here, and Falmouth was only a short drive away. Myrtle could come and live here, and perhaps someone to help in the house. The few remaining staff at Manor Withiel could continue as at present, to keep all in relative order until such time as Joss could decide and take action on what to do with the property.

To his surprise Clementine acquiesced in all this. Joss bought the house with part of the furnishings to speed the move, saying Clementine could furnish it to her liking as and when she felt inclined. Mr Borlace, his solicitor, was informed of newer, slightly more generous financial arrangements for Clementine.

The move was hastily facilitated and Clementine seemed glad to be away from Withiel and its sad reminders. She was uncharacteristically quiet and wept frequently. She tolerated Joss and seemed quietly grateful for what he was doing. Her behaviour when he had been about to leave but stayed when Margaret was found dead and Clementine had flung herself upon him beseeching him to stay with her, was not repeated.

She did not ask him to share her bed and for all this Joss was thankful. He had put his arms about her to comfort her. Her sorrow at their son, Theodore's death was genuine, and in this he

304

had compassion for her. Feelings for her in a physical sense were not dead, non-existent, quite the reverse. The gut feeling that she was something vile and untouchable that night when she informed him that his mother was ill and saying the words 'I hope she's bloody dead' were seared in his memory. In that moment he had wished *her* dead. If he had not been in such haste to get to his mother's cottage in Tiggy Lane he could have throttled her! The intense anger, hatred, had abated but the repugnance remained. He had no wish to touch even the garments she wore, much less share her bed!

But he had married her, made her his wife, and he had a responsibility, a duty to her. It was not in his nature to shirk his responsibilities, and in their shared sorrow he did wish to do what he could and should to ease her suffering.

Jonathan, now slightly taller than Polly but not yet as tall as Edwin, had left the mainstream of the boys in Mr Nicholls' form. He was on his way home from Falmouth Grammar School, a fine new granite building which replaced the former school building in Killigrew Street, and was about to enter a narrow side road which was a short cut. Before turning the corner he heard sounds of a scuffle and a boy cry out. He quickened his steps and turning the corner, saw Ossie Colman, a boy in the senior school, delivering body punches to a fat but much younger boy he knew to be new at the school.

Jonathan took pity on the fat boy. He had instant recall of some of the ragging and the punching he took when he was new to the school, but never from the older boys. That wasn't done.

Oswald Colman was known for being a bully. In seconds he reached the pair and Colman received a quick upper-cut to the jaw which sent him reeling backwards against a granite wall, the impact causing him to bang his head in the process. Taken by surprise, the older boy gave his head a shake, as though he were trying to flick off the pain then, with a snarl, lunged at Jonathan who had his fists raised ready for this reaction. Jonathan's punch again connected but Ossie Colman grabbed him in a clinch and the two locked together, endeavouring to hold one another close in order to each rain blows with the one free fist.

A loud voice brought the fight to an abrupt end.

'Cease this disgraceful behaviour this instant!'

Both Ossie Colman and Jonathan released their hold on one another and stared open-mouthed at Mr Ephraim Nicholls, Jonathan's form master.

'What is the reason for this disgraceful conduct?' the master demanded.

Neither boy made a reply. Jonathan reached for his handkerchief and wiped his nose, discovering as he did so that what was dripping from his nostrils was blood. The fat, young, new boy was nowhere to be seen.

'Very well,' said Mr Nicholls. 'I have no intention of conducting an inquisition here in a public place. The Head will be questioning you in his study, probably tomorrow morning. Meanwhile put on your caps, button your jackets and endeavour to *act* like gentlemen, even though you evidently are not. Now be on your way.'

'Yes, sir,' said Jonathan, which prompted Colman to repeat the reply, and Jonathan and Ossie Colman departed, going in opposite directions.

It was Mary's turn to cook the evening meal and Jonathan was thankful to be home before his mother.

'Hello, Jonathan,' Mary said as he entered the kitchen. 'Oh, dear Lord, whatever have you done to yourself?'

'Don't tell Mum, Aunt Mary,' Jonathan pleaded.

'I think she'll see for herself,' Mary answered. 'Been in a fight?' This was more of a statement than a question.

'Couldn't avoid it,' he confirmed. 'It was just one of those things. I'm sure it looks much worse than it really is.' By now his nose had stopped bleeding.

'You've got drips of blood all down your shirt,' Mary said. 'Go and change and give me your shirt and that handkerchief and I'll wash them for you before your mother gets here. Are you sure you're not really badly hurt?'

'Thanks, Aunt Mary, I'm fine.'

But on arrival home both Polly and Edwin noticed his nose was swollen and red.

'Is it?' Jonathan said, as though this was news to him, then added, 'Well, you know what it's like sometimes, when a crowd of boys get together.'

Next morning after assembly the Headmaster announced he

306

wished Jonathan Pendleton to report to his study and for Oswald Colman to wait outside the study. A murmur went round the assembled boys. Someone was for it!

When questioned, Jonathan refused to answer questions except to agree there had been a fight. The Head walked to the door and opened it for Jonathan to leave. 'Wait outside,' he said, and bade the waiting Oswald Colman, complete with darkened, half-closed swollen eye, to enter.

Jonathan lowered himself to a seat next to where Colman had been sitting in the passage outside the Headmaster's study. He could hear voices, mostly the Head's, but could not distinguish what was being said. The study door again opened and the Head who reminded him of a judge in his black gown, ordered him back into the study.

'Colman tells me you struck the first blow,' he announced when he and Jonathan were both seated. He gave Jonathan a penetrating stare. 'Is that correct?'

Jonathan paused. 'It was I who struck Colman the first blow,' Jonathan admitted.

It was the Head's turn to pause as he digested the possible slight difference in the implication of this remark and the wording of his question. At last, with eyes fixed on Colman, he slowly enunciated a question.

'Was there a third person involved in this fight?'

Quickly the older boy averted his gaze and did not speak.

'I'm waiting.'

Colman hesitated, still turning over in his mind the best way to word his answer. 'No, sir,' he replied.

The Headmaster turned his attention to Jonathan.

'Pendleton, do you say there was no third person involved?'

Jonathan stared straight ahead as though he had not heard, and remained silent.

With an impatient slap of his palm on the desk the Headmaster rose, saying, 'You will both have detention every day for the next two weeks, for a time and doing work to be decided by your own form masters. You will also miss sports instruction for the same period of time. In future you will remember the boys of this school, particularly the Upper School,' he glared at Oswald Colman as he spoke, 'do not brawl nor fight in the streets.'

'But he hit me first,' Colman protested. He was clearly not well pleased to be punished.

'That will do, Colman.' The Head's tone was angry.

Colman shot Jonathan a furious look which Jonathan reciprocated.

However, the fracas, unbeknown to Jonathan, turned out to have done the young new boy some good. At break he was eager to relate the story of his being attacked by the big boy in the Upper School, and of the Penryn boy in Mr Nicholls' form coming to his aid and fighting the villainous senior boy, who was known to pick on smaller boys. With enviable imagination he embellished the story thereby adding substantially to the excitement. All the other boys in his form wanted to hear the gory details. Suddenly the fat new boy became accepted and popular.

Chapter Forty-two

Joss's conviction that the entry into the War of the United States of America would hasten its end, was well-founded. On 11th November 1918 Armistice was signed. All over the country mourning for the dead and maimed combined with joy and celebration that the carnage was over. Victory was theirs, but at what a price! Never again would such a catastrophe take place! This was the war to end all wars!

To the joy and relief of Nell, Mary and Polly, Jack returned with nothing more serious than a few minor injuries which would mend, and a slight cough which he attributed to the wet trenches.

Immediately on his arrival home in dear old Penryn there was a family reunion when Jack saw his rosy-faced little daughter, Amy Elizabeth, for the first time since he was on leave when she was only a few weeks old, as well as a lively Jack Junior. He felt choked with joy. He had returned to home and sanity after a living nightmare.

But he was so thin, his pale face pinched and his blue eyes had a round, staring look about them. He was quieter and sometimes seemed far away; and Nell was concerned that with several people going down with influenza, with his cough he too would catch it.

Later, when at last Jack and Mary were alone in their cottage and Jack Junior and Amy tucked up in bed, Jack sank wearily but happily onto the velour covered sofa and pulled Mary to him. With arms about one another they kissed, long and tenderly; then Jack leant back and, with one arm encircling his wife said softly, 'I can't tell you how I dreamed of this, my love.'

'I did too,' Mary said, staring up at him with brimming eyes. 'All in one piece,' she went on thankfully. 'Two arms, two legs two eyes . . . '

'Makes you feel guilty,' Jack mused

'Guilty?' Mary questioned.

'So many didn't,' Jack answered. 'And I've got quite a few families in Penryn, Mabe and Falmouth to visit whose sons and husbands won't be returning.'

Mary stared up at his thin sombre face. 'Try not to think about it now,' she murmured. 'Just be thankful to God you're here and alive. I certainly am.'

Friends and neighbours called in a continuous stream to welcome Jack home. How good it was to be back in Cornwall. Whoever wrote the words 'Be it ever so humble there's no place like home', knew what he was talking about.

Lottie and George had received the good news that Eric was in this country and a week later Oliver arrived. Both were expected to be demobilised in a few weeks. Lottie had cases half packed, ready for her and George to depart for a week to see them both as soon as they received word that their sons were home.

Their only worry now was for Nora, who had had no word of Alec and, though she rarely spoke of it, was clearly desperately worried and dejected by the lack of news. There had been no 'Missing presumed dead' communication. Just the horrid suspense of knowing nothing.

Penryn, in common with towns and villages all over the country, began to count their human losses and plans were being made to erect memorials listing the names of all those who had made the supreme sacrifice. In some instances churches also decided to erect memorials to the memory of those who had perished from their own particular parish. Everywhere mothers mourned the loss of sons, and sweethearts faced a lifetime of grinding on alone into old-age without a life-partner or children of their own. For their generation the future would be in a land with a plethora of females. Nora began to fear that she might never see Alec again . . . that she would later be one of the superfluous females.

Her parents, Lottie and George, had been away to visit Eric and Oliver who had now returned home from the war. Eric was recovering from flesh wounds and was minus an eye. The left side of Oliver's face and throat was scarred pale pink from burns from an explosion in the engine room of his ship. Both Lottie and

310

George were thankful their sons were alive! They had injuries yes, but the injuries were not life threatening nor did they cause serious disability. They were far luckier than so many others.

Nora's fears for Alec deepened. She had no word of him and didn't know if he was dead or alive but it was beginning to look ... bleak ...

'Please God, please, God . . . let him be alive. Perhaps he has lost his memory? As long as he's alive there is hope; just let him be alive.'

One evening, weeks later, Nora and her mother and father were sitting round the fireside. George was reading, Lottie tacking the side-seams of a skirt and chatting to Nora, who was knitting a pullover for Alec and forcing herself to believe he was alive, but fearing in her heart he might never wear it, when there was a rap on the front door.

'I'll see who it is,' Nora said as she rose to her feet, and pulling shut without fastening the cosy middle room door, moved along the darkened passageway, opened the inner door, then the front door and stared at the black silhouette of a man's tallish frame. Unable to distinguish who it was, and momentarily puzzled, Nora was about to say 'Good evening' when the man forestalled her.

'Nora . . . don't you recognise me?' said a familiar northern voice.

'Alec!' A scream of joy rent the still blackness of the starless night as Nora flung her arms around the neck of the man she feared had perished. At the same time Alec's arms were about her, lifting her off her feet and swinging her round in the joy of reunion.

How long they remained clinging to one another Nora did not know. They eventually were aware of Nora's mother in the sudden shaft of light from the opened middle room door and the sound of her voice shouting, 'George . . . Come here. Alec's back!'

Alec and Nora partially released their hold on one another and her parents hugged and shook hands with the returning seafarer. Then they all moved into the warmth of the cosy room, where Alec and Nora, who was both laughing and crying at the same time, feasted their eyes on one another. Lottie reached in her pocket for her handkerchief and also did a little eye-dabbing.

Alec's face was thinner, less boyish, and he looked pinched, as did so many returning young men. Eventually it was noticed he had a slight limp, due to an injured leg. How he sustained the injury when the ship was torpedoed he did not know. He felt nothing at the time, but it was not uncommon for terrible injures to be suffered without, when it actually happened, the victim feeling anything.

It transpired Alec's ship was struck without warning by the torpedo. He was standing on the bridge. He thought several crew below deck and in the engine-room would not have stood a chance of survival. He and a few others managed to cling to large spars of wood and after a time were picked up by a foreign merchant ship on its way to Brazil. They remained in Brazil for some time until a Greek ship allowed them to return with them, hoping to hail a British vessel en route. Eventually they transferred from the Greek vessel in the waters off Gibraltar, the entrance to the Mediterranean, and from thereon were under the wing of the Royal Navy. But obviously assisting them to get back to England was not the Navy's top priority. Eventually though, they did make it, as Nora and her parents could now see.

But on mental calculation of the dates and lengths of time. Nora suddenly demanded to know why it took Alec so long to get in touch. She had been worried sick! Then Alec was forced to admit he had been quite ill. The injury to his leg became infected and he was taken to a castle in Scotland which had been converted into a hospital for war casualties with serious injuries. For a time it was feared amputation would be necessary. Until he was certain he would not lose his leg or his ability to continue his career, he did not try to contact Nora.

'I could kill you!' Nora ejaculated, 'You rotten . . . rotten . . . ' she spluttered, and lost for an appropriate word flung her arms about Alec's neck and burst into a flood of tears. 'Do you think it would have mattered to me?' she sobbed, when she mustered enough composure.

'I think I was a fool,' Alec said in a soft voice, alternately stroking and kissing the head which rested with buried face on his shoulder.

They scarcely noticed that Lottie and George had silently retreated to the kitchen on the pretext of making them all a hot drink.

Promptly at 10 p.m. Lottie and George bid Nora and Alec goodnight. 'It's our bedtime,' Lottie explained to Alec. 'I have to be at work in the morning. But you take the day off Nora.'

'Oh, may I, Mother,' Nora said, delighted.

'If Polly were here, I'm sure she would positively insist.'

'Thanks. That'll be lovely.'

'By the way, Alec,' Lottie addressed Nora's young man, 'the bed in the small front bedroom is made up and ready.'

Alec grinned. 'Thanks, Mrs Simpson.'

Goodnights said, Lottie and George mounted the stairs, leaving the young couple to themselves.

'I hoped she'd let me off work tomorrow, and I didn't even have to ask,' Nora said, as she turned to Alec.

'I'm glad too, because there's something I want us to do,' Alec said as they sat holding hands.

'What's that?' Nora demanded.

'I want us to go out and buy something.'

'I thought you didn't like shopping.'

'I shall like it this time, if you say 'yes' . . . Nora, I love you . . . will you marry me?'

For a moment Nora, taken aback, couldn't speak. But her dark eyes shone as she gazed into Alec's grey ones and Alec knew Nora had no doubts.

'Yes . . . yes, I'll marry you, Alec,' Nora said in a small but firm voice.

Alec's face beamed. 'Good,' he said. 'Tomorrow we'll buy the ring.' Their arms instantly encircled one another.

Lottie was unable to get to sleep with the excitement of Alec's return and relief at her daughter's happiness. She realised how fortunate she had been; both her sons returned from the war, one with relatively minor injuries. And now the solid young seafarer who, she began to hope, might one day be her son-in-law.

An hour after retiring she heard Nora and Alec creeping up the stairs and pausing a couple of minutes on the landing before whispered 'goodnights' when they separated to go to their rooms.

Next morning Polly was delighted at the joyful news. 'Nora must take as much time off as she wants,' Polly insisted.

When it was nearing lunch-time and the morning shoppers dwindling, Alec and Nora, arm in arm with smiling faces, called at the shop.

'Alec . . . it's lovely to see you safely back,' Polly said, warmly shaking the young officer's hand. 'And you've put a smile back

o

on Nora's face . . . we were getting quite concerned about her.'

Alec turned to gaze down at the pretty young girl who had been so worried about him. Under his jacket his bosom swelled with pride and emotion. Nora, unaware of his tender glance, was beaming at Polly.

'Is mother about?' she asked.

At that moment Lottie, who had heard their voices, came rushing down the stairs.

'Mother, come here,' Nora said, then held up her left hand for Polly and her mother to inspect.

'Oh, congratulations!' Lottie said, with an approving smile. The words were almost simultaneously repeated by Polly.

Lottie, then Polly, hugged and kissed them both, then more closely inspected the engagement ring, a wide gold band embedded with alternating diamonds and sapphires.

'It's beautiful,' they both echoed.

'We were going to look in all the jeweller's shops before finally deciding,' Nora said. 'But as soon as I saw this one, I knew I wouldn't see one I liked better.'

'Only she insisted she didn't want me to buy it,' Alec chipped in.

'Of course I didn't want you to buy anything that expensive,' Nora expostulated, then turning to her mother said, 'He didn't get much change out of £30!'

'Phew!' Lottie whistled. 'Still . . . you only have one engagement ring.'

'I hope so,' Alec said with a grin.

Next day Lottie and George learned that Alec would like to take Nora to his home to meet his mother. Though a northerner, she lived in Sussex. The move to the south of England was made because she had become a widow and wanted to be near her married daughter, Stella who, with her husband, ran a hotel in Brighton. Mrs Stevens lived in Rottingdean, a short distance away. Alec assured the two it would be for only a few days.

So a visit was arranged for early the next week. Nora was both nervous and excited. She had never been further than Plymouth. And Mrs Stevens was going to be her mother-in-law! Would she think Nora good enough to be her son's wife? Nora could not call herself a good cook; she only knew how to bake a few things: rock buns, heavy cake and . . . what else . . . ? She could fry breakfast, make porridge, she could make a pasty but wasn't sure she could bake it . . . What else . . . ? Oh yes, jam tarts, apple or apple and blackberry tart. That was all. Stew seemed easy, she thought she could soon learn to master that. Oh dear. There was such a lot she didn't know.

Nora confided her thoughts to Polly, knowing her mother would only dismiss her fears and tell her she'd manage all right.

'Do you know, except for those who have actually worked in kitchens, I think every girl feels like that when she's getting married; I know I did.'

'Did you?' Nora interrupted, surprised. Polly always seemed so efficient at everything she touched.

'I certainly did,' Polly confirmed. 'But if you don't mind taking a bit of advice from your mother and you get in a little practice, you'll soon get the hang of it. Try cooking the Sunday roast a few times with your mother's assistance. You'll soon be able to manage on your own.'

'I'll do that. But it will have to be after Alec's leave is over,' Nora promised, feeling a little more confident.

Nora, wanting to make a good impression, left for Sussex a few days later with several smart outfits, the diamond and sapphire ring on her finger, and her precious Alec. How fortunate she was, and how excited! She was also a little scared. Would her mother-in-law-to-be like her?

Meanwhile Joss's work for the coal-mining industry need not end immediately. Peacetime fuel requirements would not be the same at those in wartime, and in peacetime it was not a matter of 'Winning the war at all costs', but of commerce. It was now necessary for assessment of which areas of mining were viable, and Joss's expertise and advice was still in demand.

Joss also had the situation at Renfree's Ranch in America to consider. He had helped his country where he could, now he had his own business to think about. But though estranged from Clementine she *was* devastated by the death of their son, their only child. While there was a possibility she needed him in her grief for Theodore, he would not leave the country or her. If necessary, someone else could be found to complete the work at the coal-mines.

Joss decided to travel south to Cornwall to see how Clementine was faring. He had his work to help occupy at least some of his thoughts, but Clementine had nothing, not even her deranged mother. Probably he would return north for a few weeks. As yet he had made no firm decisions. He would first assess the situation at home. Some of the bitterness had gone from his heart; he and Clementine still had one thing in common, their shared sorrow at Theodore's death.

The trains were filled with soldiers, sailors and a sprinkling of airmen, many with bandaged heads, limbs, and with slings and crutches. For much of the tedious journey Joss and other civilians stood to allow wounded young servicemen the benefit of their seats.

As soon as circumstances allowed and he was sure Clementine was well enough to be left, he would return to Renfree's Ranch and look into business affairs there. He had an arrangement with a bank in the United States and Bill Boaden would have paid the net profits into his account. An occasional letter had been received by him to the effect that all was going well.

At Truro he alighted and took the branch-line Falmouth train, getting off at Penryn Station. There he hailed a cab and instructed the driver where to go. The driver secured Joss's case and the massive horse trotted down Helston Road and through the main street, passing the old Town Hall with its lofty clock-tower, and turned towards Lowenna Square. But as the cab was about to draw near Joss saw a uniformed man mounting the steps to the front door of his home. There was something familiar about him.

'Slow down driver,' he called.

'Whoa,' called the driver to his horse, and speeded the procedure by pulling on the long-handled hand brake.

Joss stared unblinking at the man in uniform. 'By hell, I was right!' he said to himself. 'Driver I've changed my mind. Take me to the Towers Hotel near the seafront in Falmouth.'

Clementine no longer had any need of his presence! If that was what she needed, as far as he was concerned she could have it! He could have picked up that slimy fop, Copeland, and thrown him over the steps, neck and crop! But he just couldn't be bothered. Clementine wasn't worth the effort. He'd stay at the Towers in Falmouth, and tomorrow he'd arrange to book his passage to America!

He'd given up on her, washed his hands. He no longer had a child or his parents to consider. Lottie would understand. Oh, Polly! What a fool I was, he thought for the umpteenth time.

Chapter Forty-three

Joss gazed out of the window of his large room overlooking Falmouth Bay in the Towers Hotel. The headland, topped with Pendennis Castle, curved seawards to the left, and to the right beyond Gyllyngvase Beach were the cliffs on the far side of Swanpool Beach. Here the cliffs curved seawards past the mouth of the lovely Helford River, way out to where the start of the fearsome Manacle Rocks could be seen jutting from the water away on the horizon where sea and sky met.

It was a beautiful view but Joss registered none of it. His mind was occupied with the imminent departure and the pain, or more precisely the anger, at the reason which prompted his hasty departure. He had been to the busy shipping office, which over-looked Falmouth harbour a short distance away on the other side of the headland and had booked a passage to New York on a ship leaving Avonmouth in six days; less than a week. He had also contacted the Yorkshire coal-mines overseer by telegram to the effect that due to unforeseen circumstances he was obliged to go abroad.

Next he visited Lottie and George, and was scolded by his sister for not coming straight to them. Joss explained that he didn't know whether Alec might be in Falmouth, and Lottie only had one spare bedroom. He didn't add that he felt so angry, not only with Clementine but with himself for being surprised that she was 'entertaining', as she called her peccadilloes, when he imagined she was grieving over the loss of their son, and that he wanted to be alone until the black anger receded. Some husbands would have done the same as many fathers did with erring, though often innocent ignorant daughters . . . removed their leather belts and dutifully administered 'a good thrashing'. To

317

Joss this was obnoxious as well as pointless. But with Clementine . . . perhaps his restraint had come to an end; and he had a feeling for his own preservation he would be wise to keep well away. She wasn't worth getting 'worked up' over. She could stew in her own juice.

Lottie and George were upset for him and disgusted with Clementine. George was inclined to agree with Joss that it could be better for him to get away to America now, and take up his business interests in the completely different atmosphere and surroundings, and to hell with Clementine.

Joss left the Towers Hotel to spend the last two nights with Lottie and George and decided to visit Polly, Edwin and Jonathan the evening before he left at about the time they would have finished their evening meal. That way he would be sure of Edwin's presence, which would help ensure he did not let his feelings, his emotions, his love for Edwin's wife, get the better of him. Saying good-bye would need every ounce of iron control. He both dreaded and yearned to see Polly, just to look at her, to hear her voice, to feel her hand in his, and the delight and dejection of a brief good-bye kiss.

Joss took a cab from Falmouth, his easy manner betraying no hint of the trepidation inside him. His hands were steady, his face appeared relaxed, but within his breast his heart beat wildly causing an aching feeling in his throat. Like stage fright, the feeling subsided when, after Joss's rap on the door, the handle turned and the door began to open. With a smile Joss raised his hand to remove his hat, expecting to be greeted by Edwin, but there stood Polly. An anxious expression on her face melted into a smile when she saw him.

'Joss, I'm so glad you've called,' she exclaimed. Joss followed her inside to the sitting-room.

'Lottie told me you are leaving for America, and we all hoped to see you before then,' Polly went on, as they both sat facing each other. 'But there's been an accident at the quarries . . . '

'Not Edwin?' Joss interrupted.

'No. One of the men, and Edwin has accompanied him to Truro Infirmary.'

'It's serious then,' Joss said sympathetically.

'It's not likely to be fatal but the man's arm was badly damaged by the machinery; and Jonathan is playing rugby against a team from another school. He'll be so sorry to have missed you.'

Joss, who had been drinking in the closeness of Polly's face, lowered his eyes. He had not expected to be alone with Polly. He felt a trembling inside him. Did Polly feel the same? He glanced up at her. She looked calm, composed.

He asked about Edwin and the accident, then about Jonathan, and Polly talked of her son at length. But suddenly, without a hint of warning, she clasped his hand in hers. 'Joss, I'm so sorry Clementine has caused you so much . . . '

Instantly Joss gazed questioningly into her eyes, and as her voice trailed away he saw her composure disintegrate as tears welled up in her eyes and her face puckered. She was suffering with him, for him.

It wasn't his intention, he didn't know he was going to, but suddenly he was standing, pulling her to him, their arms about each other, his kisses rapidly covering her cheeks now wet with salty tears that had brimmed over.

'Don't worry for me, darling. I'll be all right,' he said softly.

'How can I help it, I love you so much, and to know she never stops making your life such a hell . . . it's so unfair.'

Joss's reply was to kiss her mouth. 'Never mind Clementine,' he whispered when he relinquished her lips. 'She might infuriate me but she could never break my heart . . . only you could do that, and I know you never will.'

They stood for what seemed a long time, their arms tight around each other, their cheeks pressed together, each drawing solace from the other.

'I must go now,' Joss said at last, without releasing his hold on her. 'We shouldn't be doing this.'

'I know, but how can we help it?' Polly sighed.

Joss kissed her again, a long passionate kiss, then, with eyes still gazing into hers, reached for his hat and completely released his hold on her.

'I must go, my love,' he murmured, and left the room. Polly followed close behind. Suddenly Joss seized her hand, kissed both the palm and the back, pressed it to his heart, as unnoticed by Polly he took the door handle with his free hand, opened the door and suddenly was gone without a backward glance. Polly swiftly closed the door and immediately burst into tears.

Next morning Lottie arrived late at 'The Lady'. She was tearful at Joss's departure.

'It's not just that he's going away, it's the reason for his going.' She dabbed her eyes, but Polly, with iron control, was dry-eyed.

'It's so unfair,' Lottie went on. 'No one could have been a better husband.'

'I know,' Polly agreed. She glanced out of the window. 'Mrs Honour Clarkson is crossing the road. I think she's coming here.'

'I'll get upstairs,' Lottie answered as she moved towards the staircase, uncomfortably aware of her reddened swollen eyelids.

Mrs Clarkson bought an off-the-rail white blouse. No sooner had she departed than Mrs Barnett and Miss Lewis entered. They needed to order funeral outfits, the order to be executed immediately. Any tell-tale signs of weeping on Lottie's face went unnoticed by the two sisters when they went upstairs to the fitting-room to have their measurements checked. Both were too distressed by their own loss, another death from influenza, this time the victim was the little eight-year-old daughter of the brother of the two sisters.

The day was indeed off to a bad start.

On disembarking in New York Joss discovered the influenza epidemic was also widespread there. Several people became ill during the crossing and one passenger died. The death cast a gloom on passengers and crew alike, seafaring men being superstitious about ill-luck associated with a ship that had a dead body aboard.

Joss spent two nights in an hotel in the bustling city, leaving early after the second night, on the journey to Michigan and Renfree's Ranch. The vast and scenically varied American countryside always fascinated him, and it was his intention to drink it all in from his view from the speeding 'Iron Horse'. But Joss could rarely get Polly, Theodore or Clementine out of his thoughts, and when he did they were replaced with Lottie and her family, Edwin and Jonathan or his mother or that dandy, Copeland.

Eventually his reflections were interrupted not by the scenery but a talkative Jewish lady who boarded and filled the vacant seat next to him. Though not specially interested in her chatter about her parents, her brothers, sisters, husband, children, cousins etc., it was a distraction from the thoughts uppermost in his mind. The following day weariness seemed to overtake him. The garrulous Jewess reached her destination and Joss, feeling languid, nodded off. At first he was thankful to doze then awoke to the realisation that he felt 'off-colour', probably from too much sitting.

With less than ten hours travel to go Joss, who rarely felt cold, began to shiver. He did not bother to go to the diner when the last meal was served on the train. It was something of a relief to find Bill Boaden with a vehicle which had Renfree's Ranch in large white lettering on its sides, awaiting him when the train screeched to a noisy halt.

'Hi there Joss, you don't look so good, boy,' said a familiar voice as Joss alighted unsteadily from the train. Bill ambled towards him. 'Here let me take your case,' he said. Uncharacteristically, Joss submitted.

'Thanks, Bill! I think I might have 'flu coming on,' Joss said as the two shook hands and delivered each other a friendly slap.

'We've all had it,' Bill admitted. 'Get in the truck.'

While Bill deposited the case in the back of the truck Joss, with unaccustomed effort, heaved himself up into the passenger seat.

'You'd best get straight to bed when we get to the ranch,' Bill said. 'Maria will look after you, she's good at nursing folk.'

Joss did not reply but welcomed the thought of bed.

'Been some changes since you left here. You'll hardly know the place . . . '

Bill chatted on but Joss paid little heed. He'd pay attention to the ranch and the whole situation tomorrow . . . or the next day.

Around five weeks later, when Joss was still feeling drained from the severe bout of influenza during which three days were completely lost to him, he received a letter from Lottie with the news that Nell, Polly's mother had succumbed to the world-wide epidemic. Names of several other Penryn and Mabe folk who did not survive the 'flu were listed, including Silas Pope, Emma's father.

By the time he received the letter the funeral would have taken place. Joss's sorrow and concern for how it would affect Polly and Jack was mixed with guilt that when he left Cornwall, in his disgust and haste to get away, he had neglected to call on Nell, Polly's dear mother who had always been such a good friend to his parents and all the family. He would write right away to Polly, though how he could put in a letter what he felt, he did not know.

Dear Nell, dear Polly . . . his thoughts turned to his own parents and to Theodore; then Lottie, George, Nora and her brothers, Edwin, Jack, Jonathan, somehow especially Jonathan, and so many others . . . just ordinary decent people. He, Joss, was flourishing. He'd made and almost lost, thanks to the Du Canes, a fortune. And here he was now, richer than ever. There was more oil than he envisaged and the money deposited greatly exceeded his expectations.

And there was Bill . . . Bill Boaden. He could have syphoned off a fortune for himself. He had been in sole charge. Joss had trusted him with everything. But Joss had not the slightest doubt that Bill had not shortchanged him a single penny . . . not a cent. Bill had been told by him to take a generous percentage for himself, which Bill at the time protested was too much, and now Bill and his wife were quite well off, more than satisfied, extremely satisfied. You couldn't put a price on trust. These friends were the salt of the earth, and they didn't even know it. Nor could you better being able to look yourself in the eye, with the respect for yourself that comes from a clear conscience.

Comparing folk like these with Clementine and Rupert was depressing, disheartening. With all his good fortune Joss's personal life had been a disaster, and no amount of money could make up for the misery, the sick despair he had unwittingly and naïvely heaped on his own head. And he also had cheated, he had taken advantage of Edwin's wife . . . Polly, oh Polly . . .

Chapter Forty-four

Alec preferred the marriage to take place when he had secured his Master's Certificate and did not want even a provisional date to be set in anticipation of his success. Like most seafaring men, he was a touch superstitious and feared that to do so would be tempting fate.

Then, due to an accident in which the First Officer on a ship about to leave this country was injured, Alec was asked to take his place. There was no other suitably qualified officer immediately available, so Alec felt he had little choice since no actual wedding date had been arranged. It was after his departure that he learned he was now qualified to the rank of Captain.

Though disappointed by the delay, for Nora this, unlike the dreadful war years, was a period of happy contemplation of a future as Alec's wife, the future Mrs Nora Stevens or, jointly, Captain and Mrs Alec Stevens. It was a time of both contentment and sweet anticipation, secure in the instinctive certainty that Alec was a 'one woman man' and she, Nora, was that woman.

At 'The Lady' business was showing signs of improvement after a lull during the war years. There had been quite a lot of orders for mourning apparel throughout this period, and the catastrophic 'flu epidemic which coincided with the final weeks of the war and beyond. Lottie had stitched the sombre black outfits with a sinking heart. Neither she nor Polly had this sort of sewing in mind when they started a Fashion House. Profit from these ladies' patronage brought no satisfaction, but seemed to add to the gloom.

During the war genteel, well-heeled ladies found for the first time there was a dearth of servants to perform every single physical task in the running of their homes. This was due to women as well as men leaving their jobs to do a wide variety of work directly or indirectly connected with the war effort. Some were posts and tasks previously performed by men; also there had been new munitions factories. Many women enrolled for nursing and a number of these went to France to help care 'behind the lines' for those injured in the fighting and the trenches, and many injured men were brought back to this country to be nursed.

This effort to 'do their bit' was not confined to one class though. Apart from the old or unfit, better-off ladies, thousands from *all* backgrounds responded to the self-imposed call of duty, and tackled whatever task they were allotted, or often volunteered for, with cheerful resolution. In many instances the performance of distasteful or dangerous undertakings brought about mutual respect and understanding between those at opposite ends of the social scale.

With worry about what had become of Alec behind her, the wedding some time ahead and, having been warmly welcomed and clearly approved by Alec's family, Nora was able to take a more positive interest in 'The Lady'.

Both Polly and Lottie sensed that now war had ended and the dreadful 'flu epidemic was behind them, when the 'dust had settled', change was bound to come. Even prior to all this change had been in the air and had stealthily manifested itself by skirts being raised, and the view of trim ankles was more than a glimpse! Dainty shoes made of kid, suede or gabardine, and high buttoned boots with slim heels and pointed toes were revealed. Life in general would not continue completely where it left off when war started. Things were becoming mechanised and a more modern era lay ahead. But quite what change in fashion would take place was hard to forecast.

With these thoughts in mind it was decided not to aim to carry a large stock of ready-made garments, at least, not as large as they did before war started. It was possible, even likely that elderly ladies, firm-set in their own era and mode of dress, would tolerate only minor alterations to their particular style of apparel, but that the majority, especially the younger ladies, would want to keep up with the latest trends. Polly and Lottie would wait, and watch which way to jump!

* * * *

Over the past year Jonathan had a growing spurt. He was taller and seemed to have turned from a boy into a young man almost overnight.

It was a singular coincidence that something of a similar occurrence to the previous scrap with Ossie Colman, now almost at the end of his time at Grammar School, once more took place. Jonathan was again on his way from school, this time walking to Penmere Halt to get the train home to Penryn. As he strode down the steep section of the twisting hill he heard a girl's annoyed and, he thought, alarmed tones.

'Stop that! . . . Let go!'

There was something familiar about the voice. Jonathan increased his pace. He heard another voice, deeper, male but crackly and immature and also familiar. As he sped into the narrow pathway to the Halt he saw . . . Ossie Colman! He appeared to be struggling with a girl in High School uniform.

By heck! It was Laura Ann! A strange, never before experienced anger surged inside him. In a flash he reached the two.

'Let go of her, you swine!' he snarled as with a leap he tackled the older boy, felling him and himself, and from his vantage position above Ossie Colman, rained punches down upon him.

'Stop Jonathan! . . . Stop!' Laura Ann shouted, her hands on Jonathan's shoulders, trying to drag him away from the dazed boy.

'Listen, Jonathan, the train's coming!'

Breathing heavily Jonathan paused, glaring down at the bewildered Ossie, who was still beneath him.

'I only wanted to carry her satchel,' Colman said, defensively, obviously fearing another attack from his enraged assailant.

'That's what you say,' Jonathan retorted with obvious disbelief.

'The train's stopping . . . come on!' Laura Ann urged.

Together they sprinted to the platform, leaving Colman to pick himself up. The train had already started to move, Jonathan wrenched open a door and both scrambled aboard. He then slammed the door and they flopped side by side and breathless, onto their seats.

For a few seconds both sat panting. Then Jonathan turned his head to look down at Laura Ann. She was staring up at him. His dark eyes gazed down into her upturned shining blue ones.

Suddenly a strange new feeling, a tenderness, an emotion, a sweet undreamt of sensation, pervaded him. It was his turn to feel stunned!

At last came news that the ship on which Alec was now serving would be returning and a date for the wedding would be fixed. What seemed a long way off was suddenly excitingly close! There would be the bride's dress as well as her 'going away outfit' to make as well as dresses for the three bridesmaids: Esme, Alec's niece, Nora's brother Eric's daughter Sophie, and Nora's cousin and friend Madge, who was soon herself to be married.

Both Polly and Lottie were determined all involved in the running of 'The Lady' would live up to the name of the establishment and be dressed by 'The Lady'. Most of the well-dressed ladies in Falmouth, Penryn and further afield were their clients, and it was clear Nora's wedding would be the focus of some attention. Preparations began to fire ahead.

When the ship reached port Alec was to have discussions at Company Headquarters, but he made a brief weekend dash to Falmouth for a talk with Nora to make a definite date for their marriage. It was decided this would now take place one month to the day.

Everything involving 'The Lady' except for the actual sewing side was Polly's province and she suggested notices to inform the public of the shop's closure on *the* wedding day should appear in local papers for three consecutive weeks.

Lottie though saw the inclusion in the guest-list of all the staff including Madam Delia as a problem for the business. Would it be bad for business? Polly viewed it as more of an advantage. A notice in the shop window plus advertising the one day closure in the local papers for three consecutive weeks, ensured almost everyone was acquainted with the fact.

Polly had kept the list of all those who had received invitations to attend the Preview when 'The Lady' was launched. Aware some lived outside the area covered by the advertisements, by cross-reference with the names in Lottie's book of clients' measurements, she was able to notify each, of the one day closure of the shop and the happy reason. Every precaution was taken to ensure absolutely all clients were notified that 'The Lady' would be closed on that day, and everyone loved a wedding . . . more so after all the gloom of recent years. It would be a bright spot in the calendar. Doubtful still, but outnumbered by Polly and Nora, Lottie agreed to the closure.

But one much-loved member of the Renfree family would be missing . . . Joss! Polly's eyes moistened as she thought of him. How was he faring so far away from home and all his loved ones? It was strange, the way the situation had become reversed. He and Clementine no longer had a child, yet thanks to Joss she felt sure, she and Edwin had a son. That was the way the picture appeared. If only she could put her arms about him and tell him . . . poor, dear Joss . . . it would be heaven for him. But such an act would cause distress and confusion for everyone else. Jonathan loved his father dearly, and Edwin positively doted on him. What heaven and hell she and Joss created that one night. But she would never regret it. So much joy had come from their one union which would all be ruined if she did not keep her guilty secret to herself. Joss would never tell; of that she was certain. But his joy probably would. What a predicament! What hell it was to know her beloved Joss was deeply unhappy, to have it in her power to turn that unhappiness into bliss, yet to deny him!

For her brother's sake, Lottie included Clementine on the list of wedding guests. George, who was helping with paperwork, groaned at this prospect, as did Lottie and Nora, only inwardly. But Clementine declined the invitation, giving no reason. All breathed a sigh of relief.

Even with Madam Delia and Nora helping full-time in the sewing room, and machining going on until late in the evenings, there was such a lot to be done.

Lottie was thankful the excessively fussy and elaborate dress styles popular in her time at Corfields Drapers Shop were no longer in vogue, but had been replaced by simpler, straighter lines. The abundance of time consuming tucks, frills, lace trimmings and flounces was out of favour, along with all the constricting underwear essential at the time. The female anatomy had taken on a more natural shape, helped along by wartime restrictions and shortages. Younger ladies declared they would never suffer the constraining corsetry their mothers had been obliged to endure. Nevertheless, Nora did favour a long, voluminously skirted dress for her wedding, but with a more up-to-date going away outfit.

'It's going to be the town's fashion event of the year,' Polly said to Lottie in a low voice one morning when they had been talking about the arrangements.

'I know,' was Lottie's whispered and somewhat jittery reply.

'Do you think Nora is aware of that?' Polly still whispered.

'Not really, and I don't want to make her edgy, she's a bit nervous as it is.'

There could be no fittings for Esme, Alec's niece, or for her grand-daughter Sophie, and Lottie had to work with measurements supplied by their mothers.

Mrs Stevens, Alec's mother, and her daughter were aware Nora's mother had a partnership in a small dress shop. But they had no idea how plush and chic it was. Impressions gained from Mrs Simpson's homely, down-to-earth manner didn't seem to tie up with the haughty demeanour Mrs Stevens so often associated with ladies involved in high fashion. She had encountered some of these females in the dress shops in Hove. They bore no resemblance to the impression gained from Alec and Nora of Lottie Simpson.

Polly's assiduous notifications and advertising of the one day closure of 'The Lady' on the wedding day had a two-fold effect. As well as ensuring not one client or prospective customer was inconvenienced, just everyone, regular customer or not, knew about the event.

On *the* day the sun shone and the narrow Falmouth streets were crowded with waiting viewers when guests began to arrive at the Church. This was situated on the corner at a bend in the road, and entered via a flight of steps which afforded every onlooker a view of each arrival.

Inside the Church, perfumed with the scent of every seasonal flower in bloom, were about eighty further well-wishers occupying the pews at the rear. Ushers in morning suits conducted the official guests to more forward seating either side of the centre aisle. An organist high above the body of the interior, played soft, dreamy music. Now guests were rapidly arriving, and the choirboys took their places either side of the altar.

There was a faint cheer when the groom and best man, Chief Engineer John Jordan, arrived and mounted the steps, and a gasp when the three bridesmaids emerged from their taxi. Their apricot tinged cream dresses had fitted bodices, puff sleeves for the smaller bridesmaids, gigot sleeves for Madge, the chief bridesmaid, and full skirts some six inches above floor level, with scallop edged hem-lines, necklines and sleeves, plus matching satin footwear and floral headbands. Each held a Victorian Posy.

Excitement mounted. The bride would be next to arrive! Talk amongst the onlookers hushed as a quick clip clopping of horses hooves was heard, rapidly getting louder. The bride and her top-hatted father arrived in an open horse-drawn carriage. All eyes were on the bride as, assisted by her father, she stepped down from the carriage and stood amidst the crowd. There were gasps and Ooos and Ahhs of approval of her frothy, virginal white gown with fitted bodice, modest neckline, edged about by a wide band of swirls of glass beading, Pagoda sleeves and yards and layers of billowing full-length skirt. Nora's face was just visible behind her veil of fine silk tulle, which was held in place with a band of traditional orange-blossom. She held a bouquet of white lilies and contrasting green ferns. Though a little nervous she had the presence of mind to smile and give a little wave to the watching crowds, which showed its appreciation with a ripple of gentle clapping.

The organ was now silent and the guests inside the Church heard the faint commotion in the street outside. There was an expectant hush.

Slowly, for fear she would step on the voluminous skirt, the bride and her father mounted the steps and stood in the porchway.

George attentively adjusted her trailing veil which had billowed slightly in a sudden gust of soft breeze, while the two small bridesmaids, guided by Madge, correctly positioned themselves behind the bride. The white-robed Verger raised his arm, clicked finger and thumb and instantly the Church was filled with the sound of the pipe organ playing Wagner's *Here Comes the Bride*.

Alec, his best man and guests all turned their heads to see the advancing vision, moving down the aisle on the arm of her proud father. Nora saw only Alec, whose gaze was fixed on his bride. Their eyes met, he smiled, then winked, and Nora's nervousness subsided.

The Vicar took a step forward as the two came to a halt, the bride and groom standing side by side, with George to Nora's left and John Jordan, the best man, to Alec's right. The chief brides-maid and two smaller bridesmaids stood a little behind the bride and groom.

The Vicar's reassuring voice broke the hushed, almost tangible silence with the well-loved time-honoured words and passages which precede the ceremonial commitments.

Next was the singing of a hymn, and Polly felt a trembling tear roll down her cheek as the sound of her brother Jack's sweet tenor voice sang effortlessly behind her. The hymn came to a close and Nora turned and handed her bouquet to Madge, glanced in Alec's direction, and the important part of the ceremony began, the vows and the commitments. There was a panicky pause when John Jordan the best man, searched the wrong pocket of his suit for the ring, but it was found safe and secure in the inner breast pocket of his jacket.

Alec spoke his responses in clear steady tones and Nora, strengthened by Alec's nearness, did the same. When the two knelt side by side before the altar, Polly saw in her mind, herself kneeling, adorned in her white bridal attire, but the man kneeling beside her was a blur. Lottie, Mrs Stevens and a few other ladies dabbed their eyes. George just let a couple of tears roll down his cheeks and trickle beneath his jaw-line as he gave away his beautiful only daughter.

Everyone relaxed for the second and final hymn, then the main participants moved to the Vestry to sign the Register and complete the marriage certificate, while the organist played and the choirboys sang a joyful hymn. Alec and Nora were man and wife!

The two, with the bridesmaids, their parents, and the best man again emerged into the body of the Church and moved up the aisle to the playing of Mendelssohn's *Wedding March*. As they neared the Church Porch a joyful pealing of Church Bells rang out, causing raucous squawking and wing-flapping as a flock of alarmed gulls flew hither and thither overhead, and an expectant murmuring from the crowd of onlookers still waiting in the street outside.

There was a pause for the photographer as, half hidden under an enveloping black-cloth, he bent over the tripod to take a photo-graph.

'Hold it,' he ordered. Then, 'Done.'

This process was repeated several times, with the bridesmaids, then with the best man and parents etc. Then they moved outside the porch to allow space for guests to be included in the photographs.

Photography completed, headed by the bride and groom, all began to descend the steps to waiting assorted conveyances, and the drive to the Royal Hotel for the Reception.

The crowd continued to watch and both Lottie and Polly noticed a sprinkling of well-to-do ladies standing among the ordinary townsfolk who had waited to see the beautiful bride and her handsome husband with what seemed to be an absolute parade of elegantly attired ladies and impeccably dressed gentlemen.

At the reception in the Hotel, Alec's mother confessed to George that she was taken aback by the elegance of so many of the guests *and* all the flurry and commotion the wedding had caused in that busy section of the town.

'So was I,' George replied. 'I never thought we'd be able to give our daughter a wedding like that. I was only an ordinary clerk in the dock's office, you know; and I don't mind telling you I feel a right . . . ' he hesitated, stopping himself from using a rather dubious adjective, 'A right twit in this "get-up",' he said, referring to his morning suit.

Mrs Stevens laughed and gave him a nudge. 'You'll do!' she approved.

When the buffet lunch was over, the cake cut and the toasts, to George's great relief, over, Alec and Nora took to the dance floor to lead the dancing. They circled the floor a few times, then George and Mrs Stevens and Lottie and the best man joined them on the dance floor. The guests clapped when the dance ended, the drink flowed, all relaxed and joined in the celebrations. Most of the men present endeavoured to partner the bride on the dance floor. But soon it was time for the bride and groom to change into their 'going away' outfits – another creation for Nora by 'The Lady', this time a just below the knee length, straight blue chemise dress with a floppy soft-brimmed hat by Madam Delia and matching bag and court shoes.

This was bang up-to-date and in contrast to the traditional mode she had favoured for her wedding gown and the brides-maids' dresses.

Their departure was not too emotional for Lottie and George as their daughter and new son-in-law planned to buy a house in Falmouth when they saw something they liked. Until then they would stay with Nora's parents, and with Alec being away at sea so much, Nora planned to resume her work at 'The Lady' after the honeymoon.

Polly confessed to Edwin how pleased she was that the event had been such a wonderful success, both for 'The Lady' as well as the bride and her parents, adding that not many parents had pockets deep enough to provide their daughter with a wedding like that.

'But Polly,' Edwin added. 'It was really thanks to you a wedding like that was possible. Lottie would never have done it without you.'

'She could have,' Polly said.

'Maybe she could and maybe she couldn't. But she definitely wouldn't,' Edwin said with finality.

Chapter Forty-five

While Nora and Alec were away on honeymoon, part of which was to be spent with Alec's sister, Stella and her husband at their hotel in Sussex, Polly read aloud to Lottie the announcement in the local paper that Victoria Pope, Emma Pope's mother had passed away.

'That's sad,' said Lottie. 'Didn't Emma Pope's father die in the 'flu epidemic?'

'Why yes, he did,' Polly remembered. 'How rotten for the poor girl. She has no brothers or sisters, has she? And I got the impression she was always with her mother. She'll miss her dreadfully.'

'She'll either be lost or like a bird out of a cage,' Lottie replied. 'My impression was her mother had her on a very tight rein. But perhaps she needed it, she always seemed to be a "daffy" sort of a girl. I understand they have plenty of money, but with a girl like Emma it could make her more vulnerable, if you know what I mean.'

But further conjecture on how Emma Pope would now fare was supplanted by the excitement of the return of Nora and Alec after two wonderful weeks away. For Alec, parting a week later when he was to embark on a ship, *his* ship, was both agonising and exciting, for he was now Captain. It was a wonderful feeling to have his 'very own ship' even if he was heading for the oppressively hot climate of the oil-producing Middle East.

Life for Nora soon settled into a normal routine, and everything carried on in Alec's absence just as before, except she was keeping an eye on the property market for a suitable home for herself and Alec. There was no desperate hurry; she would wait until she saw just what she wanted.

Eventually a house became available which she really liked. It was in a crescent of rather nice, relatively spacious houses, just a few minutes walk from both the shipyard on the harbour side of Pendennis Headland and the beaches on the south-facing side of the headland. The walk to the shops was on level ground and the small rear garden, surrounded by high walls, was just the right size. With Alec away so much and being a working wife and not a particularly keen gardener, a larger garden would not have been advantageous.

Alec had told her, 'If you see a house you like . . . buy it. If *you* are happy with it *I* shall be. Just pay the deposit and it will be fine.'

At Nora's request, Lottie and George, Polly and Edwin and Jack all went late one afternoon to view and assess its suitability, Nora being entrusted by the Estate Agent with the key. Mary stayed at home because of the children.

'It's so spacious,' Lottie said as they inspected the four-bedroomed property. There was a large bathroom with an enormous bath. Lottie said it looked like a 'family bath!' 'It all makes me quite envious,' she went on, but George reminded her that with Nora moving out, the little terraced house where they reared their three children would be quite big enough for them.

'Apart from that,' he jokingly groaned, 'I'm the one who seems to do most of the housework these days.'

So Nora agreed to buy the house. Both her mother and Polly liked it, but the approval of her father, and Edwin Pendleton and Jack Pascoe, who paid more attention to the structure, gave her the assurance she needed to go ahead. It somehow seemed appropriate that a sea-captain and his wife would live there. A few weeks later Captain and Mrs Alec Stevens were the owners of a house in Marine Crescent.

Nora decided to curtain the front windows to make the house look lived-in, and to acquire just enough furniture for her and Alec to have somewhere to sleep and sit to eat, and they could then shop together to furnish the new home. Meanwhile, until his trip was over, she would stay at her parents' home. But with her attention no longer focused on the property market, Nora found herself studying furnishings, and every now and then would see an item she just knew Alec would love, so before Alec was due to return, the house was part way to being completely furnished.

It was all so exciting, and Lottie, George and Polly shared in the excitement with her. For them it was like reliving the past . . . the things they and almost every young married couple did, including their parents and their grandparents, and would be repeated in the future by their children and grandchildren. Continuity was good, and it was worth striving and working for, to make the future for your children just a little better than you yourself had. Polly's home was an absolute palace compared to the small cottage her parents and Lottie's parents had. Yet they were so happy with their tiny and primitive homes. Now the improvements between one generation and the next moved at such a pace! Where would it all lead? Surely it would have to stop somewhere. She couldn't imagine anything better than she, and now Nora, already had. What further improvements could there possibly be?

With the war and the dreadful 'flu epidemic past and over, and feeling that her only daughter had a happy marriage and future, Eric, Oliver and George keeping well, for Lottie life was beginning to feel good again.

But life was not now so good for Polly. 'The Lady' was flourishing, her precious Jonathan was well, nearly six feet tall, and had applied to become an articled pupil in the Surveyor's Department of Plymouth City Council.

The granite business though was continuing to decline. Edwin's workforce was down to a mere handful of men and it made him despondent. The granite industry of the Penryn area, once such a huge concern, seemed to be in its dying throes and it saddened Edwin along with all the other granite merchants and hundreds of other men, husbands, fathers, whose past had depended on it and whose future was frighteningly uncertain.

For some years there had been a continual stream of emigration by out-of-work granite workers along with tinners from the tin mining areas of Cornwall. Edwin had always hoped for a son who would inherit and carry on a thriving family business. This, clearly, would not now happen. Naturally Edwin's gloom was transmitted to Polly. It made her sad to see the result of Edwin's efforts and striving crumble before his eyes. He was thankful his father was not alive to witness the downfall of the firm.

But as Polly frequently reminded Edwin, everyone in the business was in the same situation. It did not reflect on Edwin, or the others. It was the changing times; what was called 'progress'.

*   *   *   *

'Do you know, I'm beginning to feel guilty,' Lottie announced to Polly one balmy day as they, along with May Bascombe and Nora, were sharing a coffee break.

'What can there be to make you feel guilty about?' Polly said, dismissively.

'Clementine!' Lottie said.

May Bascombe sniggered out loud. To her, with recollections of the Preview the day before 'The Lady' opened to the public, and knowledge of a few other unpleasant incidents, the thought that Lottie or anyone should now feel guilty about the woman she regarded as a stuck-up Jezebel, was inconceivable.

'Why?' Polly said, incredulously. 'Why ever should you feel guilty about her?'

'Well, like it or not, she is Joss's wife, and she *has* lost Theodore. I'm sure that hit her hard,' Lottie explained. There was a pause as Polly considered.

'Don't waste your time on her, Mum,' Nora said. Lottie did not reply but awaited Polly's reaction.

'I see what you mean,' Polly said at last; then added, 'I think.'

'It's just that if I go to see her I don't know how she'll react. I don't want any more upsets. I might lose my temper again like at the Preview, and say too much.'

'I'll go with you if you like,' Polly volunteered.

'Would you? Would you really?' Lottie's face lit up. 'I know George wouldn't. He won't even approve of me going.'

Polly grinned. She didn't imagine he would. 'When shall we go?' she said.

'What about Wednesday afternoon?' Lottie suggested.

'Early closing day. Fine.' Polly agreed. This used to be her afternoon for seeing her mother.

Two days later they met at 2.45 p.m. under Penryn Town Clock, and made their way to the little square where the three-storey double-fronted granite house stood sentinel, mounted the steps to the wide front door and Lottie rapped on the slightly tarnished brass knocker. After a pause approaching footsteps were heard. A now white-haired Myrtle opened the door.

'We've called to see Mrs Renfree, if she's at home,' Lottie said.

'Step inside, Mrs Simpson,' Myrtle answered, evidently remembering Lottie was her employer's sister. She led the way to a front-facing drawing room. 'I'll see if she can see you,' she said with an obliging nod and a smile.

They listened to the sound of her footsteps receding down a long passage, then heard distant voices. Their call seemed to be the cause of some discussion. Then lighter approaching footsteps were heard and Clementine, dressed in a straight cut, mid-calf length carrot coloured dress entered the room.

'Well . this is a surprise,' Clementine said.

My goodness, she's changed! Polly thought, noting the thinning, frizzy grey hair, the lined, dried up skin along with a distinct whiff of alcohol.

'I'm sorry not to let you know,' Lottie said. 'But as you couldn't come to Nora's wedding and we've seen nothing of you for a long time, I wondered whether you are well. We came on the off-chance,' she added.

Clementine looked slightly perplexed. 'Sit down, please,' she said and herself moved to a comfortable chair. 'You're right, I haven't been too wonderful,' she agreed.

'It's only to be expected, after your sad loss,' Lottie said, endeavouring to adopt a friendly attitude.

'Oh, yes, Mother,' she said. 'And the Manor, and I have been so disgracefully treated.'

Lottie and Polly glanced swiftly at one another. Lottie's lips were pursed. Polly read Lottie's thoughts. Was she referring to Joss?

The door was pushed open and Myrtle entered with a tea-tray.

'I thought you would like some tea ma'am. Shall I pour?'

'Yes, thank you, Myrtle,' Clementine said.

Myrtle passed around the cups of tea and Clementine offered a plate of biscuits. She seemed uncommonly quiet despite the provocative remark she had just made.

'I've been quite busy with the wedding and one thing and another, and Nora has bought a house for Alec and her to live in. You remember Alec, I expect,' Lottie said in an effort to make conversation.

'Alec,' Clementine repeated and pondered for a few seconds. 'Oh, yes. He was at the party we gave for Theodore. Yes . . . a sombre-looking young man. Very nice though. But he couldn't hold a candle to Theodore, so polished, so gentlemanly *and* so handsome.' She eyed Lottie and Polly in turn.

'Yes, very handsome,' they chorused, both taking care not to say he *was* very handsome.

'I dare say the young man will suit Nora well enough,' Clementine continued, a barb in her tone . . . She's a very pretty girl though.' This remark prompted Clementine to giggle, and she bent forward to them as though she feared being overheard and, still giggling and breathing the smell of alcohol over them, said in a low tone, 'I just don't know where she gets it from!'

Lottie's eyes widened. Had Clementine forgotten Nora was *her* daughter?

'I suppose you get quite a few visitors?' Polly remarked, changing the subject and hoping to get some information on the weird situation.

'Not as many as before the Manor was burned down.' Her face and voice hardened. 'It wouldn't have happened if Joss had been at home.'

'No, it wouldn't,' Lottie said, sharply.

But Clementine seemed not to notice. 'Victoria Pope died you know. Something flew. What was it, oh yes, a clot.' She nodded her head. 'It was a clot, you know.'

'It must be very sad for her poor daughter,' Polly said. 'Emma, isn't it?'

'Don't talk to me about Emma Pope!' was Clementine's swift rejoinder. 'Sad for me, you mean . . . not Emma Pope. She couldn't be more delighted!' Clementine made a sound which resembled a snort. 'She's a damnable little bitch, only in her case, not so little!'

Lottie and Polly were dumbstruck! Was Clementine off her head, or was she drunk? Then Lottie remembered a rumour she heard after Theodore died that Emma had been upset and Mrs Pope blamed Clementine for encouraging her daughter to believe there was something between them. Not knowing what to say, Lottie raised her cup and swallowed what was left of the tea, then noisily replaced the cup in its saucer. Conversation was proving difficult and she had made up her mind to steer clear of mentioning Joss. That would be courting trouble.

'What do you think of the new dress styles, Clementine?' Polly asked, again guiding the conversation to a different topic.

'It rather depends on what sort of legs you have, doesn't it?' Clementine replied, pushing both her feet forward to inspect. 'I

338

have nice ankles and legs. Emma Pope has legs like tree trunks! They should be kept covered and out of sight, especially from men. Quite unladylike, not feminine; seeing legs like that could make men impotent! And do you know . . . I'm quite intelligent, you know . . . that comes from superior breeding . . . if *men* become impotent . . . *people* would become extinct!' She laughed. 'Emma Pope could be responsible for ending the human race! And all by shortening her skirt!' She laughed hysterically and tears rolled down her cheeks, dousing a dozen dried-up cracks.

Totally bewildered, Lottie and Polly endeavoured unconvincingly to fake amusement. If she doesn't stop laughing she'll be crying in a minute, Polly thought. But Clementine, wiping her nose with an inadequate handkerchief, composed herself. 'Oh dear,' she said. 'That was what Myrtle calls a silly five minutes, wasn't it?'

'It was indeed,' Lottie agreed with a forced laugh. 'I'm glad you're keeping reasonably well, Clementine. We really mustn't keep you any longer, and I have to get home and cook George's meal.'

'And I,' Polly said. 'Thank you for the tea, Clementine, it was very welcome.' Lottie and Polly were now on their feet and Clementine rose from her chair. 'Would you like something else before you leave? Something warming . . . out of a bottle?'

'No, really. Thank you,' Lottie and Polly chorused.

'An aspirin? Some liver salts?'

Again Lottie and Polly affected amusement, not sure whether this was meant to be witty.

'Ha ha . . . No, thank you very much, Clementine. It's been very pleasant seeing you,' Lottie lied, gallantly.

'It has indeed,' Polly said, taking her cue from Lottie. The two departed and walked a short distance. Polly was first to break the silence. 'Wasn't she peculiar?'

'That's what I thought,' Lottie agreed. 'And I'm going back!'

'Whatever for?' Polly said, puzzled.

'I left my bag behind.'

'Oh.'

'It was deliberate. Myrtle will answer the door and I want to find out if she's really gone a bit strange.'

Lottie returned to the house, mounted the steps and again rapped the knocker. Polly waited a short distance away. As she anticipated, Myrtle opened the door and Lottie explained she had left her handbag in the drawing-room. Myrtle promptly fetched it.

'Thank you Myrtle,' Lottie said, and with a slight nod of her head towards the interior of the house, asked in a low voice, 'Is something wrong with Mrs Renfree; she doesn't seem to be herself?'

Myrtle hesitated. 'Well yes and no,' she said. 'Sometimes she seems odd but the rest of the time she is quite normal – normal for her that is, only she doesn't have so many friends now.'

'Is losing Theodore upsetting her?'

'Partly, I think,' Myrtle replied. 'But a friend . . .' she hesitated as though not knowing how to word the information. 'A Friend, if you know what I mean, deserted her, and that seems to have been the straw that broke the camel's back. She's been drinking a lot more and you never know what sort of mood she will be in. Today she is more affable . . . I think that's the word . . . but she can seem pleasant and then say something quite nasty. You never know.'

'I see,' Lottie raised her voice to normal. 'Thank you, Myrtle. My keys as well as my purse are inside it. I would have had problems without them.'

'You're very welcome ma'am,' Myrtle also raised her voice.

Lottie hurried to where Polly stood waiting and related what happened as they walked towards Lower Market Street.

'It can't have been a lady-friend,' she reasoned. 'She'd never get that upset over a woman.'

Polly made no reply, but guessed Lottie was probably right.

Lottie gave a deep sigh. 'My poor brother,' she said.

'Yes, poor Joss,' Polly agreed, as they parted company at the bus stop. With a heavy heart and the image of Joss's face before her, Polly made her way home to Villa Gwidden.

The 'Crinoline Bell' rang and Polly emerged from the kitchen of The Lady where she had been sketching the latest creation for her portfolio.

Thinking 'talk of the devil', she said, 'Good morning, Miss Pope. How nice to see you.'

'Good morning,' Emma replied breathlessly, her face pink and her bosom heaving.

'Can I be of help?' Polly asked.

'Yes. I want to order a wedding gown!' Emma tried unsuccessfully to repress a wide triumphant smile as her shining eyes stared into Polly's.

'Oh!' Polly was taken aback. 'That's wonderful news; my congratulations.'

'Thank you,' Emma beamed. 'I want something special.'

'Of course you do,' Polly agreed. 'Every wedding is special. Do I know the lucky gentleman, I wonder, or shouldn't I ask?'

'I doubt if you would know him,' Emma said. 'He's a Customs Officer. His name is Copeland, Charles Brendon Copeland.'

Polly hoped her face did not betray the astonishment she felt. Emma Pope held out her hand for Polly to inspect the diamond encrusted ring which sparkled on her ring finger.

'It's beautiful,' Polly said, then pretended to search her memory. 'His name does ring a bell . . . I think I must have met him at some function or event.'

'He *is* quite good-looking, so I can understand you would remember him if you did ever meet,' Emma said. The freedom from her hawk-eyed mother and the acquisition of a large income and now a man, had endowed Emma with a confidence which in earlier times she seemed to lack.

'If you wait a moment, I'll call Mrs Simpson, you'll need to discuss your requirements with her. I'll only be a minute,' Polly said, and climbed the two flights of stairs to the workroom. She closed the workroom door behind her.

'You've a client to see you, Lottie.'

'Who's that?' Lottie said as she rose from her seat at the sewing machine.

'It's Emma Pope, and guess what . . . she wants a wedding dress!'

'Never!' Lottie said, her mouth agape with amazement, then said meaningfully, 'Well, she *has* got money now.'

'Yes,' Polly agreed, 'but guess who to!'

'I've no idea.'

'Charles Brendon Copeland!'

'What! I don't believe it!'

'It's as true as I'm standing here.'

'So *that's* what upset Clementine! *That* is the last straw that Myrtle said broke the camel's back. The . . . ' Lottie managed to

341

stop herself saying the low but apt word which described her brother's wife.

'I think it is,' Polly agreed.

'Crikey!' Lottie exclaimed, and they both hurried down the steep upper staircase.

It was well over an hour before Emma Pope completed the order having thoroughly discussed with both Lottie and Polly and selected the material and the style for the dress. Emma explained that having neither nephews nor nieces she was having only one bridesmaid, a cousin, Miss Matilda Jennings. Miss Jennings would be coming from Truro next week and together they would visit to select material, style, etc. The wedding was to be in six or seven weeks, a firm date not having been finalised.

'My fiancé is a little older than I,' she informed them, 'and he said he's waited so long to find "Miss Right" that he doesn't want any more precious time to be wasted in marrying her.' She tried unsuccessfully to repress an excited giggle. 'I shall also need a honeymoon outfit, but we haven't yet decided where to go.' Then added, 'It's not going to be a big wedding. I don't have a lot of relatives. Charles has two brothers, but they and their families live abroad and Charles is in such a hurry to wed me, there wouldn't be time for them to make all the arrangements.'

Although Lottie had a record of Emma's measurements, she thought it prudent to take them again. 'Can't afford to take chances with such an important item as a wedding dress,' she said. She and Emma went upstairs to the fitting room, Emma chatting and giggling non-stop. As Lottie's tape-measure encircled her, Emma bemoaned the size of her chest.

'I know what you mean,' Lottie said, sympathetically.

'I used to be a fashionable shape,' Emma said.

She's deluding herself, Lottie thought.

'But today's styles are all for flat-chested women,' Emma went on, plaintively. Then a coy look spread over her face. 'But Charles said he likes me the way I am.' She hung her head shyly but her eyes turned upwards to look at Lottie. 'He said I'm very feminine . . . all woman, he said. And that's what a red-blooded man prefers!' Emma smiled with satisfaction.

'I wouldn't know,' Lottie replied, dismissively, a tone of disapproval in her voice.

But Emma was not to be deterred. 'Charles is emphatic we

have a *quiet* wedding, with as few guests as possible. He doesn't like the limelight you know. I allowed him his way in this,' she went on, giving the impression she was 'ruling the roost'. 'But I told him. I insist on having the traditional White Wedding. It's symbolic. He said . . .' She paused to control her giggles. 'He said . . . he didn't mind what I wore. I could turn up not wearing a . . . oh dear, hee hee hee,' she giggled. 'He said, ha . . . I daren't repeat it . . . well, as long as he marries me he doesn't mind what I wear!'

Lottie's mouth formed a forced smile. 'Measurements all done now, Miss Pope.'

'Oh . . . thank you . . . I must fly; so much to do,' she jabbered as together they went down the stairs to the ground floor showroom. Lottie and Polly both bade 'Good-byes' and Emma, still giggling uncontrollably, departed.

'Well,' Lottie said. 'Talk about the cat that got the cream!'

'She might as well enjoy it,' Polly said. 'I fear this is going to be another case of,' she quoted another saying often repeated by her mother about the expectation being better than the realisation.

'I wonder if she'll invite Clementine, or whether Copeland will persuade her not to.'

'The sparks will certainly fly if she does,' Polly said. 'No wonder he wants a quiet wedding!'

'Mother! I've heard!'

'Heard what, dear?' Polly's voice sounded a mite weary.

'Don't tell me you've forgotten, Mum,' Jonathan replied, some of the enthusiasm gone from his tone.

'Your application,' Polly suddenly remembered. 'What did they say?'

The excitement was back in Jonathan's voice. 'They've accepted me. Isn't it wonderful?'

'What's all this?' Edwin, who arrived just after Polly, demanded.

'Plymouth City Council has replied. The Chief of the Surveyor's Department has accepted me as an Articled Pupil. I start in less than three weeks, and they have included a list of places where I could get lodgings!'

'That's fine, my boy, if you're sure it's what you want to do.'

'I do, Father. It's what I would like. I've got all the necessary school qualifications and at the moment I'm just marking time at school.'

'Congratulations, Jonathan,' Edwin said, and gave him a slap on the back.

'It's a good thing Mary was putting a stew on a low gas for us, I'm too excited to think about cooking,' Polly admitted.

'Jonathan G. Pendleton, Surveyor. Sounds good,' Edwin laughed. 'It calls for a little celebration.'

'I'm going out with a couple of lads this evening,' Jonathan said.

'I expect you've got room for a small one,' Edwin smiled as he poured three small glasses. He passed Polly and Jonathan each a glass and raised his. 'To our son's future,' he said.

'To our son's future,' Polly echoed.

Chapter Forty-six

Joss's life had settled into a routine of work and visits to the nearest saloon. The oil business was flourishing but success lacked excitement, the thrill he experienced when he was young. Starting with nothing and a wife and hoped for family to support, gave a zest which was missing when you were no longer poor, no longer young, no longer had dreams; perhaps most of all when you no longer had anyone to work for.

The production team had taken on two Redruth tinners and they seemed to have a depressing effect on Bill, which was strange since he liked the two young Cornishmen. In fact everyone in the team liked the jokey, good-natured pair.

Then, in a flash, it dawned on Joss. Bill was homesick; he wanted to see home, parents and Cornwall again. If that were the cause why didn't he go? As far as Joss was concerned he could have taken six months off any time he wanted, had he wanted. After all this time he was entitled to longer. He guessed the reason must be Maria, his half Mexican half Scottish wife.

Joss always shared a meal with the Boadens after work. This was at their insistence. 'It is as easy to cook for six as it is for five,' Maria always said. 'And I know what you men are like. You'll "push away", as Bill says, with anything rather than cook for yourselves.' She was right.

After the meal Joss either returned to his home or drove to the saloon where men yarned, drank and sometimes played cards. When Maria was about to clear the dishes Joss said, 'I've got something to discuss with you, but I'll wait until Maria has finished in the kitchen.'

'Carry on and talk to Bill while I do the washing up,' Maria replied.

'No. I want you too, Maria,' Joss insisted. 'This is not about work, quite the reverse.'

Maria returned and took a seat next to her husband and opposite Joss.

'What's the problem, Joss?' Bill said.

'Bill, you've not seemed yourself lately. I'm wondering if you are hankering to go home and visit. You've only returned home once and that was years ago, long before you and Maria were married. I'm here keeping an eye on things. There's nothing to stop you from visiting home.'

His remarks were greeted with silence.

'It's my fault,' Maria, with head bowed, said at last.

Joss paused, thinking how best to reply.

'She's afraid of water,' Bill said, simply.

'Have you ever been on a ship?' Joss looked at Maria.

She shook her head.

'Ever seen one?'

Again she shook her head.

'I think you'll find a lot more people die because of accidents at work than from going across the Atlantic Ocean.'

'What about the *Titanic*?' Maria countered.

'That was years ago, before the war. It was news all over the world. Why do you think it was news everywhere and people still talk about it?'

'Because it was so terrible,' Maria said.

'Granted,' Joss agreed, 'but also because it was so unusual. Hundreds of people die every year in road accidents, work accidents, accidents in the home, at sport, but nobody hears about it except the people involved. You and I don't hear. It's probably safer crossing the Atlantic than being here so relatively close to the oil and the drilling.'

'I didn't think about it like that,' Maria admitted, after another pause.

Bill spoke. 'Joss, you are right. I would like to go home and see my old parents before it's too late. But we'll think about it.'

'No. We won't think about it, we'll go,' Maria said. 'I was selfish. I should have known you would want to see your mother and father.'

'Are you sure?' Bill said to Maria, staring fixedly into his wife's face.

'I can see now how selfish I've been . . . Yes, I'm sure.'

A smile spread across Bill's face. 'That's wonderful.' He hugged his wife, who suddenly realised how much this meant to him.

Bill turned to Joss; 'Ma did say in her last letter Father was not well.'

'I thought there was something,' Joss said.

'I should have guessed too,' said Maria.

Joss left Maria and Bill to discuss and, he hoped, plan the visit to Bill's parents back home in Mawnan Smith. He strolled to his tiny wooden home. It was too late to go to the saloon.

Inevitably his thoughts turned to Polly. Suddenly Joss felt deeply weary. America was vast and varied. Much was beautiful, some brash, all was exciting. He really liked America and in earlier times was stimulated by the country's boundless energy. But excitement no longer appealed to Joss. He knew that although he had affection for the country, his heart was home in Cornwall, with its warm people, its green hills which blazed golden here and there with gorse, the sea, the beautiful beaches and dunes on the Atlantic coast, the thundering Atlantic seas and breakers, the cliffs which towered above, the caves where smugglers once hid their contraband, etc., and where the seas came crashing in at high tide. Then, closer to home were the gentler waters and the beautiful Rivers Fal and Helford, and Polly, the woman he truly loved, and Lottie, his dear sister, and Nora. And though his son Theodore was no more and this greatly saddened him, he somehow could not help loving his Godson, Jonathan. His sad sweet memories were suddenly eclipsed . . . and there was his wife, Clementine!

On the Saturdays when Jonathan was returning home from Plymouth for the weekend, as Polly closed 'The Lady' at the end of the working day and turned the key in the lock, she felt a thrill of excitement. In Edwin's life and hers, Jonathan's visits were the highlight. Today Jonathan was not coming on the early train, but would arrive in Penryn around ten minutes after Polly normally reached home.

When she entered Villa Gwidden Edwin was not there to greet her. This was unusual. Before she had removed her hat, Mary

347

appeared from the kitchen. Polly was just asking her where Edwin was when Jonathan arrived. After the customary greetings Mary said that Edwin had gone to the quarries and that he wouldn't be long.

'Do you know why?' Polly asked.

'He said he couldn't remember whether he had locked the door to the Magazine Store,' Mary replied.

Polly turned to look at Jonathan. 'I'm getting worried about your father. He's been so anxious lately, though he doesn't say much. But I can tell he is distracted, he is so forgetful, like now, not remembering whether he locked the door. He is normally so particular about keeping that black explosive powder under lock and key.'

'There's stew on the stove,' Mary said. 'Would you like it now?'

'I'll go up to the quarries to him,' Jonathan said, dropping his overnight case in the entrance hall.

'We'll wait,' Polly said to Mary as Jonathan departed. 'Edwin is so conscientious about ensuring the Magazine Store is always safely locked.'

'Different to the way Bert Bohenna looks after his black explosive stuff,' was Mary's rejoinder.

Polly's anxious expression broke into a smile. It was a well-known secret that Bert took the dubious precaution of keeping his black explosive powder under his bed, the bed in which his wife delivered their six children.

Meanwhile, Edwin, who struggled to hurry, found the walk to Gwarda Quarries heavy going. He had already noticed that it seemed to take longer than formerly, when he first began to walk to work, Bessie by then being too old for the long pull to the quarries. She had died almost a year ago and Edwin did not get a replacement. He reached the place where there was a track across the land, high up where the grass was short and somewhat sparse. From the high ground rainwater quickly drained away but further down the hill the grass was thicker and more lush. He walked along the almost flat track formed by traction engines and horses pulling specially designed carts laden with granite, plus the workforce all on foot, and made his way to the Magazine Store which was on the opposite side of the quarries to the other sheds and shacks. The store *was* locked. Edwin's face relaxed and he smiled with satisfaction, reassured that he hadn't lost his grip.

He then strolled to the nearest quarry and gazed down. A crane winch at the bottom looked like a toy. The sheer, hard, cliff-like pale grey sides of the quarry glinted pink, blue, green and here and there, yellow ochre. To fall would almost certainly be fatal.

Edwin moved to the second quarry, then the third. This was a quarry which regularly collected water, and it was important that the water should not be allowed to rise too much. His facial muscles tightened as he looked down into the greenish lake of dark, murky water, below which would be a tangle of slimy weeds and sludge. By Monday the water would have risen further. He would syphon some of it off before the light faded. With the valves open at both ends, the water would run into the stream overnight.

With one end of the tubing lowered into both the lake and the foot-valve around eighty to ninety feet below, and the other end high above, where there was another valve, the hand pump would be operated to draw the water up and on into a two inch pipe. The pipe ran along the surface and downwards to a stream. As soon as the valve at the end of the surface pipe was opened, the water would drain out and into the stream.

Edwin began to prime the syphon, grasping the pumping handle and moving it sideways, forth and back, rising in a semi-circular movement as he did so. The syphon made a hammering sound and shuddered to a halt.

As occasionally happened, it refused to run. Edwin tried again with the same result. There must be sludge in the foot-valve, he thought. This was often sucked past the filter and up into the valve.

He took off his jacket and rolled up his sleeves, then began to dismantle the syphon by pulling the tubing up out of the water. He quickly descended the steps and ledges to where he could open the flap of the foot-valve, then felt with his hand for the offending matter which blocked the flow. It was a mass of weeds, slime and sludge which had seized up and bonded together, blocking the foot-valve. Expertly Edwin removed this and replaced the tubing into position. He wiped his hands on a tuft of grass which had managed to root on the ledge, again wiping with his handkerchief any remaining muck as he made his way back to the quarry top.

Intent on what he was doing, Edwin did not see his son coming up the track. Jonathan saw his father emerge from the quarry, and the outline of the familiar syphon pipe silhouetted against the rays of the setting sun. Edwin again attempted to prime the syphon. Jonathan hurried to where his father stood and was close enough to shout to his father that he would run down to open the valve where the surface pipe ended to allow water to flow out into the stream, but something made him hold back.

As Edwin recommenced working the pumping handle the part to which it was attached seemed to suddenly judder. Was it that which caused Edwin to lose his balance and fall backwards over the edge of the quarry!?

'Father!' Jonathan shouted, as he rushed to the quarry edge. As he somersaulted downwards Edwin's eyes gazed for a split second into the stricken face of his beloved son.

Instantly Jonathan raced down the steps and ledges to where, far below, he drew level with the lake, and stared into the thick, dark water. As he did so he saw his father's back, face down, rise to the surface. Swiftly he swam to the spot, then disappeared under the water, resurfacing a few seconds later having retrieved his father and, ensuring Edwin's face was above water, swam with him back to the ledge with all the speed he could muster.

Blood ran down the side of Edwin's head. He must have struck an underwater boulder. A hasty check established breathing had stopped, and gently but swiftly Jonathan turned his father over, with arms bent upwards to allow his face to rest on his hands and to keep the airways clear. It seemed an age since Jonathan had instruction in the Holger-Nielson Method of Artificial Respiration. Miraculously he had instant recall of what to do. There was enough space to kneel in front of Edwin's prone figure to place his hands over the shoulder blades, thumbs to the middle line, and fingers spread to apply gentle pressure. He counted rhythmically to three, then gradually released the pressure and at the count of four, slid his hands to just above the elbows and raised his father to a further count of seven. At eight he lowered his father and commenced the rhythmic process over again.

After a number of repeats of the procedure Jonathan paused to check his father's breathing. It seemed Edwin was not breathing. There was no pulse nor any other sign of recovery. Jonathan let out a sound like a sob and frantically restarted the artificial respiration process. He did not hear footsteps hurrying down into the quarry.

'What's wrong?' said a voice. 'Oh, my God! It's Edwin!' It was Marcus Treloar, out walking his dog. 'He fell into the quarry?'

Jonathan nodded without pausing in his efforts to revive his father.

'How long ago?'

'I don't know,' Jonathan replied. 'Ten minutes, or more.'

Marcus Treloar knelt beside Edwin. 'Let me take a look, lad.' Jonathan completed the sequence, then paused to let Marcus check. He lifted Edwin's eyelids, then closed them again and felt in his neck for a pulse. Seconds dragged. Softly Marcus spoke. 'It's no good my handsome. He's dead.'

Jonathan lifted his now tear-stained face and stared into Marcus Treloar's shocked watery-eyed gaze. A long drip hung from the end of Marcus's nose. Turning his father to him, Jonathan cradled Edwin's head and shoulders, rocking to and fro in grief, his arms tight about him and, pressing his own wet cheek against his father's head, his tears mingled with his father's blood.

Joss received two letters from England within a few days. The first was from Mr Borlace, his solicitor. It brought news that Miss Trembath had died after a short illness. Mr Borlace had made all the arrangements for her funeral so that, as Mr Renfree had instructed, she should not have a pauper's burial. This was sad news, but at Miss Trembath's age, could be expected.

The second letter, in Lottie's handwriting, was unexpected. Joss had received one from her a little over a week before and she usually wrote once a month. Eagerness and anxiety combined as Joss tore open the envelope. But his face fell as he read Lottie's opening sentence. 'I am sorry to be the bearer of bad news. You, like all of us, will be shocked to learn Edwin, Polly's husband, died a week ago . . . '

The news hit Joss like a thump in the stomach and he suddenly needed to sit down. Edwin dead! Poor Polly! Poor Jonathan! What was he doing here, so far away in America and not a soul to whom he could speak about it, not even Bill who, with his family, was now at home in Cornwall. If only he were nearer and could offer his support. He knew Polly must be deeply upset, and he

351

never grudged Edwin his privilege in being Polly's husband. Joss had unwittingly missed his opportunity with Polly; and clearly she would marry someone, as he himself had done. He was glad it had been Edwin. At least she had fared better than he himself had done, and had been wiser in her choice.

Joss brought out the writing pad, but after several attempts to write a letter of condolence, none of which conveyed the feeling he wished to express, he decided to try again later and instead reached for the bottle in an attempt to assuage the emptiness inside him.

Chapter Forty-seven

Just over a month after Edwin's death, Alec's tanker docked at Falmouth. He and Nora shared precious idyllic weeks in their home in Marine Crescent. Alec was absolutely delighted with Nora's choice of property.

Mrs Stevens came to spend a week with them and she too, praised Nora's choice. She enjoyed the soft, balmy climate, so different from the northern counties and even from Rottingdean in Sussex, where the wind from the east could at times be so cutting. They went on little char-a-banc and boat trips where Nora showed both Alec and her mother-in-law her favourite beauty spots, the chief one being the Helford River. She was delighted to find both were enraptured.

But when you are happy time flies. All too soon Alec's ship had to leave and, assisted by a few tugs, was out of Falmouth Harbour and beyond Black Rock. It would be a while before Nora saw her husband again.

A few weeks later Nora began to have a certain suspicion. In a few more weeks her suspicion was confirmed. She was going to have a baby!

Polly had returned to work at 'The Lady' but, understandably, lacked her old enthusiasm and made no effort to do any designing. Conversely Nora found herself thinking up quite a few ideas for designs which were in keeping with the latest fashion trends. She began to attempt sketching her ideas but did not show her efforts to anyone. She was aware the shop was Polly's idea and the outfits made so expertly by her mother were Polly's designs. She didn't want Polly to think she was trying to take over her province. But as time went by, Nora's interest in fashion was replaced with thoughts of baby clothes and knitting.

*　　*　　*　　*

When the birth date was nearing, Nora stopped work. She planned to do something similar to that which Polly had done when Jonathan was born . . . to stay at home caring for the baby for six-months. Then perhaps Madge, who by now had married and had a three month old baby girl, would look after her baby too.

It seemed providential Alec arrived home two weeks before the baby was due. Nora told him of her ideas to ensure he approved. At first Alec looked doubtful, then said, 'I'm sure you wouldn't leave our baby with anyone you couldn't trust to take good care of it. And if that is really what you want, then go ahead. You don't often have my company and it would be good for you to have an outside interest, provided it isn't all too much for you.'

Alec seemed far more excited than Nora at the prospect of the baby's arrival, and though he tried not to show it, became panicky when her pains started. He summoned the midwife, Lottie and the doctor before even Nora herself felt sure.

Nora smiled inwardly. Alec had clearly been so brave and valiant throughout the terrible wartime ordeals, the sinking of the ship, the horrific injuries and sights, but the imminent arrival of his baby, their baby, had such a shattering effect on him. She wondered if he feared the baby would arrive before the others did.

Lottie was first on the scene, and she helped Nora get to bed. While this was going on Alec admitted the doctor, closely followed by the midwife. Less than five minutes later the doctor, putting his bowler hat on his head, came out of the bedroom.

'I'll be back later,' he told Alec.

Alec was aghast. 'You're not going to leave her?' he said as he followed the doctor down the stairs.

The doctor answered his question with another. 'First baby?'

'Yes,' Alec replied.

The doctor gave both a grin and a contemptuous snort and walked out without saying another word.

Lottie had overheard and went to Alec. 'Don't worry,' she said. 'The midwife often knows better than doctors.'

For what seemed an age, Alec alternately smoked and drank cups of tea, between times pacing the landing outside the bedroom door and boiling kettles of water at the midwife's command. His heart hammered and he wiped his brow with his handkerchief at the sound of a few muffled shrieks from Nora.

Then came an unmistakable sound. The cries of his newborn baby!

Alec relaxed, let go, and his tears tumbled in a mixture of relief and joy. He hadn't cried since he was a child! As well as crying he was laughing too. He once saw something similar happen to a man when his leg was blown off!

Smiling broadly Lottie emerged from the bedroom. 'It's a little girl. Congratulations!' she said. Then, seeing the unexpected state Alec was in, put her arms about him and they kissed and hugged one another.

'The nurse is going to bath the baby, then you can see her,' she told him.

'How is Nora?' Alec asked, anxiously.

'Tired, but she'll be fine.'

'Thank God!' He hugged Lottie again.

'It won't be so bad next time,' she comforted.

'Next time! I don't think I could stand it!' he replied.

It was a little longer before he was allowed into the room to see Nora and his little daughter. He could tell his wife was glad to see him. After kissing her and telling her how wonderful she had been the midwife gave him the baby to hold, but only for a couple of minutes, for Nora had taken a few sips of tea her mother had brought in and was falling asleep.

As Alec emerged from the room, Lottie was letting the doctor in at the front door. It was Alec's turn to grin. 'Your timing was a little adrift doctor. But never mind, *I* managed very well for a first timer.'

During the 'lying-in' period Nora, with Alec's agreement to return to her work at the shop in six months time, began to enlarge on her plans for Madge caring for baby Sylvia. She mulled it over, and waited for a convenient moment to put the idea to Alec. On the evening of the eighth day, when baby Sylvia had been fed and was sleeping contentedly and, being early evening there were as yet, no callers, Alec came in to collect her plate, etc., to do the washing-up. Taking on the wife's role was a new experience for him, but he was managing, even liking it, in the short term. He felt quite pleased with his new achievements.

'Darling,' Nora said.

'Yes, dear,' he paused to listen.

'When you've done that, could we have a "Chat?" '

'Chat?'

'I've got something to suggest to you.'

Alec seemed not to move a muscle, but his eyes darted to one side, then stared back at Nora. She could read his thoughts . . . What's she thought up this time?

'I'll wash the dishes,' he said.

'All right, darling,' Nora replied.

As he applied himself to the washing up he pondered on what Nora's latest idea could be. She had already spoken to Madge who clearly welcomed the suggestion to look after their little baby, and Madge and her husband welcomed the idea of the extra money. What more could she want?

He left the clean plates, pots etc. stacked on the wooden draining board and made his way upstairs.

'All done,' he said. 'I'll dry them later.'

'I'll be up and relieving you of all the chores soon,' Nora said with a grateful smile.

'There's no rush,' Alec replied. 'Now, you wanted a chat.'

'Well, you know Madge has agreed to look after the baby when I return to work. I think it might be a lot easier all round if she, Ken her husband and the baby came here to live.'

At this a frown creased Alec's forehead. 'All in together! I don't think that's a good idea,' he said.

'No. Not all living together. Madge and Ken could have the big back bedroom, with the small back room for their baby, plus the dining-room, and we could have the large front bedroom for you and me and the small front bedroom for our baby, and the sitting-room for ourselves. We can easily share the kitchen and bathroom, after all, it's a good size kitchen and Madge and I have always got on well together. We'd have our own separate main rooms.'

Alec's face relaxed somewhat. He didn't immediately answer.

'What do you think?' Nora said at last.

'Let me sleep on it, Nora,' he said.

Nora made up her mind to wait patiently until he raised the matter. To hustle Alec might not be wise, after all, although a reasonably friendly person, Alec did have a private side to him.

But she did not have long to wait. After breakfast Alec told her he thought her suggestion was excellent all round. All would benefit. The house was only a few minutes walk from the shipyard where Ken worked on ships' engines. Both Nora and Madge were there on hand for the inevitable minor emergencies. Madge could save the rent she was paying, plus a modest payment for looking after baby Sylvia, which would enable her and Ken to save towards their ambition – a home of their own. It would enable both couples to have an evening out now and then. Yes, he thought the plan would work if Madge and Ken approved. Nora thought they would approve, and she was right. The idea certainly raised considerably Madge and Ken's hopes of one day buying their own home.

Although Polly was glad to have the shop to keep her occupied after the initial terrible weeks following Edwin's death, she was now, at times, beginning to feel she was losing her flair. Her loss of aptitude and zest happened with the shock of Edwin's death, as was to be expected, but she showed no sign of recovering her enthusiasm, despite being glad of 'The Lady' to occupy her time and her thoughts. She referred almost all her ideas to Nora as well as to Lottie, except for older established clients whose tastes and preferences she knew.

Nora of course, knew just what would appeal to the younger set, just as Polly once had. But Polly now, not without reason, sometimes doubted her own ideas. Nora judged the time right for showing Polly sketches of some of her latest ideas, and had tried her hand at making a portfolio of designs, most of which Polly approved but did not say there were some she didn't care for. Lottie made the assorted garments and both Lottie and Polly found they sold quickly though almost all the buyers were younger than themselves. Nora, it seemed, had shot ahead of them both.

Though Lottie's sewing ability was undiminished, when doing the fitting of a garment, she also often sought her daughter's advice on whether there should be a tuck here and there to give more shape, or whether it should hang straight. Designs had changed and she was losing her instinctive feel for the newer styles.

Also Lottie, older now and having more to do at home was

frequently weary. George was much slower and often too tired and breathless to do anything. Work at the business, which she formerly enjoyed, was becoming a burden. Eventually she confided this to Polly.

'It's funny,' Polly said, 'I've had exactly the same thoughts myself.'

'We can't both leave together,' Lottie said.

'Of course not,' Polly agreed. 'Your need is greater than mine, Lottie. You leave first, and I'll stay on until such time as there is really good replacement staff, with Nora as manageress of both the shop and the workroom. She's excellent in both departments. In addition she has learned how to put onto paper designs and illustrations of new garments she can see in her head, though in truth, she really is a natural.'

'That all sounds fair,' Lottie agreed.

'Lottie, I've also been thinking. If Nora is agreeable to take over the management of the shop she should be made a partner in the business. We shall not be working. The day is definitely coming when Nora could take over the management of every-thing. We shall not be getting a pay packet but we shall still be sharing the profits, I think Nora should have a share in it.'

'That's generous of you, Polly. My goodness, you've got it all worked out. What sort of share did you have in mind?' Lottie said. 'I hadn't gone as far as working out details.'

'The property, the building, is yours and mine, but I think Nora should have one-third share of the net profit instead of the usual bonus like the staff have always been given when profit is good, all to be effective from the time we give up. I could stand in at the shop for emergencies, sickness, and at holiday breaks, and when Alec is home on leave.'

'Yes,' Lottie was becoming excited. 'And I dare say I would do the same in the workroom. Shall we put the idea to Nora?'

'I don't see why not,' Polly replied.

The arrangement was put into operation and, as it turned out, not a moment too soon. Lottie had been retired only three weeks when George died suddenly.

Polly felt deeply for all the family, especially for Lottie. It brought back vividly Edwin's death and the harrowing days, weeks and months which followed.

For months Jonathan had returned home to spend every

minute he possibly could with his mother, and Laura Ann visited frequently.

Then, suddenly, Jonathan missed two weekend trips home, and the weekend following that when he did visit, Laura Ann did not come to the house, neither did he make an attempt to see her. Had he found a lady-friend? That could be the answer and Polly thought it probably was. She would tell him not to feel obliged to come home every weekend. But Jonathan continued to pay the weekly visit.

'If you've got a friend you'd like to come with you, he or she would be very welcome, dear,' she said.

'There isn't anyone, Mother,' Jonathan replied.

To Joss's surprise, Bill and his family stayed away back home in Mawnan Smith much longer than the agreed six months. He didn't even write to explain. Something unforeseen must have happened. Bill would not let him down. But late one evening Bill himself turned up unannounced.

After greeting each other, Bill was anxious to explain. 'I'm here because I didn't want to write,' he told Joss. Joss's face took on a concerned expression. 'What's up, Bill?' he asked.

'The thing is, Ma and Father are too old to carry on with the farm, and I don't think Father can last much longer. They've got a farmhand and he is very good, but he can't do two men's work. I haven't said anything but for years I've been hankering to return home for good, Joss, only I didn't know Maria would like it there so much. But she and Betsy do, they love it. Betsy has been going to the village school and gets on well with the other children. The other two have virtually left home, James working in New York and Nancy away at College and planning to study law. She won't want to live at the Ranch any more. They love the farm and the small hedged fields, Maenporth Beach is only a short distance away and the Helford River. My father still has his boat and they go fishing and swimming. Maria loves it all including boating on the Helford River and having towns – Penryn and Falmouth – only a short bus ride away, and they've been made to feel very welcome in the village.'

'And you don't want to leave your parents or home any more,' Joss finished the explanation.

Bill did not smile, but stared into Joss's eyes. 'Equally, Joss, I don't want to let *you* down. That's why I'm here. To talk it over with you. If it's letting you down, after all you've done for me, I will not leave.' Bill meant what he said, and his unwavering gaze continued to hold Joss's.

'I know the feeling, old mate. But you go and don't give it another thought. I was thankful I returned and spent time with my father and mother before it was too late . . . and there is nowhere like home.'

'You're sure?' Bill said, his steady gaze unaltered.

'Of course I'm sure.' Joss reached for a bottle and glass. 'Here, have a drink,' he passed a glass to Bill. 'And stop looking so worried. Are you all right for money?'

'I'm well-off,' Bill replied, smiling at last. 'Rolling it in according to people back home!'

Joss laughed and Bill's expression relaxed. 'I appreciate your coming back here to discuss it with me,' Joss said. 'Though knowing you, I'm not surprised.'

Bill, suddenly embarrassed, gave a wry grin. He remained with Joss a week, and before leaving made a point of seeing and saying good-bye to the oil-drilling and production team, among them being the couple of young tinners from Redruth who always called each other and everyone else, 'Pard'. Bill promised to visit their families in Redruth.

Bill left for New York from the nearest pick-up point, driven there by Joss. As the train pulled up Joss and Bill shook hands and briefly with their left hands hugged each other, then Bill boarded the train.

It seemed strange that two weeks after Bill sailed from New York a letter arrived from Lottie, telling him George had died!

Joss felt suddenly cold. What was he doing here in America? He never intended to stay. It had always been his intention, his plan to return. Lottie's family would try to be supportive to her, but they were busy with their own lives. *Lottie needed him now.* At this rate, if he didn't return home soon, there would be no loved-ones left for him to return to. Bill had gone. Why should he stay? He now again had all the money he needed and much more. He had come here on impulse, and he would go the same way. He'd had several offers to buy the oil-field over the years. Lottie would certainly be glad to see him return home. She was his sister and blood was thicker than water.

Before the day was done Joss saw the manager of the oil production team to tell him he was going to sell the land along with his rights in the oil as soon as he had a buyer. The manager seized the opportunity. 'If I can find a partner and between us raise the money, would you sell to me?' he asked.

'I don't mind who I sell to,' was Joss's reply.

He agreed to wait one week before putting the business on the market, and one week later a deal was struck. The bank did not hesitate. The two men were in the oil business and one was the actual production manager of the oil-field he wished to secure. Who could know better whether it was a good investment. With the land and oil fields as surety, it couldn't go wrong.

After all the routine formalities had been dealt with, no longer the owner of the land and oil which lay under it, but in possession of a fat bank balance which he was now going to transfer to England, Joss left for New York and while awaiting the departure date, spent his time shopping for gifts for what remained of his family and close friends.

q

Chapter Forty-eight

Joss did not write home to say he was returning. There was no point, he would almost certainly be there before any letters.

The key to his front door was still on his key ring but he rang the doorbell. To appear in the house after a long absence and without prior warning could be a shock. He heard approaching footsteps and the door was opened by Myrtle.

'Oh! . . . My dear . . . 'tis Mr Renfree! Come on in, don't stand out their on your own doorstep, sir. You could knock me down with a feather!'

Have to be some feather Joss thought, noticing Myrtle had now almost doubled her girth and her hair was white, but her face had become rounded and was unlined.

'Nice to see you, Myrtle,' he said as he shook her hand.

'And you, sir . . . Mrs Renfree,' she raised her voice. 'Mr Renfree's home.'

Clementine appeared from the sitting-room. 'Well see who's here,' she said, her face expressionless. Her now wispy grey hair was frizzed around her lined face, mounted on a scraggy neck, but she still maintained a slim, youthful figure which enabled her to keep up-to-date with the latest styles in dress, even though inappropriate.

'How are you Clemmie?' he enquired, giving her a brief peck on the cheek.

'I suppose the answer is "bearing up",' Clementine said.

'Shall I make tea, Mrs Renfree?' Myrtle enquired.

'Yes, thank you Myrtle,' Clementine replied and Myrtle hurried away.

Joss left his luggage in the hall and followed Clementine into the sitting-room.

'Is this a temporary visit?' she said, coldly.

'No, I'm home for good.'

'Oh. Are you?'

Joss found conversation hard work. Clementine was not co-operative. He started to enquire about mutual acquaintances but Clementine rose to her feet and moved to the door.

'Why are you taking so long with the tea, Myrtle?' she shouted.

'Almost ready, Mrs Renfree,' came the reply.

But it was still a further five minutes before Myrtle appeared with tea, small sandwiches, cakes and buttered scones with a cut-glass dish of home-made strawberry jam.

'Huh! I suppose Mr Renfree is the reason for all this largess,' Clementine said, obviously annoyed that Myrtle was taking such good care of him.

'Well, Mrs Renfree, I know you have a dainty appetite. You eat like a sparrow,' Myrtle soothed.

'Ah yes, I suppose I do,' Clementine replied, appeased. Fortunately she did not see the look on Myrtle's face as she walked away.

'You've put on weight,' she said to Joss in a tone which was both accusatory and triumphant.

'Getting older,' Joss said.

'Don't you mean too much drink?' came the reply.

'It's not a crime, my dear,' he said. 'But I don't, in fact, normally drink to excess.'

Clementine poured the tea and as she handed a cup to Joss she looked, with an aloof expression, directly into his face for the first time.

'You left without bothering to come home, and without a word.'

There was no point in trying to smooth this one over. 'I did come home, Clementine, but it was better for you, me, and everyone else that I left the way I did.' Joss's voice was quiet and unhurried.

'What do you mean?' Clementine retorted.

'At Penryn Station I took a cab home, and when I reached the house who did I see mounting the steps to *my* front door?'

'Well . . . Who did you see?' Clementine's tone was haughty.

'Charles Brendon Copeland.'

Joss's words were interrupted by Clementine's enraged voice. 'Don't mention that name to me! The money-grubbing swine!'

This was strange, her anger was with Copeland! Joss's brown eyes narrowed in contemplation. Obviously Copeland had deserted her for someone with more money. Was it because he now kept her allowance on a tight rein, though one his parents would have thought ridiculously extravagant. Or was it because Copeland had found another, wealthier woman, or one uncluttered with a husband? Or was there a well set-up younger woman whose looks had not yet faded? Money grubbing must have meant money had entered into it. Was it possible the lady had both attributes? No. Who with looks, youth and money would bother with this ageing lothario?

To try to change the precarious subject and continue a conversation would have been useless.

He had long since stopped caring enough to be bothered. Joss went into the hall to take his luggage upstairs and left it on the spacious landing instead of cluttering up the bedroom and would unpack tomorrow. He'd been sitting practically all day and would go out and stretch his legs.

The tide was high and Joss strolled down to Penryn Bridge, leaned against the wall, staring at the river. He had bought a gold necklace with sapphire and diamond droplets for Clementine and would have given them to her, along with a gold watch for Myrtle, but Clementine was not in a mood to be pleased with the Crown Jewels. He'd do it another time.

'Hey, Joss, didn't know you were home. How are you, me old pal?' The man who spoke, Dickie Polwin, was mooring his boat alongside the quay. Joss walked towards him and the two shook hands. A little group of men, some working on their boats and others just chatting, joined them. An hour later Joss returned home with a plump bass which Dickie insisted on giving him and to which both Myrtle and he were partial. The meal was prompt on time as Clementine had two friends coming that evening. They arrived around 7.30 p.m. So Joss, who did not wish to be an unexpected and probably unwelcome participant in 'women's talk' said he would leave them and pay a visit to his sister.

On opening the front door and finding the caller was her brother, Lottie shrieked with delight. She clung to him, then began to weep, as joy at seeing him and sadness at George's absence mingled.

Once inside they exchanged news, though Lottie had far more to tell. The wound caused by George's passing was still raw, but seeing Joss and telling him about Nora, Alec and the newest grandchild gave her joy, something that made life still worth-while. Also, since Joss's original return from America, years before the World War when it became obvious his marriage was little more than a sham, she had the feeling she must watch over him. Neither she nor Joss wished their parents to know and inevitably worry about the situation.

Time passed quickly and Joss learned to his amazement that Copeland had married Emma Pope. Now he knew the reason for Clementine's outburst! Emma had inherited her parents' very sizeable estate and the parasitical Copeland now, no doubt, had full control. And Clementine's eye-catching charms had definitely faded, plus the bottom of her personal monetary pit was now less deep. They chatted until late, then Joss returned home.

He found Myrtle up, awaiting his return.

'Whatever are you doing still up, Myrtle?'

'I wasn't sure where you wanted to sleep, sir, so I lit a fire in the room you used to use, just in case,' Myrtle replied. 'And shall I make a hot drink?'

'No thanks. I had one before leaving my sister's. And I shall be using the room where you made a fire, thank you, Myrtle. Now I'm going to bed and I think you should do the same.'

'Yes, sir. Thank you.' Myrtle began to move away.

'Oh, Myrtle.'

'Yes, sir.'

'How has Mrs Renfree been while I've been in America?'

'Much quieter than she once was. Not so many visitors or outings.' Joss recognised the double-meaning in what Myrtle said. 'And I hope you don't think I'm speaking out of turn, sir, but at times she seems a little odd.'

'Odd. In what way?'

'Strange,' Myrtle said. 'Up here,' she put a finger to her forehead. 'It's not often, just once in a while.'

'More troublesome?' Joss asked.

'Not really. Sometimes she's more . . . ' Myrtle grappled in her mind for a suitable word. 'Child-like . . . but children do have tantrums. I think she sometimes gets irritable because she doesn't have as many . . . er . . . friends as she once did.'

'Thanks, Myrtle, don't let me keep you any longer.'

'Goodnight then, sir. It's good to have you home again.'

'Thank you, Myrtle. Goodnight,' Joss replied.

Joss could see why Clementine no longer held attraction for a certain type of male. She no longer had her looks, and the coquettish ways which attracted some, now seemed ludicrous, though he felt she was unaware of this. Neither did she have a lot of money to squander to impress others, nor a grand manor to flaunt. Joss made his way upstairs and was asleep within seconds of getting into bed.

As was his habit, Joss was up early and listened to the wireless as he waited for water to boil for tea. After the tea he strolled to the nearest newsagent. There was a new name over the door and he didn't know the man who was undoing the strings which held together the bundles of assorted papers. He chose both the *Daily Herald* and the *Daily Mail*, then returned home to enjoy the breakfast Myrtle had prepared. He then went to the sitting-room and sat in a comfortable chair near the window to read his papers. By the time he finished reading the *Daily Mail* he heard Clementine descend the stairs. She went to the dining-room to breakfast, it being beneath her to eat in the breakfast room which was next to the kitchen, near the smells of cooking and the sounds and clatter of pots and pans. Joss had almost finished the second newspaper when she bounced into the room.

'What are you doing here?' she demanded. 'I thought you stayed out last night with some female?'

She doesn't want me, but she wants me to want her, Joss thought, and she's annoyed because I didn't go to her room.

'I stopped sharing a room with you years ago, as you know Clementine. And I've no wish to alter that arrangement,' Joss said. She might as well know where she stood from the start of his return.

'When I woke up I thought your return was a bad dream.'

'Good or bad it was not a dream. I'm here, and I'm here to stay.'

'What a prospect,' Clementine replied in a hard-done-by tone.

'If you prefer to live in either what's habitable of Manor Withiel or the cottage, you are welcome to do so,' Joss replied, evenly.

366

Clementine did not like the way the conversation was going.

'Don't you take that tone with me,' she screeched.

'Quit the nonsense about my non-existent tone. If you're wise you'll take me seriously,' Joss said. 'You like using this room, don't you?'

'No, I do not! But it's the best of a poor lot.'

'Well, when I have finished reading my papers I shall move out and into the room on the opposite side of the hallway to this one. Now that I know there has been no improvement in your temper, you might as well realise I'm too old for your tantrums, Clementine, and I've no intention of ever bothering to try again. If you can live peacefully with me, then I will live peacefully with you. If not, one of us is going to Withiel and it won't be me. Meanwhile I will keep separate rooms.'

Clementine's jaw had dropped before Joss finished speaking. He returned his attention to his newspaper and Clementine turned on her heel and left the room, giving the door an almighty slam.

After reading the remainder of the *Daily Herald* Joss surveyed the room opposite the sitting-room. He would get rid of some of the furniture and have a roll-top desk which locked, and some armchairs to his liking. But first he would get rid of the wallpaper covered in pink flowers and have something plain or striped.

He had been in Penryn almost twenty-four hours and was impatient to see Polly. He knew from the letters that both Lottie and Polly had retired from working at 'The Lady', though both helped out quite frequently and enjoyed doing so. But how would Polly receive him now that Edwin was dead? Surely it would be all right to visit now and then. He'd call this morning. No afternoon would look more correct. But she might not be at home. Then he would leave a calling card saying he would come another time.

There had been only a little correspondence between them since he suddenly left for America. Edwin was alive then, and either he or occasionally Polly wrote with news of Jonathan his Godson in mind. It was a rare and special communication with the woman he loved. But no mention of their feelings for one another was ever made and too many letters would serve to fan the embers.

Myrtle had prepared the bass for Joss and herself for lunch, but Clementine, who did not like bass, said she would have veal.

Myrtle told Joss she had taken the surplus fish to a widow she knew in Shute Lane, who had eight children to feed. She was sure he would approve, which he did.

When the meal was over Joss strolled up the ridge-like hill to Villa Gwidden. As soon as Polly opened the door and he saw the smile of welcome coupled with disbelief, Joss's vague feeling of uncertainty vanished. It was the same Polly, more mature, less slender, but still shapely, hair streaked with silver, but to Joss her smile and her face were unchanged, and there was still that special look in her eyes. Grief for Edwin had not diminished her feelings for him. They were as they always had been, constant. Joss took her hand in his and brushed her cheeks with a brief kiss.

'Joss! What a surprise! Come in. Why didn't you let me know you were coming home?'

'It was a spur of the moment decision, Polly. And a letter would probably arrive after I had.'

'What brought that about?' Polly asked. 'George's death?'

They went into the sitting-room and sat facing each other. 'You know me better than I know myself,' Joss replied.

'Edwin used to say that about me,' Polly said with a wistful smile.

'I was so sorry to learn about Edwin.'

'I never doubted that.' Polly stared up into his still velvety brown eyes.

'I think it was his sad death that planted the hankering for home in my mind. All the folk I knew, the people I grew up with, so many no longer around. And when I heard George had died and Lottie was a widow, I knew I must return home or it could be too late. There might be no one to come home to.'

'What about Clementine?' Polly said.

For a few moments Joss did not answer. Then, almost under his breath he said, 'She's the sort of wife who keeps you from coming home . . . '

'Oh, yes,' Polly said, her voice soft, remembering the reason for Joss's swift departure.

'When did you arrive in Penryn?' Polly said, changing a subject Joss clearly preferred not to discuss.

'Less then twenty-four hours ago. And I shall never move away again,' he replied, as a tailpiece to the previous topic.

Polly smiled and patted the back of his hand. 'I'm glad,' she

368

said.

Joss felt his bosom swell with deep satisfaction. He wasn't some hot-blooded youngster. To see the woman he loved now and then, to sit and chat, a gentle kiss, a touch or pressure of the hand. Quiet, happy togetherness; two spirits who had known a lifetime of closeness. That, to Joss, would be blessed fulfilment. He could not ever contemplate marrying Polly, he was not free. But if he could be with her, just sometimes, he'd be satisfied, happy.

They chatted on about Lottie, Nora, 'The Lady', etc. 'I know Mary and Jack will be delighted to see you,' Polly said. 'But Jack will still be at work.'

'We'll see each other one evening,' Joss said, then asked about Polly's mother who succumbed to the Great 'Flu Epidemic.

'I'll tell you when I've made us a cup of tea,' Polly replied. But Joss followed her to the kitchen and they chatted on, Polly suggesting that he and Clementine come for a meal one weekend when Jonathan was at home.

'I'd like that very much. Polly, you're so blessed to have Jonathan.'

'I know I am,' Polly said, looking up into Joss's suddenly sombre face. 'And losing Theodore must have been a terrible blow.'

'Yes,' Joss said and again changed the subject, telling Polly how he intended to surprise Bill Boaden with an unexpected visit to him and his family at Mawnan Smith. Then he looked at his watch. 'Is it that time! I must go. Isn't it a pity that time goes so fast when you're enjoying yourself.'

'And drags when you're not,' Polly said. 'I've thoroughly enjoyed it too Joss. Come again, any time.'

Joss walked home, his spirits high. It had been a lovely afternoon. Just a chat and a cup of tea, but with Polly. What a wonderful feeling it gave. How happy, how at peace he felt. Money couldn't buy that. He'd love to do it again and again, and again.

That night Joss lay awake, thinking the afternoon over. When Edwin was alive he felt a certain guilt to discover he was in love with Edwin's wife, Polly, the girl he had always known so closely. Now, with Edwin dead for over two years, he still felt guilty about Edwin. His son, Theodore was dead, though it still didn't seem possible, and his marriage was a sham. Everyone who mattered knew it, and quite a few who didn't matter. Surely there was more to life than this. If all the struggling at the beginning was to this end, it just wasn't worth it. How many more times would he tell himself what a fool he was not to wait for Polly. But at the time such a thing never entered his head. He always loved her but in his youth, when she was just a child, it was more as a sister. And when he arrived home from America but somehow was not successful in meeting Polly until the night of the party, still it never entered his head that when his face beheld hers, when at last he gazed into her eyes, he would fall madly in love for what he then realised was the first time, for always and for ever. Fool, fool, fool.

Polly saw and knew the mistake he was making when she was only a child. But there was nothing she could do and she would have been laughed at and treated as the year's biggest joke if she had tried.

Now Polly was without a husband and he, Joss, might as well be a widower. He and his wife did not even share the same sitting-room. He and Polly could not marry, but at least they might spend a little time together. With this prospect in mind, Joss drifted into sleep.

Since Edwin's death, Polly was always thankful for two things: Her son Jonathan, and the nights when she could sleep soundly. For weeks and months a good night's sleep was few and far between. It was the brief relief from misery she craved. In the last year she slept well.

Tonight though, she was wide awake and wished to remain so. She had again seen Joss! Her Joss! She lived again the touch of his fingers, the quick brush of his lips against her face, every word, every glance! She'd tried to be loyal to Edwin, except for her one weak moment, one lapse, when love overcame loyalty, about which at the time and for several years after she had been desperately unhappy. Yet the child which she felt sure had been the result of this, brought joy to everyone, and none more than Edwin. She was the only one who knew, the only one who carried the heavy burden of guilt. And so she should. But was she so bad, so sinful for loving Joss? It wasn't as though she chose to love him. They were made for one another.

But she loved Edwin too, and worried desperately how best to do the right thing, first and foremost for Edwin. And ultimately she realised she did do what was best for Edwin's happiness. Jonathan gave him all the joy in the world he wanted. For her, from that time onwards, although there was joy, she was never completely free of guilt. And Edwin was such a trusting husband, which had the effect of heightening her self-condemnation.

But, looking back, had she ever regretted the love between herself and Joss? No. Never. She never had and she knew she never would, guilt or no guilt.

Chapter Forty-nine

The day after his visit to Polly, Joss went again to see his sister. Company, especially family, did help in times of bereavement and he could tell Lottie was missing George more than she allowed to show.

It was a while before Joss's knock on the door brought any response, and his sister's swollen eyes were evidence she had been trying to compose herself before facing whoever it was at the door. Once inside the house Joss put his comforting arms around her. Lottie relaxed and the tears flowed.

'Let it go. Don't bottle anything up on my account,' he said.

After a few minutes Lottie became calmer. Joss steered her towards a comfortable chair, telling her he would make them both a good cup of strong, sweet tea.

'Thanks, Joss, I'm sorry about that,' Lottie said, blowing her nose in the large handkerchief her brother handed to her.

'Don't you worry Lottie,' Joss assured her. 'I'm glad I was here. It's not good to be alone too much.'

'I was about to start making a pasty when it all came over me, just *one* pasty when it was never less than two,' she explained.

'If I stay and have one with you it still will be two,' Joss said.

'Oh Joss, would you?' Lottie said, smiling through her tears.

'Nothing I'd like better,' Joss said as he poured tea and handed a cup to her.

Lottie took a swallow. 'That feels better,' she said and gave her brother a smile.

'I'll help with the pasties,' Joss volunteered when they had finished the tea.

'I've made the pastry,' Lottie told him.

'I'll cut up the meat, while you do the potatoes. I can't cut them wafer thin like you do, and I'll chop the onions. Can't have you crying again.'

Lottie smiled at this. 'All right, I'll roll out the pastry and do the potatoes and turnip. It shouldn't take us long.'

'I saw Polly yesterday,' Joss said as they worked at either end of the kitchen table.

'Oh, how was she?' Lottie said, briefly forgetting her own sadness.

'Interested to hear any news of her old friend and partner.'

They spent the rest of the morning chatting and by the time the pasties were ready to eat, Lottie had brightened visibly.

'Have you any commitments this afternoon?' Joss asked.

'Not a thing,' Lottie replied.

'I feel like a little ride out,' he said. 'Come with me.'

'You and Clementine?' Lottie said, hoping her voice didn't reveal she was dubious about an afternoon out with her brother's wife.

'No, not Clementine. Just you and me.'

Lottie's face brightened. 'I'd like that. Where were you thinking of going?'

'Any place that takes our fancy,' Joss grinned.

'Buses won't take you any place you fancy,' Lottie said.

'Who said bus? We'll hire a car or else have a taxi.'

'That's much too extravagant!' Lottie expostulated.

'Lottie,' Joss's face was serious. 'I've come home quite well off. Rich in fact. The money won't make any difference. And if there's anything at all you want, anything, just say the word and it's yours.'

'Polly and I did very well out of "The Lady" Joss,' Lottie replied. 'We're both comfortably off, and as you will know, we still get an income from the business. We are still the owners.'

'I realise that, and I know you haven't got extravagant tastes. Being a successful business woman hasn't gone to your head. But money is there if you ever want anything, or Nora, or the boys and their families. Neither Clementine nor any of her lot will squander it this time.'

The afternoon drive was delightful. They stopped for a walk along the cliff-tops, the salty sea air cleared the congestion from Lottie's head, and she felt lighter. Then they stopped at a creekside teahouse for a cream tea.

373

'It's a pity Polly's not here. She would have enjoyed this,' Lottie remarked.

'That's true,' Joss agreed, pleased that Lottie had thought of this. 'We'll ask her to come with us next time.'

'It *will* be extravagant to do this often,' Lottie chided. 'And how will Clementine take it if she keeps getting left out?'

'She's already made it clear she doesn't want my company. In any event, I plan to buy a car sometime soon. But your idea for the three of us is good. You must miss each other after all the years you've spent working together.'

During the following two weeks Joss, with Lottie, visited Nora and little Sylvia at Marine Crescent, and Lottie and Polly enjoyed a few most pleasant afternoon and day trips. Polly and Lottie chatted almost non-stop and Lottie's spirits noticeably lifted during these outings. Neighbours called or invited her in for a coffee, and George's sister who lived nearby was a frequent visitor. The company relieved the gloom and often brought a genuine smile to Lottie's face.

Joss joined one of the local sailing clubs and bought a sailing boat and resumed his lifelong interest in Penryn Rugby Club. Despite his hostile wife, who behaved like a spoiled four-year-old, he was enjoying life, especially the couple of hours he spent usually twice a week with Polly. He hadn't yet found time to look around for a car, but now learned Lottie was going to help in the workroom at 'The Lady' for a few days as Nora had to fit in several orders for funeral outfits due to the death of a well-known Falmouth Alderman. Polly was also going to help in the showroom for just two days. Tomorrow was Tuesday. Clementine was always at home on Tuesdays. He would go out to choose a car tomorrow.

It was when he was breakfasting next day that Joss wondered whether perhaps Clementine would like to accompany him to choose a car. Life was not so good for her now, though most if not all her difficulties were of her own making. When Clementine came down to breakfast Joss went to the dining-room.

'I'm going out to choose a new car,' he said. 'Would you like to come with me, Clemmie?'

Clementine paused before replying. 'It depends,' she replied,

374

languidly. 'Walking and going on a bus would be out of the question. Horse-drawn or motorised transport?'

'Spargo's taxi I think.'

'Very well then,' Clementine said, condescendingly. 'I'll get ready when I've finished breakfast.'

'I'll order the taxi for ten o'clock,' Joss replied. He mused on how a few hours, possibly a day out with Clementine would work out.

Clementine was ready only five or six minutes after the arrival of the taxi. She wore a corn-coloured deep crowned cloche hat with a cascade of small matching feathers, and a matching coat which tapered downwards from the shoulders, with court shoes, bag and gloves all in a deeper shade. She still looked eye-catchingly attractive, viewed from a little distance and with a hat covering her bobbed and frizzy hair.

They looked in at a Falmouth display, then went for a coffee. A couple of friends Clementine had not seen for some time were there sitting at a table overlooking the harbour. Clementine was very aware she looked smart, and chatting with them put her in an even better humour.

At the next garage and show area, Joss decided to settle for a William Morris Bullnose. Clementine wrinkled her nose in distaste.

'It's a cheap, second-rate thing made in a factory,' she derided. 'A poor car made to cater for poor people!'

'I can assure you no poor person could buy a car of any kind,' Joss said. 'And I was not looking at the price, nor for something ostentatious, but its suitability for use on the narrow streets and winding roads and lanes here in Cornwall. I might consider buying another more spacious one to keep for longer journeys.'

At this Clementine brightened. 'It's nice to hear you are contemplating *spending* money for a change, instead of continually harping about how much money is being spent.'

Privately Joss also thought a larger vehicle would be nice to take Lottie, Nora and the family out sometimes, along with Polly anytime she felt like joining them. Perhaps he would let Clementine use the Bullnose now and then. She wouldn't be up to the sort of games he found her at in the hotel in Truro, would she? Surely not. Besides now he was home again, he would pay all the household bills. Her personal allowance would not be affected. It was ample for what it was intended, clothes and personal needs. But she couldn't go completely wild with it.

They decided to lunch in one of the smart modern seafront hotels. It was a little late, but there would still be a choice of dishes. The driver parked the taxi and they entered the hotel and moved towards the reception area when suddenly Clementine froze. There at the counter was Charles Brendon Copeland, apparently settling a bill. For a few seconds Clementine remained motionless and silent, then found her power of speech.

'Copeland . . . You swine . . . you lecherous, bed-hopping, womanising swine!'

Copeland spun round, his mouth open though no sound issued forth, his eyes staring horror-struck at Clementine and Joss. The receptionist, a passing porter and a well dressed guest all became rigid, momentarily rooted.

By now Emma was on the scene and had heard.

'How dare you speak to my husband like that,' she shouted in high-pitched defence of her husband. The guest continued on his way, the receptionist and porter stood gaping.

'I dare to speak like that because that is what he is . . . I should know, I've known him a damn sight longer than you have.'

As she spoke Joss took a firm grip on his wife's arm. 'Come away, Clementine.' His voice was grim as she struggled to free herself from his grasp.

'Yes, let's get away from this,' the white-faced Copeland said to Emma, but Emma seemed not to hear his words.

'That's because you're so old,' she fired back at Clementine. 'You wrinkled old bat, old has-been, old man-mad bitch!'

By now the manager and the head waiter, as well as the porter, were hovering close by.

'You stupid little greenhorn,' Clementine hissed at Emma, endeavouring with mad strength to free herself from Joss's grip. 'Do you imagine he would give a great waddling lump like you a second glance before you came into possession of your parents' money?'

Emma, drawing herself up to her full five foot nothing, interrupted. 'Charles is in love with *me*, and *I* am his only true love.'

'Ladies and gentlemen,' the manager intervened in soothing tones, 'would you please leave these premises and settle your differences elsewhere.'

376

At these words the taxi driver, who was to have been provided with a meal in a room near the kitchen, walked out, but neither Clementine nor Emma heeded what the manager said. Despite her frenzied struggling Joss had dragged Clementine to the door by which they had entered, but Clementine seized the ornamental brass door handle and hung on to it, twisting her head to face Emma.

'True lover,' she spat the scorn-filled words. 'Take a look in the mirror, you outsized, pudding-faced hippopotamus . . . '

'You say that because you're jealous of me,' Emma cut in, her expression once more resembled the cat that got the cream. 'I'd rather be a little plump than have a face like a shrivelled prune, with a bag of bones for a body . . . and Charles would too . . . he told me so . . . those were his very words!'

The white-faced Charles Brendon Copeland looked aghast at Emma's admission.

'Oh, Charles did, did he,' Clementine hissed while still trying to maintain her hold on the door handle. 'And did he also tell you how much he truly *loves* your money, and *why*? It's because he's got three or four bastards scattered about needing to be fed and clothed, the bills for which, since you seem unaware, it is now *your* privilege to foot! One of the brats must be taller than you though minus your girth!'

The smugness had by now gone from Emma's face. She stood, staring, paralysed, speechless, jaw hanging, mouth wide open, thunderstruck!

'Never mind, my dear,' Clementine gleefully leered at the sight of Emma's pitiful distress, the evidence of her own victory. 'You shall have the pleasure of caring for him in his gouty, whisky-sodden old age, signs of which are already apparent, especially round the back of his scrawny neck and the few spread-out hairs on top of his balding head.'

At this Emma let out an earsplitting scream and, shocked beyond tears, like a landed, floundering fish, began to gasp for air, her strangled panting interspersed with breathless squeaks, squawks and choked screams.

Clementine's grip on the door-handle relaxed at the sight of her triumph over the demented Emma, and Joss roughly hauled her through the doorway, leaving the deathly-white Copeland endeavouring to both comfort and placate his wife, and desperately trying to explain away the damning remarks Clementine had made.

Joss and Clementine reached the taxi where the driver sat waiting. 'Take us home, driver,' Joss said. Clementine did not appear to notice that Joss's face was also white. Not as with Copeland from fear, but with rage at Clementine's behaviour.

'That'll teach the silly bitch,' she said with a satisfied smirk as though expecting concurrence.

'Shut up or get out and walk,' Joss snarled. 'How dare you speak to the girl like that. You and that Copeland idiot are two of a kind. It is disgusting that you should vent your jealousy on a gullible young woman.'

Realisation had dawned that if what Clementine said about Copeland having a scattering of bastards were true, it might be possible some were old enough for her to have been supplying his money to pay for at least one, all those years ago. His recollection of when she was getting through so much money around the time of the scene with her and Copeland in the hotel in Truro, was blindingly vivid. He seethed at the possibility.

'You can let me out here, driver,' he said, then looked towards Clementine and spat the words, 'I can't bear to sit next to you.'

He got out of the taxi and handed two large white five pound notes to the driver.

'You've given me one too many, sir,' the driver said. 'And you have change to come.'

'Keep it,' Joss replied. 'With my apologies to you for having to witness such a disgusting scene.'

Joss alighted at Western Terrace. He could cut across Cambridge Place from where he could get to The Terraces which overlooked the harbour and were only yards from where Lottie lived. He didn't want to see her, she would instantly spot something was wrong. It was his problem. He hastened across the road at Wodehouse Terrace, then down zigzagging steps and short steep hills, traversing parallel roads, until he reached Church Corner in the main street, and the Parish Church. A flight of steps separated the Church from the King's Head; he hastened down the steps and entered the bar.

The barman had one remaining pasty in a glass compartment which stood on the counter. Joss settled for the pasty along with a pint of beer. Uncharacteristically he did not join in the conversation with a group of men about the fastest of the Falmouth Working Boats, but sat alone at a corner table mulling over Clementine's behaviour and the possibility that *she* had actually handed over his money to support the misbegotten bastards of that dandified apology for a man, Copeland.

The memory of old wounds came flooding back. The times in America, when he was often immersed in work. Clementine was anxious for him to make a fortune. She said she felt sure he could. And he did. At the time he understood she had a far more affluent background than his own and that she took for normal a lifestyle which would have been an unbelievable, even wicked extravagance to people from his background. At first, for a few times, she grumbled that Joss's work prevented him from escorting her to social events. Then suddenly she seemed not to mind. Joss naïvely assumed she appreciated the situation, until one night when, at the last moment, he arrived home in time to accompany her to a party and found his presence had the opposite effect to the welcome he expected. Instead of being glad, she seemed displeased at being escorted by him. He was puzzled, then the seeds of suspicion were planted and he found she had been involved with an Embassy man from Europe who moved in select circles. She protested it was all innocent, he was only keeping her company at parties, partnering her for dancing because she had no escort or partner.

The lead up to and birth of Theodore put a brake on her activities for a time, and Joss, more firmly involved and established in his business affairs, found it easier to accompany her. Also most invitations now came via *his* business contacts and because of *his* standing in the higher ranks of business and in certain governmental departments.

But Clementine subsequently again became involved with a man, Italian in origin, with good looks and a bad reputation. Joss was on the point of divorcing her. At first she didn't seem to care, then found her Latin lover's passion did not run particularly deep, and he baulked at the idea that he should take Joss's place as her husband. Clementine begged Joss's forgiveness. Joss hesitated. There was Theodore, who was close to his seventh birthday, to consider. He would be the one to suffer; a small child, helpless and totally dependent on the preferences and decisions of Clementine and himself. Joss's fortune was now more than enough to meet even the high requirements of the Du Canes. In the south of Cornwall, the far flung southwesterly tip of England, there was not the social whirl which oiled the wheels of business as in this particular part of America.

Joss pondered the situation for a few days then told Clementine he would overlook her unfaithfulness provided she agreed to return home and settle down to normal married life. Clementine hesitated a few seconds, then apparently came to the conclusion that she had little choice. 'Of course I agree, darling. I think that's an excellent idea. When would you like us to go?'

Joss surprised himself at the relief he felt at Clementine's answer. Divorce was another word for disgrace and the burden of sorrow which his family back home would have had to endure if he had gone ahead with this had been lifted, as well as the repercussions which would have fallen on his son. They would all go home and try to mend the rift.

Then there was Copeland and the disgraceful episode at the hotel in Truro; then coming home finding the Manor ruined by the fire when Clementine entertained Hugo Farnell in her bed while he himself was absent in Hampshire seeing their son's Headmaster.

Joss's temper rocketed when he recalled with smouldering rage her telling him he was required at his mother's bedside and her words 'I hope she's bloody dead!' followed by the twisted smile of malice as she witnessed and savoured his anguish at this news. Yes, he was glad to be home in Cornwall, but he'd put up with Clementine no longer!

Joss swallowed the remains of his beer and, leaving the pasty half eaten, strode out of the saloon and hurried to the taxi rank, where he directed the driver of the nearest vehicle to his home.

On arriving he started to mount the steps to his front door, but as the taxi drove off, he turned, descended the steps and walked away. It wasn't the fracas between Clementine and Emma which now so enraged him It was the sitting, reliving old and bitter scenes of past outrageous behaviour and wounding, never to be forgotten words, which raised his temper to a level where he doubted the likelihood of his being able to keep his own actions under control. One more word out-of-place and he might not be able to stop himself from throttling her. For himself he didn't give a damn. But Lottie, what would such a horrible scandal do to her, to have her brother guilty of a hanging offence. He couldn't, mustn't crucify her or his beloved Polly, with such a dreadful outcome to his calamitous marriage.

The thought of how Polly, Lottie and her family would suffer should his temper get the better of him had a sobering effect and Joss walked towards Eastwood on the far side of Penryn Bridge, and headed towards College Woods. He didn't want to meet anyone or chat to anyone. He needed to be alone and was unlikely to encounter anyone there; with this bitter rage inside him he wasn't fit to see anyone.

He walked for a long time, then sat on the remains of a fallen tree trunk in the woods. How long he sat he did not know, but suddenly, except for what felt like a fire in his head and a burning face, the heat drained from every part of his body, and he began to shiver. He refrained from taking a warming nip from the brandy flask in his pocket. He needed his head to cool.

It was now early evening and he arrived home as Myrtle was about to serve the meal. He went to the kitchen. Myrtle looked up from the soup she was stirring.

'Serve mine in the breakfast-room, Myrtle,' he said.

'I've not set a place for you in the breakfast-room, Mr Renfree,' Myrtle replied, a perplexed expression an her face. *Mrs* Renfree was the one who shunned *Mr* Renfree, not the other way round. But she had come home in a strange 'strung-up' state. Something stormy must have happened while they were out.

'That's all right,' Joss replied as he helped himself to cutlery. 'I can do that.'

He'd wait until after they'd eaten, to tackle Clementine. Now he needed something hot inside him. As soon as he finished eating, he rose and went to the dining-room. Clementine was raising her coffee cup to her lips.

'What do you want?' she said, her tone hostile.

'Instead of having separate rooms, Clementine, we're having separate homes. Tomorrow morning *you* are going to Withiel Cottage.'

'Good,' came Clementine's swift reply. 'I shall be glad to see the back of you and return to *my home* you skinflint bastard.'

'*My property*,' Joss reminded her. 'Not yours.'

He went to the door. 'Myrtle,' he said, as she came out of the breakfast room with the dishes from his meal. 'Would you come here a moment.'

'Yes, sir,' Myrtle obliged.

'I'll wash the dishes,' Joss said. 'Mrs Renfree is leaving for Withiel Cottage early in the morning, and I want you to pack her things and yours or as much of it as you can.'

At this news Myrtle's face crumpled.

'What's wrong, Myrtle?' Joss said.

'She doesn't want to go,' Clementine said. 'But she won't have to go to Withiel Cottage. I was going to dismiss her anyway. Jane McBride is leaving Greenbank to go and live with her daughter, and I shall be getting rid of Myrtle and engaging Jane's cook-housekeeper; she's a much superior servant.'

'Oh,' Myrtle screeched in anguish and two trembling tears began to roll down her cheeks.

'You do not employ Myrtle, I do,' Joss addressed his wife. Clementine pursed her mouth and her eyes narrowed. Joss turned to Myrtle. 'You shall stay here with me, Myrtle.'

'Oh, thank you, sir. Thank you, thank you.' Myrtle, overcome with relief gratefully clasped his hand as she was speaking.

'Ugh!' Clementine exclaimed. She had always been jealous of the servants' willingness to please her husband, be they male or female.

'That's all right, Myrtle,' Joss said. 'Now you go and pack Mrs Renfree's things.'

'Yes, sir. Thank you,' Myrtle said, and loudly blowing her nose, hurried away.

Joss turned to Clementine. 'You may have Jane McBride's cook, and she can remain with you for as long as you don't make any further nuisance of yourself.'

Joss left the room, surprised that this did not bring a vitriolic rejoinder from his wife. Instead she turned on the wireless to a lively programme of the latest music and, just to demonstrate she didn't give a damn, began singing in a tone-deaf way.

Joss provided Myrtle with a trunk and suitcases from the attic, then packed a box of food from the store cupboard. It was only when this was completed that he went to his room opposite to Clementine's sitting-room. He poured himself the first drink of the evening, turned on his wireless to hear the news and sank wearily into an armchair. Who, he wondered, would look after Clementine at Withiel Cottage until Jane McBride's cook arrived.

Mrs Soloman he supposed. And if Mrs Soloman refused? She would have to do it herself. Joss pictured her at the kitchen sink, peeling potatoes, and smiled mirthlessly.

He heard Myrtle bring Clementine her milky drink and biscuits and a quarter of an hour later, Clementine went to bed. Myrtle came and asked if he would like a hot drink. 'No thanks. You get to bed, Myrtle,' he replied.

Joss, though physically weary, was in no hurry to retire; his brain was too active after the storms of the day. At last he poured a relaxing brandy, leant back in his comfortable chair and slowly sipped the drink. He felt his senses beginning to dull, and decided to make his way upstairs before he fell asleep in the chair. Once in his room he peeled off his clothes and flopped into bed, not noticing something he valued was missing from the room.

Chapter Fifty

As usual, Joss was first up in the morning. Myrtle was close after him. Joss concluded a taxi would not have enough space for all the luggage. He would hire a taxi to take him to collect the Morris Bullnose, and see if Ron Paull was available to transfer the trunk, etc., with his horse and cart.

'What time do you want me to call?'

'Around ten,' Joss said. 'But my wife is unlikely to be ready and waiting, whatever time we arrange.'

Ron grinned and nodded. ' 'Nough said, my handsome. That don't matter to me.'

Joss parked the car near to the house in Lowenna Square, but left room for Ron's horse and small cart. As he opened the front door Clementine was coming down the stairs.

'Your things are being collected at ten o'clock, so you'd better make sure you've got everything you want,' he said, brusquely.

Clementine swept into the dining-room without replying. She did though, take notice of what he said and after breakfast collected the wireless from her sitting-room and most of the contents of her escritoire, which she instructed Myrtle to pack into boxes.

Ron Paull arrived just before ten o'clock. 'Come on in, Ron,' Joss said. 'The trunk is up on the landing. Come upstairs and we'll carry it down between us.' Ron followed Joss up the stairs.

'Hang on a second,' Joss said as Ron bent to lift one end of the trunk. 'I forgot to put my watch on.' Joss had replaced the out-dated watch and chain with a wristwatch.

As his gaze went to the top of the chest-of-drawers, he halted, then turned and rushed down the stairs, his face darkening like a thunder-cloud. Ron Paull ambled a short distance behind him.

'Clementine!' he shouted, his voice furious. 'What have you done with my picture of Theodore?'

From midway of the stairs Ron saw Clementine unhurriedly emerge from the sitting-room.

'I've got it,' she said.

'Get it,' Joss ordered.

'Certainly,' Clementine said coolly, and moved towards the staircase. Ron hastened down the lower treads to get out of her way. Clementine, looking through him, ascended the stairs and a few moments later returned and handed Joss a shoe box.

'It can't be in a shoe box, the picture is too wide,' Joss said as he took it from her and pulled off the lid. All colour drained from his face as open-mouthed and temporarily speechless he stared at the contents, a smashed frame, broken glass and a torn-up picture of Theodore!

'You mad bitch,' he said in a quiet shocked voice. 'How could you do that?'

'Because you're not entitled to it.'

'Not entitled! What do you mean?' She must be trying to goad him.

'I know it is assumed he got his fair hair and blue eyes from me, but the shades were quite different.'

'So what?' Joss growled, the volume of his voice rising.

'Perhaps you remember in America, when you were always too busy to take me to parties, the handsome blonde gentleman from one of the European Embassies was only too pleased to perform your duties for you,' Clementine replied. Then meaningfully added, 'All of them.' She had the same look of triumph in her eyes as when she devastated the dreams of Emma Copeland the previous day.

'You don't mean he . . . '

'Oh yes I do,' Clementine interrupted, a twisted grin contorting her face and her eyes cruelly gleaming with pleasure at the hurt she was inflicting.

In a flash Joss remembered the tall Nordic man from one of the Embassies. He'd never noticed the likeness to Theodore. As a child it was not apparent, only for a short time before he died, when he reached manhood, and Joss had completely forgotten the man he knew briefly and who disappeared from the scene when Joss became available to escort his wife, so many years ago. But

r

recollection of the man came to him yesterday, like an ill omen. He, Joss, was not Theodore's father!

From low in his throat Joss's voice rose, crescendoing like the rumble of a fast approaching train. 'You evil, foul, slut!'

He flung himself towards her, his large hands circling her throat!

'Don't, Joss,' Ron Paull shouted and sprang at Joss, struggling with all his might to haul him from his wife, while Clementine frantically kicked and clawed his hands. Myrtle came running and equally frantically tried to prise Joss's fingers from the throat they gripped with such deadly strength.

'Joss! She's not worth it, she's not worth it,' Ron shouted. Two gurgles issued from Clementine's throat and under partially closed lids her eyes turned upwards and her body became limp.

'She's not worth it, Mr Renfree,' Myrtle repeated, a sob in her voice.

The accuracy of her remarks, and the sob of anguish, must have penetrated Joss's senses. He suddenly let go of Clementine and she thudded heavily to the floor, her face darkened to near purple.

Ron Paull picked her up, carried her up the stairs, plonked her on the bed in Joss's room and stared at her until her eyelids flickered and she began to recover consciousness. Then Ron left her to Myrtle's ministrations; his concern was for Joss. He found him in the sitting-room, seated in an armchair bent forward, elbows on knees and his head resting in his hands.

Ron Paull placed a hand on Joss's shoulder, and gave a comforting squeeze. 'She's coming round,' he said, then looked about for a bottle. He found the brandy and went to the kitchen, put four cups from the dresser onto the kitchen table and poured into each a small quantity of water from the kettle simmering on the hob. He then stirred in sugar and brandy and returned to Joss and handed him a cup.

'Drink this, my handsome, it'll steady you,' he said.

Leaving a cup for himself on the round wine table, he bounded upstairs and went into the bedroom. Throwing a brief glance in Clementine's direction he noted her eyes were half open and her colour changing to something approaching normal. He handed the two cups to Myrtle, saying, 'Here's one for you and one for her,' without again looking in Clementine's direction. 'Make her sip it,' he said and returned to Joss.

They sat in silence for a while, then Ron Paull said, 'I'd like you to know I don't blame you for what you did, old pal. I'd have done exactly the same, but probably sooner.'

Joss raised his head a little, his eyes turned upwards to glance at Ron Paull. He nodded. 'Thanks Ron,' he said. 'But I don't want to set eyes on her again. I can't trust myself, not after what she said.'

'It might not be true, perhaps she . . . '

But Ron Paull's words were interrupted. 'No, for once she was speaking the truth,' Joss said in a flat voice. 'I remember him, and Theodore is . . . was . . . a replica of the man.' A groan escaped from his throat. 'She's got to get out of here,' Joss uttered through clenched teeth.

Myrtle's footsteps were heard heavily clopping down the stairs. Ron rose, picked up the two empty cups and followed Myrtle out into the kitchen. 'How is she?' he asked.

'She's shocked, and so she should be,' Myrtle said, her face white and grim.

'Is she fit to leave?'

'I don't know whether she's fit, but I think she should leave. She won't improve here . . . she's dead scared of Mr Renfree now, and she never was before. She's too shallow to understand a man like Mr Renfree.'

'She won't object to going today, then?'

Myrtle shook her head. 'No, I don't think so. She'll bounce back, make no mistake. She's tough . . . But how is Mr Renfree?'

'He's escaped a hanging offence by a whisker, Myrtle, and I think he's now realising what *that* would have done to Lottie and all the others,' Ron Paull replied. 'He's shattered!'

It was on the Tuesday morning, over a week later, that there was a rap on Joss's front door. Myrtle answered. Joss heard a familiar voice and got to his feet.

'Come in, Mrs Simpson,' he heard Myrtle say, and as he opened the door to his room Lottie stepped inside the house and Myrtle closed the wide front door.

'Hello, Lottie,' he said.

Lottie spun round and saw him standing there. The smile

disappeared from her face.

'Joss! I've called to see if you're all right. It's been such a long time, I feared something was wrong . . . and I can see I was right.'

Joss was unshaven and pallid, with dark circles under his eyes. Lottie flung her arms about him and held her cheek against his bristly face.

'Come in here,' he said, and they moved into his sitting-room. He pulled a chair close to his. 'Sit down, Lottie,' he said.

'What's happened, Joss?'

'Clementine and I had a big row,' he said, and took his seat near to his sister.

'What's she done this time?'

'It's not worth talking about. And you can stop worrying about me,' Joss said. 'She won't be living here any more, we're finished.'

'You're divorcing her?'

'No. We're just not living together. She's gone back to Withiel Cottage.'

'Did she walk out on you? Or did you . . . ' Joss didn't wait for her to finish.

'Yes, I booted her out.'

'I'm glad,' Lottie said, with a sigh of relief. 'Now you must pull yourself together and just start enjoying life.'

'Yes, you're right Lottie. That's just what I'll do.'

Lottie didn't press her brother to tell her what the row was about, which was as well as Joss had no intention of needlessly distressing her with that knowledge.

Uncharacteristically, Joss had little to say, and it was left to Lottie to make conversation. This indicated to her that her brother was deeply upset and the recent situations were reversed. She must now cheer him up.

'I must go soon,' she said. 'I've got a dish of marinaded mackerel in the oven . . . I know you like marinaded mackerel. Come home with me and we'll share a meal.'

'All right, Lottie,' Joss agreed almost reluctantly. 'I'll have a quick shave and change, and then get the car out.'

'I didn't know you had bought a car.'

'That's because I haven't seen you.'

'Yes. I suppose. Mind you don't cut yourself with that cut-throat razor,' she warned Joss as he moved towards the door,

388

doubting his mind would be on what he was doing.

'I'll be all right, Lottie. Don't fuss.'

An hour later they were about to start the meal and Joss, in the comfortable company of his sister, began to feel a little lighter. Lottie, who could tell he was no longer quite so distracted, chatted on.

'I saw Polly yesterday,' she said.

Joss stopped eating and looked up, but did not speak.

'She said she had been expecting a visit and wondered whether you or Clementine were unwell.'

'I'll call on her sometime,' Joss said dismissively, and continued eating. After the trauma of what happened with the woman who was his wife in name and nothing else, who bore him a son he had not fathered, to call on Polly, the woman he truly loved but who could never be his, was too painful, too emotive to contemplate. He would see his beloved Polly when he felt he could stand her presence without the solace of her comforting arms about him, without the feel of her lips, her face pressed against his. He had not yet the strength to see her after what transpired between him and Clementine, when his control snapped on learning Theodore, the child, the boy, the young man he so often worried over and was exasperated by, but loved so dearly, was *not* his son but a cuckoo in the nest. It was not Theodore's fault. He didn't know he was, in effect, a bastard, a by-blow. The lad was innocent of it all. But it did not alter the fact that Joss really had no son. This was Theodore's death all over again and he was living again the agony of bereavement, but this time an even more bitter, deeper bereavement. And all his work and success in America had been for absolutely nothing.

'Joss you're miles away,' Lottie said.

He did not reply.

'Joss.'

'Huh . . . Oh, sorry Lottie. Did you say something?'

'I want you to come to my home tomorrow morning, any time to suit you. We'll have a meal and then go for a little ride in your car in the afternoon. Will you do that?'

'Yes. All right, Lottie.'

'You won't forget?'

'No, I won't forget.'

'Would you like to ask Polly to come?'

'Not this time. Just you and me. We'll ask Polly when I'm more . . . when I'm more sociable.'

'All right. We'll have a day together tomorrow.'

After a week of Lottie's attention Joss convinced himself he was over the blackest time. He was beginning to improve. His neglect of Polly, or what to her must seem like neglect, began to bother him. He must see her and give her some explanation for this . . . the truth. The same truth he gave to Lottie . . . that he had a big row with Clementine and they were now living apart. It would not be the whole truth, but there was no need to say more.

Late that evening Joss walked to Villa Gwidden and put a note through Polly's letter-box apologising for not coming before and saying he would do so on the next afternoon, if convenient to her. He felt he would now be able to behave normally, and to keep his emotions and shock hidden.

On arrival at Polly's home, she answered his knock promptly, as though she had been watching for him, and as soon as she shut the front door, threw her arms about him in a brief hug, kissed him and led the way into the sitting-room.

'I was so sorry to learn there's been an upset with Clementine,' she said.

Joss was taken aback! Polly already knew! But of course she would. The Renfrees and the Pascoes had always been like family. Lottie would have told or written to Polly.

As he entered the sitting-room, there on the mantelpiece as though staring at him, was a picture of Jonathan, Polly's son. A shock wave ran through him. He wasn't over it yet! He should have realised!

How fortunate Polly had been. A good husband, a good mother. It was only to be expected they would produce a fine son.

Polly turned and saw Joss staring at the picture. Of course seeing Jonathan's picture would remind him of the sad death of his own son, especially at times like this.

Joss didn't speak but walked across the room and stood with his back to her, staring out of the window. She guessed he was trying to compose himself, to hide his emotions.

'I think I'll make us both a cup of tea *now*,' she said. 'We can have our usual tea later on.'

Polly left Joss and went to the kitchen. He did not follow her, chatting all the way as he usually did. On her return, with a cup of tea in each hand, she found him where she had left him, still with his broad back to her, staring out and seeing nothing.

He turned, his face pale and unsmiling, and took the tea she handed to him.

'Thanks, Polly!'

'Sit down, Joss,' she said.

He sat in the armchair as usual, and Polly sat on the settee cornerwise to him.

'Lottie told me you have a new car,' she said.

'Yes,' he replied.

He's not himself at all, Polly thought, and wondered whether there was more to his difference with Clementine than Lottie let on, or possibly even knew.

Again his eyes strayed to the picture.

'I suppose Jonathan's picture reminds you of Theodore,' she said.

Joss got to his feet and again moved to the window, his back once more to Polly, so that she could not see his face.

'Joss,' she said at last. 'What's wrong? I'd like to help if I can.'

Again there was a long pause, then Joss half turned and glanced at her. 'You can't help Polly. But don't worry, dear, I expect it will ease with time.'

'I noticed you looking at Jonathan's picture. Is the loss of your son still upsetting you so much?'

Another pause, then suddenly Joss blurted it out.

'I have no son, I had no son.' He paced up and down the room as he said the words.

It was Polly's turn to be speechless. 'What do you mean?' she said in a small, shocked voice.

'I did not father Theodore!' Another pause.

'But can you be sure?'

'The timing is right and he was the absolute image of the man she said is the father.'

He stopped pacing and turned his gaze towards her, and she saw the torture, and the torment in his eyes.

'My wife was a slut, and I reared a bastard as my own child, loved him as my own. To add to it, telling me gave Clementine such pleasure . . . I almost killed her, Polly. If it hadn't been for

391

Ron Paull and Myrtle, she would be dead and I would be a murderer.'

The teacup in Polly's hand made a rattling descent into its saucer, spilling tea as it did so, while Polly burst into tears.

In a flash Joss was on his knees beside her, taking the cup and saucer from her violently trembling hand, while his gaze never left her face.

'Whatever is it my dearest? What's wrong? Has what I said upset you that much? It's all right now, and I should not have told you. I didn't mean to. It's really all right and I *am* getting over it. And Clementine is, you can be sure of that.'

But Polly's agitation only increased. Joss, mystified, rose from his knees and sat on the settee beside her, putting his arms about her, attempting to hold her close, to comfort her, to reassure her all was now well. But Polly, wrenching herself free, jumped to her feet and moved away.

'Polly . . . I don't understand . . . whatever is it? You're not afraid of me, surely? I'd never hurt you.'

Polly found it almost impossible to speak. With wracking sobs which made her words almost incoherent she blurted out the disjointed words.

'You've been . . . describing me . . . I'm a slut, a cheat . . . ' Joss's jaw dropped in disbelief. 'I didn't . . . tell Edwin . . . he was not the father. I cheated everybody . . . I deceived everybody . . . all the people I love . . . I betrayed . . . '

Joss's arms were about her and her head flopped forward, resting limply against his chest as she continued to be convulsed with sobs. Joss just stood there, one hand patting her shoulder, as the sobs diminished.

'Polly,' he said at last. 'You are over-wrought. You are not making sense, dearest. Tell me another time when you are yourself and composed.'

But Polly had become more composed. She felt drained but steady. 'I think you are wrong to say you had no son, Joss. And I did exactly the same as Clementine. I'm almost positive Edwin didn't father Jonathan, but I let him think he did.' She gulped, then went on, 'I didn't mean to, but I did.'

At last Polly glanced up into Joss's face. His eyes seemed to stare, unseeing, his mouth hung open as if wanting to speak but unable to comprehend or reply to the words he had heard.

'Don't you remember that night we were alone here, when I . . . when I encouraged you, more than encouraged . . . I threw myself at you, seduced you!'

'I never thought of it like that,' Joss's voice was soft, almost as though he were thinking aloud. 'You loved me . . . we were meant for each other, only I was a young fool and . . . ' he paused and his breathing quickened. 'You're not saying Jonathan is . . . ?' He daren't say it.

'Yes! Yes . . . he's yours . . . your son,' Polly said. 'I'm almost certain.'

Joss did not react. Polly read his thoughts. 'Almost certain' meant 'not certain'.

'Joss . . . did Theodore have a small pinky-red, crescent-shaped mark on his hip?'

Again his eyes strayed to the picture.

'No!' Joss looked slightly puzzled. Then, as if remembering something, he said, 'I have.'

'Anyone else in your family that you know of?'

'Yes, now you mention it, my father did . . . and I believe his father before him.'

'Joss . . . ' Joss stared at her. 'Jonathan has a crescent-moon shaped mark on his hip.'

A jolt visibly shot through Joss's body and, mouth open, he stood dumbstruck, rigid, stiff as a ramrod. Anxiously Polly awaited his reaction. It seemed an age before he spoke.

'Polly, you don't mean . . . ' He couldn't bring himself to think it, much less say it.

'Yes. Yes, I do. Jonathan is *your* son.'

Again Joss stood motionless. This was too good to be true!

'It's true, Joss. I didn't intend ever to say it. But when I saw you I couldn't help myself.'

Joss sat down, his eyes never blinking nor leaving hers, and suddenly a straight horizontal line moved slowly downwards from somewhere above his hairline. As it moved down his forehead his pale, almost grey pallor changed to a fresh, pinkish shade. The straight line continued down his face and down his throat until it disappeared under his stiff collar, and all tension left his face, while his eyes which less than a minute before were dull and almost dead-looking with unspeakable sadness, looked into her's brimming and sparkling with wonder. Suddenly for Joss it all registered. Revitalised he bounded towards her and swept her up into his arms dancing and whirling her around in delight.

'Polly, Polly, you've made me the happiest man in the world,' he said, as he rained swift ecstatic kisses all over her head and face. 'Jonathan is *my* son!'

Again he whirled her around, and when he gently dropped her he held onto her hand which he kept clasped in his as he guided her to the settee where they sat side by side.

'It's a funny thing,' he said, putting his arm around her shoulder, 'but I've always loved Jonathan. I don't know why, I just couldn't help it. Mother loved him too. I know she did.'

Then he suddenly stopped speaking as he recalled her dying words when she tried to tell him . . . 'The baw . . . ' she must have meant 'boy' was his. Joss turned to Polly. 'I think mother knew,' he said. 'She was trying to tell me something just before she died.'

Polly lowered her head. 'I think she knew too,' she said, and looked up into his face. 'And please, I don't want Jonathan to ever know you are his father.' Her eyes gazed pleadingly into his. 'He loves you. But he loved Edwin.'

Joss sobered a little. 'I understand,' he said. 'And I don't want anyone to know Theodore was not my son. I still love him and it would be like betrayal; also it would upset Lottie so much.' He paused, then added, 'And I see the terrible predicament you were in.'

'I couldn't tell a soul,' Polly cried. 'Not even my own mother.'

'Knowing you as I do, I can imagine how hard it all must have been for you, Polly, to have to pretend he was Edwin's.'

'It was hell,' Polly said. 'But Edwin worshipped him!'

Joss, gazing down at her, watched her eyes fill and as a tear brimmed over, gently he patted it dry with his handkerchief.

'I'm glad Jonathan made Edwin so happy,' he said.

'He was the proudest man on earth,' Polly interrupted.

'And now I'm proud, overjoyed, that he is really my son,' Joss said, ecstatically, and again his gaze was concentrated on the framed photograph which stood on the mantelpiece opposite to where they both sat. Polly rose to her feet and disappeared, returning a couple of minutes later with a brown paper bag which she handed to Joss. 'You have this,' she said. Joss took out the photograph which was inside. It was a photograph of Jonathan like the one on Polly's mantelpiece, but unframed. Joss seemed mesmerised by the image of the face which seemed to gaze back at him. His lower lip trembled slightly and his eyes remained transfixed.

Then he looked down at Polly who was now sitting beside him. 'Thank you, Polly, dear Polly, mother of *my* child. You can be sure neither Jonathan nor anyone else will ever know. I'll keep that joy, that privilege, in my heart. *I know*, and that knowledge will sustain me through anything and everything. It makes up twenty times over for all the disappointments and bad things in my life.'

Polly knew he was referring to Theodore and to the fact that he had never known the blessing of having a 'proper' wife.

Joss looked at his wristwatch. 'I must go now, dearest,' he said, getting to his feet. 'But there's a lot I'd like to hear and share in. Could I come up again tomorrow? I'm so longing to hear more. But there is something I must see to.'

'Certainly you can come tomorrow, Joss. We'll have a good talk.'

'I did have something to work for in America after all, only I didn't know it.' Polly didn't know what he meant but Joss kissed her gently. 'When I arrived here this afternoon I felt I was the most miserable man imaginable, Polly. You can't believe the difference you've made telling me that I'm the father of Jonathan . . . he's *my* boy. I'm bursting with happiness and pride.'

Polly sighed. 'I'm feeling relieved that at last you know the truth,' she answered. 'The burden of guilt and the doubt about what was the right thing to do, crucified me and still bothers me at times.'

At this remark Joss paused. 'It's strange,' he said. 'I don't feel guilty any more either.'

'What could possibly make you feel guilty?' Polly asked.

'There have been times when I felt ashamed of Theodore,' Joss replied. 'And I felt I was at fault; because I had fathered him, but somehow that feeling of guilt has gone. I still love him though.'

'Of course you do,' Polly murmured.

Joss bent to briefly hug and kiss Polly. 'See you tomorrow, my love,' he said, and hurriedly left.

Chapter Fifty-one

'Your meal is in the oven keeping warm, Mr Renfree,' Myrtle said, as Joss entered the house on his return.

'Sorry I'm so late, Myrtle.'

'Don't apologise, sir,' Myrtle interrupted, noting with pleasure that her employer looked better and seemed so much brighter.

'I was unexpectedly held up,' Joss explained.

'Mr Renfree, would you mind if I leave now?'

'Oh, it's your W.I. night, Myrtle. I forgot,' Joss said.

'That's all right, Mr Renfree, only tonight Penryn W.I. have got entertainers coming from Falmouth W.I. and I promised to help prepare refreshments for them to have afterwards.'

'You go ahead,' Joss said as he removed his coat and trilby hat. 'It'll do you good. You've been cooped up in here with me quite enough.'

'And glad to do so, Mr Renfree, sir. I'll get ready to leave now, if that's all right with you?'

'Yes. Carry on and enjoy yourself.'

Joss went into what he still regarded as 'his' sitting-room, lowered himself into his favourite armchair next to which was the round wine table with a brandy bottle and glass standing on it. He settled himself in the chair, opened the paper bag and took out Jonathan's picture. For a while he just sat gazing at it and smiling. Then he started to sing to himself, quietly and slowly.

Myrtle, passing his sitting-room on her way out, heard him and departed smiling. Mr Renfree was better.

Polly looked forward to Joss's visit. After her confession to him the previous day, she felt a weight had been lifted from her, for she had never quite lost the feeling she had not only cheated Edwin, she had cheated Joss. But after the terrible blow he suffered she just had to let him know the truth. She was thankful she was able to turn the abject misery of the man she had loved from childhood into unexpected and unparalleled joy.

It was Edwin's delight in the baby he believed to be his, that convinced her she had done the right thing in keeping to herself the overwhelming doubt about which of the two men fathered her little son. But it was Emily's subsequent brief but unmistakable shock at seeing something unexpected in the baby that confirmed what she herself believed.

She looked at the clock. Joss was late. Seconds seemed like minutes. At 4.30, the time when Joss usually left, except for yesterday when strangely, though there was so much he wanted to hear about, he left earlier than usual. It was as though there was something he *had* to do, something that must not and could not wait. Yesterday, when he wiped a tear from her cheek with his handkerchief, he left the handkerchief behind on the settee. She had washed and ironed it, and it was waiting for him in the sitting-room on a small low table. She would go and return it to him and at the same time discover if something was amiss.

Polly put on her brown cloche hat and matching coat, walked downhill to Joss's home and rapped on the heavy front-door knocker. Myrtle answered and, with a broad smile, welcomed her.

'Come in, Mrs Pendleton. Was it Mr Renfree you wanted to see?'

'Well, yes,' Polly said, as she entered what had been Clementine's sitting-room. 'He had something he wanted to discuss with me and said he would call this afternoon. He didn't call, and it's so unlike him not to keep to an arrangement. I wondered if there was something wrong.'

'I might be able to explain it. He came in late last evening . . . '

'Late?' Polly interrupted Myrtle, remembering he had left Villa Gwidden early.

'Yes,' Myrtle went on, 'and he seemed completely well. I haven't seen him look so happy for years. I was going to the W.I. and his dinner was in the oven keeping warm. When I got back he'd washed his plate and put it away, only he forgot to turn the oven off; it was on low heat, keeping his meal warm. But he's been sleeping so badly lately, I expect now he seems to have got over his upset, he is making up for it with a good long sleep. I didn't want to disturb him, I thought a sound sleep would do him good. As a matter of fact, I was just thinking I should wake him up or he won't sleep tonight, and then get on with cooking a meal.' Polly nodded. Myrtle lowered her voice. 'Between you and me, Mrs Pendleton, I expect he had a brandy or two as well.'

Polly paused to consider what Myrtle had said.

'Did he start eating his dinner before you left?'

'Er, no. He'd only been in a few minutes and went into his room.' She tilted her head in the direction of Joss's sitting-room on the opposite side of the passage.

'Let's check he did eat it,' Polly said, and she and Myrtle went together to the kitchen and Myrtle opened the oven door.

'Oh, dear God! It's still there!' she said as she brought out a plate of dried-up cottage pie and vegetables covered with an upturned dish.

'Let's look in his bedroom,' Polly suggested.

Myrtle led the way and they both mounted the stairs. With Polly close behind, Myrtle rushed across the landing, knocked on the door and without waiting for a reply, entered.

'The bed's not been slept in!' she exclaimed, panic in her voice.

Polly turned and dashed down the stairs, Myrtle, panting with alarm, followed behind. Polly threw open the door of Joss's sitting-room. There was Joss, seemingly asleep in his chair, one arm hanging downwards, with Jonathan's photograph on the floor beneath his dangling hand.

'Joss,' Polly shouted, and gently shook his shoulder, while Myrtle hovered close by. Joss did not respond. Polly picked up the glass near the brandy bottle, sniffed it, and looked up at Myrtle.

'He's *not* had anything to drink,' she said. 'Joss, Joss!' She shook him more urgently, holding her breath, awaiting some response. Myrtle, wringing her hands, stood looking on. Polly put the back of her hand against his cheek and the colour drained from her face.

'Myrtle! Run up the road to the doctor's house. I think. I think . . . Oh, God.'

From Myrtle's throat came a choking sound and, without removing her pinafore or donning a coat, she ran from the house.

Frantically Polly tried to rub warmth into Joss's hands, but to no avail, and as the doctor, followed by Myrtle, rushed into the room, gave a stifled sob of despair.

The doctor spent a few minutes examining and checking, then looked up.

'I'm afraid it's too late,' he said. 'He knew it could happen any time. He's had a heart attack.'

The muscles of Polly's white face tightened, while Myrtle loudly sniffed.

'He's been under a lot of strain lately,' the doctor went on. 'How was he yesterday?'

He looked towards Myrtle who again blew her nose loudly before attempting to speak. 'The same, sir. But when he came in last evening he was fine . . . his old self, like he used to be years ago. I heard him singing to himself in this room as I went out, and I haven't heard him sing for years, though he only sang the first two lines.' She paused, overcome, then with a sob in her voice added, 'I'll never forget the words.'

'What words?' Polly said quickly.

Myrtle drew a deep breath, then, as if summoning up her strength and with a struggle, haltingly repeated the words of the song, 'When you come . . . to the end . . . of a perfect day . . . and you sit alone . . . with your thoughts . . . '

Polly, with a loud cry, burst into tears.

Epilogue

On a cold, blustery day, on the high ground where, amid the quarries, facing down towards the Penryn River, and the more distant rooftops of Falmouth, Joss was buried in the same cemetery close to where rested his parents Emily and John Renfree and his grandparents; Polly's parents, Nell and Daniel Pascoe; also Edwin and his parents, Cordelia and George Pendleton; and where Polly knew, she would one day join them. All were within a few yards of each other.

Clementine did not attend the funeral, excusing herself as having a bad cold. Lottie, Nora, Stanley and Eric Simpson and their wives were present, also Polly and Jonathan, Jack and Mary, Agnes and Caleb Collins, Ada and Wilfred Pearce, Mary Jane and Fred Phillips, Bill and Maria Boaden, Ron and Jim Paull and their wives, Marcus and Mary Treloar, William Parnell, Ben Spargo, Will Triggs, Dickie Polwin, the Penhales and the Thomas's, the Trembaths and the Pellows, Myrtle and the remaining staff at Manor Withiel, Mr Borlace, Solicitor, Dr Laity, numerous friends from Mabe, Penryn, Falmouth, Flushing, Mawnan Smith as well as old quarry workers and tin miners from Lanner, Redruth and Camborne. All gathered in the chapel and afterwards around the graveside, the men bare-headed.

The funeral tea took place afterwards at Joss's home in Penryn. Clementine was present for this and awaiting the return of the mourners after the funeral, when relatives would remain behind after for the solicitor to read the Will.

Lottie tried to persuade Polly to remain behind after the refreshments but both Polly and Jonathan were adamant they would leave and were on the point of departing when Mr Borlace, the solicitor, requested their presence.

Before commencing to read the Will, Mr Borlace seated himself at an opened gateleg table on which he had placed his document case. He looked around over the top of his spectacles. 'Perhaps I should tell you all, Mr Renfree very recently changed his Will. Nevertheless, this was not a sudden decision. He had been intending to do so for a number of years, but due to . . . er . . . unforeseen circumstances his departure to America was sooner than anticipated.' Lottie shot a withering glance at Clementine. 'Before he left the United States to return to England he learned he had a heart condition which could possibly bring about his sudden demise.'

Lottie's hand flew to her mouth as she drew in a gasp of surprise at this statement. Mr Borlace paused and raised his head to look about and make sure all were ready for him to continue, then adjusted his spectacles and carried on speaking.

'This was the first opportunity he had to put his affairs in order since his fairly recent return from the States. I have to say it is providential that he did so, otherwise there could have been untold difficulties.' Mr Borlace then commenced to read the customary wording about last will and testament; then came the bequests.

'To my wife, Clementine Louisa I wish payment to be made at the same monthly allowance as at present, the use of Withiel Cottage during her lifetime and Edmund Borlace, that is myself of course, or whosoever might subsequently take over from him, is empowered to arrange for employment of a maid or cook and any medical care which may be required.' Mr Borlace paused.

Clementine waited, then said, 'Is that all?'

'It seems very satisfactory . . . and, I might add, very generous.' Mr Borlace said in a quiet unruffled tone. Clementine vehemently complained and walked out. Unperturbed, Mr Borlace continued.

A substantial bequest was made to Lottie, also generous bequests to Nora, Stanley and Eric and to each of their children, also to his one-time neighbours and lifetime friends, Polly Pendleton and Jack Pascoe. A bequest of one hundred pounds was made to Myrtle plus two pounds per week, to be paid monthly; she was also to have use for the remainder of her lifetime, of the cottage in which his parents had lived. Bequests were also made to Manor Withiel staff and numerous charities. Then came the words: 'Consequent upon the death of my dear son, Theodore Edward Charles, I bequeath to my dear Godson, Jonathan Guy Pendleton, the remainder of my estate.'

Jonathan's jaw dropped and Polly gasped as fear took hold. Her gaze flew to Lottie. Would this cause a rift between her and her dear friend? Lottie's gaze was already upon her. Though grief-stricken she managed to smile and nodded approval. Relief, mixed with amazement flooded Polly. Then a thought suddenly struck her. Could Lottie have guessed? But what did it matter, as long as their friendship remained unharmed.

Mr Borlace coughed meaningfully and Polly's anxious gaze left Lottie's face. Mr Borlace then spoke, directing his words at Jonathan. 'Mr Pendleton, you are now a man of substance!'

After Jonathan and Polly went home, both totally dazed, neither hungry, they had a simple meal of just tea, bread, butter and jam. Polly sat in a chair by the fire and, exhausted, fell asleep. She dreamt of Joss, just as he was years ago, when he was young and before he married Clementine. Then she heard his voice . . . 'Wake up.'

Polly opened her eyes and there he stood, smiling down at her, a cup of tea in his hand.

'Thanks Joss, that's just what I need.'

'You're dreaming, mother. It's me, Jonathan.'

'Oh, Jonathan, you're right. I was dreaming.'

She smiled and took the tea from him, suddenly knowing in her heart Joss had not completely left her. She still had something to hold onto. In Jonathan she still had in flesh, blood and a hundred different ways the regeneration of Joss, their son, their only son, the perpetuation of their love, created from a combination of them both.

Polly sipped the tea and vowed to await, to patiently await, the ultimate reunion.

Three months later the world was shocked by news of the Wall Street crash in America. This had some effect on the estate Joss had left, but Jonathan, his only beloved son, was still a man of means.